catfish

LYNDA THROSBY

Cover photograph by Emma Hayes & Stuart Reardon
Featuring Stuart Reardon
Cover design by Sybil Wilson / Pop Kitty Designs
Formatted by Cassy Roop @ PinkInk Designs
ISBN 978-1-9993150-0-9
Lynda Throsby Publishing

E-Mail ljtpublishing@gmail.com

Dedication

This would not have been possible without the
support I received from my Hubby Peter.
He continuously told me to get on with it. Running our business,
making the time for me to write. He's my champion and my hero.

My second bestie Stuart, who continually said, 'do it', don't be a
chicken, even when I wanted to quit and for doing
the stunning pictures for my cover.

Reviews

I really hope that you enjoy this story. Reviews are lovely! Honestly, they are! And they also help other people to make an informed decision before buying this book.

I would really appreciate it if you took a few seconds to do just that.

Thank you!
Amazon
Goodreads
Bookbub

Lynda Throsby Xx

*I close my eyes to old ends
It's time to start something new
To open my heart to new beginnings
And trust the magic of all that's new.*

ONLINE DATING MEANINGS

Stashing – When you start seeing someone, but they keep you a secret and stash you away—usually because they are married or seeing other people. You are their secret.

Ghosting – When you start seeing someone, and they just disappear and vanish without a trace. They don't return your messages and even block you from social media and dating sites. This is so they don't have to tell you they are breaking up with you verbally.

Zombieing – If you have been ghosted the culprit may resurface back on the sites. This is usually a fair bit of time after they ghosted you. They try to make contact, only to probably ghost you again.

Benching – This is before you discuss exclusivity, and they bench you like in a football game while they look for someone better. You are their backup option. They may come back to you if no one better comes along.

Catch and release – Where someone persistently pursues you as they love the chase, but as soon as you agree to a date they release you, as you're not a conquest any more.

Breadcrumbing – This is where someone seems to be pursuing you, but really, they have no intention of being in a relationship with you. It could just be the chase they like, or it's a game as they are already in a relationship. They message and chase, leaving you breadcrumbs with no outcome.

Cushioning – When you're dating, but they know it's not going anywhere or will not end well so instead of cutting you loose they prepare you for the break up by chatting and flirting with others online to cushion the blow to you.

Kittenfishing – Someone who has out-dated images of themselves and lies about their age, height, job, hair etc. If you were to meet you would know they were lying.

Catfishing – The pinnacle of online dating deception. Where someone pretends to be someone else. They use fake images to lure you in and use false information to make them seem more interesting. This can be dangerous if you decide to meet up, although you would never know until you decided to go that far and by that time it could be too late for you.

catfish

CHARLOTTE

MUCH LOVE

LINDA xx

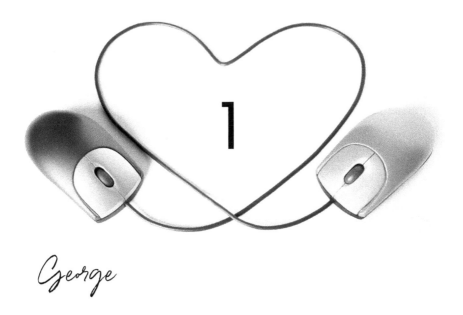

George

IT HAS TAKEN ME A LONG TIME to reel this one in and get her to finally agree to meet me for a date. It's been too long now since my last catch, just over a year ago now. This one is going to suffer because i've waited for so long, I've missed out on others while I've been chasing her, and my need is growing more and more. It's getting harder each day—both figuratively and literally. The things I'm going to do to this bitch now... I can't wait, and boy will she regret making me. I am a very impatient man.

The minute I laid eyes on her profile picture while scanning the hordes of whores for my next catch, I knew I had to have her. It was the long mousey brown hair and the hazel eyes, although the others had looked similar, this whore was the spitting image of my fucking bitch of a mother.

My brow is wet from sweat, and I'm shaking, knowing I will finally have her tomorrow. I'm so fucking hard right now just looking at her picture. God help me when I get my hands on her. She will regret ever responding to my messages and playing with me, stringing me along. Why the fuck I get hard for these whores that look like my mother is a mystery to me. They should repulse me, but I can't help myself, and it makes me hate myself even more. I feel sick to the stomach. Now I need to take care of my fucking cock. That bitch, Katherine has done this to me yet again.

Katherine

WHAT HAVE I DONE? I SAID I wouldn't date for a long time, so why have I just agreed to meet this Lewis guy. Why am I doing this? Why do I put myself through this? It's not like I need someone. I have my own business, right here in the city, which takes up most of my time. But still… it's lonely, and his pictures are hot. I mean, those abs and biceps and the tattoos… Oh, god, they make me drool. But it's the bright, mesmerising, light brown eyes with long eyelashes and black curly short hair that made me succumb. He is just so pretty in a masculine way. I still think this is too good to be true. Why would someone that looks like him be on a dating site? Surely, he can get any woman he wants.

I've had such bad experiences with men in my life, going back to my family. I had no father to speak of. He left mum, my brother Brad, and me when I was two, so I never knew him. Brad is three years older than me, and although he did look out for me in school and was very protective as most big brothers are, he's an arsehole.

He has a wife now, Cindy, and he is mean to her like he used to be mean to me. Not the hitting, but he does have some serious anger issues, and I'm sure it stems from him being so young when our dad left.

Brad used to get angry a lot and hit me, and if I ventured into his room, all hell broke loose. He even broke my arm one time when I was eleven. He had a girl in his room; mum was at work as usual. He was on top of her, grunting away, and all I saw was his arse, but he jumped off that bed so quickly, grabbed me and threw me hard on the floor of the landing that my arm snapped. He was sorry, of course, and persuaded me to tell mum I'd fallen. That was just one of the times in my childhood that I ended up at the hospital, being told how clumsy I was.

Mum worked two jobs. She was the only one bringing money in for the three of us. She was a room cleaner in a hotel in London during the day, starting at 6.30 a.m., she finished that job at 3 p.m. just in time for me to get home from school and see her for half an hour before she had to work the evening shift from 5 p.m. to midnight down at the local petrol station.

She trusted Brad to look after me, being my big older brother, but it was best I stayed away from him as much as possible, or I ended up with bruises. I never told mum he did that to me. She had enough to worry about.

So yeah, men! Dad left—arsehole, and Brad hit me—another arsehole.

THERE WAS MY first boyfriend at fourteen. Luke Jones. At first, he was really nice and made me feel special, but it became clear that was only because of what he wanted from me.

We were going steady for about three months and we'd only ever kissed, that was a trauma in itself the first time. I had no experience, and when he stuck his tongue in my mouth and tried to push it down my throat, I almost puked in his mouth, much to his dismay. Having never had a boyfriend before; I didn't want to go any further than kissing, although he did try to put his hand under my skirt or up my top a few times.

He even tried to put my hand on his erection over his trousers, but I was scared and naive, so in the end, he got fed up and called me a cock-tease because I wouldn't have sex with him or let him feel my boobs.

He told all the boys in school not to waste their time with me because they would get nowhere, and he told everyone who would listen that I was a frigid bitch. The girls in school picked on me anyway. I thought it was because I was quiet and kept to myself, but both Brad and Luke told me they were all jealous of me because I was pretty, and I had a good figure for my age, that the other girls felt threatened by me. When Luke dumped me, it just got worse with the mean girls. They had more ammunition to throw at me just because I wasn't a slut like them.

I REALLY THINK I should cancel on Lewis. It's just he is so sweet in our messages, saying how beautiful I am and asking if I've ever considered modelling. He wants to meet to talk and get to know me. Nothing more, he said he has no expectations as he respects me. I mean who does that these days? It's usually 'wham bam thank you, ma'am'.

I just can't see someone like him wanting to get to know someone like me. I don't think I'm ugly. I'm curvy in all the right places and in some not-so-right places, but I'm not a size zero by any means. I'm more a comfortable fourteen to sixteen in clothes.

I'm successful in my business, and it takes up most of my time, I've worked hard to get it where it is today. Porter Properties is one of the top property investor/developers in the city, and I'm proud of that. It's so hard being a woman at the top in a man's world, but I have this knack of knowing a good deal when I see one. I own several commercial buildings and apartment blocks.

I have a penthouse apartment in Knightsbridge, not far from my office, which I use during the week, and at the weekends I head to my five-bedroomed house in a lovely area of Chelmsford. I bought a big house because I was hoping mum would move in with me and quit her jobs, but it wasn't meant to be. It's very quiet where I live. I love the peace and tranquillity, and I know mum would have loved it too.

3

George

JUST ONE MORE NIGHT AND I will have that bitch. My thirteenth catch. I may prolong it. Make her suffer like that bitch has made me suffer for weeks. I've checked her out on social media, and from what I can tell, she doesn't socialise much. There are some work references and a few pictures with work colleagues, that's it. After digging, I found she owns the company, but other than that, there is not much about family or friends. I just hope, as I suspect, she lives alone. They nearly always do or why would they be looking for love on these shitty dating sites?

In our messages on the dating site: LookingforLove.com, she never gave much away about herself. She was always quite vague and guarded, and I suspect she's had bad experiences with tossers who go on these dating sites purely to get free sex with no intentions of dating. I can't blame the wankers really. Why get tied down with some whore permanently when you can have pussy on tap? Looking for love, what a load of bollocks. I know why I go on the dating sites. It's to rid the world of anyone who looks like my useless mother. They don't belong here—don't deserve to live, just like she didn't. She used to say she loved me, yeah right, like fuck she did. What mother would let her waste of a husband do the things he did to me, do nothing about it, even joining in herself? Sick fuckers—both of them were.

Who needs love and all that crap when you can just take what you want and then do away with them? Love: what is it anyway? Is it what my father showed me when he used to punch and burn me while stubbing out his cigarettes on me when he couldn't be bothered getting off his lazy fat arse to find an ashtray?

He would make me sit in the room with him while he jerked off to his porn. I would have to sit on the floor next to his chair and get him anything he needed. I was his personal slave. 'Boy get me a beer.' 'Boy get me something to eat.' 'Boy get me my playboy magazine.' 'Boy, light me a cigarette.' The only thing I didn't do was shit and piss for him. I had to have tissues ready for him jerking off, or it would be my hands used to clean him up. He even made me suck him clean sometimes, telling me to lick every drop or he would beat me. He used to make me lift my t-shirt up, if I was wearing one that is, so he could pinch and twist my body when he was about to shoot his load. If I cried from the pain, he would kick me so hard that I would fall over and end up bruised, knocked out, or with broken bones. Once, he kicked me so hard, I sailed across the room, knocking the T.V. over. He flew out of his chair to make sure I hadn't broken it. I had never seen him move so fast, and for that, I got punched in the stomach and kidneys, a black eye and bloody lip. He never once looked or asked me if I was okay. Never. He didn't care what he did to me.

I never went to school. No one knew I existed. No one ever came to our house, and I was never allowed to leave except on the rare occasion I was allowed out to help mum with shopping when he'd severely beaten her and she couldn't move properly. When the man at the shop asked who I was, she just said I was a visiting nephew. I didn't know if we had any other family or not.

My mother used to work all day at a café in town to keep the money coming in for my dad's booze. God forbid if there was no beer or whiskey in the house for him, then he would lay into her with his fists—always on her body, never visible because she needed to go back to work. He couldn't have her staying off work and not bringing in the money. I would go days without food, and when they finally gave me something, it was only something basic like rice or porridge oats. Even though she sometimes brought leftovers from the café, I never got any. He got everything, and she was just as bad. She let him treat me like shit.

He wanted to watch me with my mother. I didn't know that what he had us doing was wrong. I had no idea. I thought all kids did it with their parents. He used to jerk off, watching me go down on my mother or with my cock in her mouth. He liked to join in sometimes and make her suck me while he ploughed into her backside. The bastard was sick. I know that now. I hated them both so much and the older I got, the worse it got. Being a teenager was a nightmare, but I was plotting in my head. Plotting to rid the world of the vile pair. I was plotting to fight back.

4

Katherine

I WISH MUM HAD BEEN AROUND to see my success. It was sudden, mum's health deteriorating. She was so proud when I passed my course to get a BA Hons in Business and Management with flying colours, but it was just after I'd finished and was building my business up but still living at home when mum fell ill. She started getting very tired. I asked her to stop working so that I could take care of her, but she liked working, it kept her active. She started falling asleep, even at work, and lost her appetite. I made her go to the doctors to get a checkup, and they weren't happy with her blood results and made an appointment for her at the hospital.

It took six weeks before we got to see someone and during that time she had got much worse. They kept her in hospital to run tests, and it turned out she had Endometrial cancer, which is cancer of the womb. If caught in time and a low grade, it can be removed, but for mum, it was too late. It had penetrated the lining of her womb and had travelled through her bloodstream and spread to other organs. The doctor said she didn't have much time left and there wasn't anything they could do for her.

Mum refused to stay in the hospital, insisting that if she didn't have long left, then she would die at home, and I agreed. It was the worst time of my life, knowing we didn't have long. We cherished every minute we could together, while we could. Brad came around most days to spend time with her too. It calmed him a lot until she died, then his anger went through the roof. She lasted two weeks after being diagnosed, and I'm thankful she didn't suffer any longer, she was progressively getting worse.

I was distraught, and Brad found out he was going to be a dad just two days after her funeral. It was bittersweet. Mum was gone, but I was going to become an aunty. Mum would never know her grandchild, and that was so sad.

I HAVE A MEETING tomorrow with a hotshot model who wants an apartment in the city. His PA phoned and asked for me personally, saying due to confidentiality, he would only speak and meet with myself. Here we go again, probably another arsehole—why do they all think they are so special? I have a lot of high-end clients. I don't care who they are or what they have. A client is a client.

I quickly finish up in my office, it's gone ten p.m., and I don't fancy driving home. Luckily, my apartment is only a ten-minute walk from here. I stop at the deli on the way to get a ham and cheese wrap and a bottle of wine to take home.

When I get to my apartment building, I greet Harry the doorman and have a quick chat with him about his five-year-old granddaughter. I like hearing Harry's stories. He's a nice man.

Once inside, I pour a glass of wine and head to my home office. I need to message Lewis and tell him I can't make the date tomorrow. I'm probably using this as an excuse but this meeting with the model might run over, and I don't want to rush it for a date. God, I hope he isn't too angry with me.

George

THAT STUPID FUCKING BITCH HAS cancelled on me. I'm tearing my hair out, pacing my shitty bedsit, kicking anything in my way. How could she do this to me? I'm in a rage. I have to calm down. I need to get out of here. I need to find a release. I storm out of my place, a rat-infested building in the slums of Brixton. I'm on the 9th floor of the high-rise, most of the time the fucking lift doesn't work, and the stairwells stink of piss and are full of graffiti. There are usually gangs of youths hanging around the stairwells selling their drugs and god knows what other shit. I run down the stairs, not even bothering to try the lift to see if it's working. I just need to get out. I need a drink fast. I need to find a pub.

I'm so enraged that I've been walking for ages, not paying attention to where I'm going, just seething. How could she do this to me? I can't get my head around it. How dare she.

I literally bump into people in the street, not seeing anyone in front of me. All I see is red—this is what happens to me. I can't explain it; there's a red cloud shrouding my vision. I hate this shit.

I don't know what went wrong. I said all the right bullshit stuff to her that women fall for: how beautiful she was and had the perfect hair, eyes, and figure. You know, the shit women need to hear. She seemed to take it all in, even agreeing to meet me. I won't give up. I will get her. She is a dead ringer for my mother—when I see her, I see my mother, and the anger and hate come back to me tenfold. I have to kill her, no question. She can't be allowed to reproduce. She can't be allowed to put any kids through the same living hell my mother put me through.

I look up, and there's a shitty pub over the road on the corner. Thank fuck. I head into it, and I can see some whores trying to get anything they can from the punters, they want booze and sex, god, why do they do that? I've seen them with cocks in their mouths and arses in these kinds of dives, usually in the hallway near the toilets. I've even been taking a piss when they have been at it in the shitter stalls—sluts the lot of them. It's always the whores to blame for it, not the pricks—they just take what's on offer to them and why the fuck not? If it's free, you don't reject pussy, no matter what the top end looks like. As long as the cock fits, who cares?

I order a neat whiskey and down it in one gulp, then order another one. I look around and spot a seat over in the back corner, right near the hallway to the toilets. Being in the back is great because it means I can see what's going on in the pub. This place is a dive. Middle-aged men are drinking themselves stupid, not wanting to go home to their wives. Who can blame them if they just get nagged at? There are some young pricks over the other side, dealing drugs with whores sat around or on them. Fuckers.

A bitch grabs one of the pricks by the hand and heads my way, in the direction of the toilets, I don't look up as they pass me, knowing exactly what they are up to.

I get up to follow. I want to watch. I need to watch. Just as I enter the hallway, I hear her giggle, the stupid whore, it's so irritating. I hear the prick, who was covered in tattoo's and had piercings in his nose, lip, and eyebrow, saying, "Shut the fuck up. Get on your fucking knees and take this big fat cock in your mouth, Stacey." They're just by the men's toilets, and they haven't seen me approach down the dim hallway. There is a small alcove just on the other wall, which I step into so I can watch. I hear her gagging as he shoves his cock roughly into her mouth. She's trying to pull him out, but he's holding her head tightly. He's thrusting and thrusting, and she's taking it because she doesn't have a choice. He's moaning, she's sucking but struggling to breathe. I'm getting fucking hard watching them, and I'm rubbing myself, trying not to make any noise. I'm going to cum in my fucking pants. I need to go somewhere quickly to sort myself out. I move towards the toilets, and he looks me straight in the eye with a big fuck off sneer on his face

"Take it, bitch, suck me hard, yes, yes, that's it." He's chanting over and over while eyeing me as I pass, thrusting harder. God, I wish that was me, and she was sucking me that deep, even though she's not my type with her bleached blond hair.

I go into the shitter cubicle to finish myself off and clean up. I needed that, but it wasn't enough to make up for my mood after the bitch cancelled our date. I had big plans for her.

Now that I have calmed down a little, I need to re-focus. I'll get her to re-schedule the date. It's a minor setback, that's all. For now, I just need to find someone I can take out my frustration on.

I'm a good-looking guy, and I keep myself fit by running and doing cardio in the park. I know I can get a whore easily—they come onto me all the fucking time. I go and get another whiskey from the bar and watch and listen to those around me, but I can't really see a whore to my liking. I think about just calling it a day, then the doors open, and one walks in. Jackpot. She doesn't look like she belongs in this shithole, but she's my type, sort of, with long brown hair, petite and curvy. I like curvy.

She heads to the prick I watched earlier in the hallway, and they start yelling at each other. He's yelling at her to get the fuck out, that it's over, and he's had enough of her possessive bullshit. She's yelling back telling him he's a tosser and she didn't know what she ever saw in his skinny arse. She marches off but not before slapping the bleached blond whore.

I can see she is upset so I finish my drink and head outside after her.

6

Katherine

I FEEL BAD. I KNOW LEWIS read my message because the little icon showed me it had been read straight away, but he didn't write back. Oh well, I didn't want a date anyway, did I? The more I sit here and look at his profile pictures though, the more I start to regret it. Maybe he will be different. Maybe he won't stand me up or try to get in my knickers on the first date. There have to be some good guys out there right? It's just I haven't met one in my twenty-seven years.

AFTER LUKE JONES, I didn't go out with anyone else in high school. I stayed away from any of the boys that tried to talk to me. I just put my head down and got on with getting good grades. I was still picked on by the mean girls, but I got through it, just. It wasn't until I was at Waltham Forest College studying Business and Management that I met Liam. We started talking occasionally, and he would come and sit with me in the cafeteria sometimes. It was all small talk, but we got on well, at least I thought we did. He used to hang around the common room with a bunch of guys and girls, but I never approached him at those times.

It was in my final year in college, I was nearly eighteen, and he asked if I would go out with him to the cinema. I was a bit reluctant at first, but I agreed.

He was the perfect gentleman.

When he saw me approach the cinema he had the biggest grin on his face that I matched. He let me choose the movie. I didn't think he would want to see a chick flick, so I opted for *Jumper* with Haden Christensen and Samuel L Jackson. He bought us drinks and popcorn, and we really enjoyed the movie. Afterwards, he asked if he could walk me home. He held my hand the entire walk, and when we got there, he told me he'd had a great night and asked if we could we do it again, to which I agreed. He kissed my cheek and waited until I had gone into my house.

After that, we went out a few times, and I really enjoyed it. Being underage, I couldn't go to pubs and clubs, so we'd often go to his house to listen to music, usually when his parents were out. We got into some heavy petting, lots of kissing, which I found I liked with him. We dated for about three months, and just like Luke, at the three-month mark, he tried to get more from me, but I wasn't ready. I eventually caved one day at his house when he asked if it was okay to 'feel my tits'. He asked me to take my top off, which I did reluctantly, but I found when he was squeezing my boobs and playing with my nipples through my bra it was doing strange things to me and making me feel wanted. I enjoyed the feelings it was giving me down below. I found my knickers were wet from my excitement.

The next time we were at his house, it went a bit farther. He said I was driving him crazy and he asked me to rub his cock. I hesitated, but then put my hand on him and started to rub and grip him through his jeans. Wow, it was so hard. He started to kiss down my neck to my exposed boobs until he took a nipple into his mouth. I moaned, rubbing him harder. I was so turned on, and that feeling was making me braver. I felt I wanted more but wasn't quite ready for sex.

He started feeling my leg, his hand rising higher under my skirt, all the while still sucking on my nipple. I tried to stop him, but he went higher, ignoring me, telling me how much I would enjoy him touching me there. He rubbed his thumb over my clit through my knickers, and it shocked me, I loved the feeling it gave me, but it felt wrong to be doing that. I jumped up, telling him I wasn't ready and I wanted to go home. He wasn't happy with me, but he walked me home anyway and said he would see me at college.

He didn't talk to me the next day. In fact, it was a few days after the incident when he approached me again, and he apologised for how he reacted. We arranged to see each other over the weekend, as his parents would be away. I was sure he wanted more, and I was nervous, but I was nearly eighteen, maybe we could go just a little further? He made me dinner of sorts, which we had with a bottle of wine. I had never had alcohol before, so one glass made me tipsy, which was probably his intention.

He took me up to his room. I felt a little awkward, standing there looking around while he was messing around near his TV. He took my hand and led me to his bed, and I got the giggles from the alcohol and nerves.

He sat on the bed and pulled me between his legs. His head was at waist level, and he started nuzzling my belly button.

He was telling me I was gorgeous and I was driving him mad,

that he needed to see me fully naked. He was whispering, telling me he couldn't wait, saying I was the most beautiful girl he had ever met. He lifted my top off and unhooked my bra—I tried to cover myself, but he removed my arms telling me I should never cover up. He took a nipple into his mouth, and I threaded my fingers in his hair urging him to suck more, I loved it. He alternated between nipples, and I didn't realise he had undone the zip on the back of my skirt until it was falling to the floor.

I gasped as his hand moved to between my legs and he started rubbing my clit over my knickers. I loved how he was making me feel. He moved my knickers to the side and started rubbing in my folds. I started to breathe heavily, jutting my hips forward the more he did it. I moaned loudly, which he took as a signal, slipping his finger inside me. I was so turned on, pressing his mouth harder to my nipple, wanting him to suck and bite harder. He started thrusting his finger in and out, harder and faster. I was moaning louder now, his thumb was rubbing at my clit, and then he put another finger inside me.

I loved it. In and out his fingers went, it was sensory overload, then I screamed out so loud. I felt electrical charges all over my body, the tingling everywhere was just the best feelings I had ever had. Then I was shuddering—my legs felt weak and wobbly like jelly. I threw my head back and screamed, there were stars in my eyes as they rolled back in my head. Oh. My. God. Wow. What the hell was that? I almost collapsed, but Liam caught me, making us fall backwards on the bed.

I felt embarrassed. My cheeks were burning so much I'm sure I looked like a tomato. He asked if I'd enjoyed it and I nodded, with my head buried in his shoulder. He laughed at me, telling me not to be shy. He said it was absolutely fucking amazing watching me cum for him. Oh my god I just had my first orgasm?

He undid the zip on his jeans and asked me if I would stroke him. He was rock hard after watching me come apart for him. Very slowly, I sat up and was amazed to see his hard cock in his hands, he was stroking himself. I had never seen a hard penis before. It kind of turned me on watching him, I started to stroke it like he was. Watching the look on his face made me brave and made me feel a little powerful. I could see the enjoyment he was getting from me stroking him. I grabbed harder and started moving up and down. He told me to grab harder, tighter. I had never done anything like this before, and I had to admit I was enjoying it, I think the wine had a lot to do with that. He was rock hard, yet it felt like velvet in my hands. I squeezed hard like he encouraged me to do.

He was gasping and saying my name over and over. I could see there was moisture at the end of his cock, he opened his eyes and saw me looking at it.

"Lick it, please, Kate, I'm desperate to feel your mouth on me."

I was inquisitive, so I bent my head slowly and stuck my tongue out to swipe the tip. He bucked underneath me and groaned out, "So fucking perfect. I want my cock in your mouth so much. Please take me in your mouth."

I lowered over the head putting his cock in my mouth. It wasn't so bad really—salty, but bitter, and smoother than I imagined. It didn't take long before he had hold of my head, gripping my hair tightly and thrusting up into my throat. I tried to move, but he wouldn't let me. He was gripping so hard, starting to ram upwards hard and fast. It hurt, and I wasn't enjoying it any longer, but he wouldn't let me go. I started to panic and tried to pull away, but he gripped me tighter and thrust harder. "Hang on, baby, just a bit more. Oh God, use your tongue as well. It's going to taste so good shooting down your throat, all thick and creamy. Can you handle that, babe? Can you feel it getting bigger? That's it. Just there like that. I'm about to blow. Oh God, Kate, Kate, Kate, aargh."

He was thrusting his hips, gripping my hair and the hot, salty taste shot down my throat. It was all too much, and I started to gag. I tried very hard to get up but he was gripping my head tightly, he was pulling my hair out, I could feel it tearing at my scalp. With his cock still in my mouth, the puke came spluttering up and projected out of the sides.

He dived up off the bed so fast that he knocked me to the floor shouting, "What the fuck, you stupid fucking bitch. That's disgusting, what the hell? Get up, you stupid slut."

I was shocked that he would talk to me like that. It wasn't my fault. He'd pushed me and forced me out of my comfort zone.

I grabbed my clothes and ran for the bathroom. I looked a mess, my hair was all over the place and knotted, with loose strands that he'd pulled out. My face was red and blotchy, and I could see bite marks on my boobs and what looked like a bruise forming. I was crying hard, mascara and eyeliner making my eyes black. My chin and down my neck was covered in cum and sick, I started gagging again.

The smell of the sick and his cum made me throw up. I quickly washed my face, rinsed my mouth out and used some of the toothpaste from the cabinet. I needed to get rid of the taste of the sick and his cum before I puked any more. I got dressed and ran down the stairs and out of the door. He didn't even come after me, the arsehole.

I didn't hear from him on Sunday, and when Monday came around, I was dreading going into college. The first time I saw him was in class, he didn't even look at me. What the hell? I thought we were seeing each other! Why was he ignoring me and treating me like this?

At lunchtime, I walked into the common room, and he was there with the usual guys and girls, all gathered around him, all laughing. When they noticed me, they started whispering and laughing louder. One of his friends shouted out, "Hey, puke-et, how's it going?"

I was mortified. He'd told them! Why would he do that? But then I realised it was worse than that, much, much, worse than him just telling them.

I could hear me moaning and calling his name as I screamed my first ever orgasm. I could hear him moaning and him saying my name, and then him calling me a stupid slut. Oh my god!

I looked over at him—he was holding his phone. When we made eye contact, he smirked at me. They were all watching me on his phone. The bastard had recorded us.

He'd totally used me. I ran out of the room and ran home and locked myself away for a week. I only had to go back to college for one remaining exam, luckily, I had aced all my coursework and had taken three exams with just the one remaining. I would have had to leave if it was halfway through the year.

I left never to see Liam again—arsehole number two.

I LOOK AT the computer screen in front of me, looking at Lewis's face, wondering could he be the one—could he be different and not use me? I'm older and wiser now. I think I can judge people better. I start typing a message to him. I suggest re-arranging our date for next Saturday so that I can't use my meetings as an excuse. I quickly press send before I change my mind, shut down the computer and head to bed. I want him to reply, don't I?

7

George

AS I LEAVE THE PUB, I CAN SEE the brown-haired bitch just over the road leaning against one of the shop windows. I start casually walking towards her, and when I get near and she hears me approach she looks up at me with tears streaming down her face. I pretend I'm just casually walking by

"Hey, are you ok, love? Are you hurt?" I ask her acting like I'm concerned.

"I'll be okay. I just broke up with my boyfriend. The knobhead was cheating on me again, and I've had enough. God, I'm so stupid, It just hurts he did that to me."

I offer to walk with her. She's a bit wary of me and weighs me up and down, but I put on my best innocent look; the one I've perfected over the years, and I know the moment she decides I'm okay and it's safe to walk with me. Her face changes and she looks like she wants to devour me. I see it a lot—women just want me as soon as they see the face and the body, they want to use me like I'm a piece of fucking meat. I keep myself trim, and it seems to get most of the girls riled up when they see a few abs—the cheap sluts, they are all so fucking shallow.

We start walking. "I'll cancel the taxi I called to pick me up," she says, "my flat is a good twenty-minute walk from here, but I think the walk would do me good and help me calm down a bit."

She tells me about what has happened in the pub. She obviously didn't see me sitting in the back, and assumes, as I intended, that I was just an innocent passer-by.

"Hey, you know not all men are arseholes, some of us are decent guys," I say winking and getting a smile from her, putting her a little at ease. She tells me her name is Cheryl and she is twenty-four years old. I tell her my name is Sam, and I'm twenty-six—just a slight lie on both accounts. I don't want her freaking out that I'm thirty-three.

"I haven't been with him for long, in fact just a couple of months, and this is the fourth time that I know off that he's cheated on me. I should have kicked his drugged-up skinny arse into touch the first time. I'll never learn!"

We walk along and chat like old friends. She grows more confident with me, which is my intention. There's no one else around, and it's quiet, which is exactly what I need. We turn a corner and are walking on a deserted road. All the houses on this road look derelict and are boarded up with metal shutters to stop people getting in or vandalising them, although they are covered in graffiti. I can see one house a little farther down the road on the opposite side that's not boarded up but has bars on the windows, and there's a light on in the upstairs room, presumably the bedroom, but that seems to be the only house that looks occupied on the whole street.

I need to make my move now and quickly before we get any closer to that house. I stop and turn to this stupid bitch, so stupid that she's walked down an empty road with a complete stranger. She stops and looks at me.

"What's wrong?" she asks. I grab her neck and before she can say anything my mouth is on hers. She tries to stop me at first, barely, pushing on my chest, but then she gives in to my kiss and returns it with full force, slipping her tongue into my mouth. Her hands start roaming my chest, feeling my abs, then one lowers to grab my cock. Like I said: stupid bitch.

I start walking her backwards with my mouth still on hers, one hand still on the back of her neck, the other now under her top pinching a nipple. I'm backing her into the garden of the house behind her. She just follows my lead. I have my eyes open and can see there is a side gate that's hanging off its hinges. I move us towards that. She puts her arms around my neck, pushing her tongue into my mouth harder and duelling with my tongue. God, I hate this much intimacy, but it's the only way to get near her without her panicking or screaming.

Once through the side gate, I can't really see anything. I don't think she even realises we've gone around the back of the house until she opens her eyes and stops kissing me. She looks around, panicked, trying to get her bearings as her eyes adjust in the darkness.

"What are we doing here?" she says to me as I pull away from her. I just stare at her. At that moment, all I can see is my mother in front of me. It's dark, but I swear it's her, the one who supposedly loved me. I hate her.

The red mist comes over me, and I grab her around the neck with both hands, squeezing hard. "You need to die you fucking bitch" I whisper in her ear. She tries to claw at my hands to get me to release her, but I can't, I'm seething.

Her eyes start to pop. I'm sure they will be bloodshot and her face red, but I can't tell in the dark. She starts to go limp and stops fighting me. I know I haven't killed her yet, she's just unconscious, which is how I need her. I let her slump to the floor. I hear her head hit the ground. Good—she deserves that. I need this release. I've waited over a year already. One more before I get the one I want won't hurt.

I use the torch on my phone to see if I can find an opening in the back of the house. I do it quickly, I'm not sure if there are houses out the back, and I don't want anyone to see the light. The back door and windows are all boarded up—fuck, now what? I can't chance making a noise by prying the metal boards off, and I need to move fast before she wakes up. With my eyes adjusting, I can see the house next door, and again it's boarded up, but the bottom panel of the backdoor has been kicked in at some point. Jackpot. I quickly make my way to that door to see if I can get it open, luckily, I can reach in and up to the handle and turn the lock. The door swings open.

I nearly retch from the stench in the kitchen. It smells like something has died in here, and it reminds me of what I did to my bastard parents. I rush out to grab the bitch, just as she starts to come too, making noises. Fuck, I lean over and punch her in the face, knocking her out. I pick her up and put her over my shoulder and manoeuvre through the broken fence and into the house next door. When I get in and shut the door, she starts to moan again. I drop her onto the floor. I need to gag her. I can't have her shouting and screaming. There is rubbish all over the place, hanging off the kitchen window is a filthy, torn net curtain. That will do. I don't have time to search for anything else. I rip it down and tear it up to make it small enough to shove in her mouth. With the remaining net, I bind her hands behind her back.

I walk out of the kitchen into a hallway, through a door to the right, into what must have been the living room. The shit smell is terrible—so many memories come back to me with that smell. I remember lying in my room—I didn't have a bed, just a dirty old blanket on the floor. When my mother wasn't at work and was at home to service him, they used to lock me in there for days sometimes and forget I was there. I didn't have anything to eat and didn't have anywhere to take a piss or shit, so I had to just do it there in the corner of my room.

Pulling myself back to the present, I notice a filthy mattress on the floor, which will do for what I need. I tear a curtain down and throw it on the mattress and go back to grab the bitch from the floor. I grab her long brown hair and drag her through to the other room. She's crying and kicking out, but with her hands tied and her mouth gagged, there isn't much she can do.

I slap her hard and throw her onto the mattress. She's manic, struggling to get up, but I push her down and climb on top of her, straddling her waist. I punch her in the face again, almost knocking her out. "Shut up, you fucking stupid bitch and keep still."

She goes rigid, and I can see her eye starting to swell and close up from the punches

"You're going to pay for that now, bitch." I rip open her top, exposing her tits. She isn't wearing a bra—what a surprise—what a slut. I edge lower over her legs so I can get to the waistband of her leggings, and I rip them open as well. She at least had a scrap of material trying to cover her up, but I rip that off too.

I open the fly on my jeans and take my cock out. I'm so fucking hard seeing her like this. I start to stroke myself. God, having this power over her is so good. She's still crying, only really hard now. "Shut the fuck up, you dumb bitch, or I will make you be quiet."

I stroke myself harder and start rocking on top of her, grinding into her, pulling, gripping faster and harder.

I can see her watching me with one eye, the stupid bitch and I don't like it.

"Close your eyes," I shout. She does, fast.

God, she looks like my mother. Their faces merge into one. I hate her for making me do the things she did with her and dad. I'm pressing down hard, then almost jumping up and down with my arse digging into her, all the while gripping my cock hard, pumping up and down so fast, I'm almost there. Oh God, I need this. I move quickly to stand up. I'm about to explode, and I want to do it all over her tits and face from above. I want her to smell me for a change, instead of me always face planted in my mother's cunt, smelling and tasting her. Ahhhhh I'm coming, thick and fast, you would never have known I'd had a release less than an hour ago in that shitty pub. I always see my mother when I'm like this. It brings out the hatred.

The bitch is whimpering below me. I let go of my cock and sit back down on her, only this time higher up her body where I can rub my cock in my cum, all over her tits and in her face. She's still crying. I can see the tears rolling down her face. I punch her again. Only this time, I knock her out cold.

Good. She deserves everything she gets. I continue to run my cock all over her face and between her tits until I'm starting to get hard again. I take the net out of her mouth and replace it with my cock while she's out cold so I can fuck her mouth without worrying about her trying to bite my cock. I shove so far down her throat that I'm going to cum again. I explode down her throat. Maybe she will drown in my cum, that would be something, death by cum, it will save me having to do it.

I shuffle farther down her body, and I start to play with her pussy, running my flaccid cock along it over her clit. I'm not going to enter her with my cock. That isn't what I want. I just want to play. Oh god, playing with her clit is making me hard again. I insert my fingers in her cunt. There's something about the soft feel of the inside. I'm moving around in there when she starts to move, unconsciously bucking her hips. Jesus, does she have no shame—even unconscious? It's been so long since I've had a woman, which must be why I cum again all over her.

This was what I had needed, to help me re-focus. Taking control. I needed to get my head back in the game and focus on getting the bitch to agree to a date with me.

I want her. I need her because she is the spitting image of my mother, and I can't let her live. I now realise this bitch doesn't look like my mother apart from the hair, but that's enough for me to want to get rid of her. The less there are in this world the better.

She starts to come around again after I finish playing. I need to finish her now. Get it over with. I wrap my hands around her throat and start to add pressure. Her eyes open and begin to go bloodshot and bulge out of her head. I love this bit, the power it gives me. To see the terror in her eyes, the terror I put there, the terror that gives me the control knowing I'm the last thing she sees. To see the last breath she will ever take and what fucking power that gives me. It makes me feel like the king of the fucking world. I never had the power with my parents—not until I killed them that night. I showed them who had the fucking power then all right. She starts gasping, trying to get air, I increase the pressure on her windpipe. She doesn't stand a chance. One last flail, one last look, one last breath. Then she stills. It's done—she's lying there, lifeless, with her bulging black eyes staring.

I leave her there, but cover her body in the torn curtain and some debris that's lying around until she just looks like a pile of crap in the corner. Unless someone moves the rubbish, you won't know anyone is there. It's getting light out. I didn't realise I had been here for so long. Time flies when you're having fun. I need to leave. I'll come back tonight to sort out the body and hope no one comes in during the day. I creep out and lock the back door by reaching up inside once I've closed it. I then straighten the panel to make it look like it's solid and secure, hopefully, to deter anyone from trying to get in.

I head back to my bedsit and hope the bitch has sent me a message.

8

Katherine

I TURN ON THE COMPUTER THE next morning after I have made my coffee and before starting to get ready for work. I'm eager to see if Lewis has replied to me. There's no new message from him, but then he only read the message at 5.33 a.m., which was less than an hour ago. He is either an earlier riser than me or he was late getting in. Maybe he works shifts?

In my office, I fire up the computer, and Clive, my secretary, comes in to run through some work with me and bring me some iced water. Clive has been with me for just over a year now, and I don't know what I ever did without him. He's the closest I have to a friend, and it probably helps that he is gay, so we have no interest in each other sexually. He can be a little protective of me though. He's a couple of years older and tries to act like my big brother.

"Right, first off, the meeting you had scheduled for this afternoon has been cancelled. I had a call from his PA, saying she was so sorry, but he was called away on business last night and would not be back in time, but could they re-schedule for Friday this week at 3 p.m. I checked your diary, and you are free unless you have something else planned?"

Great! I cancelled my date tonight with Lewis for nothing. I shake my head. "No, I have nothing else planned. It just sucks because I changed some plans I had for tonight in case it ran over." I roll my eyes. I hope Lewis gets back to me then it won't have been for nothing. Maybe I won't hear from him again anyway. Maybe he'll bench me like I have been once before. I've had nothing but bad experiences with online dating. I'm not sure how much longer I can persevere with it.

NOT LONG AFTER I started online dating, I met someone who looked really nice. We sent each other messages, getting to know each other. We met up and hit it off straight away, although, I was so cautious after the last two arseholes. His name was Leo Worse, and he was lovely. I was still young and in uni, and because I didn't do the whole student partying thing and preferred to study, I thought I'd join the online dating site for some company.

Leo was in his final year at Oxford Uni to be an architect, he was a little older than me. With me starting out in the property world, I found him interesting and we had a lot to talk about. He never tried anything on with me, which I was pleased about, but we did kiss and cuddle a lot. I'd been seeing him for a while and he only ever came to visit me, he never suggested I visit him or meet his family, even though I introduced him to mum, who thought he was sweet.

We did eventually go further in the relationship. He was visiting, and my mum was out at bingo one Saturday night. We were watching a movie, and I was snuggled up to him on the couch, he turned and started kissing me, then lowered me to my back.

He got on top of me, and I could feel how hard he was. He started grinding slowly into me, I was getting aroused. He lifted my top and started to suck on my boobs. His hand moved lower under the waistband of my skirt and into my knickers where he started to stroke me. I was moaning for him not to stop.

He sat up and started to kiss down my stomach while pushing my skirt and knickers as far down my legs as he could get them so I was naked apart from my bra.

He then knelt on the floor in front of the couch and swung my legs around so my feet were on the floor and he parted my legs, exposing me to him fully. I was mortified to have him right there, staring into my most private parts, and I covered my face with my hands. I had never been so exposed to someone before.

He nudged between my legs, ran his fingers between my folds and bent his head to kiss my tummy before moving lower and lower, smothering me with kisses and licking his way downwards towards my core.

He spread me open with his fingers, bent his head and licked very slowly right down my folds. I gasped out loud, trying to close my legs and get up off the couch. Wow, what just happened?

"Don't, baby, you taste so good," he said as he prised my legs open again after pushing me back down. He then lifted one leg at a time and put each one over his shoulders, so my core was directly in his face. He licked again, only this time he latched onto my clit and started to suck. OH.MY.GOD. It was pure bliss. He kept licking and sucking then he dipped two fingers into me and started moving in and out, getting faster and faster. I could hear how wet I was, but I didn't care—it felt amazing. I was floating in complete ecstasy. I had never felt anything like it and didn't want it to stop. I grabbed hold of his head, pulling him harder into my core, I needed more. I was pushing myself into him as hard as I could whilt pulling his head in. He may drown down there but at that moment I didn't care.

To say I loved what he was doing was an understatement and without any warning, I had the biggest and loudest orgasm I had ever had. I saw stars as my eyes rolled back, and I think I may have blacked out for a few seconds. My body was shaking, and wow, I wanted that again and again. It was heaven. I had tingly feelings running all through my body from the explosion.

I opened my eyes to see him sitting back on his legs, smiling at me. "You really liked that, didn't you, baby? That's the sweetest pussy I have ever tasted."

I felt embarrassed, not just at his words, but also because I loved it so much and the way I reacted to it. I let my eyes drift down his body. I don't remember him taking his top off, but when I got lower, I could see he was rock hard. I unzipped his jeans and took his cock out. He was huge, and I wanted to return the favour and taste him. I bent my head and started to lick the top of him just like I would an ice cream. Then I remembered my disaster with Liam. I stood up quickly. "Where's your phone?" I asked him.

"It's in my jacket pocket in the kitchen, why?" He was looking at me with a confused smile on his face.

"I'm sorry. I had a really bad experience in college when an ex-boyfriend videoed me when we were fooling around, and showed it to all his friends."

"I would never dream of doing anything like that, babe. What a dick."

I started stroking his cock, gripping harder, and he started moaning just like I had been doing five minutes earlier. I lowered my head to take him into my mouth, I started to lick the tip and suck the pre-cum from him. I stopped and looked up, a little embarrassed. "Please can you not cum in my mouth?"

I lowered my head again and started to wrap my mouth around him before he could ask me any questions. Oh, wow, he only just fit. Oh god, how was I going to do this? I had only ever done it once before so wasn't sure what I was doing. He started thrusting forward, holding onto my hair, but he was being gentle, unlike Liam. I still panicked though and started gagging with him thrusting harder and deeper. He was nearly in my throat, and I didn't know what to do, I grabbed the base of his cock, so I could try and control how much I could fit in my mouth. I started pumping with my hand as well as sucking and licking. He was moaning loudly. "Oh god, baby. Take it all, just like that."

I felt him start to expand, and I knew he was close. I started to move my mouth, trying to lift my head up, but he gripped me harder, keeping me there and not letting go, thrusting faster and harder. The next thing I knew, he was coming in my mouth, and it was spurting down my throat. It was bitterer than I remembered and very salty all at the same time.

I was going to be sick, again. He was still thrusting hard, and I was crying. I clamped down with my teeth hard to get him to release me, and it worked. I quickly scrambled away from him and got up, running up the stairs to the bathroom, and threw up in the toilet.

I cleaned my face and brushed my teeth, then went into my bedroom to put on my dressing gown before going back down to him.

"You bitch. What the fuck did you do that for?" were his first words to me once I entered the living room. He was still naked, nursing his cock.

Why does this keep happening to me? Why do they treat me so badly? I was fuming. "I told you not to cum in my fucking mouth, you wanker, what part of that did you not understand? Just get dressed and leave."

He looked at me like I was mad, still nursing his cock, which did look a bit red.

"Leave, Leo, before mum comes home."

He stood up, pulled his jeans on and put his top back on. To my surprise, he came over and wrapped me in his arms. "I'm sorry, baby, I just lost control. I didn't do it on purpose. I had every intention of pulling out and coming all over your amazing tits, but you just did something to me, and I couldn't stop. I promise it won't happen again. Don't be mad at me, please…" He bent to look me in the eyes before peppering my face with kisses.

My anger dissipated at his words. "Ok. I'm sorry too, but you still need to leave. Mum will be here in the next twenty minutes. I'll speak to you tomorrow, okay?"

He hugged me, and then kissed me so sweetly that I was melting. I was sure he'd meant what he said. Then he left.

We did speak the next day, and he apologised again and said he was leaving to go back to Oxford in the next hour, and he would see me again soon. We didn't speak for a few days, so I texted him to Facetime me, which he did fifty minutes later.

He seemed a bit flustered but said he was out when I texted, and he had just run back to his room so he could Facetime with me.

I asked when I could see him next and offered to go to Oxford, but he gave me the usual spiel of how I couldn't go to his shared house as it wasn't allowed, and he wasn't going to his parents for a while.

I was beginning to get a complex, thinking he didn't want me to meet his friends or family. Little did I know, I was right all along.

I decided, as he couldn't make it to mine this weekend and I couldn't stay at his that I would book into a Premier Inn hotel near his university. I would surprise him at his shared house by just showing up, and then he could stay with me at the hotel.

I got the train early on Saturday morning so I would arrive at his house by 8 a.m. Perfect, as I was sure he would be there at that time.

When I arrived, I was really surprised at how nice and big it was. I knocked on the door, waiting for someone to answer, but no one did. Just as I was about to leave, a man came jogging up to me, all sweaty; he had obviously been out running.

"Can I help you?" he asked.

I must have looked surprised because he cocked his head to the side and frowned at me. This man was middle-aged, he wasn't a student sharing accommodation for uni, but he also looked familiar to me.

"Sorry, I must have the wrong address. I was looking for my boyfriend, Leo. I thought this was it. Shared student accommodation?

The man laughed. "Oh, it's shared alright, between me and my son Leo. When will he fucking learn? The dipshit." I must have looked shocked and confused.

"Look, love, I'm sorry, and I'm also ashamed, but I have had enough of his bullshit. You'd better come inside."

I hesitated when he opened the door and beckoned me inside ahead of him, but stepped into the hallway. There were stairs ahead of me to the right, and the hallway down the side of the stairs led to what looked like the kitchen.

"There's a door just down the hallway there, before you get to the kitchen, on your right. It's under the stairs, and it leads to Leo's apartment in the basement. I'm sorry about this and what you will walk into." He looked at me with a sorrowful look on his face before he headed up the stairs.

I was a bit shocked, not sure what to think or do. I was just rooted to the spot as I watched the man disappear up the stairs. Should I just leave? What if it was a trap? I had no idea if this was real or if this man was a psycho, but my curiosity got the better of me.

I edged down the hallway, all the while listening for the man upstairs to make sure he wasn't coming down to trap me in his basement.

I approached the door under the stairs and saw a plaque that said "Leo's Pad". I guessed that answered my question then. I tried the handle, and it opened. It was dark down there, but with the light from the hallway, I could see the stairs in front of me. I noticed a light cord hanging down, I pulled it, and it lit the stairwell for me.

It was nicely carpeted and there were pictures on the wall leading down, mainly of football stadiums.

I started to descend, being as quiet as I could, not knowing what to expect. When I got to the bottom, there was a small lounge area with a sectional sofa and a plasma TV on the wall with a PlayStation in a unit under the TV. I could see two doorways leading off the small room.

I found another light switch and put it on, and headed to one of the door's, which was slightly ajar. I peeked in, and with the light shining in from the lounge area I could make out a toilet—this was a bathroom. I started to make my way to the next door but stopped when I heard noises coming from behind it.

I reached for the handle, trying to be as quiet as I could and slowly started to open the door, not sure what to expect or even if it was going to be my Leo in there or not.

It was dark in the room, but the noises were unmistakable.

I felt for a light switch on the wall and flicked it. There was a girl sat on top of a guy, riding him. She turned to look at me. "What the fuck, who are you?" Leo's head popped up at her question, and in a panicked voice, "Holy shit, what the fuck are you doing here? How did you get in here, Katherine?"

I was frozen, trying to take in what I was seeing. There were clothes all over the place, both male and female, and in the open wardrobe, there were women's clothes hanging up. There was a unit of drawers to the side of the door with all kinds of women's things: makeup, perfume, and hair straighteners.

The girl who was still on top of Leo scowled at me then looked back at him. "Who the fuck is she, Leo? Why do you know her name? You better tell me straight, or I will cut your balls off here and now." He looked horrified as he looked from her to me then back to her. "Babe, it's not what you think, my dad must have let her in. What the fuck are you doing here, Katherine?"

Him saying my name again brought me out of my shock. "I came to see you, Leo. You weren't coming to me this weekend, so I thought I would surprise you. Who the fuck is she and why is this your dad's house? You told me you lived in shared accommodation with other students, and that you weren't allowed to have anyone stay over?"

I stood with my hands on my hips, waiting for his reply. The girl got off the bed and headed towards me, stark naked. "I'm his fucking fiancée. Who the fuck are you?"

I looked from Leo to her. "You're his fiancée? I'm his girlfriend, or so I thought. We met online a few months back, and he's been coming to my house every other weekend."

She glared at him, and then lunged for him, punching and slapping him. "You fucking bastard. You told me you'd closed those dating site accounts months ago—after the last one. What the fuck is wrong with you? Am I not enough for you that you have to go chasing more pussy, you fucking pathetic worthless bastard? We are so done this time. You can go and screw as many as you want now, but don't come begging me to take you back this time. You screwed up royally. Don't expect a job with my dad now."

With that, she punched him a few more times, then got a bag and started to shove her stuff into it. She left the room but not before picking up a speaker and throwing it at him. I walked over to the side of the bed, looking down at him, still naked and still hard. I bent down to speak to him, and at the same time, I grabbed his cock, dug my nails into it and started twisting it so hard he was screaming for me to stop.

"You fucking bastard, you had a fiancée this whole time," I screamed at him. "That's why you wouldn't let me come and visit you in your 'shared' accommodation or visit your parents? You were just stringing me along all this time. Was I the only one or are there more?"

He started to scream like a little girl, and because of the hold I had on his cock, he couldn't answer. I let go and turned to leave.

As I approached the door, I turned to look at his pathetic form curled up on the bed holding his cock in pain. Served him right, the arsehole, and just like his fiancée, I picked up the other speaker and threw it at him. I went back into the lounge where the other girl had just come out of the bathroom

"I'm so sorry. I had no idea he had a fiancée. I wanted to surprise him. I guess it was us that got the surprise." I thought she was going to lay into me, but she just grabbed her bag and headed up the stairs, cursing all the way. I pulled out his PlayStation and smashed it on the floor, and picking up a guitar next that I hadn't seen earlier, I then smashed that over the PlayStation before I headed up the stairs to leave. That was arsehole number three. I had been stashed—someone's secret.

Wow, WHERE HAD the day gone? I'd been so engrossed in the new contracts that it was time to leave. I wanted to go home to my house tonight, not stay in the apartment, so I got my stuff together and headed out of my office. Clive was still here. He needed to leave. He had a boyfriend to get back to. "Why are you still here, Clive? You need to get back to that gorgeous man of yours."

"He's away on business tonight. I wanted to finish stuff here before heading out. I'll see you tomorrow afternoon when you're back in the office."

I had an appointment at 10 a.m. to see a building I was interested in purchasing just outside of the city and on my way back in from my Chelmsford house. Another reason to go there tonight.

I'm anxious to see if Lewis has got back to me about rearranging the date yet.

9

George

Now I have to decide what to do with the whore I have in that shitty house. I can't leave her there. She will be found sooner or later, and my cum is all over her. I don't want my samples on their records.

No one knows I exist. They never have. No one knew my parents had me. They never told me why or how. I don't know if she gave birth to me at home or if I even belonged to them. Did they take me from someone else? I will never know now that they're dead.

I have never been in trouble with the police, and obviously, I have never been caught for killing my parents or the other whores that looked like my fucking mother. So even if they find the bodies and get my DNA from them, I'm not in the system, they won't be able to trace them to me.

I have a secret place where I take the bodies on Tottenham Marshes in very dense woodlands. Nothing has been found in the sixteen years since I killed my parents. I suspect one day they will be found. It's just a matter of time, it's a waiting game. Until then I will keep dumping more bodies.

My preferred method was strangulation, and that's how I killed my mother and all the other whores. It was my father that was different. I stabbed him over and over while he slept in his dirty chair in front of the TV, passed out on too much wanking and too much whiskey.

It was easy enough, but if I had tried to strangle him, he could have woken up and possibly overpowered me. It was too risky, so I killed him first. I was seventeen and big. He didn't order me around as much as he used to, probably because he thought if he pushed me now I could fight back, because of my height and muscles I gained through working out in my room.

From the age of fourteen, I seemed to shoot up, and around that age, I started working out. I had nothing else to do being locked in my room for days. I did anything I could do, quietly. I grew in height and width as I built up my muscles. He still wanked in front of me and had me wank myself at the same time while watching his porn, and we still all had sex together, but it was getting less and less the bigger I got. I still did what they said. I didn't know at that point it was wrong, wrong and disgusting to do that with your parents because it was all I had ever known. I thought it was what everyone did. My filthy mother couldn't get enough of me though, from the age of fifteen. With my physique changing so much and my cock growing, she fucking loved nothing more than riding it or sucking it. She grew more and more needy, but she only wanted me, never my dad. She wanted to do everything with me, and half the time he was so pissed he didn't care, he just sat wanking while watching us as though we were his own private porn show. Other times he took her hard and made me watch. Filthy bastards.

One day, after being downstairs most of the day with him and being his slave I snapped. I was pacing my room thinking of all the shit they had me do, thinking how wrong it all felt, and something seemed to snap in my head. It was the first time I saw the red mist. I just knew I had to do something to stop them. I had to kill them. It was the only way out for me. It was time. My mother was in her bedroom. I could hear her snoring, and I knew my father was more than likely passed out downstairs.

I headed for the kitchen and took a bread knife out of the drawer, then walked into the living room and sure enough he was passed out in his chair with the porn still playing and his flaccid cock hanging out of his jogging pants. I took the knife and raised it above his chest—I was going straight for the heart. I kicked his legs, making him wake up. I wanted to see the fear in his eyes when he realised what was going to happen to him.

He didn't move as I kicked him, so I did it again harder. This time he started to move and slowly opened his eyes. "What the fuck are you doing, boy, move you…" he started to say. The look in his eyes when he realised I had the knife held above him was priceless.

I brought that knife down straight through his heart. His eyes went so wide that I thought they were going to pop out of his head. He started making gurgling noises as he tried to speak but blood was pouring from his mouth. I took the knife out and brought it down, again and again, harder each time, giving me my first taste of power and control. Finally, after all this time I had the fucking power.

"You fucking bastard, you deserve this and more. I hope you rot in hell!" I screamed at him.

He went still, the blood oozing out of his mouth and the holes in his chest. He was gone, his wide eyes just staring but blank. The life had gone out of him once and for all. Thank fuck for that. I felt a sense of relief and great satisfaction.

I heard movement upstairs, and I knew I had woken my mother with my rage, shouting as I stabbed him. I moved behind the living room door when I heard her coming down the stairs. As she walked into the room, she came to an abrupt halt, trying to comprehend what she was seeing. I crept up behind her and covered her mouth with one of my hand's so she couldn't scream and put the other round her throat.

"Hello mother, your turn, you filthy whore. You deserve to suffer as much as him. You're no fucking mother. You never loved me or protected me from him when he hurt me. You enjoyed it all, just like the whores on the TV. You haven't been able to get enough of me since I got bigger. I could see how much you enjoyed it, you filthy bitch."

She tried to speak, but it was muffled with my hand over her mouth. She was becoming hysterical, trying to grab my hand from her mouth, so I dragged her to my dad, to his lifeless body and let her take it in, him lying there, eyes wide open, blank and staring, blood everywhere and a flaccid tiny cock hanging out. I released my hold on her.

"Take his cock in your hand, NOW!" She bent down slightly and with shaking hands grabbed his cock.

"Take the knife out of his chest and cut his cock off." She was violently shaking now as she tried to pull the knife out.

"Do it, bitch or your death will be very slow and painful." She pulled at the knife a few times but it was wedged in. She finally pulled it out.

"Cut his cock off, and make it quick."

"No, George, please don't make me do that. Please don't hurt me. You know I love you. I'm your mum. You're my big boy, George."

"YOU NEVER LOVED ME!" I shout right in her face. "Fucking do it NOW! Cut his cock off."

She started to hack at his cock. The knife was serrated, but it was still difficult. It took her a while to do, trying to saw and stab to separate it from his body, all while she was crying and sniffling, but she managed to cut it off. There was blood everywhere.

I took the cock from her hand, then grabbed her hair, yanked her head back and shoved it in her mouth before she had a chance to scream.

"That's what you deserve, to choke on his cock after where he's been sticking it all these years. Choke on it, you bitch."

She was gagging, with his cock stuck in her mouth. I covered her mouth with my hand again, so she couldn't try to spit it out or scream. I brought my other hand to the front of her neck and started to squeeze tightly. She grabbed at my hands, trying to pry my fingers away from her neck to get me to release her. She was turning a nice shade of purple. It was so satisfying watching the life being drained from her like this. The sense of relief that came over me was immense. I wanted to cry, but I wouldn't until she was dead. I didn't want her thinking I was crying over her. Maybe I was, but only in relief that it was finally over, my hell—my seventeen years of torture. I watched her closely; letting her see right into my eyes and the hatred I had there for her. I watched as she took her last breath with a cock shoved in her mouth. The ecstasy I felt was immense and so fucking satisfying, the relief was so powerful and having this control was a feeling I would never forget. I felt like I could rule the fucking world right not with all this power.

She fell to the floor with a thud, cracking her head on my dad's knee on the way down. I just stood and stared at them both. Then, I burst into tears. The emotions were so overwhelming, but I was free at last.

Then it hit me like a big fucking boom. Shit, what do I do now?

When I got back to my bedsit this morning at about 5.30 a.m., I switched on the computer and was flooded with relief that the bitch had sent me another message. I couldn't read it fast enough. She was apologising for cancelling and asking to reschedule our date for Saturday. Thank fuck for that. I've got my catch back. I will finally get her.

Then it hit me. Why couldn't she have said about rearranging it when she cancelled? I wouldn't have needed to go out last night and kill that whore. That bitch's death was her fault, and she would fucking pay.

10

Katherine

Iget back to my house in Chelmsford around 8 p.m. I park my car in the double garage, which is separate from the house, then walk along the gravel path. There's a noise just as I start to put my key in the door. "Jeez, what the hell was that?" I say out loud before I see what looks like a badger running from the side of the house. I'm so jittery and have no reason to be. Luckily, I have a bottle of wine in the house. I need a drink.

It's cold inside. I don't programme my heating system to come on automatically because I never really know when I will be home. I throw my briefcase onto the hall table, and I run up the stairs to get out of my suit and into my sweatpants and hoodie. I then go down and into the kitchen put the heating on and set about making some cheese on toast and grab the wine. I go into the living room after getting my laptop. I'm anxious to see if Lewis has replied, and I don't even know why? I've had so many disasters, and this is bound to be another one. I just know it.

AFTER BEING 'STASHED' by arsehole number three, Leo, I stayed away from dating again for a long time, although I was still on the dating sites—I liked to see what was out there. I had been contacted by a lot of men looking for love but none that I took any interest to until one, Joseph Ball, who was quite persistent.

Joseph seemed really nice from his profile and bio. I messaged him back, and we started talking quite a bit. He was twenty-three so a little older than me at twenty-two and still in uni. He said he worked as an accounts assistant for a large company on Canary Wharf. We met up and really hit it off. He was so sweet and wanted to take me out all the time. We saw each other for about six months in total. It was mainly kissing and heavy petting—just us feeling each other up, and I started to think that he might be the first guy I would sleep with.

Joseph would come to mum's and stay at our house sometimes, and even though I was twenty-two, my mum insisted he sleep in Brad's old room. She had old-fashioned values, and no hanky-panky went on under her roof. Sometimes, I would go to his flat and stay there. It was only a very small flat, more like a bedsit really, with a partition to separate the living/bedroom from the kitchen, so it was cosy. Although we had a lot of foreplay, we never actually had sex. I just wasn't ready for that, and he seemed to be fine with it. We both had fantastic orgasms.

His flat was really sparse, even though it was small, there didn't seem to be any personal items around like pictures of his family, or books, and magazines—nothing really. He told me his parents lived in Manchester, and that's where he was from. He had a younger brother that lived with his parents and an older sister who also lived in Manchester with her partner. I never really thought much of it until it was too late. He never told me the name of the company he worked for in Canary Wharf and thinking about it afterwards, it all made sense.

I hadn't heard from him for a few days. I had texted, but he never responded, so I tried calling him but got no answer. I decided to go to his flat to see him one evening and got no answer. I was just leaving when an elderly neighbour came out.

"Excuse me, but have you seen Joseph, the guy who lives here?" I asked her. She looked at me strangely. "I'm his girlfriend, but I don't seem to be able to reach him."

She picked up the newspaper she had dropped. "Well, that's because he moved out last weekend. He was only flat-sitting for Duncan, the man who owns the flat, while he was off travelling for six months in Australia. He's a lovely boy, Duncan, have you met him? You should you know, he's a lot nicer than that chap who was living there. He was a bit weird if you ask me. Sorry, love." I was shocked and didn't know what to say, so I just thanked her and left. I walked back to my mums in a daze. He just left and never said a word? Did he even work in Canary Wharf or have family in Manchester? Was it all a lie? Thank heavens I didn't sleep with him.

When I got home, I checked the dating site, and his profile was gone. He'd just vanished as though he never existed?

So, disaster number four with arsehole number four. I'd been ghosted! What's wrong with me? Do I give off some kind of vibe that says, "Hey, treat me like shit? I don't mind?"

11

George

I'M EXCITED, WHICH IS A NEW feeling for me. I'm going to get her on Saturday. It's Wednesday now, so not that long to wait, although she could have been mine last night if she hadn't cancelled, bitch. I still have to go and sort out the whore in the derelict house and get rid of her body before someone went in and found it.

I don't reply to the bitch straight away. I'm going to make her wait.

I go back to the derelict house, just after midnight, when there's no one around. I park my car around the back, so no one will see—as luck would have it there is an alley out back, which makes it easier for me.

I've got my saw in the back seat, along with a roll of plastic sheeting and some black plastic bags, all down the back of the driver's seat just in case someone looks in. The spade is in the boot ready for when I get to the woodland by the marshes.

I find the house easily enough and enter through the back door, the way we had last night. I roll out the plastic sheeting and place her body on it, then set about removing her limbs and head to make it easier to carry her. I wrap them all up in the plastic and then put them into a few black plastic bags, so they just look like rubbish. This part always takes me back to finding a burial ground for my parents, and how I survived after them.

AFTER I KILLED them, I had to leave them in the living room, rotting until I knew what to do with them. I had hardly been out of the house in my life, only to the local shop once or twice, and I didn't know the address of where I lived or even where it was. I could barely read my own name. I couldn't write. I couldn't drive, even though I knew my dad had an old banger out in the back alley, which I found the keys to. I knew nothing of money, or technology, except for the TV. I didn't know how to interact with people. I was like a fucking alien. I was so screwed. My clothes didn't fit me—they were all too small and filthy. I had to put my dad's shitty clothes on that were too big but were better than mine. Everything I knew, I had learnt from the TV, but that was mainly porn films, very occasionally, the news.

I did wander out of the house the day after I killed them. I walked around, exploring where I lived and concentrated on landmarks so I could find my way back home. I went out when it was dark because I didn't want anyone seeing me coming and going from my house when no one knew I existed.

I went past a couple of, what I now know are pubs, and there were always whores and guys outside, smoking. One time I was walking past and this trashy whore with a barely-there skirt and a top that only just covered her tits came up to me.

"Hey there, big boy. You're a handsome one. Do you want to come and party with me? I can show you a good time." She started touching my arm, trying to get me to stop, but I shrugged her off. She was older than I first thought up close, and her face was thick with make-up you could probably scrape off with a trowel, and her hair was greasy and plastered to her head. I ignored her and kept walking muttering, "slut."

This was going to be hard. I had to decide what to do with the bodies and quick because the smell was getting bad. I didn't want anyone reporting it or knocking on the door. I left the TV on all day and night, as that was the norm with my dad, so if we had neighbours, they wouldn't think it was weird that it had gone quiet.

On one of my nightly explorations I came across a wide-open area of land, and behind the land, was water. If I could just find the right place that I didn't think people would go near, then I could bury them there. I would need to do it during the night, and I needed to cut them up then I could carry them there bit by bit. I also need something to make holes in the ground with, and I would need to be really careful putting the grass back, so it didn't look like it had been moved. So much to fucking think about.

Just to the side of the open area, I could see trees, lots of trees, so I went to take a look. I walked for ages into the trees. They were dense, therefore a brilliant place to bury the bodies. The ground was uneven and not disturbed, there was no rubbish around, so it didn't look like anyone walked in the area. Perfect.

I'd found mum's secret stash of money—I didn't know how much because I couldn't fucking count. I needed to learn to read, write, and count. I took some of the money, and I went to the big store, and I asked someone to tell me where the thing for digging was. Luckily, the guy took me to the spades. I took one to the till and handed one of my notes, hoping it was right. It must have been because they gave me some back. Once I'd sorted my parents' bodies, I would need to find someone to help me. I had to. I would not survive this world on my own.

I went back to the place I found in the trees every night for a week, watching to make sure there was no one around. It was so dark that it was hard to see anything. I picked out a spot, right in the thick of the trees. I had to mark out where I was going to put them, so when I returned each night, I knew exactly where I was going. I found a big red carry bag in my house, with wheels on it. I was going to have to make a few trips. I had to go back to that big shop and look around for something to make it easier to cut them up with. My serrated bread knife wouldn't be any good. I found this big long metal thing that was sharp on the edges, it was like a huge version of my bread knife, and the man called it a saw—that would do. I also got some big black plastic bags.

I went home and set about cutting them up. Thank God I had bought the black plastic bags. Even in pieces, they were heavier than I thought. It took me four trips to get them both there, but I managed it in one night and buried them, making sure to put all the grass and leaves back on top. You couldn't even tell. Thank God that was done.

The next night, I went back to one of the places I had seen a few days ago where the slut tried to speak to me. I needed to get friendly with someone and hoped they could help me learn to read and write. When I approached one of the places, a whore came up to me to see if I wanted to party. I played along with her, and she took me to the back of the building and sucked my cock until I came down her throat. I despised her for that. I didn't know it was what everyone did. I thought it was just for parents and children. I told her I was twenty-two, and my name was Carter. She seemed to like me, so I latched on to her. Her name was Lucy, and she was twenty-three. I saw her nearly every day for that first week. She had her own flat, which we went to a lot until I'd practically moved in with her.

I told Lucy I had recently lost my mum. That she had been ill my whole life, and I had to look after her, which is why I never went to school and that's why I couldn't read or write. She went out and bought children's books. She taught me how to read and write, and she taught me everything I needed to know to survive, all about technology, she even bought me a mobile phone—not that I had anyone to phone, but she taught me all about the Internet—wow what a thing! I never knew there was so much at my fingertips.

Lucy told me she loved me. I had to have sex with her a lot, but it was a small price to pay to learn all I needed to from her. I will always be grateful to her for that. I eventually broke it off with her when she wanted to get serious. I had lived with her for nearly two years. She was devastated, but I told her I met someone else, that way I could make a clean break.

Now I could read and write, I found out it was Tottenham Marshes where I had buried my parents. I had been back to the house I grew up in, just after I'd moved in with Lucy, and I took what I needed—not that there was much there of mine. Looking in that house you'd never know a kid lived there at all. I had bought bleach and cleaned up the blood residue. I took the keys to his car and the tin with the money in. My mum had saved about £5000 in that tin. Maybe she had been saving it so she could leave him and maybe she would have taken me with her, but I will never know.

I watched videos on YouTube on how to drive, and I taught myself, so now I had wheels. I got myself a bedsit in Brixton, in the slums. It suited me fine keeping low key. I'd discovered charity shops when I was with Lucy. I couldn't believe the stuff I could get there for next to nothing, and I looked and felt good. I even bought a couple of suits so I could visit nicer places because that's where you found the classier whores. I bought a second-hand TV and computer, and that's where my search for whores that reminded me of my mum started. That's where I signed onto the dating sites.

WHEN I GET back to my bedsit at 4 a.m., it's still dark, and luckily, I don't have to be at work until later, so I can get a couple of hours sleep. I might reply to the bitch later tonight to tell her yes, we are on for Saturday.

Katherine

THIS WILL MAKE A GREAT INVESTMENT. I'm at my 10 a.m. appointment viewing an old warehouse situated on the embankment of the Thames, not far from the financial district of Canary Wharf. This place hasn't been touched for many years, but the area is starting to rejuvenate, and I think this will be an amazing opportunity to turn into apartments.

There's a basement, which will be great for secure parking. On the ground floor would be a foyer, with a doorman to make it secure. There's plenty of room, to maybe put a state-of-the-art gym for the residence to use, all as part of their annual management fees of course. I could maybe get 15 apartments in this building. With space being at a premium in London, they will sell for a substantial amount, especially if I make them all high-end, with all the latest appliances and features, such as marble bathrooms, in-wall sound systems, underfloor heating, floor to ceiling windows, the list is endless. I can really see the vision of this place.

I haven't been this excited about a building in a long time. It's going to take a massive outlay of money, but I can manage this, no problem. My company has grown so fast, I'll have no problem funding a build like this.

The agent showing me around is a young guy, very nervous and inexperienced. He has a file with information, but it takes him a while to find the answers to my questions. It's lucky I'm patient, having done this job when I was in uni.

"Do you know if you are selling the building next door?"

He looks at me blankly. "Let me just, erm, phone the office, and, erm, find out for you." He's flustered and walks out of earshot to make his call while I wander around, assessing the place. This is going to be a huge project to take on, but I know I can do it.

"Yes, we're selling that one for the holding company as well, would you like to see it? I have the keys. It's almost a mirror image of this one. They were all built at the same time and used by the same company," he says taking me from my thoughts.

"Yes, I would like to see that one, please." Buying both of these buildings is going to be by far the biggest project I have ever taken on. It makes sense though. They are both next to each other and share the road access and the gate to the land, so why not do them both at the same time? Identical layouts, same features and landscapes. That way I can offer secure gated access with secure parking and maybe use the basements for swimming pools. So much potential and so many ideas.

Yes. I can do this.

After my meeting, I speak to the agents selling the properties and tell them I'm really interested but need to make an appointment to go back with my structural designer, and architect before I put in an offer. I'm really excited about this project. This could make me millions in profit and put my company at the top of the list of investment properties in the city.

I wish I had mum or someone to share this with. Brad doesn't share my enthusiasm. He's settled being an accountant and having his family, who I love to bits. Cindy is such a lovely caring person and they have Simon who is now four and Lottie who was born last year and is such a princess. Being this excited and not having anyone to share it with is hard. I suppose one of the reasons I still search on the dating sites is to see if I can find that special person, even after my disasters…

THERE IS A list of online dating terms, and I swear I am going through them all.

Two months after successfully ghosting me, Joseph—arsehole number four, actually had the nerve to message me on the dating website. Just like that, he tried to contact me to see if I fancied meeting up with him.

Like hell I did—the arsehole just left without a word. I wasn't going to allow him to zombie me. He messaged me a few times, but I totally ignored him. I wasn't falling for that again, not trusting him not to do it again, so even though I would have liked to hear his explanation, I blocked him.

CLIVE HAS INVITED me to his flat this evening. He's as excited about the warehouse project as I am. I stay for a while, just chatting and laughing with him and is partner Zane . It's great to have people to speak to, and I really enjoy their company.

Back at my apartment, I put on my laptop. I'm eager to see if Lewis has been in touch. I thought about him a lot this afternoon.

George

AFTER JUST A FEW HOURS OF sleep, I get up in a bad mood. I'm not sure why because I got rid of the body last night, and I'm getting that bitch in just two more days.

My job is in a meat-packing factory about thirty minutes from my bedsit. It's not legitimate, but that's not my concern. I just keep my head down and get on with it. I fucking hate the job, but it's cash in hand, no questions asked, which is great, as I still don't exist.

The pay is lousy, as expected, but it's enough at the end of the month for my rent and bills and some food. I still have most of the money left that I found in my mum's room, as Lucy paid for everything when we lived together. I'm glad I never hurt her in any way apart from when I left. I didn't have real feelings for her. I don't think I could ever have feelings for anyone. I'm sure my brain is not wired that way.

My job is usually eight hours a day, ten till six, and it keeps me fit, lugging carcasses around. I've grown so much over the years with all the exercise I manage to do. Most people keep their heads down when they meet me and don't make eye contact. I suspect with my shaggy, curly black hair, six foot three height, bulky build and the many tattoos I have on my arms and body, not to mention my rugged looks and don't-fuck-with-me face, I must be a bit scary to some. I certainly attract the whores easily enough.

Two days and I get the bitch. I really need this. I think that's what my mood is about today. I need to message her to let her know I will meet her on Saturday. I don't want her changing her mind again. If she does, I think I will flip my shit for real.

I need to plan what I'm going to do. I'm finishing work at four today. I said I had an appointment with my parole officer. I told them when I started I had done time in prison, which is why I'm not so good with reading and writing. All bullshit of course but they bought it.

I did a search on the bitch this morning and found out where she works. I'm going to go over there to see if I can watch her coming out of the building and see where she goes. If she gets in a car and drives, then I'll be screwed, but really, I just want to see her in the flesh.

At four, I leave the factory, stinking of meat, blood, and guts. It takes a lot to get rid of the smell each day. I get to my shitty bedsit in record time, especially for this time of day, and have a quick shower to scrub off the smell. I slick my hair back to make it look neater, and I wear a suit, that way I won't look odd loitering outside her building, and it covers most of my tattoo's.

I find her building in a good area with lots of office buildings around. I wonder if she owns it? Across the street, there is a cafe with outdoor seating. As it's cold out, I go over to the cafe and order a black Americano, pick up one of their free newspapers and sit outside facing her building pretending to read. I must have fit right in as no one even glances twice at me, apart from a couple of women ogling me as they pass. Whores! Why do they make it so obvious? They eye-fuck me all the damn time. Do they think I'm just going to drop my pants for them?

I've been here for a while, and I'm now on my second coffee. I'm trying to make them last, so I don't look too odd. It's almost seven p.m. when I spot her coming out of the building. I just stare. I can't help it. She looks so much like my mum. The red mist comes down on me, and all I want to do is go over there and kill the bitch. All I can see now is my mum standing over there, looking at me with a sneer on her face. I must be nuts—my mind playing tricks on me. I killed my fucking mum.

This bitch is fumbling in her bag. She must have been looking for her phone because she pulls it out to answer a call. She then turns and goes back into the building. What the fuck now? I haven't sat here all this time for her to just disappear back into the building.

I wait and wait, still sitting outside, and I end up getting another coffee. It's really cold now, even though my blood is boiling inside.

Finally, at around 8.20 p.m., she comes back out of the building. I'm seething that she's made me wait all this fucking time. Who the fuck does she think she is? She starts to walk down the street, and I start to follow her but on my side of the street, keeping a good distance back. I have the newspaper tucked under my arm. In my suit, I just look like a normal office worker who's just left the office for the day.

We walk for about five minutes, and I watch her enter a sandwich shop. I cross over, and I go into the shop myself. I could do with a sandwich. I stand next to her at the counter. I just want to be near her. I close my eyes at the smell of her. Being so near is making me dizzy—making me want her. I could just reach out, wrap my hands around her throat and finish her right here, right now. God, her smell is driving me crazy. I want to fuck her hard and make her scream loud. I have to step back slightly because I don't want to draw attention to myself. I don't want her to notice me.

She suddenly turns and smiles at me. I turn quickly and look away with a slight scowl. I don't want her seeing my face. I look at the counter full of meat and sandwich fillings. Hers is being made up by the old man serving.

He looks at me. "What can I get you, sir?"

I look at what he is making. "I'll have a tuna mayo on white please." I take a side glance at the bitch, not face on, and she looks at me again and smiles, but she has a look on her face I can't work out.

She cocks her head slightly.

"Have we met before, you look familiar?" she says.

I freeze, looking at the meat counter. I wanted as little eye contact as possible, but she's just like the other whores, coming onto me just because I have a pretty face and a nice body. I can feel her still looking at me, and I can see her reflection in the glass of the meat counter. She's waiting for my answer. "Erm no, I don't think so. I'm new to the area," I say still not looking at her and trying to disguise my voice, making it gruff.

She lets out a small laugh. God, my cock is getting hard. I hope my jacket hides it, but I can't look down to check.

"Sorry, you just look familiar, and I was seeing if I could place where I had seen your face before. It was rude of me to stare like that." With that she gets her order off the guy and hands over some money.

"Thanks, George. I'll see you soon, no doubt." My heart nearly thumps out of my chest, and I stand there, frozen. Is she talking to me? Does she know me or who I am? Has she worked it out?

The old guy replies to her, "See you, Kate, have a good weekend." I blow out the breath I'm holding. The old man is called George. Thank fuck for that. Once my heart has settled down, I realise that if she'd recognised me, she would have called me Lewis anyway—what a dickhead I am. I get my order from him and leave.

I cross the street again. I can see her way ahead of me. I see her enter a glass door to a building that is being held open by a doorman. As I'm approaching on the opposite side, I can see she is still standing inside, talking to the doorman. I walk past with my head down so she doesn't notice me. I think she must live in this building. She told me she lived in Chelmsford. Maybe she's visiting someone, or maybe the rich bitch has a place here as well.

I can't wait for Saturday night now. This has just made me hunger for her more than ever. First, I need to get back to my shitty bedsit. I need to relieve myself before I find a whore to do it. I can't risk killing another one so close to getting the bitch—not now.

The first thing I do when I get back though is put on my computer to send the bitch a message that we are on for Saturday.

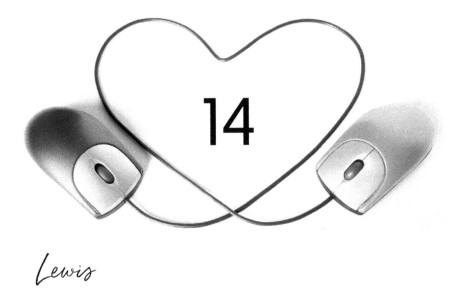

Lewis

I T'S THURSDAY NIGHT ALREADY. With being called away suddenly on Tuesday for a shoot, I had to cancel all my appointments and this week has just flown by. I have a date tonight with Sadie, the hot new model for Victoria's Secrets. She's in London, doing some promo work for their new campaign. I got an invite to the catwalk, I mean, who wouldn't go to a VS catwalk show? Even my close friend Nigel, who's gay, would be up for that!

Being the most famous British male model, I get invited to a lot of fashion events, some I attend, others I don't, but VS I would never pass up. I had been invited backstage as usual and being VS there were scantily clad women all over. Ok, nothing new for me, but it never gets old and, wow, these ladies are something else. That's where I met Sadie and we arranged a date.

My agent keeps pushing me to have a hot model as a girlfriend for my image, but I don't buy into all that. I haven't had a steady girlfriend since my break up with Susan.

I HAD BEEN with Susan for five years, and I was sure we would get married. We got engaged, then we moved in together, but then three months later she was gone. She cheated on me with the new personal trainer at the gym. She said we had got too serious, too fast. That she needed time to explore herself more, whatever that meant. Five years was not too fast in my books, and I loved her so fucking much, she broke my heart. I spiralled into a deep depression after that. It took me a long time to get over her, and I've never trusted anyone else since.

Maybe Susan and I wouldn't have lasted when I became famous, and I do believe everything happens for a reason. If I love, I love hard. It's just my sensitive side, and I expect that in return, and I certainly am not the type to cheat. She burnt me so badly.

Now I just play the field, which is easy in my job.

"LUCE, WHAT TIME is my appointment tomorrow with that property woman?" I shout through the half-open door. I'm staying in the Mandarin Oriental in a suite. Lucinda is in the living area, and I'm sitting at the desk in my bedroom, looking at my laptop. I need to get ready to meet Sadie soon.

"It's at 3 p.m. so don't worry if you have a late night tonight. Your schedule is clear in the morning until that appointment. You do, however, have a shoot on Saturday for Gucci.

Lucinda is a godsend and has been my PA for four years now and was my best friend. I was a nobody when we met, just a struggling personal trainer trying to pick myself up after my breakup with Susan. Luce helped me so much. I could never repay her for her friendship.

MY LIFE HAS changed dramatically since meeting Luce, down to her and the confidence she had in me. She actually lived near me and got in touch via messenger to see if we could meet for a coffee, she had an idea she wanted to run by me.

I was intrigued and met with her and her husband, Mark. She explained that she'd seen my PT images and thought I'd be great as a model in the book industry. Specifically, book covers. I had no idea about the world of self-publishing, but she guided me and arranged for me to have a photo shoot with a local photographer, we posted the images on my social media, and it exploded. I had so much interest from authors wanting to use me on the cover of their books. I was amazed. It just went wild and took off from there. We then made appointments with a couple of modelling agencies here in London, and Elite Models immediately signed me. They wanted to send me to L.A. to their headquarters, so off we went. They sent me to a casting call to be the new face of Calvin Klein.

I will never forget that day. My first ever casting call being a model. I had no confidence and when I walked in and saw all the young models I turned around to leave. No way in hell would they pick me. It was Lucinda that made me stay, "If you even think about walking Lewis, it may be the biggest mistake of your life. You have as much chance as any of the guys in this room. You can do this Lewis. You just need a bit of confidence in yourself. You are better than any of these guys in here." I scowled at her, but I did, she gave me the boost I needed and I got to be the new face of CK.

I've never looked back, and I've been the face of many advertising campaigns in the last four years.

I'VE DATED QUITE a few models and actresses in the four years since, but only casually, never anything serious. In fact, the longest I have seen someone is about two months, and even then, on and off. With my work schedule, I don't have the time to date, plus my trust issues after my break up mean I'm not looking for anything more.

I sometimes think that I need to settle down. Honestly, I would love a family. I'm thirty-three now and time is passing me by, plus the modelling will slow down the older I get.

I need to get ready for my date with Sadie. "Lucinda, did we bring my grey pinstripe Armani suit with us? I want to wear it tonight."

15

Katherine

I TALK TO HARRY FOR A LITTLE bit in the foyer before heading to my apartment. I glance at the doors while Harry is talking to me, and I swear I see that guy from the deli passing on the other side of the street. Maybe it's my imagination? He looked so familiar, but I just couldn't place him. I was thinking about him on my way back here, trying to think where I had seen him before, but I didn't get the best look because each time I looked at him, he looked away from me. Even when he spoke to me, he wouldn't make eye contact with me. Very strange.

Once in my apartment, I head straight to the kitchen to put the Nespresso machine on for a coffee to have with my wrap. I go to get my sweats and a t-shirt on while the water is heating up and then grab my laptop from my briefcase and set it on the dining table. I have a lot of research to do ready for tomorrow's meeting with Mr Model, and I need to pull out my best penthouse apartments for him to view. I'm searching through my portfolio of properties, as I'm not sure what area he wants to view, so I have to pull up several different ones for him. I'll show him the options, then if he wants to go and view any, I will take him. This may be a long meeting, which is why it's best later in the afternoon, in case it runs over.

The icon for the dating site at the bottom of my screen tells me I have messages. I click on, hoping Lewis has replied. I have butterflies when I see there's a message from him. Oh god, is he cancelling or is he going to meet me? I hover over the message. I can't believe I feel like this. I have never felt like this with any of the guys I've talked to on here or by text. I don't know what it is about him. I mean, yes, I am massively attracted to him. Who wouldn't be? It's that hair and those piercing brown eyes, but I'm nervous about meeting him. I keep changing my mind, should I meet him or not? It takes me back to yet another disaster with arsehole number five.

I WAS REALLY into growing Porter Properties at twenty-four and just before my twenty-fifth birthday in February, I started getting messages from a guy called Seb. He looked so cute in his pictures, even though they were a bit grainy, He was twenty-nine, very athletic looking, with nice brown hair.

I started to talk to him through messenger, and we seemed to get on very well. He was a loss adjuster for a big insurance company. We exchanged numbers, and we started talking on the phone a lot. He would make me laugh. He was funny and had a very dry sense of humour—I liked that. He told me how beautiful I was, and he couldn't wait to meet me.

We arranged several dates, but apart from one where I had to cancel due to a meeting, he cancelled them all, usually right at the last minute. He was at a meeting that ran over, or his mum was ill—there was always something, he also lived in Nottingham, and I was mostly in the city, so that was a factor. It wasn't like we lived around the corner from each other.

We carried on talking a lot, nearly every day, and we became quite comfortable with each other. I asked to Facetime or Skype but again there was always an excuse—he had an older phone so couldn't Facetime and said he was rubbish with Skype. We did eventually Skype, but I couldn't see him because the camera wasn't working on his laptop, but he could see me okay. He was happy with that, me, not so much. I never thought anything of it.

As time went on, it was like we were boyfriend and girlfriend but without ever actually meeting. On the phone, he started telling me how sexy I was, and he couldn't wait to finally meet me. He hoped I wouldn't be disappointed in him. I told him not to be ridiculous. I wouldn't be disappointed at all. That he was lovely and funny.

One time, I was in bed, and he knew, he had asked me what I was doing.

"What are you wearing, baby?"

"I have shorts and a vest on, not really sexy," I said laughing.

"Can we switch to Skype so I can see you, beautiful, even though my camera is still not working?" I hung up and dialled into Skype on my laptop after making sure I looked okay.

"Wow, baby, you're stunning, you literally take my breath away. Just seeing you there in bed does things to me. I can see the swell of your breast peeping out of your top. Can you pull the covers off and let me see lower?" I was a little embarrassed, especially as I couldn't see him, and it was all one-sided, but I pulled the covers down and moved the laptop so he could see down my body.

"I'm so hard right now. I'm stroking my cock, Kate. God, I wish I was with you, and I could stroke your body. Baby, can you do me a huge favour?" he said to me, and I could hear his breathing was getting quite erratic.

"Can you take your top and bottoms off, and let me see you naked? If you don't feel comfortable, then I completely understand it's just, wow, you are fucking perfect, and I wish you could see what you have done to me. My cock has never been so hard, and my balls are so tight, I think I may explode at any moment." I was getting aroused myself from what he was saying, but I was also embarrassed about him seeing me without me seeing him.

I was comfortable with him, after all, we had been chatting for just over two months now, so I started to remove my top and my shorts. I didn't have any underwear on.

"Fuck, I can see your tits. They are so perky and perfect. I wish I could suck on them and make you squirm. Can you lower the laptop, baby and let me see the rest of you? Rest it on your legs so I can see all of you up to your face." I did what he said, getting over the embarrassment. He was making me hot and brave.

"Seb, I wish I could see you and what you're doing to yourself."

"Babe, I wish you were here doing it to me. I would be sucking on your tits, then I would go lower, and I would get between your thighs, and I would smell you. I bet you smell so fucking sweet, and I bet you taste even sweeter. I would turn around so my cock was in your mouth, and I would suck on your clit so hard, swiping my tongue up and down your perfect pussy before inserting it into you and making you scream. All while you sucked on my cock. I would be fucking you with my cock and my tongue."

Wow, I was about ready to combust at his words alone. I could hear his breathing, ragged in between his words, and I could hear him pumping away.

"Baby, can you play with your clit? I have the best view in the fucking world here of your perfect pussy and tits. Put the laptop on the bed, lift your legs either side of it with your feet on the bed, bent at the knees so I can see right into that pussy." I did as he said and opened up my lips and started rubbing. I was so wet from his words and what I could hear him doing. I inserted two fingers inside and started moaning. With my other hand, I rubbed my clit. I was lost in the moment, listening to Seb jerking off, moaning my name all the time, encouraging me more and more.

"Baby, I'm going to come so hard, can you hear me? You're amazing. I want to fuck you so bad. Oh god, oh god..." I could hear how wet he was and as he was breathing and moaning my name, I exploded on myself.

"Oh God, Seb. That was amazing."

"Oh, babe, I'm in awe watching you like this. Thank you for doing that for me. You are gorgeous, and I can't wait to meet you and do those things in person. Soon, babe, I promise."

With that, we said good night, and I went to the bathroom to clean up. I couldn't believe I had done that not seeing him. I really wanted to meet him now.

We had a few more bedtime episodes like that, even though Seb's camera on his laptop was still broken, then we agreed to meet one Saturday and spend the day together. I was so excited to finally meet him. I thought I was falling for him if that was possible just from conversations alone. The day arrived. I got to the Costa Coffee early, and I sat with a coffee in the window watching everyone go by, looking for Seb. It was past ten o'clock—the time we arranged to meet, and I was getting worried he wasn't coming. I kept checking my phone, and there were no messages. Every time the door went, I looked to see if it was him. 10.45 a.m. and still no Seb. I was beginning to feel like a fool. I sent him a text message, but after twenty minutes I still hadn't heard anything.

The door went again, and an older guy came through the door. He looked straight at me with a very sheepish grin on his face. He looked really familiar. He made his way over to me but didn't really look me in the eye until he stood in front of me.

"Kate," he said, and I just knew from his voice and the way he said my name that this man, who was well into his fifties, quite rounded with thin greyish/brownish hair, was Seb.

I just stared at him, trying to comprehend this situation. This could be his dad or an uncle, and he'd sent him to apologise. My brain was trying to come up with the reason that this older man, who was old enough to be my dad, was so like the pictures of Seb, and had the same voice. But I knew deep down that this was the Seb I had been seeing and having one-way sex sessions with—it all became clear now: the broken camera and old phone and the cancelled meetings. I just put my head in my hands, shaking it, trying not to let the tears come.

"Kate, baby, you are even more beautiful in person. I'm so sorry I am not what you expected. Please don't hate me. I couldn't help it. You drew me to you."

"Just stop, Seb." I gritted my teeth seething at him. "How could you do this? How the fuck did I get into this? How old are you? Is your name even Seb?"

He hung his head. "Yes, my name is Seb, and I'm 59. I'm sorry I didn't tell you the truth. I knew you wouldn't be interested in me if you saw me as I am now."

"Are you delusional, Seb? Of course I wouldn't have bothered with you, for God's sake! You're sick. You're old enough to be my granddad, let alone my dad." I was mortified. This old man had made me do things to myself, and he had watched me like a pervert. I stood up, grabbing my bag to leave. He reached for me.

"Please stay, Kate. Let's talk like we do on the phone. Nothing has to change. I'm still the same person you have been talking to and having Internet sex with these past few months. I didn't mean to deceive you, but I fell for you hard."

"Will you just stop? You are disgusting, preying on a woman thirty-four years younger than you and not telling her the truth. Do you even have a job or was that a lie as well? In fact, don't tell me. I really don't care. Do not try to contact me again. I never want to speak to you. I feel like you have violated me, and I feel sick to the stomach thinking about it." Oh God, I was going to throw up. I ran to the toilet, heaved and brought my coffee back up. I felt used and stupid. How the fuck could I have done the things I did and not actually have seen him? How pathetic was I? I needed to leave. I headed out of the toilets and saw he was in the chair just waiting for me. I headed straight for the door and got out of there as fast as I could.

I did a bit of research when I got back to my apartment, and I found out that I had been Kitten-fished. Great! Arsehole number five and yet another online dating disaster.

I CLICK ON the message from Lewis. After just remembering arsehole number five, I'm tempted to tell him to forget it, but I read the message from him, and he is really quite sweet.

Katherine,

I am so pleased you wanted to re-arrange our date instead of cancelling it altogether, and yes, I would love to meet you this

Saturday. Shall we say the same place at 7 p.m.? Is that good for you? Please let me know if you need to change the time. I can't wait for Saturday now.

You are a beautiful intelligent woman and I'm sure we will get along amazingly.

Till Saturday, Kate, take care, beautiful. Lewis x

He even put a little kiss at the end. How can this man be real? I'm nervous now for Saturday after recollecting my previous disasters. I quickly reply to his message and tell him I will see him at 7 p.m. at Russell's Restaurant on Saturday, and I'm looking forward to it. I hit send.

I finish up with the properties I've found for Mr Model, close my laptop and go to bed.

16

Lewis

Wow, last night was a fucking disaster. Sadie was on fire. She was hot and couldn't keep her hands off me, but I didn't actually stay and sleep with her. Let's just say, when I found out her true age, I freaked out and left in a hurry. I know she is the newest VS model and they are usually young, but I honestly thought she was in her mid-twenties, so when it came out in conversation, in her hotel room, that she was only seventeen, I was horrified!

I stepped away from her, looking for my jacket so I could leave. I felt sick! Seventeen, and I would have done all sorts to her. It's bad enough, in the club after the meal she was all over me, straddling me, rubbing and making my cock so hard I nearly came. I even went there, dipping my fingers under her thong and stroking her until she was shuddering with her release on my lap. We left after that, rushing to get to her room because it was nearer, trying not to do anything in public that would get us both arrested.

I could see the tears forming in her eyes. "I will be eighteen next month. I'm legal now anyway, so what difference does it make if we can't keep our hands off each other? Lewis, you're the hottest man I have ever met. I want to have you all night. I want to ride your dick and suck it till you scream my name. I'm not a naïve little girl you know." Holy fuck, I needed to leave, this was so wrong. I wasn't going there with a seventeen-year-old, even if it was legal and she was fucking gorgeous.

"Sorry, Sadie. It's my loss, but you are way too young for me, sweetie. Please don't be upset. This is all me. I really thought you were a lot older."

She looked devastated, standing there, almost naked and tears rolling down her cheeks. She was about to beg me to stay, I could see it in her face, so I leant forward and kissed her cheek. "Bye, sweetie," I said then turned, grabbed my jacket and left.

I headed back to the Mandarin, thinking what a close call that was. I got back to my room and headed for the mini bar and poured myself a big glass of neat Haig Club whiskey before going to bed. I had my meeting tomorrow with the property woman, so at least I would have a clear head, ready to find myself a place in the city.

I wake up feeling rough. I hadn't drunk much last night, so maybe the rather large neat whiskey was the last straw. I feel like shit with everything that happened or rather didn't happen with Sadie—she's a nice kid, I hope she wasn't too upset and doesn't start trouble. That's the last thing I need. I look and see its 6.45 a.m. I'll go for a run around Hyde Park, then hit the gym when I get back.

Lucinda arrives at the suite just after 2 p.m. "Hey, Lewis, how was your date last night?" Is the first thing out of her mouth as I knew it would be.

"Let's just say, I won't be seeing the very YOUNG Sadie again," I say emphasising the word young so she gets my drift.

"Oh, ok. So just how young is she?" she asks me with a concerned look on her face.

"Well it was a good night up until the point we got back to her room, and I discovered she was seventeen. I legged it out of her suite as quickly as I could, but we had already got into some heavy petting at the club. Oh God, Luce, I hope she doesn't turn sour and start rumours."

"I hope not too. She's of legal age but that isn't the image we want of you. I'm sure she will be professional about it as her VS contract is probably quite strict on the publicity side as well."

"Thanks, you always know what to say to make me feel better." I get my jacket from the back of the chair, ready to head out.

We get a taxi outside the hotel and head off to Knightsbridge where Porter Properties offices are. I have been told they are the best in the city and like Lucinda always says, only the best will do. I do have a house, in a lovely place called Little Waltham, which is not too far from Chelmsford, but I spend a lot of time here in the city, so thought it wise to invest in a property that I could use, rather than spending a fortune in hotels.

We arrive fifteen minutes early and make our way up to the reception area where we are told to take a seat and that Ms Porter will be with us very soon. The receptionist brings some water, and just as I'm about to take a sip, I see in my eye line a stunning woman walking towards us. She suddenly comes to a halt in the hallway, looking at me, quizzically. Here we go again, she's reconginsed who I am. When she realises that I have noticed her, she starts walking again towards us.

I can't help but stare at her. She is perfection. Such stunning beauty, with her mousy brown hair, pulled back into a braid. Her lips are red and sensual, but it's her figure—she's curvy in all the right places, and those hips just sway from side to side. God, what I could do holding onto those hips... I'm sure I look like a fool, sitting there with my hand in mid-air, mouth open, just staring at her. I hope she's heading to us. I hope she is Ms Porter. The closer she gets the more captivated I am by her.

I can see the hesitation in her steps the closer she gets and the suspicious look she's giving me as she approaches, but she keeps professional. She must recognise me? Or maybe we've met before? No, I would definitely remember this goddess if we had.

"Good afternoon," she says as she reaches us.

"You must be Mrs Turner, and you are?" she says, turning to me and reaching out her hand to shake mine. I can't move, struck by her beauty. I mean, I have dated some women in the last five years and a lot of them, beautiful, but this woman in front of me has rendered me speechless with her natural beauty and all-woman figure. Yep, I look like an idiot, sat here gawking.

Lucinda steps in to save me as usual. "This is Lewis Clancy, and you can call me Lucinda. I'm Lewis's PA."

"Lovely to meet you. I'm Katherine Porter," she says as I eventually take her offered hand. Wow, what the hell. The electricity surges between us, just from that one touch. I drop her hand quickly. Did she feel it too? Her face doesn't give anything away. Just me then.

"Shall we head to my office so I can show you the apartments I have marked out for you to look at, and you can let me know exactly what you are looking for?"

"YOU" I shout in my head. I'm looking for you!

I manage to pull myself together, nod and stand up.

"Yes, please, Ms Porter, lead the way."

Katherine

Holy shit. Lewis is the guy I'm supposed to be going on a date with tomorrow! What is he doing here? Chrissie, my receptionist rang through to tell me my three o'clock was here and I didn't want to keep them waiting in reception long, but when I stepped out of my office and started down the hallway, I just stopped, frozen on the spot.

How is he here?

Did he know I worked here?

How does he know?

Has he been stalking me?

He noticed me as he was about to take a drink of his water and he just froze like I did. He was staring at me, and I was staring at him. I needed to move. I had to walk so it didn't look strange. I must have had a quizzical look on my face because I was baffled trying to work this out.

As I reach the table, the woman introduces them both. "This is Lewis Clancy, and you can call me Lucinda. I'm Lewis's PA." Shit, it is him.

I offer my hand to him, and he just stares at me, frozen. Does he know it's me?

He must surely recognise me from my pictures on the dating site or why else would he not speak? He seems to come around, he takes my hand to shake it, but drops it just as quickly. Oh God, the electricity from that one little touch alone. Wow. Did he feel that? He dropped my hand, so maybe he didn't feel it.

I force myself to speak. "Shall we head to my office so I can show you the apartments I have marked out for you to look at, and you can let me know exactly what you are looking for?"

I turn and head back down the hallway to my office. I have a large office, with a mahogany, L-shaped desk, holding two large side-by-side monitors. To the left is a dresser, with lots of my stuff, both work and personal. I spend a lot of time in here, and I want it to be homely with some ornaments and plants and pictures of Simon and Lottie. To the side of the dresser is a door, which leads to my private bathroom. To the right, as you enter, is my viewing area. I have a small conference table with six chairs around it, facing the back wall where I have a seventy-five-inch flat screen monitor so I can show the properties to clients from my laptop on the table.

"Please, take a seat." I gesture to the chairs as I make my way to the table and stand by the chair where the laptop is set up. "I have some properties lined up for you to see on the screen, then if there are any you would like to go and view, my driver, will take us to them this afternoon. If that suits you, Mr Clancy?"

"Please, call me Lewis," he replies as he sits down at the table, not facing the screen but facing me. Just then, Clive enters with a tray holding a carafe of fresh coffee, some iced water and a tray of assorted Marks and Spencer's biscuits.

"What can I get you to drink?" he asks Lewis and Lucinda as he passes me my iced water.

"Just water for me, please," Lewis answers and Lucinda asks for the coffee. Clive leaves after making sure we have everything we need.

"So, Mr Clan, err sorry, Lewis, do you know what it is you are looking for? Do you know what area you would like to be in? What price bracket? Lucinda did mention to Clive you were looking at a penthouse, so I have pulled some out around Knightsbridge and Chelsea, depending on your budget." Why is he staring at me like he wants to devour me? Has he even heard a word I've said?

Looking at him, this close, he is beautiful in a very masculine way. His eyes look golden, and his eyelashes are so long, any woman would be envious of them. He's not quite got a full beard, but it's on its way, and he has lots of black hair, which is very curly. He is stunning. His pictures do not do him justice, and he looks different to the images on the dating site, they must be older pictures, he looks older now and much more distinguished. He is even more spectacular in person. Why on earth would he need to be on a dating site? He could have his pick of anyone and probably does. Oh god, I'm staring at him now. Maybe he doesn't understand my reaction to seeing him here. I'm so confused right now, but I must get on with the meeting and stop staring at him, no matter how hard it is. Just his presence is making me flustered. I need to be professional here and do this presentation, but if he keeps staring at me like that, I'm not sure I can.

"Sorry, Katherine, may I call you Katherine? What did you ask me, I was miles away?"

Oh God, this is going to be a nightmare. I don't know if I can endure a few hours of this and not say anything to him, asking why exactly he is here when we have a date tomorrow. Did he know it was me he was meeting or is this a shock to him as well? Maybe that's why he is staring at me so much—it's shock.

We go through the list of things he would like in the apartment. He doesn't really mind too much where it is, but he said because he works out a lot he would like a gym in the building. I show him a few properties, three of them are within walking distance from here, one of them being in my building, unfortunately. I wish I didn't have that one to show him—it could become quite awkward. He decides he wanted to see the ones closest to here first. Then, if he doesn't like them, he will see the others. The one in my building has caught his eye, as it has a pool as well as a gym in the basement.

The one in my building is farthest, so we leave that until last. He seems to like the first two—the first apartment more than the second one but he prefers the gym at the second one. "Wow, Katherine, these buildings are amazing. Do you own the buildings themselves or just some of the apartments in them?"

"Well, the first one, I own the building and the second one, I own the top five floors. The next one we are going to see is also my building."

We approach my building, and I let us in. It's Alfred on the desk today. Harry normally works nights.

"Hi, Alfred, how are you? I haven't seen you for a while, and how is your wife Dot doing now? I hope she has got over her flu?"

"Oh, Ms Porter, how lovely to see you. Yes I'm well, and Dot is better, thank you. It took a long time for her to shake the darn thing, but she's all good now, thanks for asking."

We make our way up to the top floor, there are only two apartments up here, and one of them is mine, although I'm not going to divulge that bit of information to Lewis. We enter apartment two, and he just seems to fall in love with the space straight away. It has floor-to-ceiling bi-folding doors all across the one wall giving a stunning view from the twelfth floor. I open the doors because it's a nice day to show the amazing balcony and outdoor living. Towards the end of the balcony, are some steps that lead to a rooftop garden, which is shared between the two apartments. If he did buy this one, we would probably bump into each other, which is why I'm hoping he doesn't go for it. The kitchen, just off the lounge area, is startling white with top-of-the-range chrome appliances, and to the right is a hallway that leads to three bedrooms. The master is en-suite with an amazing wet room and a walk-in closet. There's also a main bathroom in the hallway, which is shared between the large double bedroom and a smaller bedroom, which I use as an office in my apartment. This apartment is a mirror image replica of my own.

Lewis is really taken by the apartment, and Lucinda seems quite stunned by the beauty and finish of it. I then take them down to the basement, where there is a state-of-the-art gym, a sauna and a rather large swimming pool. I'd already explained about the large annual management fees because of these facilities, so I presume Lewis can afford it.

I can't stop looking at him, the beauty of him, no wonder he is a model. Just being near him makes my head fog and when he gets really close; I feel it all through my body. I try to keep my distance without being obvious.

"Wow, Katherine, I don't think you are going to beat this one. I love it, and the location is amazing. Can we walk down the road to see what restaurants and shops there are within walking distance, please? Though, I think you have sold me on this apartment. I don't think I want to see the others," he says getting closer, into my personal apace as he talks.

"Of course we can, Lewis. It's a lovely area of Knightsbridge with great transportation links nearby, lots of trendy bars and restaurants along the street, and a lovely deli that makes to-die-for wraps and sandwiches. You can't go wrong here, and if you intend to use the gym and pool then the management fees are worth it, just for the convenience alone," I tell him trying to step away. He seems to have made his mind up.

After showing Lewis the surrounding area, he's sold. He loves this area and the apartment, especially the facilities. We go back to my office to discuss proceeding, but Lucinda doesn't come back with us, as she has to get to an appointment. Oh, boy, Just the two of us, I need to find out what he is playing at. If he knew it was me he was seeing today and if he deliberately chose Porter Properties? Maybe he had put two and two together with my name being Porter...

I also need to try and keep my distance. He keeps getting in my personal space, and it's making me all hot and bothered. I kept forgetting my sales pitch. No one has ever really had this effect on me before, not even the five arseholes before him.

"I really would like to proceed with the last apartment. It is the one for me. I know it's quick but to be honest, I'm in the city so much, and it costs me a fortune staying at the Mandarin all the time. Can you send all the paperwork for the property to my solicitor please?" He reaches into his wallet to pull out the business card of his solicitor.

"Stollock and Co. Ah yes, I've worked with Jason Stollock on a few properties," I say taking the card from him. Our fingers brush, and it sends electric pulses through me. I gasp and look at him at the same time as he looks straight at me. Did he feel it too?

"Will you go out for a drink with me, Katherine? After you've finished here, or maybe grab a bite to eat?" I just gawp at him; stunned he's asked me for a drink now when we have a date tomorrow. I'm rooted to the spot, only his voice shaking me out of it. "Katherine, are you okay? Look, I'm sorry if I've offended you in some way," he says with a nervous laugh.

"I'm confused because you're asking me out for a drink now when we have a date tomorrow? Are you playing some sort of game with me here, Lewis? Did you know it was me you were seeing today?" I'm livid. Is he fucking playing me? Is this another online dating trick that I haven't discovered before?

"Sorry, you've lost me, Katherine, what date tomorrow? Of course, I knew I was seeing you. I had heard you were the best in the business in the city, and I only wanted the best, but I've never met you before or arranged a date. I don't know what you're talking about."

"Holy shit, I think its best you leave, Lewis. I'm sorry, but I don't think we should do business. You must think I'm easy or stupid or something. Have all our conversations the last few weeks been for nothing? Couldn't you wait until tomorrow night because I cancelled on Wednesday?" I start yelling at him, Clive knocks on the door to make sure I'm okay and asks if I need him to stay.

"No, Clive, thank you. Mr Clancy was just leaving. We will not be doing business with him." I glare at Lewis.

"Goodbye, Mr Clancy. I would say it's been a pleasure getting to know you, but I'm afraid I would be lying." With that, I turn my back on him and go to sit in my chair behind my desk.

18

Lewis

I'M STUNNED—JUST STARING AT HER. Has she gone mad? I have never even laid eyes on this deranged woman before, and I thought she was perfect, beautiful, and very smart. I thought we had some kind of connection. I think it best I just leave. Shit, I really liked that fucking apartment as well—who am I kidding, I really like her.

I turn for the door, and Clive is standing there, looking like he's ready to kick me out by the looks of it. Well, fuck him, I can walk out on my own.

Shit, no wait, I need to know what I did wrong. I only asked if she fancied getting a drink. I have never had that reaction before and what is she on about 'all our conversations'? I turn to face her, but she has her head down, pretending to read some papers on her desk. Well, screw that, baby—you will hear me out.

"What the hell are you talking about, Katherine? I have never met, spoken, or seen you until I walked into your office today. I think you must have me confused with someone else. I thought we hit it off, which is why I asked if you fancied a drink or something to eat, but if that's your reaction, I've obviously read you wrong. Nice to have met you, I think, and sorry we couldn't do business."

"Wait, what do you mean you have never spoken to me before? We've been messaging each other for a few weeks now, and you've been after a date for a while. What bullshit are you pulling, Lewis? Is this some sort of fucked up game to you, messing with people's feelings?"

I'm baffled, rooted to the spot. I start twirling my beard which is my tell of nerves, frustration and anxiety, I have no idea what she is talking about. I walk towards her desk, and Clive moves towards me from the door. I hold up my hands. "Look Clive, no disrespect, mate, but I think Katherine and I need to find out what's going on here. I have no idea what she's talking about, but I intend to find out. Katherine?"

She looks up at me and glares. If looks could kill, I would be dead by now. "Are you or are you not on a dating site?" she asks, her cheeks flushing as she hangs her head slightly as though embarrassed. God, I wish I was making her cheeks go red for a different reason, but I need to sort this out. "No, I'm not blowing my own trumpet here, but do I look like I need to go on any dating sites?" I say to her not meaning it to be cocky in any way but Jesus, I go out with VS models for Christ's sake.

"So, you are not on LookingforLove.com," she says as she starts to tap away on her keyboard before addressing Clive. "Clive, it's okay, thank you. I think I need to talk to Lewis alone and sort this out."

Clive starts to leave. "Just shout if you need me," he says as he gets near the door then turns to me and glares at me. What the fuck?

I turn to Katherine who is on her computer. "Look, Katherine, I have never joined a dating site in my life. I have never sent you any messages—maybe you need to tell me what this is about? Is someone pretending to be me on a dating site? Because it wouldn't be the first time. Usually, Lucinda gets in touch with the site to report them, or if that fails, she gets in touch with the person using my images and threatens legal action. So I can assure you if you have been talking to someone using my images, it most certainly is not me," I say to her sitting on the chair in front of her desk. God, she is beautiful.

She turns the monitor to let me see what's on the screen and sure enough, there is my photo, but not only my picture, it's my fucking name as well. Some sick bastard has stolen my whole identity. I get up and perch on the desk to get a closer look. "Wow, this guy has done his research. He knows my age, height, weight. So, you've been talking to this guy, thinking it's me, for some time and now you have a date with him tomorrow? I have to say, Kate, I don't like that at all. He could be anybody. He could be dangerous. He could be some kind of predator."

"You're right. I need to cancel the date straight away. I can't possibly go now. I don't know who it is. God, I'm so sorry, Lewis. I've been confused all day. You've been looking at me strangely, and I couldn't understand what you were playing at and if you were doing this on purpose. I feel a complete idiot now for telling you to leave."

She opens up her messages and starts to type to him. "Stop, Kate, don't message him yet. This guy could be a psycho; I think we need to do something. What if he does this a lot, and you're not the first to fall for it? He might have done things to other women, or wants to? This is scary shit, Kate. You could have gone tomorrow to meet this guy only to be stood up, but the guy who is behind this could have been lying in wait to follow you home without you knowing. Let's face it; most women on these sites are looking for love and companionship because they don't have anyone waiting for them at home. I take it you live on your own?" She nods at me, wide-eyed and in shock. "So, this dickhead could follow you home tomorrow night and then do who knows what to you when you put the key in your door. God, Kate, it doesn't bear thinking about. Maybe we need to go to the police, but then I doubt they would do anything, there is nothing to report and no crime committed, yet."

I stand, pacing the room, rubbing the scruff of my chin and raking my hands through my hair in frustration. We need to do something. He may not be a psycho—he might just get off on the chase, but then if he didn't have any other intentions why would he pretend to be someone else and arrange a date? I hate these fucking dating sites. Why can't people meet how they used to: in pubs, clubs or work, even in the gym or park?

"Kate, can we get out of here and go and get a drink? I could do with a brandy right now, and I need to think what to do about this."

"Yeah, sure, there's a quiet little bar over the road. I really am sorry, Lewis. I'm so stupid. I should have known you were too good to be true on the site. I even questioned why someone who looks like you would be on a dating site and why you would be interested in someone who looks like me. I'm a complete idiot. In fact I'm mortified. I've heard of this before, it's called Catfishing. Believe me, there is a list of online dating terms, and I'm making my way through the complete list. Well, never again. I'm through with this now, if I end up a spinster with twenty cats, then so be it."

Wow! From that I gather that she doesn't think she is special and that she's attracted to me. I need to tell her just how special and beautiful she actually is and maybe some good might come out of the shit storm that's about to happen.

19

George

FRIDAY NIGHT. THANK FUCK FOR that. Almost Saturday, and I will have that bitch once and for all.

My mood is still low. I don't understand this feeling I have. Is it the anticipation? I need to get out of here. If I stay in this shithole for the evening, I will go mental. I just saw she started typing a message to me because the little dots appeared, but then nothing. I start to panic thinking she might be cancelling again, the bitch. I'll get her one way or another if she does cancel again.

I grab my jacket. I need to go and find some kind of release. I'm not going to fuck anyone, but I could go and hang out in one of the seedy pubs where there is always some whore trying to get laid.

I start to walk down the road to the pub not too far away. It's still early so I should get my corner near the hallway to the toilets. I can watch everyone around and just wait for some slag to take a guy down the hallway. It almost always happens when I go to the dive I'm headed for.

I head inside and get myself a whiskey, and take it to the darkened corner near the hallway. It's quite busy. I was lucky to get this table, but then again most of them are around the pool table getting noisy. I can see there are three men and two whores in skirts that hardly cover their arses, and tits hanging out of their barely-there tops. One whore doesn't even have a bra on, and her tits are hanging out of the side of her sleeveless vest top. The way they dress, they're asking for it.

One of the guys cops a feel as she passes him, but then she does pass really closely, rubbing her tits against his chest. I'm sure she grabs his cock at the same time as he grabs her tit. Fucking whores, the lot of them. She passes me, but I keep my head down and just focus on the glass in my hand swirling the liquid, that way she doesn't notice me. The last thing I want is her unwanted attention. Half the time they only look at me once, then they are all over me.

I keep my eye on the guy and the whore as they say a few words when she returns from the toilets. She stays talking to him, standing very close, rubbing herself up on him, getting him all aroused, but it doesn't seem to take much. He whispers something in her ear, and she cocks her head in the direction of the hallway. It's on, and I've only been in here for twenty fucking minutes.

She grabs his hand and leads him towards the toilets. Again, I keep my head down. I don't want them to notice me. They barely make it to the hallway, and he pulls her back and spins her around so that she's facing him, then he grabs her arse and yanks her tight to his chest. He walks her backwards, farther into the hallway. I stand to see how far they have gone and to check if I can edge nearer to watch them. I can't, they haven't moved down the hall much.

Just as I turn around to sit back at my table, the other whore at the pool table catches my eye. She's all over one of the two remaining guys, straddling him and rubbing her pussy on his leg as he leans against the pool table. It looks like they are going to go at it right there. The third guy starts towards them, and he grabs her arse while she's rubbing and pressed against the other guy. The two guys look at each other with knowing looks and smirk. The one she is rubbing against suddenly grabs her wrist and starts pulling her roughly towards me. I sit down quickly.

He's being rough with her, and she's nearly running trying to keep up. "Shit, slow down, Ben, you're hurting my arm." "Come on, Gill. I can't wait. I need my cock in your mouth, and I want to watch Steve fuck you from behind while you're sucking me. Then I'm going to eat you out so much that you will be screaming and begging me to stop. You have got me so worked up, girl. I'm about to lose my load."

Once they pass me, I get up and follow them. They're heading straight to the toilets. They reach the first two where the first whore has his cock in her mouth, and he's thrusting in so hard that she's gagging, and they stop to watch. I'm sure she'll be puking any minute now, especially when he blows.

"Easy there, Zac lad, she's gonna puke all over your cock if you're not careful."

"I (thrust) don't (thrust) give (thrust) a fuck (thrust) she can take it all... Aargh..." He blows his load right down her throat. She struggles to take it all, and his cum is dripping out of her mouth and down her chin onto her top. She starts to heave as though she's going to throw up.

"Don't you dare throw up on my cock, you bitch, or I won't eat you out." She manages to calm herself while he finishes his release, then she licks him clean like a pro, smirking up at him. The second couple have been joined by the third guy, who now has his hand up the second whore's skirt and is finger fucking her while they all watch the first couple. She starts gyrating harder on his hand as Ben—guy number two, starts to take his cock out to shove in her mouth.

"Come on up here a bit, Gill, where it's a bit darker." He moves farther towards the toilets then he gets on his knees and drags her down with him. He has his cock in his hand and is stroking himself, then he grabs her head and shoves his cock in her mouth. The other guy kneels behind her and lifts her skirt up—she obviously didn't have any knickers on—and he just shoves really hard into her. It might be her arse he's fucking rather than her pussy. It's hard to see from this angle.

The first couple have moved past them and gone into the toilets. That means I can get closer to the other three without them seeing me. There is a small alcove where I can hide, just near them but out of view. This is better, much, much better. The noises from her sucking and the other one fucking her from behind are really doing it for my cock now. It's solid like steel. I start rubbing myself hard. This is what I need to see and hear, these three going at it.

I can also hear the first whore in the toilets starting to scream with her release, the noises from all of them are really getting to me. I'm not going to last long myself. This is far better than watching a porno.

The three I can see are now all moaning, and it looks like the two guys are blowing their load at the same time. She can't scream because of the cock in her mouth, but she's bucking as her orgasm approaches. God, what a show this is.

The two guys swap ends. They start all over again. She is fucking loving this, the dirty whore. She's panting hard and moaning loudly, thrusting her arse out more, the one behind has laid on his back and is licking her pussy, as he sticks a finger or two in her arse. She's being licked, sucked, and fucked in all holes at this point. She's a fucking whore. I take my cock out of my pants, stroking and pulling hard. I'm about to explode right there in the alcove. God, I have to be quiet. I don't want any of them to hear me. Although, with everything that's going on, I doubt any of them will notice me anyway. I'm timing it just right so that when she screams out as she cums, I shoot my load all over the wall in front of me, grunting as quietly as I can.

I quickly tuck myself away while she's coming down from her orgasm, even though both guys are still going at her. The others in the toilet are still going at it, and she is screaming in pleasure. I slowly start to move away back towards the bar so they won't see me. My drink is still on the table. I grab it and throw it down my neck then go to get another one. God, I needed that release and the drink. Now I will be ready for tomorrow. I'll go home to prepare and plan exactly what I'm going to do to the bitch.

Katherine

I'M MORTIFIED. I CANNOT BELIEVE what an absolute idiot I am, and how I have embarrassed myself so much in front of Lewis. I knew it was too good to be true—that this stunningly beautiful man would be on a dating site and actually want to go out on a date with plain old curvy me. I should have stopped talking to him online when I questioned it myself, but no, I was too caught up in it, yet again. When will I ever learn?

Lewis is annoyed as well. I can see it in his face and posture. When he puts it to me that this idiot could follow me home because I would have no clue who he was, it scared the shit out of me.

We leave my office and head over to the little bar on the corner across the road. Lewis goes to the bar while I grab a table. He comes over, carrying a tray with a bottle of wine, two wine glasses, and two tumblers with amber liquid in them.

"Brandy, neat. Do you want one, Kate?"

"Yes, please. I think I need it, even though I don't normally drink it.

Lewis, I'm so sorry you are being dragged into this. Really, I can just cancel the date and go to the police. I can report him to the dating site as well."

Lewis drinks his brandy in one go, then grabs the wine bottle and fills our glasses to the top. "No, Kate, we need to think about what to do here, but I don't want you in any danger. The police will do nothing, so it's up to us to catch him out, or prove he has other intentions. Although, I hate to imagine what they are… I can't have that on my conscience even though it has nothing to do with me. It's my image he's using. I just can't get over how stupid someone must be to use someone who is well known as his profile image."

I feel really bad because Lewis is well known in the model world but only if you follow the tabloids and the celebrity gossips. I clearly didn't know who he was.

"Sorry, Lewis, I guess I am stupid too, I didn't know you were a model, or that you were well known until I met you today, and only then because Clive had told me we had a famous model coming in to see me. He didn't even tell me your name. I don't really follow the gossip mags or tabloids, I'm always too busy with work and building my business."

Lewis chuckles at me. "It's okay, Kate. I know I'm not an A-list celebrity and that suits me fine, to be honest. The publicity I get now is bad enough. I don't think I could cope if I were famous. It's great I can sit in here and have a drink without anyone recognising me." Just as the words are out of his mouth, three young girls appear at our table. I can't help the smile on my face as they ask for his autograph.

"You spoke too soon, Lewis," I say once the girls have gone, after taking lots of selfies with him that will no doubt end up all over social media.

"Sorry about that, Kate. I suspect now that people have seen them making a fuss, it's drawn attention to us, and it won't be the last. That's how it usually goes once I've been spotted. I think it's fair to say that even though I'm not an A-list celebrity, having your face and body plastered all over the billboards in the big cities does draw attention to you, although a lot don't usually recognise me with clothes on."

"I'm sorry for being so ignorant, but what do you model?"

"No, don't be sorry, it's not ignorance, Kate, and to be honest, it's refreshing that you don't know me and who I am. I got my first big break being the face of Calvin Klein underwear, which is why I say a lot don't recognise me with clothes on. It wasn't me implying anything else." He's looking a little embarrassed at me and a bit sheepish.

"That's great, and it's great you have made it as a model. I do know it's a hard industry to get into. I have other famous clients, some A-listers as you call them. Just because they chose a different profession than I have, doesn't make them any better than me, and I don't mean that disrespectfully, it's just that some that I have had the pleasure of showing apartments to seem to think they are royalty just because they are well known and have money. I have money, but it doesn't make me any better than the people who work in the supermarket I go to. We all choose our paths, and some make it, and some don't. You try your best, and that is all you can do."

Lewis just stares at me.

"I'm sorry, Lewis. I tend to get on my soapbox when people think they are better than everyone else. So far, I'm pleased to say you do not fit into that box. I also seem to be apologising a lot tonight."

He has the biggest smile on his face and is looking at me like he wants to pounce on me. Just then, two women this time, appear at the table, all smiles and sass. They must have had a little to drink as one pulls up the spare chair right next to Lewis and sits down so that they are thigh to thigh. They both completely ignore the fact I'm with him at the table. The one sitting next to him starts touching his arm and squeezing his biceps. Lewis, ever the gentleman, is so polite to them, but he keeps throwing me apologetic glances. I'm quite amused by the fact that this is what happens, and the women totally ignore the fact he's with someone else. This goes on for a good ten minutes. I just sit, bemused by it while they fawn all over him and then take some selfies with him.

"Ladies it was a real pleasure meeting you, thank you so much for the support you give me." I guess this is his way of politely letting them know their time is up. They take the hint and say their goodbyes by giving him hugs and kisses. One of them gives me a really sly look as she starts to leave the table, but I just politely smile.

"Kate, again I'm so sorry. Look, this is going to keep happening now I've been spotted. I don't want you to think anything of it, but I have a suite at the Mandarin Oriental if you would rather we go there to discuss what to do about tomorrow night?"

My apartment is only a short walk away, but I don't want him to know that the apartment he's interested in is right next door to mine. On the other hand, I'm also unsure about going to his hotel. The lesser of the two evils is my place.

"My apartment is just a short walk from here if you would rather we go there? I don't want to be photographed getting out of a taxi with you at your hotel. Is that okay?"

He drinks the remainder of his wine, then stands up and grabs the wine bottle that's still half full. "Let's go then before I get stopped again."

21

Lewis

W E LEAVE THE LITTLE BAR, AND I have the bottle of wine wrapped in my jacket as it's against the law to have alcohol on the streets of London in certain areas. I'm following Kate's lead, as I have no idea where her apartment is.

"I'm sorry about that, Kate. It gives you a small glimpse into what it's like being out in public with me. I hope it hasn't put you off?"

She looks at me, a bit confused by my statement, and I'm not sure how she's taken it. I really like her, and I hope when we have sorted out this mess tomorrow, we can go out on a date. I know she isn't my usual type, but I'm over all that, especially after Sadie. I want someone normal like Kate, not to mention she is beautiful, and we have this chemistry, I can feel it. I think normality is what I need if I want to settle down and start a family. I am thirty-three after all, so I need to do something.

"It's okay, Lewis, honestly, although it would drive me potty if that were me it was happening to. It must get to you sometimes. All types of women fawning over you like you're a piece of property and you belong to them. They see you as an object rather than a person, and that must really get you down sometimes."

She's hit the nail right on the head. It's true. I am seen as an object by so many people; both female and male. I'm so grateful to my fans, don't get me wrong, but it would be nice to be treated like a person sometimes, and not just a body. Kate really seems to understand me.

"You're right, a lot of them do see me as an object, and it does get to me sometimes, but I really appreciate my fans, especially the book world ones that follow me. That's where it all started for me, and I am so grateful for that."

"Book world fans? Do you write books as well? Oh, how interesting. What kind of books?" she asks looking at me, amazed.

"I don't write, no," I answer with a laugh. "Have you ever heard of Fabio Lanzoni? He's a famous cover model from the 80's and 90's. He was on a few hundred book covers back then. Well, Lucinda calls me Fabio as a joke because I'm on a lot of romance book covers. It all started there for me, getting into the book world, I used to go to book signings as a cover model. I met so many amazing people doing that, and I'm so thankful for it. It was after that when Lucinda arrange for me to join some model agencies, that I got sent on a casting call for CK and got the job. The rest, as they say, is history."

We are walking along the street, talking happily, and I haven't paid attention to where we are going, and when I look around, I recognise the place from the little tour of apartments Kate took me on earlier. We are at the building with the apartment I want to buy from Kate.

"Well, this is me then," Kate says as she stops at the huge glass double doors. She looks up at me, waiting for my reaction when I recognise where we are. Just then, the doorman opens the door for her. It isn't the same one from earlier, but he knows Kate.

"Thanks, Harry and how are you today?"

"Just great thank you, Kate, can't complain too much when I'm fit and healthy."

"Harry, this is Lewis, a friend of mine and he's interested in the penthouse next to mine, so he may become a new tenant," she says turning to me with a smile on her face.

"Nice to meet you, Harry. Yes, I really love this place. I'm considering buying the apartment I saw earlier today," I say reaching out my hand to shake his.

"I'm sure you will like it here, sir, it's by far the best place I have worked, and the boss is really nice to work for too," he says while shaking my hand and winking at Kate. She laughs at him. You can see how fond of each other they are and that they have a great relationship, not just boss-employee. They seem to know each other well.

"I hope Lillia hasn't been giving you the run around again today. You know she keeps her grandad on his toes," she says to him laughing.

"No, I didn't get to see her today. She wasn't very well, she had a bit of a tummy bug and was sick, and my daughter thought it best not to come so she didn't pass any bugs onto me. She said at my age I have to be careful of getting any kind of bug, as they can knock you for six! The cheeky little minx, what does she mean, at my age? I'm only fifty, after all." He said this winking and smiling at Kate, as he is obviously older than fifty.

"Whatever does she mean?" Kate says laughing at him.

She moves away towards the lifts. "You take care now Harry, see you later." With that, she presses the button for the lift, and the doors open immediately.

"That was good timing," she says walking into the lift and pressing the button for the penthouse apartments.

"You didn't mention you lived here," I say glancing down at her. I'm so close to her in this small space that I can smell her perfume. I don't recognise it, but I love it on her. My heart is beating faster, standing this close, she's a little shorter than me but not by much. I'm looking down on her, and she's twiddling with her hair. What is it about Kate? She's beautiful, no doubt about that. She is all woman from what I can see, even if that isn't a lot with her suit on. She's intelligent, smart, stunning and I can't help but be attracted to her. She lets go of the strand of hair she's twiddling, and I automatically reach forward to swipe it behind her ear. She gasps as I touch her cheek, and I swear I feel sparks in my fingertips.

"Sorry, that was just automatic. I didn't mean to startle you," I say looking straight into her beautiful hazel eyes. I could have sworn they were green earlier, but now they look brown.

"You surprised me, that's all."

The lift reaches the top floor, and we walk out really close to each other. I follow Kate to the right. She takes her card key out and taps it on the door. We enter the apartment, and it is the same as the one I viewed earlier today, just mirrored.

"Welcome to my place. Here, give me the bottle. You sit on the couch over there while I get the drinks, then we can sort out what to do about tomorrow night."

Kate then heads to the kitchen, as I move over to the bank of floor-to-ceiling windows near the couch.

"This view is spectacular, Kate," I say when she returns. I can't help but stare at her.

"I love the view at night, all the twinkly lights of the city and on a clear night you can see for miles." She looks up at me and catches me staring at her. She smiles shyly. I can feel the pull I have to her. I'm sure she can feel it too by the way she's looking at me. It's like we are in a trance and can't pull our eyes away from each other. Like there is an invisible thread joining us and drawing us closer, I could just lean in now and kiss her, and I'm sure she would be into it as much as me. I know I can't do that though, we need to sort out this dating site mess.

I move away from the window to break the connection between us and to save my own embarrassment because I can feel my cock stirring being so close to her, and I don't want her to see what she is doing to me right now.

"Do you think if you postponed the date from tomorrow to one-night next week that he would go for that? I'm just thinking of buying us a bit more time, you know, so we can think this through properly before going in their half-cock." Oh shit, why did I say cock out loud? Now he is rock hard. I move to the couch quickly and sit down, shit. Luckily, she has only put on a small table lamp, so at least it's not too bright in here.

Kate moves from the windows, glass in hand and sits on the couch opposite me, putting her glass on the table. I refuse to move, keeping my cock hidden until he settles down.

"I already cancelled on him once because of my meeting with you earlier in the week. I don't think he was happy because he didn't reply to me for a while. I could get my laptop from my bag and see what he says? It's worth a try. Like you say, it's better to go in with a proper plan than a half-cocked one."

Shit, now she said cock. That's it, he's not going down anytime soon. I'll be staying put for a while. When did she take her jacket off? Oh no, I can see her bra through the white blouse she has on, and it's a lacey one. Stop looking at her tits, idiot, look at her face.

"Yeah okay, get your laptop. Tell him something has come up and ask if you can cancel until next Friday or Saturday. I just need to check with Lucinda to make sure I'm here in London next weekend." She heads to get her laptop, and I quickly stand up to get my phone out of my pocket before she comes back then I dial Luce to see what my schedule is for next week.

22

Katherine

I GRAB MY BRIEFCASE, TAKE OUT MY laptop and start making my way back to the living area. I can hear Lewis talking as I approach, so, rather than listen into his conversation, I take the time to get changed out of my suit and put on my casuals.

I look in the mirror, and I'm horrified to see my cheeks are red. I'm all flustered from being so close to him. It's hard to deny the sparks I feel.

He is stunningly beautiful, so handsome, and I feel this pull of chemistry between us, but then I look at him—this famous supermodel and plain old me. He can't possibly feel anything between us. I'm sure he dates supermodels and famous people so there is no way he will be in the slightest bit interested in me. I'm just me: plain, mousy brown hair, boring hazel eyes, curvy, so no Victoria's Secret body here.

However, I do love how he wants to try and stop this imposter from doing anything to me or any other women. I love the protective way he wants to help people. He is such a nice humble guy, especially for someone famous. Most famous people I come across are so arrogant, but he is completely the opposite.

I get changed into my sweatpants and a short, tight-fitting t-shirt which are my usual house clothes when I'm just relaxing with a glass of wine, and as I enter the living area, Lewis is still on the phone. He turns when he hears me enter and he gawps at me with his mouth hanging open. I look down to see what the problem is, thinking my knickers are over my sweats or something, but I don't see a problem, so I look back at him and frown. I put my laptop down on the coffee table, still confused. Does he have a problem with me or something? I mean, I don't really know him, we've only just met, but he keeps looking at me strangely.

He looks away embarrassed then realises whoever is on the phone has spoken to him.

"Oh sorry, Luce, yes, yes, thank you, that's great. Can you send me the schedule on my phone, please? Of course, you've already done that, and I should have checked first, but you know what a scatterbrain I am sometimes. I will. Enjoy the rest of your evening. Goodnight, Luce."

He hangs up the phone and puts it on the arm of the couch. He's staring at me again. Gee whizz, he's giving me a complex here.

"Umm, Lewis, is something wrong? Only you keep giving me funny looks."

He takes his wine and gulps it down.

"Sorry, Kate, I don't mean to give you funny looks. You just surprised me being in your casual clothes, that's all."

Okay then, maybe I should have stayed in my suit or possibly put on something smart-casual like slacks and a sweater, but I'm hot after the wine and walk, so didn't want to put a sweater on. I get another bottle of wine and top up our glasses, sit on the couch opposite him and grab the laptop to fire it up.

"Do you think this person pretending to be me will re-schedule the date? I don't want him to change his mind. I feel we need to pursue this and find out what he's up to." He takes a sip from his wine again and moves a little in his seat as though he's uncomfortable.

Maybe I should have gone and put that sweater on after all.

Maybe he doesn't like curvy girls, and that's why he's been giving me funny looks.

Maybe he thinks I should be more covered up, so he doesn't have to look at me. Now I feel uncomfortable. I think I'll go put a sweater on while the laptop boots up.

As I come back to the couch in my hoody, he speaks. "Were you cold, Kate?"

"Just a little, yes. I thought it best to put a sweater on than turn the heat up in case you're warm." I am now sweating in my sweater. Great. Well, he won't be here for long, so he won't have to look at me for much longer.

I log onto my dating account. There are no new messages from fake Lewis, so as far as I'm aware the date is still on for tomorrow.

"What do you think I should tell him to make it believable?"

"Maybe say your mum is sick and you had to go and stay with her for the weekend."

I don't look at him. It still cuts deep.

"My mum died, Lewis. I've already told fake Lewis that she is no longer around. That it's just my brother and me now." I choke out the words, trying not to get emotional, he'll think I'm a wreck, but it's still raw after four years. I miss her so much.

"Oh, Kate. I'm so sorry. I had no idea. Was it recent? I understand if you don't want to tell me. I had no intentions of upsetting you."

"It was four years ago now, but it still feels like it was yesterday. I lived with mum—we were very close. She got cancer, and by the time we found out she didn't last long at all. In fact, by the time they found out, the cancer had spread, and she only lived for two more weeks. It's just me and my older brother, Brad and his family now. We don't have any other relatives. He has a wife, Cindy and they have two children, Simon and Lottie, who I adore immensely." I look back at the laptop and start to write to fake Lewis.

23

George

W HAT THE FUCK! NO WAY IS SHE doing this to me, no fucking way. How fucking dare she cancel on me again? Who the fuck does she think she is, the stupid bitch. This is not happening. I'm going to get that bitch tomorrow night. I will get her if it's the last thing I do. The rage inside me is so immense I want to smash everything to bits. I see the red mist. I need an out, now, before I lose my mind. She's going to make me lose it big time. I get up, not knowing what I'm doing or where I'm going. I need her. I need to rid the world of her before she hurts anyone. What if she has a child and does to them what she did to me? She has to go for good.

I find myself outside, not even remembering leaving my shithole of a bedsit. I'm sitting on a bench in the park near Tottenham Marshes. How the hell did I get here and why have I come here of all places? I need to leave, get away from here and go back home before anyone sees me near here. Fuck my life.

When I get back to my shithole, I see that the front door is slightly open. Shit, is someone in there? I listen at the door to see if I can hear anyone, but I can't. I slowly open the door a bit more, and it creaks. If anyone is in there, I just gave myself away. Still no noise, so I edge in. Shit, it looks like a bomb has gone off in here. My chair is flipped over, and there are smashed plates and cups on the floor. Luckily, my PC is still sitting on the table, undamaged. But my bed is turned upside down, and the pictures on my wall have been ripped off. Who would do this? No one knows me. Fuck, has someone found out?

I go to the chair and pick it up, then my bed. I pick up the crappy pictures then I start to pick up the broken dishes. I sit on the chair in front of my PC and tap the keyboard. There on the screen is the message from the bitch cancelling our date tomorrow. Now it comes back to me. I went ape-shit after reading her message, and I guess the red mist descended. I must have trashed the place before leaving and ending up in the park. Thank fuck it was me and no one else.

I read her message to me.

Dear Lewis,

I am so sorry to have to do this, but I need to cancel our date tomorrow night. I know this is the second time now and it's short notice, but my brother phoned me to say my niece has been rushed into hospital. He has asked if I will go and stay with them to look after my nephew while they are at the hospital.

I am sorry, Lewis. It's a family emergency.

Please can we re-arrange for next weekend?

I look forward to hearing from you..

Best Regards,

Katherine

THAT FUCKING BITCH.

24

Lewis

"**D**O YOU THINK HE WILL BUY that Kate? I hate that you had to use your family to lie to him. If he goes for it, then we need to plan this out and think about what we need to do to make sure he isn't a danger to anyone." I'm standing behind the couch, behind Kate, looking over her shoulder at the message she had just sent to fake Lewis. My rock hard cock has now deflated, thankfully. It helped that she put a sweater on because her tits in that tight T-Shirt were nearly making me blow my load. She has the perfect figure, and when she walked in wearing the sweats and that top, I nearly lost it completely.

"I know I'm asking a lot of you, to do this with me, but I feel it's my responsibility in some way." I hope to God he just enjoys the chase, but my gut is telling me this isn't right, and this is a bad person.

She turns her head to look up at me "I know Lewis, and I do want to help. I'm just scared. The more I think about what you said, the more it scares me." She turns away to face the laptop and brings up the pictures fake Lewis had used. Most of them are old pictures from before I had started modelling; back in my PT days—when my hair was a lot shorter and curlier, and my beard was wild. I suppose that made more sense than using the recent ones that millions of people had seen all over the world. Plus, I wear glasses more now than I used to, even in my shoots.

"Do you need another top up of wine?" I ask Kate when I see her glass is empty. She nods and passes me her glass.

"I think we need to wait until he replies to you before we decide what our next step is. My gut is telling me he will reply." I head to the kitchen to top up our glasses. Kate's kitchen is almost the same as the apartment next door, just homelier with all her finishing touches.

"Kate, you never answered me before when I said you didn't tell me you lived here. If I buy the apartment that will make us neighbours," I shout to her from the kitchen before I head back in with our wines.

"Thank you. Well, I don't make it a habit of letting people I have just met know where I live. Especially when I'm showing an apartment in the same building." She smiles as she takes a sip from her wine.

"Good point, we don't know each other… Yet." Shit, did I just say that out loud? From the look on her face, I think I must have because it looks like I've scared her, again. She blinks and then goes to say something, but then takes another sip of wine instead. I need to change the subject quickly. I think the wine is going to my head. "Any reply from fake Lewis, yet? Does it show if he's read the message?"

She looks at her laptop. "Yes, he's read the message, but he hasn't replied to me. Last time I cancelled, it was a day or two before he contacted me again and that was only after I sent him another message to say about re-arranging the date."

I think I've changed the subject from getting to know her. I can't do anything about this attraction I have to her, not until we have sorted out what is going to happen with this psycho.

"I think we need to wait and see if he replies to me. Then we can take it from there. I don't think I will hear back from him tonight. It's quite late now."

"Yes, I agree. I should get back to my hotel. Like you say, it's late. Let me give you my number, and then if you hear back from him, you can ring or text me, and we can take it from there." I stand up and grab my glass, which is now empty and take it into the kitchen, but Kate takes it from me and puts it to the sink herself. I follow behind her and lean on the counter as she washes the glasses out. I have to say that I love the view from here. She has the most perfect arse. Not too small, just lovely and curvy. I need to stop thinking about it, now I'm starting to get hard again, and I can't hide it.

"Can I use the toilet before I head out please, Kate?" I ask so I can make a getaway before she sees how hard I am. I turn so I'm not facing her, ready to make my way to the toilet.

"Yeah, sure, the guest bathroom is just down the hallway, second door on the left. Do you want me to call an Uber for you?"

"That would be great, yes, please." I head for the bathroom, hoping by the time I get there my cock will have deflated. I haven't reacted to anyone like this in such a long time, in fact. I didn't even have these reactions with Susan, and I thought she was it for me until she broke my heart. It just goes to show everything happens for a reason, and I'm starting to see that she was not meant to be the one for me.

When I go back to the living area, Kate is sitting on the couch with her phone in her hand, Uber app open. She looks up at me. "Uber is on the way and will be outside in a few minutes."

"Thanks for the wine, Kate. I'm sorry you're going through this with the fake Lewis. If you change your mind and decide you don't want to meet up with him I completely understand. The last thing I want is you scared or in any danger." I turn around and start walking to the front door so I can call the lift. Just as I reach the door, Kate pulls on my sleeve to make me turn in her direction.

"Lewis, this is on me. It's me on a stupid dating site looking for love. I'm really grateful we met today, or I would never have known the danger I could be in. Please don't apologise for something that you have no control over. Just because some idiot uses your images, that is not your fault, no matter what you say. Give me your number, and I'll call you if he gets in touch," she says this a bit sheepishly.

"Pass me your phone. I'll put my number in for you." After she hands me the phone, I put my contact details in, then I press ring, so her phone rings mine.

"There, I have your number now as well."

I open the front door, and she follows me to the lift where I press the call button.

"Don't forget to call me, Kate, as soon as you hear from him. If I don't answer, text me because I'm on a shoot tomorrow, and I may not have my phone on me. It's hard to hide a phone when you're just in your undies." I smile at her trying to make light of the evening.

"I had a good evening tonight, thank you." I lean forward and kiss her on the cheek.

She gasps as I do and blushes. Sparks shoot through me. She must feel them as well—it can't be just me. I step into the lift and press the button for the ground floor.

"Goodnight, Kate, hopefully speak to you soon, sweetheart."

The doors close on her shocked face.

25

Katherine

Wow, I can't breathe. Did he just actually do that? Kiss me on the cheek? I've only known him a few hours, yet the sparks I got from that his touch again shot right to my lady parts. Shit. I have never reacted to anyone like that before. But he is such a sweet guy.

He said hopefully he would see me soon. Does that mean he wants to get to know me? I'm so confused. Is it my feelings for him making me think he likes me? He could have anyone he wanted. I need a shower now and maybe some sort of release. I am so wound up.

Still nothing from fake Lewis, but I'm not losing any sleep over him. I will, however, lose sleep over the real Lewis. I'm sure. I turn all the lights out and head to my bedroom so I can take a shower before bed.

In the shower, I can't stop thinking of Lewis. Every time we touched I felt the sparks of electricity running through me. He is gorgeous. It's those eyes and hell those lips. I'm getting so turned on thinking about him. I turn the head of the shower to power jet then I open up my folds and let the jets massage my clit. God, that feels so good. I close my eyes and picture Lewis kneeling down in front of me. He makes me spread my legs wide, so he can dip his head and taste me. While thinking of Lewis doing that I insert two fingers inside me, and moan, imagining it's his tongue. The water is still massaging my clit, and I'm pumping in and out faster with my fingers. It doesn't take me long to explode. I slide down the wall to the floor as I come down from my orgasm before my knees buckle. I have never in my life come so hard on my own.

I get out of the shower, feeling relaxed and sated. I put my boy shorts and tank top on and get into bed. I find it hard to sleep, tossing and turning, thinking of Lewis. Thankfully, it's Saturday tomorrow, so I don't have to get up too early, although I am planning on going into the office for a while before I head home to Chelmsford. I have some prep to do for my showing on Monday afternoon after my meeting at the old warehouse project that I'm excited to be buying.

Sleep comes to me after what feels like forever lying in bed mainly thinking of Lewis but also about the catfish situation. I don't wake up until 9.33 a.m. I don't honestly remember the last time I slept in till this time.

I get a shower, get some coffee, and make some toast then head out to the office.

In the office there is a note from Clive sat on Chrissie's desk at reception, reminding me he's not in the office now until next Thursday, as he's away in Spain to celebrate Zane's birthday for a few days. Good job he reminded me, I had forgotten about it. He said I could still contact him if there is something I need to know and that he has sent my meeting schedule to my planner on my phone and to make sure I check it. I'm terrible at checking my planner. I rely on Clive far too much. He ends the note with a smiley face and some kisses.

I fire up my PC, then get some iced water. I check and see if fake Lewis has contacted me first. He hasn't written back, but I'm not going to worry about it. If he doesn't respond, that's fine by me. Except then I won't have an excuse to message Lewis. I'll just have to hope he goes ahead with buying the apartment. Will it be weird being neighbours? Maybe we will become friends, who knows? We got on really well last night. It was like we had known each other for ages, not just a few hours.

Just then my phone pings with a text message. I think it's probably Clive reminding me about something else for next week, but when I pick it up, I see it's Lewis? I nearly drop the phone. My heart beats fast as I look at the message.

Lewis – Morning, beautiful, just checking in to see if you've heard anything from the psycho this morning?

Kate – Good Morning, Lewis. No, he hasn't replied to my message yet.

Lewis – On my way to a shoot. Let me know if you hear anything. Speak to you soon.

Kate – Yes, will do. Have a good shoot. Speak soon.

I love how caring he is. I also love that he called me beautiful. When I read that I had butterflies in my tummy. I sit there, sipping my water for a few minutes with a smile on my face re reading the text's. The fact that he thought to text me makes me go all gooey for him. I'm in trouble.

I have Dave, my structural engineer, Tom, my architect I used for my last project, and also my trusted project manager, Alf, meeting me at the old warehouse buildings on Monday morning so that we can go over the buildings and make sure that they are structurally safe and a good investment. Hopefully, I can get a rough costing analysis done for the renovations. With the price of the buildings—I really want them both—and then the renovation costs, I'm going to need an investor or a hefty bridging loan from the bank.

I'm praying Dave says the buildings are sound, and that Tom can see my vision.

I've been here a few hours, putting together a proposal for the bank or investors. Provided my team approve everything on Monday, I will be putting in an offer for the buildings, so I have that letter ready to go as well.

I look at the clock and its 3.30 p.m. already. I decide to call it a day and head home to Chelmsford for the rest of the weekend. I lock the offices up and head back to my apartment block to get the car. I nip into the deli on the way to grab a tuna wrap and decide to eat it in the park before my drive.

I get this weird feeling as I leave the deli that someone is watching me. I look around, but I don't see anyone else apart from cars passing by. I head to the park to enjoy the fresh air while eating.

I sit on the bench in the park, which is relatively quiet apart from a dog walker and one woman pushing her child on the swing, and I suddenly think to check my phone, as it's been on silent. There is another text from Lewis. I have a big grin on my face and butterflies in my tummy again. What is he doing to me?

Lewis – Hey, beautiful. Just finished the shoot, and thought I would check in with you to see if you have heard back yet from the catfish. I'm in the car on the way back to the hotel and will be back there soon. Don't worry if you're busy. Just let me know when you can.

The butterflies are doing somersaults in my tummy, he called me beautiful again. The message was 40 minutes ago. He will probably be back at the hotel. I send a reply anyway.

Kate – Hi there. I'm just sitting in the park eating a wrap before I head on home. Sorry, I haven't checked my messages since this morning, was too busy in the office. I'll check when I get home. It will probably be around six, depending on the traffic.

Lewis – No worries. What park are you in? That's a long drive back home?

I haven't told him about my house in Chelmsford. I decide to be open. I'm not starting a friendship on lies.

Kate – It's a park just near my apartment. When I say home, I actually live in Chelmsford. The apartment is my London place for during the week.

Lewis – Ah ok. I was going to see if you fancied a drink tonight? Don't worry. We can catch up when you're back.

Oh no. I would have definitely said yes to that. I must look so stupid, sitting here with a big grin on my face. He wants to see me again tonight. We only saw each other last night.

Kate – Sorry, Lewis. I would have really liked that. I'm back here on Monday for the week. I will also let you know if I hear anything from FL (Fake Lewis). Speak to you soon.

Lewis – Ok, Kate and drive safe. Let me know when you get home please? We can have that drink on Monday then if you like? Speak to you soon.

I finish my wrap and check my e-mails. I still feel as though someone is watching me. I look around, but I don't see anyone. I then make my way back to get the car to get on the road home.

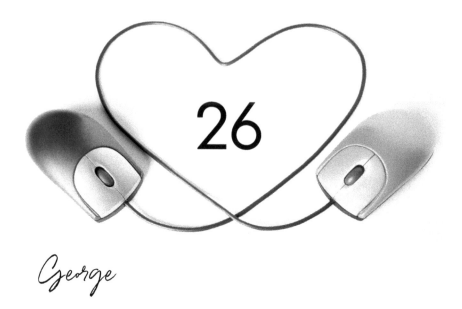

George

I WAKE UP EARLY, MY HEAD WON'T switch off, thinking about that fucking bitch, and I'm still pissed at her. Well, fuck her. I'm taking back control. I'll write back later and re-arrange for next weekend, but there is no way in hell I'm waiting that long. I intend to strike before then. Especially now I know where she works and lives. I need a plan.

I get up. I need to burn off some of this anger and frustration. I do a workout in my little shithole. I have just enough room to do press-ups, sit-ups, lunges, squats, and weights that I keep under my bed. I have a pull-up bar across the only door there is, which leads into the bathroom and set about doing one hundred pull-ups to finish my workout.

Nearly two hours later and I'm dripping with sweat by the time I've finished. I head into the bathroom to take a much-needed cold shower, just as well, as I don't have any hot water.

While in the shower I think of the bitch and I get hard. Fuck, just what I need right now. I jack off to give me some release, but it doesn't do much for me. Shit, I can't be in this state all day. I decide I'm going to her apartment to see if she's there. I don't trust the bitch. I think she's lying to me. I want to see for myself.

I finish in the shower and check the time. It's still only 7.30 a.m. Still early for a Saturday morning, if I get dressed and head to her apartment, I can watch her building from across the road and out of sight.

I make it to her building by 8.55 a.m. and wait. It's now 9.55 a.m. and still no sign of her. I'll stay here though until I'm sure she isn't here.

10.45 a.m. and there she is. I knew it. She was lying to me. She's on her own, no kid with her. She's heading in the direction of her office. I get up to follow her but make sure I keep well back so she doesn't notice.

She approaches her office building and goes inside. I go to the café opposite, the one I sat in the other day in my suit. I go in and use the toilet, then order a coffee, grab one of the free newspapers, and sit at a table in the window where I can keep an eye on the building. I could be here all fucking day.

I've been here for ages. My phone says 2.45 now, I've had three coffees and I'm on my second bottle of water. I had to swap newspapers a couple of times. Finally, at 3.40 she appears at the front of the building. She's practically done a day's work, and I've sat here bored shitless. She starts to head back in the direction of her apartment building. I get up and start to follow her, staying on my side of the road and way behind so as not to look suspicious. She turns into the same deli she went into the other day. I stay back where I am, not near enough that she would notice me even if she looked in this direction. I'm just a guy in a baseball cap standing with his phone.

She comes out of the shop and looks around up and down the street as though she's looking for someone before she starts back towards her apartment building. I edge forward but then at the first side road she comes to, she turns right and heads down it. Oh shit, has she seen me and is trying to lose me? I speed up a bit, so I don't lose sight of her for too long.

I approach the side road she turned down and turn cautiously just in case she's there. She isn't. Shit, where did she go? I walk faster down the road. I'm alert, my eyes darting everywhere in case she's in one of the buildings along this road, but I don't see her. I come to a crossroads and look left, then right. I still don't see her. Fucking great. I can't even tail the bitch properly. I decide to cross over the road and turn left, still heading in the same direction as her apartment but just on a different road. I'm walking past what looks like a little park area that's all fenced off. There is a swing set and slide and then a very small grassed area with benches and fuck me, she is sitting on one of them.

Luckily, she isn't looking. She seems engrossed in her phone. I move back a bit so I'm shielded behind a large tree and a small hedge. I can still see her, but she won't be able to see me. She finishes her food and then suddenly looks around as if looking for someone. I quickly move out of her line of sight behind the tree so she doesn't see me.

I don't look back for a couple of minutes, in case she's still looking, but then when I do look, I start to panic as she's up and making her way towards the gate to come back out onto the road. Shit, I move quickly in the opposite direction so she doesn't see me. I think I make it around the corner on the other side of the park without her noticing. I can see her leaving the park from this side view. That was close. Fuck, I don't think I'm cut out for this stalking bullshit. I'd just rather get it over and done with.

I still manage to follow, keeping my distance. She's heading back to her apartment. She reaches her building, but she heads down the ramp at the side towards the underground parking instead of up to her apartment. I stay where I am on the road and get my phone out of my pocket and pretend I'm on it, talking.

A few minutes later, I see a blue Mercedes appear and notice she's driving. Shit, I can't follow her anymore. She turns right onto the road away from me.

Fuck, what a wasted day that was. I still don't know if she was telling me the truth, because she could be heading to her brother's now. I think she was bullshitting me, and that pisses me off.

27

Lewis

W HEN I GOT BACK TO THE HOTEL last night, I needed a
shower and a release. I just couldn't stop thinking about
Kate. She's the most beautiful, curvaceous woman I have ever met. I
could hardly sleep all night, which is not good when you have a shoot
the next day. The last thing I needed was to look like I had been out
partying the night before. A bit of concealer can hide dark circles, but
I never want the photographers or producers to think I don't take
this seriously. I have no idea how long the modelling will last. I do
love my job, and I will keep at it for as long as I'm in demand.

At 5.30 a.m., I decided enough was enough. I got my running
gear on and went out in Hyde Park. It really rejuvenated me. Once I
got back to the hotel, I got changed into my workout clothes. I need
to look ripped for this shoot. It's for a new fragrance by Gucci for
men, launching just in time for Christmas. I'm almost naked in the
commercial, so I just had a protein shake for breakfast.

Lucinda comes to get me at 10 a.m. We have to travel to a studio in Shepherds Bush for the shoot. The traffic is bad for a Saturday morning. I get my phone out to see if Kate has messaged me, but nothing. I decide to text her, just to see if she has heard from the psycho yet. That's what I tell myself anyway. Really, I just want to make sure she's okay.

She texts me right back. I'm not sure if I'm disappointed that she hasn't heard back from him or not. I want to keep her safe. She intrigues me. She's nothing like I have ever gone for and maybe that's my problem.

I have to get to wardrobe, and although my agent sent me the script for the commercial, I need to run through with the director and producer to find out exactly what they want me to do today.

This is only my third commercial, so I'm a bit nervous. Thankfully, there are no lines to learn. It's not a speaking commercial, just a visual one.

"How are they going to make it look like I'm in some kind of palace with a big ballroom in this little studio?" I ask Luce.

"They are only doing some of the shots here, Lewis. We are going to Venice, Italy on Tuesday to film the rest of it in the magnificent Palazzo Pisani Moretta. We are there for two nights. It's in your schedule. If you looked at it for once instead of relying on me to tell you your every move, you'd know!" She's smiling at me now. I was so wrapped up with Kate last night, I didn't check when Luce sent it through, and I only asked her if I was free next weekend, not what I was doing this week.

Shit, I'm going to be out of the country for a couple of nights this week, and I wanted to see Kate. I need to concentrate on filming this commercial and not think about her, but that's easier said than done.

We are on set for about four hours in all, which isn't too bad, and the producer and the marketing team from Gucci seemed to be pleased with the way it has all gone.

We get into the car to head back to the hotel, and I pull out my phone to see if Kate has texted me. There are no messages from her, so I take it she hasn't heard anything yet. I'm going to see if she wants to have a drink with me tonight. I really need to see her again.

God, I have it bad already, and I have only spent a few hours with her.

Once I get back to the hotel, I order room service and go onto the balcony to relax for a bit and catch up on my social media.

My phone dings with a text from Kate. My heart flutters, and I get butterflies in my tummy—a reaction that shocks me. We message for a bit, and I discover she actually lives in Chelmsford. I have a house there too. This is no coincidence—it's fate. I hope she agrees to a drink on Monday.

28

Katherine

THE DRIVE HOME IS GOOD. NO TRAFFIC, so it doesn't take me too long to get here. I love coming home. I do miss it here. It's so quiet and peaceful, especially after being in the city all week. I downloaded a new album by a new artist called Tokio Myers. He's a pianist with a twist. I listened to that on the drive home, and it really chilled me out.

I arrived at 5.45 p.m., and I'm looking forward to just relaxing and reading tonight with a nice bottle of wine.

I make myself some tuna pasta, then I shower and am now in my boy shorts and tank top with a glass of wine and reading a book in front of my real wood fire. I love the fire in my house. Last time I looked at the time on my phone, it was 7.45 p.m., but I look up as it pings with a text message and it's 10.30 p.m. Wow, nearly three hours I've been sitting here, relaxing, engrossed in my book.

I look at the message and see it's Lewis. My heart skips a beat, and the butterflies in my tummy are doing somersaults again.

Lewis – Hi, beautiful, just wanted to check in with you again and make sure you arrived home safely and to see if you had heard anything from the catfisher yet?

Oh crap. I'd forgotten to check if FL had messaged me back. I'd best check before I reply to Lewis. I grab my laptop and log onto the dating site, but there is no message from him yet. I really don't think I'll hear from him again. I don't want to hear from him. I would much rather go out for drinks with the real Lewis. I text him back.

Kate – Hey, Lewis. Sorry, I said I would let you know that I got home okay, but yes, I did, thank you. I'm just not used to letting anyone know where I am or what I'm doing. No, I haven't heard anything from FL. I don't think I will to be honest.

Lewis – Sorry, I wasn't checking up on you. I just wanted to make sure you were safe. Glad you got there okay. I didn't know you lived in Chelmsford. I live not far from there.

Kate – Wow, do you? I didn't realize. So is it just an apartment for when you are in London you are looking for? I thought it was for a permanent place to live. I don't mind you asking if I got home safe—it's nice to have someone who cares enough to ask.

Lewis – I have a house in a small village called Little Waltham not far from Chelmsford. I love that house. It's really quiet at times, but then it's not too far from the village pub and the little village shop.

I do care enough to ask, Kate.

It's sad you don't have anyone to ask you. A bit like me really, besides Lucinda, I don't have anyone who cares enough.

Kate – Well then, let's make a pact to care enough about each other that we want to ask. Deal?

Lewis – Yes, that's a deal I would like to make. What are you up to tonight? I know it's late. I hope I didn't wake you.

Kate – No, I was reading in front of my log fire with a glass of wine, just chilling. To be honest, I've been so engrossed in my book I didn't realize the time until your text came through. I'm really tired though. I didn't sleep well last night.

Lewis – I'm just in my suite at the hotel on my own. I was browsing through the internet finding out about dating sites. Did you know there are lots of terms used for the different types of people on these sites? I remembered you saying last night that this was you being catfished, that's why I looked them up. Why didn't you sleep well? Are you okay?

Kate – Yes, I found out a lot about the terms used on these dating sites, and I've probably had 70% used on me, but I won't go into that now and bore you. I just couldn't sleep. I had too much going around in my head. This stuff with FL, then with work. I'm looking to buy some new buildings to convert... and then you

Why did I say that?

Lewis – Me?

Kate – Yeah, you. I couldn't stop thinking about you as well. About what a coincidence it was, you coming to me looking for an apartment, and the guy I have been talking to using your picture. What are the chances of that happening? Thinking that everything happens for a reason, and maybe you are my white knight. Also, what if I hadn't met you yesterday? Who knows what would have happened tonight? It terrifies me, Lewis, thinking about it. I don't normally scare easily, but this has gotten to me.

Lewis – I'm so pleased we did meet, Kate. I daren't think about what could have happened. It makes my blood boil. I couldn't sleep last night either. The same reasons as you really, but mainly I couldn't stop thinking about you.

Oh wow. He was thinking about me last night. Is that just because of FL or because he likes me. My tummy is doing somersaults again.

Kate – Me? As in you saved me?

Lewis – As in I really like you, Kate, and I want to get to know you more. I know you said you would have liked to have a drink tonight if you were still in the City so can we meet up on Monday for a drink?

I'm shocked that he's pursuing this! I'm a plain Jane who is a bit hefty. I bet if I did a search on the internet for Lewis Clancy I would see lots of pictures of him with models and actresses at star-studded events. He's way out of my league. I don't go to events where people snap pictures of you. I don't have all the designer clothes like the models wear, mainly because they stop at a size twelve. I don't fit into Lewis's life. I'm a nobody.

Lewis – You there, Kate?

Kate – Yes, sorry, Lewis. You just shocked me.

Lewis – Why?

Kate – Just because…. I don't suppose I'm your usual type, that's all.

Lewis – What do you mean? What is my usual type?

Kate – Come on, Lewis. You know what I mean. I'm not exactly model material.

Is this getting a bit too heavy now? What is it about writing to someone and not speaking face to face or on the phone? I seem to be more open and say things I wouldn't normally say face to face?

Lewis – Kate I don't really have a usual type? But I can tell you that you are most definitely my type. I haven't stopped thinking about you all day today. You are a beautiful smart woman who I would like to get to know. How about that drink on Monday? PLEASE, pretty PLEASE–I'm not beyond begging. In fact, I'm on my knees now haha

Shit, he really does want to get to know me. I like him more and more and he seems so lovely and caring. Will it hurt to go out for a drink with him? Maybe he should come to mine again if Friday was anything to go by, with his fans coming and interrupting us. Would he think it too forward if I suggest he comes to my apartment?

Lewis – Kate? Have I scared you off?

Maybe I can do this. Why not. I am good enough for anyone, just because my past experiences have been horrendous, why should I settle for less? I think I should take the chance.

Lewis – Sorry if I upset you, Kate. I didn't mean to overstep the mark, I can't help what I feel, and if the chemistry last night was anything to go by, you must have felt it too?

Kate – Sorry, Lewis. I'm here. Just thinking. Yes, I would like to have a drink with you on Monday. I thought it was just me that felt that last night. I was so embarrassed after you left. Do you want to come to mine on Monday, or I could come to yours? That's not me being forward, please don't think that. I'm just thinking how it was in that bar last night and how your fans kept approaching you. It would be difficult to talk with that happening?

Lewis – Phew. I thought it was just me. Glad you felt it too. I would love nothing more than for us to spend time together alone rather than be interrupted all the time. I don't mind either way, if your happy, I will come to you. I know you feel better that way.

Kate – Yes, okay then. If you come to mine around seven p.m., I should be home by then. Do you want me to do some pasta? I will see you on Monday. Loved speaking to you tonight. I'm off to bed now. Goodnight, Lewis. Xx

Lewis – Pasta is my favourite. I would love that, thank you. See you at seven p.m. on Monday. Let me know tomorrow if you hear from FL, please, Kate. Goodnight, beautiful. Hope you manage to sleep better tonight. I know I will now. X

What have I done? A real-life date with a real person that I didn't meet on a dating site and a famous model of all people. I need to pinch myself. Oh well, if I don't take the chance, I will never know.

I go to bed and do fall asleep fairly quickly, and I have a great night's sleep this time.

George

I'M GOING STIR CRAZY HERE. I went back to her apartment building late last night, well more like early this morning, and I snuck down the ramp to the parking garage. I was in black sweats, jacket and black beanie hat with the hood of my hoodie pulled up so the security cameras couldn't see my face. I knew there would be security cameras in a place like that. The parking garage was only the one level thankfully, so I could get in and out quickly before someone came to see what I was doing. I couldn't see her blue Mercedes anywhere. She didn't come home last night, the filthy whore. Is she seeing someone else? Is that why she cancelled on me?

I came back home to think about what to do? The bitch is lying to me and messing me around. I have to get rid of her for good. I can't just leave it and find someone else. She's in my head. She's the spitting image of my so-called mother. I can't let her live and do things to her children like my mother did to me. I have got to do this and rid her from this earth.

I trained for over two hours, and still I felt the anger. I went back to her apartment building at 10 a.m. to see if her car was there and it wasn't. I hung around for a couple of hours just down the road where I could see the entrance to the garage ramp. There were cars coming and going but not hers. Where the fuck is she? Why is she doing this to me? She just wants to mess with my head. Well, just you wait, bitch, I will mess with your head.

I went to the pub, the one I was at the other night watching those other whores. I wanted to see if I could get rid of this anger by watching them. It was nearly empty; the only women in there were old, haggard ones looking for free drinks from anyone that would buy them one. Filthy whores, the lot of them. I stayed for a couple of hours, knocking back a few whiskeys before coming back to my shithole.

It's now 2.30 p.m., and I'm in front of my computer looking at her message to me. Maybe that's where she is, at her brother's looking after her nephew. Maybe she hasn't lied to me. Who am I kidding? They all fucking lie. I start to write, telling her I understand and that we can re-arrange to next Saturday, along with other bullshit I have to put to make it sound genuine, blah blah blah. I won't be able to wait that long. I know that for a fact, I will get her this week, one way or another.

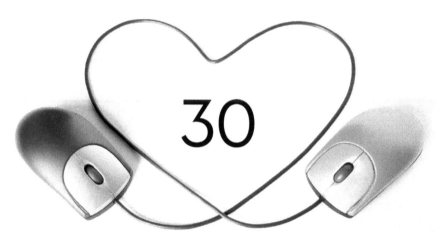

30

Katherine

I HAD A GOOD NIGHT'S SLEEP, AND feel refreshed this morning. I'm on a walk in the fresh air near my home. There are fields around where I live with public footpaths for the ramblers. It's nice but fresh out, so I wrapped up with my woolly scarf, hat and gloves, and put my wellies on. I love it around here at this time of year. It's just coming into autumn.

It also gives me time to think, walking through the fields. I checked before I left and there was no message from FL on the dating site. I am beginning to hope I don't hear from him again. I know Lewis is worried he's dangerous predator and wants to stop him from hurting anyone, but it still scares me.

I shudder at the thought of what could have happened if I'd met him last night. It really is scary when you think about all the possibilities. I think if I ever do this again, on a dating site, I will make sure I Facetime or Skype the person I'm going to meet so I know exactly who it is I'm meeting. I suppose you learn by your mistakes, but to what expense. I could have been raped or killed last night. Wow, I'm actually crying at the thought and possibilities and the embarrassment at being stupid to put myself in this predicament.

I start heading home. I pass a few couples out walking, mainly with dogs. It's at times like this I really want a relationship, for those moments, out walking a dog or going out just to the pub for lunch or cosying up on the couch in front of the log fire, watching films and drinking wine. It's the company I crave as well. I hate being alone. Since mum died, it's been hard. I miss her so much. I think I will go and see Brad and Cindy and give my lovely niece and nephew big cuddles. It's what I need today.

When I get home, I make a mug of coffee and go and sit on the cushioned seat in the window recess in the kitchen. The view from here is of my back garden, then beyond the garden is a vast field, housing horses.

I phone Brad to see if he and Cindy are in and up for a visit and arrange to go over a little later on after I've done some more research on the buildings I want to buy. Cindy shouts to Brad to tell me to stay for dinner, that they have plenty. I say I will be there at four p.m. for dinner and cuddles.

After a couple of hours, I decide I've done enough research. The buildings I want are sounding better and better to me. I'm so excited about these buildings. I'm so confident when it comes to my business, why can't I be like that with men?

I check the dating site before I get ready to head to Brad and Cindy's, and my heart drops to my stomach when I see that FL has messaged.

Katherine,

I am so sorry to hear the news about your little niece. I do hope she's doing okay and that it's nothing too serious.

I completely understand, family comes first.

As long as everything is okay with your family, then I would love to re-arrange and make it for next Saturday.

We have waited this long, so what's a few more days, although I cannot wait to finally meet you in person. I hope you feel the same.

Please let me know how your niece is doing.

Shall we say Saturday the same time and the same place providing everything is ok?

Please don't worry and just concentrate on helping your family.

Hope to hear from you soon.

Lewis

Wow, I did not expect that. He is very understanding and so genuine. I would have had no problem believing he meant what he said if I hadn't met the real Lewis. It's so scary how deceiving people can be. I need to let Lewis know I've had a message back from FL.

Kate – Hi, Lewis, just wanted to let you know that FL has messaged me back and he wants to re-arrange the date for next Saturday. He was really nice in his reply and very genuine, which is scary. I'm going to my brother's for dinner and cuddles with my niece and nephew. I will speak to you when I get back home later if you're around? Maybe we can Facetime or Skype? Xx

I send the message, then go and get ready to head out to Brad's. I'll reply to FL once I've spoken to Lewis, hopefully later on. Now I'm really nervous about how we will get him.

I need to head to the shops before they close. There is a toy store on the retail park not far from where Brad lives, and I want to get Simon and Lottie something. I like to spoil them when I do get to see them, but Cindy doesn't like them having sweets, which I tend to agree with, so a toy it is.

I get to Brad's just after four p.m. I give him a kiss on the cheek then rush in to see Simon and Lottie.

Simon screams, "Tanty Kate, Tanty Kate," and runs at me like a bull. I scoop him up in my arms. "Wow, Simon, you've grown so big. You're getting too big for Aunty Kate. Soon you will be lifting me up into your arms." He laughs at me. "Tanty Kate. Tats silly. I'm small. You can lift me for this long," he says spreading his arms wide. I put him down and tickle his tummy and sides. Lottie comes crawling over to me and grabs my leg while Simon is laughing so hard on the floor from the tickling. Lottie pulls herself up to a standing position, gripping my leg. She wobbles a little bit, but she's able to stand up on her own. "Oh wow, Lots, look at you, my little pudding, standing up all on your own, you big girl."

I reach down to lift her into my arms and give her a big cuddle. I blow a raspberry on her cheek, and she starts to giggle. She tries to do it to my cheek, and I end up with slaver all over me. She's just the cutest thing ever. I squeeze her to me, and she starts squirming and grabs hold of my hair.

"Ouch, don't pull my hair, Lots. Give Aunty Kate a big kiss and a cuddle. I've missed you, my little pudding." Lottie giggles again in my arms. "Down, Down," she squeals. I put her down where she crawls to Simon, who is looking in the bag I put near the kitchen door.

"Hey, Mr Nosey, out of the bag." He looks at me with the biggest grin on his face.

"But, Tanty Kate, there is a truck in the bag and a teddy bear. Are they for us?" He looks at me with those big brown eyes he has and long eyelashes fluttering at me, looking like a little cherub. How can I resist that look? Lottie is also trying to see what's in the bag. I move to them and take the bag off the floor. I pull out a big box that has a fire truck in it, and a big teddy bear that has different materials on it to touch, and his arms and legs make sounds when you move them.

"You spoil them, Kate, but, thank you," Cindy says to me from behind.

"I'm allowed to spoil my niece and nephew. I don't see them anywhere near as much as I would like," I say to her. "Besides, don't thank me yet. That fire truck makes a lot of noise," I tell her laughing.

Brad brings me a cup of tea, and I hand Cindy a couple of envelopes.

"Kate will you stop with the envelopes every time you come. The only reason I take them is to put the money away in the savings accounts I've set up for them."

"I know Cindy, but it's up to me. It's my money." I shrug and smile at her.

"If you have accounts set up for them give me the account numbers, then I can just put some money in as and when, and you don't need to take the envelopes from me anymore." It's what I will do for any children I may have—if I ever have any. But for the time being, I can do this for my niece and nephew.

Brad doesn't like me doing this. He thinks it's his job to provide everything for his family. He hates that I'm successful and have money. I wish he would just be proud of me. He's all I have left.

After dinner, its playtime before bath and then bed. I help bath them and then help put them to bed. I love doing this. It makes me feel like I belong somewhere and have a purpose. I'm a successful businesswoman with one of the biggest and soon-to-be biggest property investment companies in London, yet, I don't feel I have a purpose or that I belong anywhere in particular.

I check my phone once the kids are in bed. Lewis has messaged me back.

Lewis – Kate, please Facetime me when you get home so we can discuss the FL situation. Hope you're having a good day with your family. Speak to you later. X

Kate – Just got your message. Having a cup of tea now the kids are in bed. Will Facetime you as soon as I get home a little later if you are around. Xx

Lewis – Oh, don't worry. I will definitely be around waiting for your call. X

Now I can't wait to get home. I have my cup of tea, make small talk before I leave around seven p.m. I will get home, have a shower, and then Facetime Lewis.

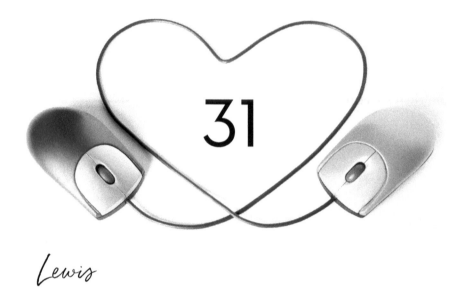

31

Lewis

I'M PACING THE LIVING AREA IN the suite, anxious for Kate to phone.

I have my phone in my hand so I don't miss her call.

I take it to the bathroom when I need the toilet so I don't miss her call.

I take it into the kitchen area of the suite so I don't miss her call.

I look again at the phone just in case I did miss her call, somehow. I notice it's 7.20 p.m. I thought she said she wouldn't be long. I'm so impatient, but I can't help it. I just want to speak to her, and I'm so glad she suggested we Facetime or Skype, my heart goes wild when I think of seeing her beautiful face again. I've got it bad for her.

Does it really happen—love at first sight, or is that just a myth? It's never happened to me, but I have strong feelings for her. I know it's quick, but I think it's possible. I wish she were here in London, so I could be with her.

I'm still pacing. I just can't settle. I thought about going for a run but it's dark outside, plus I didn't want to miss her call. I hope she's alright. It's 8.15 p.m. now. Surely, she should be home? I think about texting her, but I'm worried she'll think I'm too eager. My phone pings, and I see her name appear. Thank God for that. My heart is pounding.

Kate — Sorry, was longer than expected at Brad's. Home now, but just jumping in the shower. Will ring you in about thirty minutes. Xx

Ok, at least she's home. I think I'll do the same. I have a shower and get into my sweats. I haven't put a top on yet, and I'm towel-drying my hair, walking out of the bathroom, when my phone goes. It's Kate, Facetiming me. I grab the phone and answer, still drying my hair

"Hey, beautiful, how are you?" Fuck, seeing her face my heart is beating so fast, she is gorgeous.

"Hey, yourself, handsome. I'm good, thank you. Oh, sorry, do you want me to call you back? It looks like you just got out of the shower."

"I have, but its fine, let me just comb my hair back, otherwise it dries all messy and curly if I don't." I reach for my comb and hold the phone in one hand so I can see her beautiful face while I comb my hair with the other hand. I then go to my bed and sit on it with my back to the headboard. "Did you get your shower?"

"Yes, I did. Are you sure you don't want to finish getting dressed I can call you back?" She's blushing, and it's then I look down and realise I don't have a top on. She must think I'm naked.

"Is it bothering you that I don't have a top on Kate? If it is, I can throw a t-shirt on. I don't want you uncomfortable. I do have my sweats on, see?" I point the camera down so she can see me, but I do it slowly down my chest to my bottom half. Shit, it's a good job my cock is behaving after seeing her, it looks like she is only wearing a cropped camisole. I can see the straps and the top of it, which shows the swell of her chest. There goes my cock. It doesn't take much. I move the camera up quickly so she doesn't see him standing to attention.

"Lewis, I'm far from uncomfortable that you don't have a top on and you didn't need to show me the bottom half. I can't see it while talking anyway, so it would be fine if you were naked because I wouldn't know…" She's blushing and has a big grin on her face. I love it. Is love too strong a word? Now she's chewing her bottom lip, and my cock is rock hard. This conversation is going in the wrong direction very quickly.

"You're a fine one to talk, beautiful. It doesn't look like you're wearing much either. It's a good job you're covered up and not topless, or we may have a problem."

"Ha, how do you know I'm covered up? I could be naked down below." She's teasing me now, and I love it. There I go again with the L word. Two can play at this game.

"I bet you really are naked down below, that's why you aren't showing me." She moves the camera down her body like I just did, slowly, torturing me. Holly shit, she has the tightest tank top on, which is showing me how turned on she is, her nipples are like bullets, standing on end. As she goes lower, I see her pierced belly button. Now, that is a surprise. Lower still, and she has the tiniest boy shorts on, showing her amazing legs. Shit, I think I am about to explode in my pants. Breath, Lewis, breath. Down boy.

"You ok, Lewis?"

"Yeah fine, Kate, just need a second, beautiful." I can't speak properly, and my voice sounds higher than normal.

"Oh, okay. Do you want me to call you back?"

"No, No, I'm fine, honestly." No not fine, going to explode any minute now, trying to look normal is killing me. I feel like I'm blushing as well. My face feels hot, and I keep scrunching my eyes shut. Shit.

"You look as though you're in agony there, Lewis, why are you screwing your eyes shut tight like that? Are you in pain?" Shit. I forgot she could see me. And she just said screwing. I'm done for. I fumble a bit and hit end quickly, just as I explode in my pants. I have never ever done that in my life. I'm stunned and mortified. I have my hand down my pants, stroking it out. My heart is racing. I'm panting. I jump off the bed and take the sweats off. I pick the towel up off the bed, the one I used to dry my hair, and I use it to clean myself up. I'm just about finished when the phone rings again. I answer it as I climb back onto the bed and sit where I was before, naked.

"Lewis, are you okay? What happened, did we lose the connection?"

"Yeah, my signal dropped. I was just about to try and phone you back when you phoned me."

"I thought you hung up on me because you looked as though you were in a lot of pain. I hope you're feeling okay. I can call you tomorrow after my meeting, or we can wait until we see each other tomorrow night."

"No, honestly, I'm not in pain, Kate, I was just, oh shit, it's embarrassing, but I was just having a moment. Do you know how hot you are, Kate? Showing me your almost naked body... I'm a red-blooded male, I reacted. Now I feel like a right pervert. I'm sorry."

"Oh my God. I am so sorry, Lewis. I didn't mean to do that to you, and would never dream you'd have a reaction like that to me. I feel terrible. But if it's any consolation, I was the same when you were showing me your almost naked body. Holy shit, I was drooling. Now I'm mortified I even told you that. I need a filter on my mouth sometimes. Shall we start again, and forget all that happened?" She's laughing now, but I can see how embarrassed she is, as am I.

"Don't worry. Let's start again then. Hi, Beautiful, how are you?"

"I'm good, thank you. How was your day?"

"Pretty boring today really. I actually had a rest day. How was the visit to your brother's?"

"It was the best. Lottie, who is nearly one, actually spoke. I was so excited she called me Tanty Kate. That's what Simon calls me. He's nearly 5. I just love them to bits. I love playing with them, cuddling them, and just spending time with them. Oh, Lewis, I wish I could spend more time with them, but with being in London all week, it's hard. I usually end up spoiling them. I miss them though." She lights up when she's talking about her niece and nephew. You can see the love she has for them. She's adorable when talking about them.

"How were your brother and his wife, Brad and Cindy, isn't it?"

"Yes, Brad was fine, we don't usually have a lot to talk about. We have never been close, but he's my only family now. I feel lost when I'm with him, I've always felt like that. He isn't happy about my success. He hates that I give Cindy money for the kids. She's set up a savings account for them both now, so I'm just going to set up a direct debit so that money goes in there each month. That way it will build up for them and hopefully help them when they are older, they can buy property or use it for college or university. I just want them to be set and not have to worry about money too much like I had to. Brad won't know I'm doing it. Sorry, I get on my soapbox, all I want to do is help Lottie and Simon."

"It's fine, Kate, I love how passionate you are when you speak about them. I can tell you love them. It's nice to see that passion and fire in you."

"Thank you, Lewis. Shall we talk about FL or shall we leave that until tomorrow? To be honest, I don't want to discuss him tonight' I'm just enjoying talking to you."

"Me too, Kate. We can discuss him tomorrow when I come over to yours. I'm looking forward to tasting your cooking. I'm a pretty decent cook myself. I will have to return the favour but it will have to be at a weekend when you're in Chelmsford, and I'm back home. Hotel suites don't have everything I need to cook."

"That would be great. I would love that, Lewis, thank you. I'm not the best cook, so don't be expecting Michelin-style food. I'm usually working late, so end up grabbing a wrap from the deli on my way home, or I just throw some pasta on."

We talk about stuff like that for a while, just general chit chat and getting to know each other. It's great that I can watch her at the same time rather than it just be a phone call. I love how relaxed she is talking to me. Again with the 'love' word.

I can't wait to see her tomorrow though. I'm still embarrassed at what happened earlier, but I will get over it if she doesn't bring it up.

"Right, it's time for me to call it a night, Lewis. I have an early start tomorrow. I'm excited about these buildings I want to buy, and I have my team meeting me there in the morning. If all goes to plan this will be my biggest project to date."

"That sounds great, Kate. I hope it all comes off for you."

"I can tell you tomorrow how it goes. Goodnight, Lewis and thanks for the chat. I've really enjoyed it."

"You are more than welcome, Kate. I look forward to seeing you tomorrow, beautiful. Goodnight, and I hope you get a good night's sleep. See you tomorrow."

"Night, Lewis."

32

Katherine

Holy smoke. I think I'm in love with Lewis Clancy. Did I just say that? He makes me feel alive, and that's only on Facetime. He's amazing. He's a caring, sweet, humble—a genuine guy. He was actually interested in what I was talking about. He asked questions. In fact, he only seemed to want to talk about me and my day.

I feel awful I didn't ask how his shoot went yesterday. I must remember to ask him tomorrow. He's really coming to mine tomorrow night. I can't believe he's even interested in me. That got a little weird for a moment though. I can't believe he had a reaction to me like that. WOW.

I need to try sleep now, although, I think it will take a while after spending an hour and a half on Facetime to Lewis. I'm so hyped up. I think I need a nightcap. A Baileys will go down great right now and it always helps me sleep. I get my drink and go to bed with it. I make sure to set my alarms. I don't want to be late for my meeting with the team.

I wake up with a start, and I'm wet, I mean soaking wet. I can't believe I'm just coming down from an orgasm in my sleep. Well, it was Lewis and his tongue that gave it to me in my dream, and it was the best orgasm of my life. He was such an expert with that tongue of his... Oh my, I'm getting turned on again—but that chest of his after seeing him topless on facetime, I was running my hands and tongue all over his abs, tracing his tattoo's in my dream. It's 6.15 a.m., time to I get up. I have a cold body shower to calm myself down, grab some coffee and toast, get my briefcase and make sure I have everything I need to head back to London for the week.

I arrive at the site of the old buildings at 8.45 a.m. I'm slightly earlier than the rest of them—we set the meeting for 9 a.m. I open the gate and decide to have a little wander around. I love this place already. I can visualise the finished effect. It will look amazing with all the landscaping out front to give it kerb appeal. My heart races with excitement.

My team start to arrive just as I'm wandering about. Alf, my project manager is first. "Good morning, Katherine and how are you, pet?" Alf has been the project manager on my last four buildings, and I trust him and his judgement. We make small talk and chat about my ideas while we wait for the others.

Dave, my structural engineer and Tom, my architect pull up at the same time. I head to greet them at the entrance and weigh up their reactions as they approach the buildings. I can see Dave looking very intrigued already, which is a good sign. Tom is looking thoughtful as he stands by his car looking on at the buildings. I'm eager to hear their opinions so dive straight in, "So, come on, first impressions, what do you think?"

"Well, Kate, I can see enormous potential, especially if you're looking at both of these buildings," Tom says putting a huge smile on my face.

"From the outside, they don't look too bad. The roofs look intact, which should mean there isn't much damage on the inside. Let's get in so I can have a better look," Dave says to us.

I confirm that I want to buy both buildings and my vision for the conversion, and we head over to the first building on the left as soon as the agent arrives. Dave heads off with his tools and gadgets, and I leave him to it, I would only get in his way. Tom is walking around with his sketch pad in hand and his camera taking lots of pictures and sketching as he is going along. Alf is also mooching around. He's gone to assess upstairs.

I'm just standing here in awe with the agent. "Have you had much interest in either of these buildings?" I ask him knowing he's going to say yes. It's a seller's pitch.

"I've shown them to three other prospective buyers since yourself, and two of them are going to come back for second viewings this week. One, like you, was interested in both buildings. As far as I know, they are only viewing them again and not bringing a team as you have. That puts you one step ahead at the moment. I can see in your face that you want these buildings."

"Yes, I do. But, it depends on the price I can get them for and also on their reports and findings," I say nodding in the direction Dave and Tom disappeared. I've got my poker-face on. I can't let him see how excited I am about these buildings.

Alf heads back to me. "Well, pet, from what I've seen, I think this building looks great. I think it would be a great project." I'm too giddy. I can't speak. I just grin, nodding my head.

Tom heads back to where Alf and I are standing, looking positive.

"We could make this building into something really special, Kate, if you have the funds to make it all high-end and up-market. It could become a highly prestigious, sought-after place to live. From what I see of the structure all around it looks in such good condition for its age. I think you're onto a winner here, sweetie."

"Oh Tom, you have no idea what hearing that means to me. I'm ready to sign on the dotted line. I just have this feeling in my gut about this site and these two magnificent buildings."

Dave comes back to us, but he doesn't say much. He never does until he's done his reports.

"Shall we head over to building two so you can all look around that one?"

The three of them once again go off and do their inspections. I stand near the door just waiting. I get my phone out to make sure I haven't missed any calls, and my heart flutters and the butterflies return when I see a text from Lewis.

Lewis – Good morning, beautiful. I just wanted to say I had a great evening talking to you last night, and I can't wait until tonight. I hope you have a good day. X

Kate – Good morning to you too, handsome. I had a great evening as well, thank you, and a good night's sleep. Looking forward to seeing you later. I hope you have a good day too. Xx

I'm just putting my phone away when Alf approaches me. "I have to say pet although this one is a bit more knackered than the first one, I still think it's got great potential."

"I agree," Tom says as he approaches.

"It does need more work, but we can make them both equally spectacular providing Dave thinks they are structurally sound." Both Alf and Tom give me the nod, and Dave confirms that he'll have his reports to me later today. I thank the agent and tell him that I'll be in touch as soon as I have all the information I need. Everyone leaves, but I stay for a few minutes trying to take it in, looking at the buildings and the surrounding area. These are going to be mine. I just know it.

I head back to my office, I have a lot of work to do, and with Clive being away it will be hard to keep up with it all. Thankfully, its only for a few days.

George

WHY DO MY MORNINGS ALWAYS start off so shit? Every day, I wake up, and I'm instantly in a bad fucking mood. I know it's down to her. She's driving me crazy. The sooner I get rid of her, the sooner I can continue with some kind of normal life. She's making my life hell just like my mother did all those years, abusing me and never protecting me.

She's read the message, but she hasn't replied I kept checking all night and nothing. Is she playing games with me and just screwing with my head? Why the fuck is she doing that to me? I bet she's out screwing other guys she thinks are better than me. No one is better than me, you dumb whore.

I went back to her building again—twice. Once at about 10 p.m. and then at about 1.30 a.m. I snuck down and her car still wasn't there either time. She's just making me mad. She's making me lose my mind. I just want rid of her after I've played, just like she's been playing me.

She has to be going to work today—it's Monday. I'll go and see if her car is back at the apartment, and I'll go to her office. I don't know whether to watch from outside or chance going into the building. I'll put my suit on just in case. I phoned in sick at work, I'm not going to get paid as I'm stalking her instead of working. Just another reason to be fucking furious with that whore.

I go to the café, again, and I get a coffee. The girl behind the counter recognises me, but she doesn't flirt with me like all the other whores, in fact she seems quite timid. I kind of like that and she is very pretty. Maybe this one is different. She has red hair and freckles, but she has such an innocent look about her.

"Oh hi, do you want your usual, black Americano?" she says blushing and barely looking at me. I may actually be able to use her. I was thinking of phoning the bitches office to see if she was in today, but I don't have internet on my phone. It's an old phone. Maybe this girl has internet, and she'll let me use hers to get the number.

"Yes, please. I'm new to the area, and I'm looking at buying a property around here."

"Oh, that sounds wonderful, you might become a regular then?"

"I hope so," I say winking at her and she blushes bright red.

"Can I ask you a favour?"

"Yes, sure," she says.

"My phone is being repaired at the moment, and I only have this old thing, and I don't have internet on it. Do you have a phone I could borrow? I just need to look up a phone number I forgot to bring it with me. I need to ring to make sure my viewing is still on."

Red, or Tania as her name badge says, reaches under the counter and pulls out her phone. She unlocks it then hands it to me.

"Thank you. I will only be a minute." In the search bar I put in Porter Properties. It brings it up straight away with links to the website and contact details. It says it's open now. I grab a napkin and ask if she has a pen I can use. Luckily, there isn't anyone at the counter, and I write the number down. I clear the field, so nothing is showing, and she can't see what I looked at.

"Thank you so much for that, Red. I really appreciate it," I say smiling at her and handing back the phone. As she grabs the phone, she touches my hand and a strange tingling sensation shoots through my body. I look at her, and she gasps. What the fuck is that all about? I must be going soft in my old age. I grab my coffee and move to where the sugar, milk, and stirrers are. I can feel Red watching me, so I turn and give her a wink, keeping her sweet. Women just can't resist me. She blushes all over again and looks away quickly, grabbing the cloth to wipe down the counter.

I move to one of the tables near the window that gives me a clear view of the building opposite, so I can see if *SHE* arrives. I get my phone out, and I dial the number I wrote down. It rings a few times, then goes to voice message, telling me to leave a message and someone will get back to me. I hang up and try again. I get the same. She isn't there, and her secretary isn't there? I slam my phone down on the table, a bit harder than I realised. Luckily it didn't smash, but I look around and see Red and a couple of other people are looking at me. I don't acknowledge them. I just turn to look out of the window again. It's 11.55 a.m. Where the fuck is she? She's been missing since Saturday. I put the napkin with the number in my pocket and take a sip of my coffee.

Just then, I see her rushing towards the door to her building. Thank fuck for that. I was beginning to worry. She's no good to me dead.

34

Katherine

I RUSH UP TO MY OFFICE, PANICKING because I just checked my planner and I have a conference call scheduled for 12.30 p.m., and it's not far off that now. I'm not even prepared for it because I was so wrapped up in the warehouse buildings and Lewis.

The office is locked up when I arrive. That's odd, where's Chrissie? She should be in, managing the phones and reception. It takes me another ten minutes to get sorted out, putting the lights on, turning the computer on, and seeing what messages there are, all things Chrissie would have done.

The first message is from Chrissie, apologising profusely that she can't make it into work today or this week in fact because she was rushed into hospital with suspected appendicitis. I phone her back immediately just to reassure her that everything is fine and not to worry. The last thing I want is her stressing out about work when she's in so much pain.

Luckily, there are only three other messages and two calls with no messages. I quickly put the kettle on and make myself a coffee, then go to my office to get ready for the conference call.

The conference call is great, but they are such an odd couple, both living in different cities, they said they hardly see each other. I start thinking about Lewis. What if we do pursue these feelings and things go further? Could I cope with being separated a lot because of his work?. Is that what I want? No, I want to be part of a couple. I want to be together and do things together. I think if it does go somewhere, it's a conversation we will need to have.

The rest of the afternoon goes by quickly mainly because Clive and Chrissie are not here and the showing I had has now been re scheduled. My computer pings to say I have an e-mail, and I glance up to see it's the structural report from Dave. My heart starts beating fast as I open the attachment.

Structural Advisement Notice for Building 1 & 2,

101 Narrow Street, London Docklands.

After examining the structure of the building, I deem this to be of sound construction and a valid investment with the exception of:-

- Windows need to be re-glazed with double glazing, and the cast iron frames need re-ironising and the style retained as this is a listed building. I will forward you the diagram of the windows in my detailed report.
- New roofs must use the same material as already on the roof which is Fesco Caledonian Heavy Slate sourced from Scotland. This is still available in today's market.
- Some of the brickwork inside and outside needs replacing due to crumbling, again with the same bricks already on the building to keep it all uniform. The lower half of the building was constructed using a plumb brick, but the upper floors used a higher quality yellow stock brick. I have checked, and you can still source both bricks in the UK.

As long as these stipulations are adhered to I see no reason why you should not make an investment into both of the buidlings, in my opinion, I consider them to be a sound investment.

The foundations are excellent. They are extremely deep to ensure stability in a marshlands area with iron rods and columns under for extra support.

All the columns and posts in the buildings are sound and do not need any construction on them. I would not advise trying to move or remove any of them. They form part of the structure and are load bearing.

As you will be stripping the insides right back, I would recommend trying to recycle the wooden floorboards and any iron works as much as possible.

Building two needs more of this work done to it than building one due to the location nearer the water's edge. They are still good investments in my opinion.

I will send you a detailed report by the end of the week.

I will also forward detailed costs for all the above. A ballpark figure would be £850 thousand to £1 Million for this work outside of your renovation costs.

If you have any questions, please let me know.

Regards

Dave

David Goodall

I'm relieved, ecstatic, excited, nervous and I can't wait. I need to get the ball rolling now. I bring up my offer letter, and after some adjustments, I email it to the estate agency. Then, I email my business manager Stacey, at the bank with my proposal for a bridging loan, and to see if I can get an appointment with the bank tomorrow afternoon. I know I won't hear until maybe tomorrow, but I will push it to get an answer in the morning.

I look at the clock, and it's 4.30 p.m. I check my schedule. I have two phone appointments tonight. One at 5.30 p.m. and the other at 6.30 p.m. That's going to be a push for Lewis coming over. I need to go to the deli on the way home to get some fresh pasta and some more wine. I decide to text Lewis to let him know I may be a bit late depending on how long the call lasts.

Kate – Hey, handsome, I have a phone appointment at 6.30 p.m., and I'm not sure how long it will last so it may make me a little late? Xx

I put my phone on silent so I can prepare for both my calls. I need to get some files from Clive's desk, so make a detour to the kitchen to make a coffee. I see movement outside the main office doors, in the corridor, near the lifts. There's a tall figure with his back to me, waiting at the lifts. What is he doing here? This floor is mine; there are no other businesses here. I didn't hear him come in. Maybe he got off on the wrong floor? I watch him while he stands, waiting for the lift. I'm near the hallway to the bathroom and the kitchen, and it's dark here, luckily, because just then he turns slightly and looks through the glass door. I can only see his side profile, but he looks familiar, I swear I've seen him before? He can't see me, but I have definitely seen him before. I just can't think where.

The lift arrives, and he steps into it. He doesn't turn to face the doors once he's in like most people would. Instead, he just stands there with his back to the doors. How strange. He's made me nervous, and as soon as the lift doors close, I head to the front office door and lock it. No one is going to be coming into the office without me knowing.

I head to the kitchen to make the coffee, pick the files up of Clive's desk, and go back to my office. My first call doesn't last long, but the 6.30 p.m. call lasts nearly an hour. By the time I'm finished, I'm panicking, thinking about Lewis. I check my phone. Shit. Four messages and two missed calls from him.

Lewis – 6.06 p.m. Hey, beautiful, it's okay, I will come over a bit later. Let me know when you're leaving the office. X

Lewis – 6.20 p.m. Hey, beautiful, you haven't read my message. I know you are probably engrossed with work. Let me know you're okay. X

Lewis – 6.45 p.m. Hey, Kate, worrying a bit here. I will come over to the office at 7 p.m. If you finish your appointment, can you wait for me, please? X

Lewis – 7.26 p.m. Kate. I'm outside your office doors, and it looks dark, are you in there? I tried calling you, but no answer and I knocked on the doors? I will wait for a few minutes. X

The last call was just two minutes ago. I jump up from my desk and rush to the front doors, but I can't see him. I have my phone in my hand, so I call him back.

"Hey, beautiful, where are you? I was at your office, and it was all dark and the doors locked, did you get my messages?"

"Lewis, I'm so sorry. I have only just taken my phone out of my drawer where I put it when I'm on calls. It was on silent. I have only just finished my six thirty appointment. I'm still in the office. Where are you now?"

"I'm just in the lobby of your office building, about to head to your place. I'll come back up now. I'm at the lifts, just getting in, see you in a minute."

I unlock the front door and then go into my office to shut everything off and get my bag and laptop. Just as I'm stepping out of my office, I jump and squeal. Lewis is stood there in front of Clive's desk. "Jeez Lewis, you scared the life out of me."

"Sorry, beautiful," he says smiling at me. How can I be scared of his gorgeous face?

I smile back at him. "Let's get out of here. I need to go to the deli to get some fresh pasta and some wine for us. I've had one hell of a long day, and I could do with a nice drink and even better company," I say, grinning back at him.

We head out of the office, and I lock up, giddy he's here and we will walk home together like a real couple. I'm ready for the evening to start so I can relax and unwind with him.

35

George

ISIT IN THE CAFÉ FOR ABOUT TWO HOURS pretending to read the newspaper while watching the building. Red brings me two more coffee's. "On the house," she says.

Just after one p.m., I decide to leave to throw Red off a bit, making it look like I have an appointment to go to. I pretend to get a message on my phone, get up and head for the door. Red comes over just as I reach it.

"See you soon, I hope."

"Yes, you will, Red. I'll be back here in a bit. I'm just going to view an apartment not too far away, then I have another appointment later. It's a good job I have the week off work to get myself sorted out," I say just before I leave the café, giving her a smile and a wink.

I head down the road a short way, but still in viewing distance of the bitch's office. I just hang around with my phone out. I keep pretending that I'm texting and then I hold it up to my ear as though

I'm on the phone and nod. All the while, watching her building but out of sight. Another hour goes by, and there's still no sign of her.

I head back to the café for yet another coffee—it's freezing out today. Red is still there when I arrive. "How did it go?" she asks me as I approach the counter.

"Ok, I wasn't that impressed, to be honest. Too small. I have another viewing in about an hour. I need to wait for the agent to text me the details first," I lie to her. I order my coffee. There are a few people in line behind me, so she asks my name to put on the sticker for the coffee mug. I think it's just an excuse to find out my name.

"John," I say picking the first name that pops into my head. She blushes, looks down, and writes John on the sticker.

"Thank you, John, you go and sit down, I'll bring it over to you."

"Thank you, Red."

I go to a table not quite in the window this time, as they are all occupied, but I face the window. I can still see the building across the road. I grab a different newspaper and sit, pretending to read it.

It's not far off 3 p.m. now, and I haven't seen her since she went into the building this morning. I hope I haven't missed her and she somehow left without me knowing. What if there is another entrance out the back?

I know Red keeps watching me when she isn't busy at the counter because she keeps flitting around me pretending to clean the tables. "You need another coffee, John?"

"No, I'm good, thank you, Red, but I wouldn't mind a glass of water. I think I've had too much caffeine for one day, already." I take my phone out of my pocket and pretend I have a text.

"Oh good, the agent sent me the details of the apartment to view. I'm meeting him there at three thirty." I look at the time on the phone. "I best make a move. Thank you, Red. Hopefully, I will see you soon."

Again I wink at her, and she blushes. "Ok, John. Yes, I hope so too. I finish my shift at four. If you're coming back this way after your viewing maybe I could wait for you and we could grab a drink?" She says this so quietly and timidly, I almost can't hear her. Shit, if I wasn't waiting on the bitch over the road, I would probably take her up on it, she is very pretty. See, that fucking bitch has even screwed this up for me now. "Ah, Red, I would have loved that, but after this viewing, I have a meeting to get to with another agent. Maybe we can arrange for some other time? I'm sure I will be popping in here again this week."

"Yeah, okay, that would be great, John. I'm in all week, so I should see you. Good look with your apartment hunting."

I leave the café and walk back in the opposite direction from the way I went earlier. All the while looking back to make sure I don't miss her coming out.

I'm getting really fed up now. She hasn't left for lunch or a meeting or anything. I pull out my phone and hit the last number I rang, which was her office. I press the call button to see if she answers. I can always just hang up, or I can ask to make an appointment. It rings and rings and no one answers. Fuck, I must have missed her, or she left through a different exit. Fuck, Fuck, Fuck. I need to go to the office and see if she's left. Risky because if she's there, she might see me and even recognise me from last week at the deli.

It's 4.16 p.m. People are coming and going all the time. I won't look out of place, but they might do I.D. checks at the reception in the lobby? I start to walk back towards her office when I spot Red walking towards me. Shit, she's the last person I want to see right now, but too late, she's seen me.

"Hey, Red, you just finished your shift?"

"Hi, John, yes. Thankfully. Now I'm heading home to Chip for a nice cuddle and a relaxing evening. I do an open university online study course, so I'll get some of that done as well. How did your viewing go?"

"Chip? Is that your boyfriend?"

"Oh no, silly, that's my little cat. He's old now, so he loves when I get home for cuddles."

"Ahh right, your cat. The viewing was okay. Still a bit small. I'm just heading to see another agent now. Must get going, see you soon, Red." I wink as she seems to really like that, and I start to walk past her. She's definitely different somehow, and it's starting to distract me. I'm turning into a fucking pussy.

"Yeah, see you soon, John. Good luck."

I head towards the building. There is a security guard at a desk in the lobby, but he's busy with some old lady who seems to be a bit lost, so I head straight for the lifts, acting as if I know where I'm going. I don't look in the direction of the guard. I don't want to draw attention to myself. Luckily there is a plaque on the wall telling you the companies in the building and what floors they are on. Porter Properties is on the 7th floor. I get in the lift when it arrives, and two other people get on with me. They greet me, and I just nod at them and look at my phone. God bless the mobile phone.

They get off on the 5th floor, so I'm on my own now, heading to her floor. The doors open and it's very quiet. Straight ahead is a glass door that says Porter Properties. It's dark inside—it looks like there isn't anyone around. I try the door, and it opens. I creep in quietly and listen to see if I can hear anyone. Where are her employees? She must have people that work for her. She's one of the biggest property investors in London, so Google says. I don't understand why no one is here.

I'm standing in what looks like the reception area. There is a desk and seats, plus a table with magazines. There is a coffee machine on a side unit and a water cooler next to that. I stay still, listening. There's a hallway to the right of the reception area, and it's dark, but I can see a light coming from under one of the doors. I move closer to the reception desk, and there's a note on the top that catches my eye. It's to Kate. I scan the note, and it says it's from Clive, and he's not back in the office until Thursday. I wonder if that is her secretary or receptionist? I move closer to the hallway, nearer to the door with the light, not making a sound. I can hear someone typing on a keyboard. She must be in there. It might not even be her. Could I risk barging in? If it's someone else, I can say I knocked, and no one answered. If it's her, then I could do this and finish her. How easy is this? I could go in there now, take her hard, and finish her to get it over with once and for all. But I need to plan. If I don't plan it could all go wrong. How would I get her out of here with the security? There will be security cameras around, no doubt, so I will have probably already been seen on camera. Fuck. Why didn't I think of that first? This is why I need to plan. It would be so easy to get her now, but I might get caught.

Just then I hear movement. Shit, is she coming out? I quickly and quietly move back to the reception area and out of the door. I call the lift, praying it opens so I can get in before she sees me. Shit, it's not here. Fuck. I can feel her. I feel her eyes on me, piercing the back of my head. She knows I'm here. I slightly turn my head, not facing her. Out of the corner of my eye, I can just make her outline out in the darkness because of the light coming from her office behind her. The lift arrives, and I get in quickly, but I don't turn around. I keep my back to the lift doors until they close. Then I turn and press the ground button. That was too fucking close. It's weird there was no one around. It's not even 5 p.m., and the place is empty on a Monday.

I make my way outside, passing the guard, not looking with my head in my phone, I feel him looking at me, but I pretend to be texting, so I don't have to look up.

"Goodnight, sir," he says as I pass.

"Night," I say, not looking up. Him seeing me might work in my favour. If I decide to visit again this week he may recognise me, and not question me.

I head down the road in the direction of her apartment. Fuck, that was close. What if she checks the security cameras and sees me skulking around? I stay out of sight, hidden behind some fake topiary bushes and leaning on a low wall, but I can see the entrance to her office building. I have my phone in my hand, and when anyone passes me, I hold it to my ear, pretending I'm on it. This fucking phone is a life saver.

I can see people entering and leaving her office building. I wait and wait. I keep checking the time on my phone. How much longer is she going to be? This woman just works and works. It's nearly 7.00 p.m. Shit, I'm getting angry. All I've done all day is wait for the bitch. Should I leave and come back tomorrow? I wait for a little bit longer, then decide to call it a day. I head back in the direction of the office to pass it as it's on my way home, but on the other side of the road just in case she comes out. I don't want her to see me.

Just as I pass the building, I turn back around, and I see her coming out. I hear her first, laughing. What the fuck is she laughing at? Wait, who is that she's with? The fucking whore is with someone else. They're walking really close together. I'm mad—the rage is building and building in me. I decide to follow. He might be someone she knows in the building, but he's in jeans and a shirt and wearing a fucking baseball cap. Very casual.

I follow from a distance on the other side of the road. They stop at the deli as she often does. I can't see him properly, but he's tall and has longish dark hair, not all hidden by the cap. From here, I can see she is being served at the counter, but he's talking to two young girls who are laughing and giggling. Why the fuck would he be flirting when he's with the bitch? He mustn't be with her. They must just be acquaintances, but then why the fuck is he in the deli with her? Why didn't he carry on to wherever he's going if he isn't with her?

I'm standing across the road, and my hands are balled up into fists. I want to punch the cocksucker for being near her. She's been served and is now waiting for him near the door. She suddenly turns and looks around outside as if looking for someone. She can sense me, I'm sure of it. We have this connection, just like I sensed her watching me near the lifts at her offices. She can't see me from here. I'm standing back in a passageway between buildings where the bins are kept.

He finishes with the girls and goes to the bitch. He takes the shopping bag from her and then he's putting his hand on her lower back, steering her out of the door. What the ever-living fuck is that all about? She isn't seeing anyone, she told me. She's going on a date with me. Why would she be with someone else when she's going on a date with me? She's just screwing with my head, the filthy whore. Just like my mother did to me. She's taunting me on purpose, I know it. They walk up the road a bit more, then they go into a store. I can't see them in this one, but they are out quick enough with yet another bag, and he puts his hand on her lower back again. I am blazing, he's fucking touching her.

I follow them, but I know where they're heading. To her apartment. No doubt to fuck.

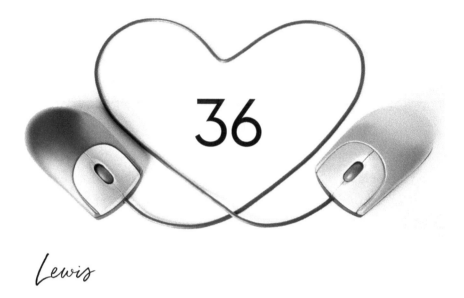

36

Lewis

I START TO PANIC WHEN SHE DOESN'T reply to my text messages. She hasn't even read the messages. I try calling, and it goes to voice message. Shit is she having second thoughts about this. Panic is setting in. I have never felt anxiety like I'm feeling right now.

I quickly shower and get ready to jump into a cab to Kate's office. I check my phone again but still nothing.

It's 7.15 p.m. now, and I was supposed to be at hers for 7. I hope she's not having second thoughts. I'm working myself up into a state here.

I get to her office, and the security guard greets me. He recognises me from being with Kate on Friday and gives me access to her floor. Her offices are all in darkness. Her phone is still going to voicemail. I try the door, but it's locked. Presuming that she's left, I get back in the lift and head to the lobby, but just as I'm leaving, she rings. Thank God.

Crisis averted and my panic attack over, we are now heading to her apartment after stopping at the deli for the fresh pasta and the off license for wine. We enter her apartment, and I'm a little nervous to be honest. I'm so attracted to Kate, and I really want to get to know her. She's all I can think about. All I want to do is take her in my arms and kiss her, and my cock immediately reacts at the thought.

"You okay, Lewis?"

I didn't realise she had turned and was looking at me because I had my eyes screwed shut.

"Are you in pain… or," she looks down at the bulge in my jeans, "are you having another moment?" She smiles a huge, victorious smile and blushes.

I smirk at her and edge closer. I'm standing right in front of her, and without warning, I take her head in both of my hands, and I lean forward slightly, brushing my lips over hers, softly. Jesus, her lips are so soft. She smells amazing. If it's possible, my cock just got bigger. I pull back slightly, and her eyes are now closed. I'm smiling at her as she opens them and looks up at me through her eyelashes, she's blushing, but she looks gorgeous.

"Kate, I just have this reaction around you. You make me feel like a fourteen-year-old schoolboy all over again. In fact, I was never like this as a fourteen-year-old. I don't know what you do to me, but I just can't control him," I say looking down at my cock. She follows my gaze and smiles. "I've wanted to kiss you since I first laid eyes on you in the hallway at your office." She's embarrassed, I can see it in her face. She turns away from me, grabs the bags she dropped when I kissed her off the floor, and heads to the kitchen. Shit too much, too soon?

I kick off my shoes and follow her to the kitchen. She has her back to me, unpacking the shopping we bought. I step up behind her, my chest almost touching her back, and I put my hands on her hips, kissing her neck near her ear. She shudders, reacting to me.

"Sorry, I didn't mean to startle you," I whisper in her ear. I kiss her neck again, and she leans back into me. She must be able to feel my cock on her arse, she ever so slightly wiggles into me. I'm not sure if it's just a reaction or she's doing it on purpose and giving me the green light. Her breathing becomes heavy as I trail kisses along her exposed neck and nibble on the bottom of her ear.

"Lewis," she breathes out my name. I start to run my hand up her arm very gently. Then I move the hand on her hip around the front and spread it over her tummy, pulling her closer to me.

"Can you feel that, Kate? You do that to me every time I see you. I can't control my cock, no matter what I do. I'm sorry if I'm taking this too fast, but this, and you, is all I seem to be able to think about since we met on Friday. I wanted to take this slowly and get to know you, but to be honest, Kate, I'm having a really hard time. Pun intended," I say as I grind my cock on her arse slowly.

"Oh god, Lewis, I've been the same. I haven't stopped thinking about you either. But I'm having a really hard time, NO pun intended, wrapping my head around the idea that you actually want me. I hate to admit it, but on Saturday, I did a Google search on you, and you're pictured with beautiful models and actresses, so how could you even look at someone like me?"

"Shit, Kate, you have no idea, do you? You rendered me speechless when I saw you on Friday. You make my cock uncontrollable. You are the sexiest, most intelligent person I have ever met. I don't care about models and actresses. I care about you. Most of the stuff on Google was for publicity. I have only ever had one relationship in my life.

I thought she was it for me, and we got engaged. Then she cheated on me, so yes, I've played the field ever since, and I have trust issues.

But you, Kate, you make me want all the things I thought I wanted in my one and only relationship. I now know that what I had then was not real. I feel more for you in a few days than I ever felt for her in the five years we were together. You have knocked me right on my arse."

I'm still standing up against her with my hand splayed on her tummy, holding her to me with my chin on her shoulder. She hasn't spoken. She's going to bolt, I know it. I've gone too far and scared her. She's tensed up, I can feel her. I gently pull her tighter into me. "You okay, beautiful?" I whisper into her ear.

She shudders and turns to me, placing her hand on my chest. "Oh, Lewis, I have trust issues as well. I've had a few boyfriends, nothing serious like you, but…" she trails off. God, she is beautiful.

"But what, Kate," I say taking her hips in my hands and pulling her towards me. She puts her hands on my chest to stop me pulling her in more. She leaves them there then looks up into my eyes. "They used me, Lewis. The ones I thought I had something with. They all used me. None of them felt anything for me, and I find it hard to open up to anyone now. I've had some really humiliating experiences, and I never want to repeat them. It's why I find it hard to believe you want anything to do with me." She hangs her head as though in shame.

I can't stand it. I lift her chin with my finger for her to look at me. "Kate, please don't hide from me, sweetheart. We can take this as slowly as you want to. I would never pressure you. I want to know you and that brilliant mind of yours. God, I love your sexy curves, don't get me wrong, and my cock will hate me for it, but, sweetheart, I can wait as long as you need to, and we can go as slow or as fast as you need to. I'm not going anywhere, anytime soon. As long as you want me around, that is?"

She doesn't say anything, just keeps looking right into my eyes as though searching for something. She looks lost and so vulnerable right now. I pull her to me and hold her. She sighs, leaning her head on my shoulder near the crook of my neck. This feels so right. I feel like we belong.

"Lewis,"

"Mmm,"

"Will you kiss me?"

I don't hesitate, not even for a heartbeat. I bow my head to hers, and I take her mouth ever so gently. I feel like I'm going to combust at any moment. I have never felt anything like this in all my years. These feelings of just gently touching her are indescribable. She opens her mouth for me, and I take the invitation before she changes her mind. I deepen the kiss, and my tongue is in her mouth duelling with hers. Her hands are running up my back, and mine have found their way to her arse. What a perfect fucking arse it is. I'm squeezing it gently with both hands. I don't want to stop the kissing or the squeezing. She pulls away from my mouth to catch her breath.

"I think I should start on dinner or we are never going to eat at this rate." She's blushing, her cheeks are a lovely rosy colour, and I love that I do that to her.

"Okay, beautiful, whatever you want. What do you want me to do? I did say I'm pretty good in the kitchen, didn't I?"

"Cocky much, Mr Clancy? You may have mentioned it in passing." She has the most perfect smile on her face right now. I can't help it, and I lean in to kiss her again. She responds immediately. This time, she instigates the tongue duel, and I love her taking control. I lift her onto the counter, and I gently edge myself between her legs, all the while still kissing her. She pulls me into her more if that's even possible. My hands are on her hips, but I move them around her back to pull her in. She surprises me and wraps her legs around my waist.

My cock is about ready to explode. I'm not sure I can take much more of this.

She can feel how hard my cock is with her legs wrapped around my waist, as my cock is right in line with her pussy, and I think, subconsciously, she is rubbing herself on me, trying to get a bit of friction.

"Kate, sweetheart, I'm seconds away from embarrassing myself yet again. I have two choices here, beautiful. I either run as fast as I can to the bathroom, like an adolescent, to take care of myself, or I take you here and now. It's your choice, but I really don't have long."

She puts her hand up to her mouth to try and hide the laughter, but it's not working.

"Okay," she says.

"Erm, can you elaborate on 'okay', sweetheart?"

"Do you have a condom, Lewis?"

"Fuck, no. Bathroom it is. I don't have a condom." With that, I walk awkwardly to the bathroom. I head to the one I know is in her bedroom, as it's the closest to me. Just as I'm nearing the bathroom door, I hear, "Lewis, come here" I turn and she is behind me next to her bed.

"Come and sit here for me." She pats the bed next to where she's standing, looking shy and embarrassed. I head over to her, and just as I reach her, she pulls me by the waistband of my jeans and starts to unbutton them.

"Kate, sweetheart, what are you doing? You do realise that touching me there is not helping me?"

"Shhh, Lewis, relax." She unbuttons my jeans and slides them down to my knees, taking my briefs with them. My cock springs free, right in her face. She pushes me so I sit on the bed. My cock is glistening at the end. She gets on her knees in front of me and looks up at me through her eyelashes.

"Sweetheart, you don't have to do this, you know. I can take care of it. I don't expect anything from you, and I don't want you to think this is all I want."

"Lewis, I want to do this. I mean, really want to do this. I have never wanted to do this before and…" She looks down at my cock who is standing loud and proud.

"What, Kate?"

"… I want to taste you, Lewis. For the first time ever, I want to do this. Because of you and the way you make me feel. I know I said I don't trust easily, but I'm actually putting some trust into you."

With that, she bends her head, and she licks the tip of my cock. I nearly shoot off the bed, and she looks at me, puzzled.

"Sweetheart, I will not last long. Just that touch sent electric shocks through me. It was like a lightning bolt through my body."

"Just one thing though, Lewis, I erm I don't swa, swallow. I, oh god, this is embarrassing…"

"Hey, look at me, that is perfectly fine. If it's not your thing, I totally understand, I will let you know when I'm ready to explode so you know to move quickly, is that okay?" She nods then lowers her head again.

This time she licks a bit harder then moves down my cock towards my balls. She licks back up then takes me into her mouth, and sucks. Fuck, can she suck and that tongue of hers…. She's a natural. I start to thrust gently. I don't want her to gag on my cock. She takes me a bit deeper each thrust, and when I feel her gag slightly, I pull back a little bit. She clamps her lips down around my cock to stop me from moving back, then grabs the base and starts pumping with her fist while sucking. Her other hand then starts to fondle my balls. Jesus Christ, she's fantastic. I know I'm going to go off like a rocket. Any second now.

"Oh fuck, sweetheart, that is so good, ahh, Kate, arrgghh, sweetheart. I'm going to cum, pull out now. I am going to explode."

"Sweetheart, now, please I'm coming." With that I explode. She takes him out of her mouth just in time, but she keeps pumping him with her fist and squeezing my balls gently. I rest my hands behind me on the bed to lean back slightly so I don't collapse back. I'm watching her, and she's smiling at me. I'm sitting here in front of the most beautiful woman I have ever met, with pure ecstasy written all over my face. I'm in love with Kate Porter. I know it. I knew it the moment I saw her in that hallway at her office. I knew it as we were viewing apartments. I fell in love with her at first sight.

37

Katherine

I'M SITTING ON MY KNEES IN FRONT of the most perfect, handsome man I have ever met. His cock in my hand, and his cum all over us both. He did as he promised and told me when he was about to cum, but, I could feel he was about to explode. His cock got thicker if that was even possible. I can't believe I just did that and voluntarily too, and I barely know the guy, yet. I hope he doesn't think I do this all the time and that I'm a whore or that I'm easy. I don't know what it is about Lewis—he makes me feel special. I can see the sincerity in his eyes. I know I'm not a good judge of character, look at my past track record, but I feel this might be right.

He has ecstasy written all over his face. He's watching me, watching him. There is something else on his face as well. He's looking at me with adoration, as though what I did to him then was the best thing ever. I blush, smile slightly and look down.

"Sweetheart, look at me." I look up to his face looking him straight in the eye.

"That was the best fucking blowjob ever!" I take my hand from around his cock, and I look down again in embarrassment. I start to rub my thumb and fingers together with his cum on them. My hands are quite wet. Without realising, I put my fingers in my mouth one at a time and suck.

"Sweetheart, you carry on doing that, and I will be coming again." I look at him with my middle finger in my mouth. He groans at me, and I can see his cock stirring again.

"Come here," he says as he reaches down for me and pulls me up so I am standing between his legs with his arms wrapped around me. He leans into me and nuzzles my tummy.

I put my hands on his head and start to run my fingers through his messy curly hair. He groans against my tummy. He starts to move his hands around towards my back, but somehow they have gotten under my top. He lifts it and peppers my abdomen with kisses. I still have his head in my hands, playing with his hair. He licks my tummy and belly button. God, that is hot. I wiggle a bit between his legs, and I can feel his cock start to get hard. He's kissing and licking, and his hand moves to the button of my trousers and undoes it. Then he pulls the zipper down. I'm soaking wet. He gently starts to push down my slacks. I'm not embarrassed by this—I'm just so turned on. He pushes them down to my feet and taps the back of my leg gently for me to lift it so he can take the slacks off completely. His head moves lower, and he is now nuzzling my pussy through my panties. He's sniffing me, and then his tongue comes out, and he licks me there.

"Ohh god, Lewis." I grab his hair and pull him harder to me. I think I had a mini orgasm just from that one lick through my panties. I stand, shuddering, gripping his head and hair.

"Mmmm, sweetheart, you smell fucking amazing, and if that little taste was anything to go by, I need these panties off now." With that, he rips them off me.

He looks up at me. "You okay with this, beautiful?" I can't speak, I just nod my head frantically with the biggest grin on my face and my eyes wide.

His hands then start to drift up my body. He's removing my shirt. I lift my arms, so he can take it off easily. I have a front fastening bra on, he unclips it and pulls the straps down each of my arms. The bra joins the other clothes on the floor. I am now naked in front of Lewis. I go to cover my boobs with my hands, but he stops me. "Oh no, you don't. They are fantastic tits. They should never be covered up while I'm around." He leans forward and takes one in his mouth. My hands go back to grabbing his hair but not too hard. He's sucking one, then the other, alternating between them both. His hand moves between my legs to stroke my pussy. I'm going to combust at any moment.

He eases my thighs apart.

"More," he says encouraging me. I spread my legs open more to give him access. He dives straight in, playing along the slit first, and spreading my juices. Then his fingers work into my folds.

"Ahh, Lewis. Oh god. That feels so good." I'm panting hard. He starts to play with my clit, then he inserts one finger, then another. So many sensations. I don't know if I can last. He is still alternating between boobs while vigorously pumping in and out of me with his fingers. I'm going to explode. I can feel it building. He looks up at me with awe on his face. "So fucking perfect, sweetheart. I can't wait to taste you properly. You're so wet; it's dripping down my fingers. I just want to lick them like you did." I explode. My knees buckle, but he keeps me upright with his free hand, pulling me closer to his face. I'm panting hard, trying to catch my breath.

"Wow, Lewis, that was just…" I don't have the words. I'm trying to catch my breath. Once he knows I'm not going to collapse, he takes his fingers out of my pussy and stares up at me, looking me right in the eyes as he brings them to his mouth and sucks all my juices from them one by one. He closes his eyes as he's licking between his fingers.

"You taste like honey, sweetheart. I could get addicted to this. You could be my own personal addiction. I would take your flavour over anything—my own special Kate flavour." I'm still breathing hard.

I look down and see his cock is rock hard again. I reach down to stroke it. He inhales sharply and looks up at me with a grin on his face. He starts to move forward on the bed slightly then slides off the end and sits on the floor right in front of me with his back to the bed. He looks up at me from the floor and takes my hips to bring me closer to him. Somehow, I manage to stay upright. I'm not sure how. This god is sitting in front of me with the biggest smile on his face, and he is staring up at me with such adoration. How did I get here like this with him?

He pulls me so close that his nose is right at my pussy. He nuzzles and sniffs, smelling me. Shit, this is so fucking hot. He rests his head on the edge of the bed. "Sweetheart, come here. I want you to straddle my upper body and sit on my face. I'm going to get addicted right here, right now. I need my fix off you, Kate. I need my tongue inside you. I need your cum dripping down my throat. I need you to scream my name as you cum." I am done for.

He grabs behind both of my thighs and pulls me so I'm directly over his mouth. I'm watching him, as his tongue darts out, and he licks along my folds from my clit all the way down. I'm in heaven.

"So fucking perfect," he manages to say between strokes of his tongue. Then he starts to flick my clit with his tongue.

"Ahhh god, Lewis. Lewis, please, more, Lewis, arrgh" I start to shudder and shake, and my knees begin to buckle, I don't know if I can stand any longer. He has his arms wrapped around the back of my thighs, holding me up. He is flicking and sucking my clit. Then he moves his tongue lower and inserts it into my pussy. I'm panting so loud, trying to catch my breath. I'm sure I must be pulling his hair out; I'm gripping it so tightly. I'm grinding on his face trying to get his tongue deeper. I'm not sure I can last.

"Fuck, Lewis, oh godddddddd, Lewisssssss." I'm screaming at him. He flicks my clit with his tongue and inserts 2 fingers into me. He's turned me into a whore. He makes me lose it, and I just let it all flow.

He's pumping and sucking, and his other hand is on my arse, kneading and making sure I stay upright. I start juddering over his face. I feel like I'm about to explode. I lurch forward suddenly, fully covering his face and resting my hands on either side of his head for support. He could be suffocating, but right at this minute, I don't care. I cum hard. It's sensation overload.

"Fuckkkkkkkk, Lewissssssssssss." I'm grinding, and jutting and shuddering on his face, screaming his name. I'm screwing my eyes shut, the waves of ecstasy shooting through my whole body over and over. I don't want it to stop. I have never felt this before. Electricity soars throughout my body. I collapse. I think I must have blacked out.

The next thing I know, Lewis is behind me. "Hey, sweetheart, you back with me?" He's stroking my back, making figure-of-eight patterns all over it and it feels amazing. My whole body is tingling. The sensations still going through me are like nothing I have ever felt. I feel euphoric, elated, delirious, and emotional.

"I lost you there for a moment, beautiful, are you okay?"

"Yeah, I think so. What happened?" I start to panic. I have

never felt anything like that before or lost control like that. Is that normal? "Lewis, did I black out? Is that normal? Is there something wrong with me?" I feel fine. In fact, I feel fantastic. I can still feel the aftershocks of the most intense orgasm of my life.

"I don't know if it's normal, sweetheart. I have heard about an orgasm being so intense it makes you pass out."

"Well, I feel okay, amazing, in fact." I smile at him. "I'm not very experienced in the bedroom, but that was by far the best orgasm of my life." He grins at me, looking pleased with himself. I'm still bent over the bed, and he's standing behind me, rubbing his cock on the crack of my arse. I turn around so I'm facing him but lie back on the bed. He stands upright. I smirk at him and look at his cock. "Don't get a big head there, handsome." I laugh at him, and the look on his face.

"Shall we go and clean up, beautiful? And then you can feed me some more," he says, winking at me. I look down at his cock. "I mean pasta," he clarifies.

We go into my bathroom to have a shower. The shower in here is big enough for us both, so he strips the rest of his clothes off and joins me. We soap each other up, exploring with our hands. It's hard keeping my hands off his perfect body. His abs are to die for. I have never been with anyone that looks like him. I can't help but keep running my hands all over his chest and abdomen. It's really hard to the touch, but it fascinates me. I'm mesmerised by his tattoo's, they are a work of art and beautiful. I am relaxed with the water washing over me from the rain shower above my head and Lewis's hands roaming all over my body.

"Sweetheart, you have the most perfect figure. Your curvy arse is amazing, your hips, and your tits—don't get me started on them. I could live between them all day, as well as your thighs. Your intelligence and drive blow my mind. But you know what I love the most?"

He just said 'love', but he doesn't mean he loves me, does he?

He puts his finger under my chin to lift my head, so I'm looking up at him. "What I love the most is the whole package. Everything. Not just a single thing, but all of it." He leans down and gives me the sweetest and most gentle of kisses. He pulls back before it can deepen.

"I think we need to get dry and then go and make that dinner before we get carried away again," he says to me as he makes sure all the soap suds are gone from us both, then turns off the shower.

We dry off in the bathroom. I leave him in the bedroom to finish off, and I head to the kitchen to start on the dinner that we were supposed to have ages ago. I put the pasta on and am mixing tuna with mayonnaise, sweetcorn, and some red onions ready to throw onto the pasta when it's cooked. I feel Lewis come up behind me and wrap his arms around my waist. He leans down and kisses me very gently on the back of my neck. I lean into him and groan.

"Shall I pour us some wine?" he says moving away to grab the bottle.

"Yes, please, the glasses are in the second top cupboard on the left."

I dish up the pasta for us both and head to the dining room table with Lewis carrying our wine behind me. "Best view ever."

"I love the view up here. I can see for miles, and there isn't anyone overlooking me at all."

"I wasn't talking about that view." I turn my head to look at him, and he is smirking and looking right at my arse. I roll my eyes at him.

"What?"

"Nothing, come on. Let's get this food down us."

We sit and start to eat. Neither of us speaks for a minute, but it's a comfortable silence.

"What are you thinking about, beautiful?"

"The truth?"

"Always the truth, never anything but the truth."

"I was thinking how can this be real? How can you be here, half-naked at my table, eating tuna pasta that I made for you? Did that just happen? What we did in the bedroom? I know that it did because I'm feeling so relaxed and so serene after it, but it's all so surreal to me."

"Oh, sweetheart. It's me that should be thinking those things. How can this be real? How can I be sitting at your table, with the most beautiful woman I know, eating tuna pasta she actually made for me? How can that beautiful woman give me the best blowjob I have ever had and then let me taste the sweetest pussy I have ever tasted in my life? I'm the luckiest man alive right now. It's all so surreal to me, sweetheart." I'm blushing. I can feel my cheeks getting hotter. I can't look at him.

We finish eating our food in silence, all the while looking at each other and just smiling. I get up to take the empty dishes into the kitchen. Lewis takes the wine glasses and the bottle into the lounge area and puts them on the table. I walk over to the sofa and am about to sit opposite him like we did on Friday.

"No, sweetheart, sit here with me." He pats the seat next to him, so I walk over and sit down, tucking my leg under me. He pulls me into his side and kisses the top of my head.

"Thank you, beautiful, that was an awesome tuna pasta."

"You're welcome, handsome." I lean up and kiss his mouth. Again, we deepen the kiss until I'm breathless. We just can't seem to stop touching and kissing. We're like a couple of teenagers.

"Hey, as much as I want to kiss you all night, we don't have any condoms, and I'm not sure I trust myself right now."

"I know, I can't help it. I feel like a giddy teenager. Now I know what your fans go through." He laughs really loud at that.

"Lewis, I don't really want to ruin the mood, but we need to talk about FL. I need to reply to him and let him know we are either on for Saturday or to forget it. Personally, I would rather never see him, but I know you would rather deal with it. If you want me to meet him so we can try and stop him, then I will, for you."

"Sweetheart. I'm not going to force you to see him if you feel uncomfortable with this. God, the last thing I want is for you to feel that or think I will be disappointed in you. I could never be disappointed in you, and we will only do this is if you feel you can, and not because you think it's what I want. I would never want to put you in any danger, and I would kill the fucker if he tried to do anything. You need to think hard about if you can do this for yourself, not for me." He looks hurt and agonised.

"I can do it, Lewis. With you there, I can do it. I think we need to know once and for all if he is dangerous or if it is all about the chase. Even if we stop him from catfishing someone else, it will be worth it." I smile at him to reassure him and kiss him gently on the side of the mouth.

"I will be there watching your every move beautiful. I won't let you out of my sight."

I put Ed Sheeran on the Bose system before I sit down, and we sit there in comfortable silence holding each other, just listening to the songs. I love this man.

38

Lewis

I'M IN COMPLETE BLISS, CUDDLING on the couch with the most beautiful woman I have ever met. My life at this moment in time is perfect. I can't help keep thinking though that this is the calm before the storm. I *AM* in love with her—without a doubt, but I have no idea if she feels the same. She must feel something deeper than attraction. She put her trust in me earlier in the bedroom, and it doesn't sound like she trusts anyone easily. The last song finishes, and it goes quiet. Time to sort out FL.

"Sweetheart, I really don't want to ruin the moment, but like you say…" I sigh not wanting to do this.

"I know Lewis, we need to sort out this mess." I'm relieved that she feels the same.

"Do you want to grab your laptop to send him a message?" I kiss the top of her head. She gets up reluctantly but turns to give me a kiss first. Then she goes to the hallway to get her bag from the table.

"Do you need a top up before I sit down?" she asks me as she detours into the kitchen.

"Ah, but the lady knows me so well already," I say laughing at her.

Kate comes back with her bag and another bottle of wine. I take the wine and pour us both another glass while she sets up her laptop on the table. She's tapping away on the keyboard, and I'm just looking at her. Looking at how beautiful she is, and she doesn't even know it.

"Hey, handsome, are you ignoring me?" I was in a world of my own.

"Sorry, I was distracted. What did you say, sweetheart?"

"Well, mister, keep your mind on what we are doing here and out of the gutter." She's laughing at me, she leans in to kiss me gently on the lips. I know we fooled around earlier, but I don't want to rush into this. I want to get to know her.

"I said, what do you think of what I have put in the message to FL. I thought you were watching me type to him, but you had a faraway look in your eyes. The one I noticed earlier when you were thinking naughty thoughts."

"Sweetheart, I can't help but think naughty thoughts with a gorgeous sex kitten beside me in shorts and tank top. Do you know what you do to me?" I say looking down at my lap where my cock is standing high and proud waiting for her attention.

I read the message she's written to FL. Short but to the point, arranging to meet up on Saturday as he suggested, but to meet at The Dog and Partridge pub instead of the restaurant they had originally arranged. Easier for me to look inconspicuous in a pub than sat in a restaurant watching. Smart woman. "Ok, you will meet him at the pub near your house in Chelmsford. I will be in there, watching. I will sit where I can see you come in and also look at what's happening around without being obvious, to see if anyone is there just watching you. You need to pay attention to where I am and sit where you can see me, so you know I will be able to see you at all times."

"But what if someone recognises you, Lewis, just like on Friday? It's hard for you to be out and about and no one recognise you?" Shit, she has a point there.

"What if I'm just in my jeans and beanie hat? Would I get away with that?"

"Oh, Lewis I don't think this is going to work. You'll get spotted, and then if he sees you, he will know something isn't right. He's using your image, so why would the real you be in the exact place he is? Plus, it's a great little country pub with roaring fires, and you might look a bit out of place in a beanie?"

"Mmm, you have a point. We need to think about this, but one thing is for sure. I will be there, and I'm not letting you out of my sight."

"I know, Lewis." She looks at me really sheepishly as though there is some doubt there. Hell, no she will not doubt me.

"I mean it, Kate, I will sort this out, and you will be safe. I would never put you in danger. I may just have to find another disguise that's all. Trust me." She leans forward and kisses me "I do Lewis."

She closes the laptop, and we sit, cuddling on the couch for a while just listening to the music—both of us in deep thought. I know she's worried about meeting this catfisher and, to be honest, I'm not sure I'm comfortable putting her in danger? Do I want to put her through this? I just can't shake the feeling that he needs to be stopped.

I look at my watch and see its almost 11.30 p.m. It's time to go. As much as I ache to stay here with her, I can't. I realise just then Kate has nodded off. I can hear how relaxed her breathing is. I'm not going to disturb her. Instead, I slowly move so my head is resting on the arm of the couch and she moves with me, now tucked more into my side. Her legs are already on the couch stretched out, so she ends up practically lying down with her top half on me. It's not the most comfortable position for me, but as long as she is comfy, I don't care. I will stay here all night if I have to.

I must have fallen asleep after listening to Kate's breathing. I suddenly wake with a stiff neck. Kate has somehow managed to tuck herself behind me, which helps, as I can now get up slowly. She's still fast asleep.

I stand in front of her for a few minutes and just watch her sleep. She looks so beautiful and peaceful—she mesmerises me. I head to her bedroom, and I pull back the duvet on her bed so I can put her straight under the covers.

I go back to the living area and gently lift her into my arms. She stirs a little, wraps her arms around my neck and nuzzles into my chest. I slowly carry her to the bedroom and place her gently on the bed then pull the duvet over her. I lean down and kiss her forehead gently, lingering, taking in her scent. "I love you, beautiful" I whisper to her.

She snuggles into the duvet, so I can barely see her. I leave the bedroom and quietly shut the door. I head to the living area and order an Uber, take the glasses and bottle into the kitchen before heading out. I rinse the glasses so Kate doesn't have to do it in the morning. I hope her alarm is set so she gets up in time for work. I'll put an alarm on my phone, then I can phone her in the morning to make sure she is up in time. I leave her apartment and head down to the lobby to wait for the uber. It's freezing out tonight. It's a good job I had my Calvin Klein cashmere duffle coat.

Harry's on the desk still, and I stop to speak to him until my Uber pulls up. He's a nice guy, and I get the feeling he's a little protective of Kate, which is great. All the time I'm talking to him, I feel like someone is watching me. I get this strange feeling, but when I look through the doors, I can't really see anyone. It's so dark outside, and the light in here is reflecting on the glass.

Out of the corner of my eye, I see a car pull up outside. I say goodnight to Harry and go out to the taxi. I don't hang around. With my head down, I head out of the door and straight into the car. I have my baseball cap on, which more often than not is my attire when I'm out, and it's low over my face. As the driver pulls away, I glance under the rim of my cap and see a tall figure just over the road, lurking in the shadows. I can't make him out, and he won't be able to see me as in here it's dark. I get the same, uncomfortable feeling that I had when talking to Harry. Why would someone be lurking in the dark at this hour? Should I be worried? I mean he could be paparazzi, waiting for me to emerge, they will do anything for a story. I'm sure he was watching me. I just had that feeling.

Once back at my hotel I remember to set my alarm for 7 a.m. so I can phone Kate and make sure she's up. I get into bed and text her.

Lewis – Good Morning, beautiful. I hope you were not too uncomfortable on the couch with me last night. I didn't want to wake you, so I put you in bed and left. I will be phoning you at 7 a.m. to make sure you're up for work. If you are up and read this first, then just send me a text to let me know. I don't want you to be late for work. Your boss might be a right tyrant. Thanks for a fantastic night, beautiful. I can't wait to see you later. I hope. Xx

39

George

THAT GUY IN THE LOBBY OF HER building is the same one she was with earlier. I knew she was a fucking whore. It's after three in the morning, and he's only just leaving. What the fuck?

I went back to my place after I left here earlier on. I had to before I did something stupid. I wanted to go in and strangle the bitch there and then, and kill the fucker she was with.

Why would she want to go on a date with me and lead me on the way she has been if she's seeing someone else? Maybe she does this all the time. Maybe she's meeting lots of guys on that dating site and leading them all on so she can get a fuck out of them. The filthy whore.

I tried to calm down once I got back to mine. The lift wasn't working in the shithole, yet again, I had to take the stairs. There were kids hanging around, as usual, they learnt a while back they don't take the piss out of me, and they back off when they see me coming. I gave them all a beating one time when I found them bullying the old man from a few floors down from me. I told the old man if he ever has any trouble with them again just to let me know, and I will sort them out for him. As far as I know, they have left him alone. They now know better than to get in my way. They darted as soon as they realised it was me. Pussies.

I wish they had said something to me; I could have taken my anger out on them. I go straight to bed, trying not to think of the whore but that's easier said than done. Was she fucking that guy while I was outside waiting to see when he left? That filthy bitch is gonna pay for that.

I'm so wound up that I don't even put the computer on to check if I have any messages.

40

Katherine

Islowly start to wake up. I stretch out. I feel amazing. I'm happy, elated, and so very relaxed. I realise I'm in my bed, but I don't remember going to bed last night. The last I remember is being snuggled up to Lewis on the couch. I sit up to see if there is any sign of him. I look at the clock, and it's 6.40 a.m. I get up, use the bathroom, then head to the living area. There's no sign of Lewis. He must have put me to bed, then left.

I grab my phone from the table, noticing he's cleaned up the glasses and wine bottle. I read the message on my phone from Lewis. I look at my watch—6.55 a.m. I send him a quick text.

Kate – Hey, handsome. I just got up. Thank you for the message and thank you for putting me to bed last night and for cleaning up. Just about to shower, then head to the office. Don't want my tyrant of a boss to fire me. Have a good day, and yes, I hope to see you later. Xx

I put the phone on the kitchen counter, put bread in the toaster, put the coffee on, then move to the shower to get ready for work. Once ready, I go into the kitchen to grab my toast to eat on the go with my cup of coffee.

I pick my phone up and notice there are two missed calls.

One from Lewis and one from Stacey, my business manager at the bank, there's a voice message. I listen, and it's Stacey just letting me know that the proposal is going through, and she should have news for me later today. She asks if I can go and see her at 3 p.m. She should know the result by then.

I reach my office, and after the scare the other day, I lock the door again as soon as I'm in. I know I will be on my own in here today and don't have any visitors planned. I switch everything on and get my glass of iced water, making sure my office door is open, so I can hear if anyone knocks. I send Stacey a quick e-mail to let her know I got her message, and that I will be there at 3 p.m.

I phone the estate agency to see if they have accepted my offer. I hold my breath while they get the paperwork out. I dropped the offer considerably, so I expect them to counteroffer, which is exactly what happens. I am willing to pay a little more, but don't want her to know that, so I tell her that I will be in touch and wait until after lunch to email my new offer.

It's so quiet without Clive or Chrissie, who is still in the hospital. I look at the clock and realise it's 1.30 p.m. I haven't stopped since arriving this morning. I need to grab some lunch, then head out to my meeting with Stacey.

I decide to nip to the deli and grab my usual wrap and a coffee and sit at one of the small bistro tables by the windows. Out of the corner of my eye, I see movement across the street. I look out of the window, and I can see a man standing over the road but tucked back into where there is an alleyway. He's wearing a suit, which you expect in this neighbourhood, but why is he hiding away? It's a bit odd. He has his head down, and I can't make him out, but I suspect he is looking at his phone.

I carry on eating my wrap, watching the man over the road discreetly. He looks up, and it strikes me that he is the same man I saw in here last week.

Then he turns and starts walking away. He must have just been on his phone, probably looking for a signal. I suppose it's not unusual to bump into the same person if he works around here.

I've been distracted, and now I need to go. I give George a wave as I leave the shop, jumping in a taxi. I haven't heard back from Lewis since he tried phoning me this morning, so I decide to text him while I'm stuck in traffic.

Kate – Hey, handsome, sorry I missed your call this morning. I was in the shower. Hope everything's okay, and I hope to see you later tonight if you're free? Let me know, and I will get something in for us. Just off to the bank for a meeting, speak to you soon.

I put the phone on my knee and look out of the window noticing that we are nearly at the bank. Stacey sees me as I enter. She excuses herself and comes straight over to me holding out her hand to shake mine.

We head into the meeting room. She has my file in front of her. Julie, the secretary, brings us coffee, and I can't wait to wrap my hands around it as they are freezing.

"Ok," Stacey says opening the file.

"This is the most nervous I have been since the very first property I bought. I've never wanted a project so much. Please put me out of my misery," I say with what I'm sure must be anxiety written all over my face.

"Well, it's good news. The bank has looked at your proposal, and they like what they see. With your track record, they are more than happy to offer you the bridging loan." She has a big smile on her face. "Now we need to discuss the terms and arrangements that suit us both, so I have some proposals already made out for you to look at."

We go through all the paperwork and iron out the finer details. I sign what feels like a million pieces of paper. I feel like I'm signing my life away, but I'm so happy. I leave the bank with the biggest smile on my face. I pull out my phone to check my e-mails to see if the agency has replied to me and they have. My offer has been accepted. I stand in the middle of the steet just clutching my phone grinning. I am a little disappointed in one respect, I was hoping to see that Lewis had called or messaged, as I want to tell him my news, so I'm disappointed there are no missed calls or texts from him. I try to phone him, but there's no answer. I send him a quick text.

Kate – Hey, handsome, hope all is okay. You're probably on a shoot or something. Just had my meeting with the bank, and I got the bridging loan for my project. I also got my offer accepted on the buildings. I'm so excited. I wanted to tell you first. I thought we could maybe celebrate tonight? Speak to you soon. Xx

I decide the next person I need to tell is Clive, so I ring him, and after the excitement of my news I decide to tell him about Lewis.

"Aaaand, I have some news, of a more personal nature…"

"Kate! Do tell!" he replies excitedly.

"Well, I had a date, kind of, with Lewis, last night," I say a bit quieter.

"Hold on, back up. You *kinda* had a date with Lewis? As in hot-as-fuck Lewis? Lewis Clancy the hottest supermodel there is? What the fuck, Kate? How did that happen?"

I tell him everything that had happened, glossing over the FL stuff, as I don't want him to worry.

"Hold on. You made him something to eat? So, does that mean he was at your place last night?"

"Yes, he was. It's just easier because the couple of times I've been with him in public people have recognised him—they want to speak to him, take selfies with him and get his autograph. So I made him some food at my place."

"And is that all? Just drinks and food?" If he could see me now, he would know something else happened, with the colour my face has gone. I can feel the heat in my cheeks.

"Kate, you there?"

"Sorry, yes, Clive, and yes, it was food and drinks. You have a dirty mind, Clive Bunce. He was the perfect gentleman. Clive, he's just everything, as well as being as hot as hell. He's kind and funny. He says all the right things, and he says he really likes me."

"Wow, Kate, it sounds like you've fallen for him. I've never heard you like this before."

"Oh, Clive, I have fallen for him hard, but I'm worried? He's this hot supermodel that has actresses and models throwing themselves at him, and I'm just old frumpy me with huge curves. I'm not a size six model. What could he possibly see in me when he could have those gorgeous women? I'm no one." I can feel a tear roll down my cheek as the reality hit's home, and all my insecurities emerge again.

"Now you listen to me, Katherine Porter. You might not be famous, but you are definitely all woman. There is nothing false about you. You tell it as it is, and you have the kindest heart and soul. You are loyal to the end, and any man would be honoured just to be in your company. Do not let me hear this from you again. You are one of the most confident women I know. You're smart and sassy. You run an empire for God's sake, Kate. Now cut it out. What does Mr Supermodel say?"

"He says I'm beautiful. He loves my curves, and that I do things to him that have never happened before. He says just talking to me or one glimpse of me, and he can't think straight. Clive, he's the sweetest, but I can't help feeling I've been here before, and I've heard it all before, only to be played. I'm scared to let anyone in." I don't know if it's me I'm trying to convince or Clive. "Lewis makes me feel like a wanted woman. He comes across as really caring and he seems to be such a genuine guy but look at my track record with men. They all seem genuine, but not one of them has been, so I feel I'm a bad judge of character.

What if he gets what he wants from me and then realises it is the beautiful models and actresses he prefers? I don't know what to do, Clive, but I've fallen for him. I'm in love with him, and I hardly know him."

I hear Clive letting out a breath on the line. He's thinking. I know whenever he goes quiet, it's because the cogs are turning.

"Kate, you're smitten. I hear it in your voice just talking about him. I knew the first time we met him that he was smitten with you too. He couldn't stop looking at you. You were speaking, and he was a million miles away, just staring at you. I could see it in his face. Don't throw it away—go with your heart on this one and see where it takes you. Give him the benefit of the doubt. If he's saying these things to you now and it's only been one date, then who knows where it will go? Please, try for me. You deserve some happiness." I do deserve a break. "In all honesty, in his line of work, it's got to be hard to find genuine people. Women probably throw themselves at him because he's famous and has money. But it must get old. He probably sees you for you, a real person with no airs and graces, and who quite frankly couldn't give a fuck if someone was famous or loaded because you don't need that in life. You're successful in your own right. Promise me you won't throw it away, and you will see what happens?"

He's right. I know he is. I have never let anyone's status sway me on anything. It makes no difference to me.

"Ok, Clive, I promise I'll see what happens and won't throw it away. But the first inkling I get that he's playing me, and I will dump him so fast his arse won't know the ground is travelling up to meet it."

"I know, Kate, but just try. I have a good feeling about him."

"Gosh, how did my celebratory call to you turn into agony aunt hour? I can't believe I actually admitted to you that I'm in love with Lewis. Wow, go me, full on. Get back to your gorgeous man, and enjoy the rest of your holiday, and I'll see you soon."

I start to walk to the tube station to head back home. The station is nearer to my office than home, but I fancy the walk even if it's freezing out.

I'm on the main road, heading towards my apartment building. It's still early evening, and there are a lot of people about on their way home from work. I get the feeling that someone is watching me again, so I stop and lean against a railing and pretend to look at something on my shoe while actually, I'm looking around to see if I can see anyone. As I look across the road, I see the back of a tall man in a suit just rounding a corner onto a side street. He looks like the guy from earlier today. There aren't many businessmen around here with that long messy black hair, so he is instantly recognisable—unless I'm just a bit paranoid. I put my shoe back on and start back to my apartment. The sooner I get there the better.

I feel so relieved to be home. I had an uneasy feeling all the way here. As soon as I remove my coat, I take my phone out of my bag to see if there are any texts or missed calls. No, nothing. It's strange, I've sent two texts to Lewis today and not heard anything back from him. The only thing was his missed call this morning while I was in the shower.

I phone his number, but it just rings out. Strange. I decide to text him again. I don't want him thinking I'm stalking him though.

Kate – Hey, Lewis, wasn't sure if you were coming round or not? I haven't heard from you, so I didn't get anything in to eat. I'm gonna have a tin of soup now, do some work, then have an early night. Catch you again, maybe.

I wonder if it's a bit curt? Maybe he's been on a shoot and couldn't use his phone? I don't know how these things work. It's all new to me. Surely he has a break though? He would have been able to text me back. I'm not going to sound desperate. That's the last text I'll send him. The ball's in his court now.

I eat my soup, do my research, and send some e-mails to my team letting them all know we have the green light on the buildings and we need to meet up this week to start arranging all the scheduling. I have a shower and do my hair, then get into bed. It's still early, so I decide to read for a bit. I look at my phone. It's 10.25 p.m., and still nothing from Lewis.

Well, screw him.

If he's that busy that he can't even reply to my text, then he obviously doesn't think that much of me, regardless of what he says. It's all bullshit. I knew it. There is no way someone like him could even look at me. I live in a dream world half the time. Well, I've had it with him. He can go to hell now. I told Clive the minute I thought I was being played that would be it for me. I'm done. Men, why do I bother? No more dating for me. Work all the way. I have my project to keep me busy now for the next twelve months or so. Screw you, Lewis Clancy.

Lewis

SHIT, SHIT, FUCK.

She is going to think the worst now. I said in my text that I hoped to see her tonight, which I had every intention of doing, but when I woke up this morning there was a message from Luce telling me she would be here at 7.30 a.m. to pick me up for the airport. The jet would be leaving at 10 a.m. Shit! Venice! Kate had been occupying my brain, and I couldn't think about anything else.

After showering and shoving my stuff into a bag, I check my phone. There's a message from Kate to say she is awake and thanking me for putting her to bed and cleaning up. She said she hoped to see me later as well! I try and ring her, but it just goes to voice message. I don't leave a message. She would see I had called and hopefully call me back.

Luce arrives dead on 7.30 a.m. and lets herself into my suite. We head straight out to the waiting car to take us to the airport. I keep checking my phone and Luce notices.

"Everything okay, Lewis? You don't look too good, and you keep checking your phone?"

"Yes, I'm okay, Luce. I didn't tell Kate about my trip because I forgot all about it. I'm worried she will think I'm lying to her."

"Kate as in property Kate? Why would she think that? Are you seeing her?"

"Yes, I'm seeing her, and when I left last night, I said I would see her tonight. I completely forgot about Venice. Now she's going to think I'm not interested in her. She already thinks it's unbelievable I would be interested in her as it is."

"So, are you interested in her, or is she just another of your flings? Sorry, Lewis, but I've seen your conquests firsthand over the years."

"No, she's different, Luce. There's something about her. She's beautiful, intelligent, sassy, funny, and I can't for the life of me stop thinking about her. I have never, ever had feelings for someone like this before. I thought Susan was the one, but my feelings for her were nothing compared to my feelings for Kate. God, I sound like a fucking wuss. I think I'm in love with her, Luce. From the moment I set eyes on her in her office last week, I just knew it then. I hardly know her, how pathetic am I?"

"No Lewis, when you know, you know, and I've never heard you talk about anyone like this before."

We arrive at the airport and drive straight to a hanger where the private jet is waiting. I can't concentrate on anything at the moment. My head is not in the game. I can't stop thinking about Kate. She's really embedded into my head and my heart.

As we settle in our seats on the plane, I check my phone to see if Kate has messaged me yet, but there's nothing. I thought she would have tried to phone me back this morning or at least texted me after she saw my missed call. I want to message, but then I would rather speak to her to explain where I am. It's better we talk in person. I don't want her thinking I'm not interested and fobbing her off. I was really looking forward to seeing her tonight, but now I have to wait two fucking days, and it's going to kill me. I won't see her until Thursday!

We land in Venice, and I switch my phone on hoping I have a message from Kate. My gut falls, there's nothing. I'm getting quite angsty and frustrated because I haven't heard from her. I sit and play with my beard twisting it.

We arrive at the hotel, and I head to my suite to get ready for the shoot. I check my phone, Still nothing. I head to the gym in the hotel first. I have time to do some quick cardio workouts before the car arrives.

It's late when we finish filming. I go straight to my bag for my phone and switch it on. I have a couple of messages and missed calls, and I scroll down my phone, to see there are three messages from Kate.

Finally, thank fuck. My heart starts racing. Shit, I'm like a schoolkid. I open the first message from her. Shit, she wanted me to answer her about going tonight and her getting some food in for us. I look at my watch, and it's 11.45 p.m. that makes it 10.45 p.m. back home. I wonder if she's awake? The second message was after the bank, and she was excited she'd got the loan and the offer on the properties was accepted. I love she wanted to share that with me. The third one was at 7.30 p.m. so that would have been 6.30 p.m. there. She was a bit abrupt in that one because I hadn't replied to the previous messages or answered when she called. Knowing her like I have gotten to know her the last week, she will be thinking I don't want to see her again. She is very insecure, and I need for her to believe in me.

I try her number. I need to speak to her. I know it's late. It goes straight to her voicemail. Shit. I'm not leaving a shitty message. I need to speak to her in person. They're picking me up at 6.30 a.m., which will be 5.30 a.m. back home so that will be too early to call her. I'll have to take a break and call her—I hope I can reach her to explain. I need to know if she has heard from FL yet as well. We need to plan that out properly.

Why is my life complicated all of a sudden?

George

I'M NOT CUT OUT FOR THIS STALKING shit. She saw me twice today. She watched me.

I saw her sitting in that deli from across the road; watching me. I don't think she suspects anything, I just pretend to be using my phone so she doesn't see my face. I keep my head down all the time. Then I walk away farther down the street but somewhere that I can still keep an eye on her.

The stupid bitch then gets into a taxi. I decide to go and wait in the café over the road from her office building, to see if she comes back.

Red is in the café when I get there. She waves at me with a big smile on her face as I walk in. I grin and nod my head as a hello. She makes me feel warm inside. What the fuck is that about? "Sit down, and I'll bring you the usual," she shouts across to me. I head for my usual table in the window where I can see the building over the road.

Red comes over with my coffee, and another one in her hand, which I guess is for herself when she sits down opposite me. Great. She's a nice enough girl, but I can't be dealing with her right now. I'm too worked up about that bitch seeing me today.

"Hey, John, how are you?"

"Hey, Red, I'm good, thank you. Just on a break, then back to work."

"Oh, I thought you had the week off? Did you find an apartment yet?"

"I meant work, looking for an apartment. No, I haven't found one yet. I'm still looking. Prices are high round here, and you don't get too much apartment for your money. Thanks for the coffee, here let me give you the money."

"No, it's fine. It's on me. I know what you mean about the apartments though. I live in a little bedsit. It's all I can manage and why I'm always in here working. I'm doing that course at night— accounting and finance so I can become a financial officer and hopefully a CFO one day."

I wish she would shut up. I have no idea what a CFO is, so can't comment on that, and I'm trying to watch the building across the road. It's a pity it's so quiet in here, or she would be serving customers. Just then, some people walk in the door, and she looks over at them. Thank fuck for that.

"Oh, looks like I need to go and make some coffees. Nice talking to you, John. Give me a shout if you need another coffee, on me, of course."

"Thank you, Red." I wink at her again. She blushes then heads off to the counter. Good. Now I can concentrate on the office opposite. But why do I feel shitty now she's left me?

I sit there for what feels like forever. Red has been hovering around me like a fly on shit. I wish she would piss off and just leave me alone. But then I don't. I am so fucking comfused right now. I would have shagged her no problem if it wasn't for that bitch over the road. I have to deal with the bitch before I go there with Red. I try to be nice to Red by winking because she loves that and blushes every time. I don't want to be mean to her. I think she's nice and different to the others. I think I actually like her. I rub my hand over my head so fucking confused. I decide I need to leave here before Red starts asking more questions or I get mean to her. I could do with a bite to eat but not here. I think I'll go to that deli. I know I may miss the bitch if she comes back, but then she usually walks past there on her way home.

I reach the deli, and like the bitch did this afternoon, I sit at the table in the window. I can see the road outside. I'm starving. I haven't had anything to eat today. I was so pissed off when I saw that dickhead she was with leaving early in the morning that when I woke from the little sleep I managed to get, I just left my shithole without having a drink or anything to eat. Not that I had any food in to eat anyway.

Suddenly, I see my mother. Holy fuck, she just came out of the tube station. I have to blink twice, but I can't mistake her, I would know that bitch anywhere. But it's not my actual mother, fuck my head is all over the place. It's the bitch. I get up and walk out as quickly as I can. I cross over the road, and I watch as she heads towards her apartment building. I follow, but at a distance.

Just then, she stops and leans on a railing, taking her shoe off. I'm sure she knows I'm there. I head down a side street. I hope she didn't see me. At least she's on her own with no man in toe this time. I cross the small road and hang back slightly. She can't see me from where I am now, but I can still make her out. She looks around, then puts her shoe back on, then carries on walking. I hold back, just edging forward so I can see her. She looks around again, as though she knows someone's watching her. I decide to stand here for a bit and let her get ahead. She always talks to the doormen of her building, so if I wait, I can walk past and make sure she's gone home.

I get near her building and see she's in there. If it's a different doorman, I might be able to slip past him, but it's the same old fucking man as usual. I'm getting to the point now where I just want to get rid of her and get her out of my life any way I can—once and for all. I'm becoming obsessed with her, which is driving me nuts and it's consuming me. I'm not sure if I can wait much longer. I know her secretary is away, and she was on her own in the office yesterday. I'm getting desperate now. I think tomorrow, I may pay her a visit at work and get this over with. I'm going to make this bitch pay. Pay for making me wait longer than I needed to and also for stringing me along and fucking others at the same time.

I can feel my blood boiling, and the red mist is starting to descend. No, not now, not here. I need to think of something else and get away from here. I turn around and head back past the deli. I'm heading for the café before I know it. Maybe I need to fuck Red—use her as a distraction and get all this anger out of me. I have to be careful though. I can't hurt her. I do like her. Can I do that, just use her? She's different, I can just tell she is and I think I would like to explore where it could go. God, I'm turning into a fucking pussy. I have never liked any woman before. Before I know it, I'm in the café, and Red is looking at me with a quizzical look on her face. It's not that long since I left.

"Hey, Red, do you fancy getting that drink?"

"Oh, wow, yes. Yes, John, let me finish cleaning up. I won't be long, just take a seat. Can I get you anything?"

We head out of the café after her shift finishes.

"So, shall we go to the pub down the road here for that drink? It's a nice little pub, have you been in it yet? The Three Kings, it's fairly small, so it does get busy."

"I would prefer somewhere a bit quieter," I say to her looking into her eyes. She blushes again and looks at me all dough-eyed. She really is pretty. I like her more and more each time I see her. What strange thoughts for me. I never think anyone is pretty. They are all whores to me, but not Red, she is different. I can feel it, she makes me feel things I've never felt before. It's all new to me.

"Well, erm, most of the pubs I know here get busy, with all the office staff going for drinks. We could, ermmm…" she hesitates and looks really sheepish like she doesn't want to suggest going back to her place in case I get the wrong idea, but that's exactly what I want.

"What, Red?"

"My place is really close. We could go back there if you want? Just for a drink. We could grab some beer or wine. It's up to you, of course, I don't mean anything by it, but it is quieter, oh…"

I turn to her and put my finger on her mouth to stop her from talking. She looks at me, still blushing. I lean in and replace my finger with a sweep of my lips. She's a bit shocked at that and gasps a little, then breaks out into the biggest smile.

"Sshhh, it's okay, Red. You don't need to be embarrassed, that's a perfect idea. It gives us some privacy, and we can relax with a drink."

We grab some beer and a bottle of wine. There is a chip shop next door, so we get some fish and chips to share back at hers. We're away from the hustle and bustle now and on a council estate that I didn't realise was this close to Knightsbridge. We approach one of the really old-looking buildings. We climb up two flights of stairs to the top floor. The carpets on the stairs are all threadbare and are probably as old as the damn building. The walls have some kind of shitty wallpaper on them, curling at the edges, and the high ceilings have paint peeling off. Still, it's better than the shithole I live in.

Just as we walk into her place and she starts to close the door, a little furball comes barreling into our legs rubbing all up hers and meowing. He's okay, just all fur.

"Hey, chip, my little pussy kins, did you miss me, baby, are you hungry?" She's bending over right in front of me stroking the damn pussy. Now I want to stroke her pussy, goddamn it.

She realises I'm right behind her, very close, and she turns and catches me staring at her arse.

"Oh, sorry, John, this is our little ritual. Chip always comes to greet me when I come home, to tell me it's tea time. Come on. There isn't much to see. It's only a small bedsit." I look around, and it's not much bigger than my place. It's just the one room. There's a bed in one corner with a small wardrobe that fits right at the end of it, flush against the far wall. Next to that is a unit with a small TV. I can see a laptop on the shelf underneath the TV, and there is a window with a small table under it with two chairs. Then, along the other wall to my right is the small kitchen, if you can call it that. Just a sink, with cupboards under it and above it. One side there is a counter top stove, a kettle, a toaster and a small oven and no room for anything else. Still, it's more than I have. There is a door next to me which I presume is her bathroom.

She watches me looking around. I look at her, and she glances down. "It's not much, I know, but its home to me. It's better than where I was a few months back. It's safe. One day I will get a bigger and better place."

I put my finger under her chin to lift her head up so she's looking at me. "Hey, I don't care what it looks like. It's your home, Red. It's perfect, just a little cosy, but that's okay, right?" I say, wiggling my eyebrows at her to try get her to smile again. Of course, she blushes.

"Thank you, John." She rises on her tiptoes and kisses my cheek. Holy shit, I like it. It gives me a funny feeling in my stomach that I've never had before and that tingly feeling I felt last time. She walks to the kitchen area, opens a cupboard, pulls out some plates, forks, and some glasses.

"Let's get this fish and chips put on plates, and the drinks poured. Will you just dish it onto these plates, please, John, while I get Chip his tea?"

"Erm, yeah, sure." I start to share the food out. We take the plates to the small table and sit to eat. She's really easy to be around, which I find surprising. I'm never comfortable in a woman's company. She is different. She isn't judging me. She's only interested in finding out about me. I lie, of course, when I have to. I make up a family I had, but no longer have.

After we've eaten, the only comfortable place to sit is on her bed. She goes to the bathroom, and I take off my shoes and lean back against her headboard. It's a single bed, and I practically fill it with my size. She comes back out and turns on the tv, then looks at me on the bed, and realises I fill it, she pulls out one of the chairs to sit on. I open my legs and tap the bed.

"No, come here, Red. Sit here with me and relax." She looks at me like a rabbit caught in headlights and blushes. She isn't sure what to do. Maybe she thinks I've gone too far, but fuck it, I want her near me, and between my legs right now is the perfect place. I wonder how long it will be before I can get her mouth around my cock. I can feel myself getting hard thinking about it. She hesitantly moves towards me, and I reach out for her hand as she gets near the bed. I pull her gently towards me. As she gets nearer the bed, I put my right leg down placing my foot on the floor. I pull her slightly so she's on the bed, awkwardly at first.

She's facing me rather than sitting between my legs. She just stares at me. I lick my lips.

"S-sorry, John, I haven't brought anyone back here ever, and I never really thought much about the space. It's usually just me and Chip." She hangs her head, and in doing so, she is looking right at my crotch. She doesn't realise she's done that.

My cock is standing up to attention just thinking of her head in that direction and being so close to her mouth. She looks right at me, and she is as red as her hair. She's noticed my cock. I shrug. "Sorry, he has a mind of his own, and when a hot-as-fuck sexy woman is looking right at him, then he stands to attention." I have no shame. She licks her lips. Fuck, I don't have any control. I pull her up my torso, and I take her mouth. She's a bit startled at first, but it doesn't take her long before she opens up to me. I have her head in my hands, and she's resting her hands on my chest. She starts to explore it.

My hands move down her neck, one hand down one of her arms, the other to her waist. I tug her forward, right onto my chest. I can feel her tits pressed against me, so she must be able to feel my cock. She can't move her hands now, but I can move mine.

My hands wonder round to her backside, and I pull her closer still by her arse. I'm gripping it in both hands. She's moaning into my mouth, and I'm moaning right back at her. She pulls away slightly, to look at me. "John, I don't ever do anything like this. Please don't think bad of me. This is all new to me. I'm nervous and scared right now."

"Baby, I don't think bad of you, and we won't do anything you don't want to do." God, I hope she wants to do more. She starts biting her bottom lip. I can see the uncertainty in her eyes. I stroke her back. Up and down right to her arse cheeks. She wriggles a little, liking what I'm doing. "Of course, if you wanted to say hi to my cock, you know, maybe go and have a conversation with him as you're so close to him, I'm sure he would appreciate it."

She pulls back from me and starts to move. Shit, Shit. "Baby it's okay, I was joking. You don't have to do anything. I promise you. I will not make you do anything. I'm not that type of guy." Red really is different. She is nothing like all the others. But I'm not sure if it's because she seems so innocent. Fuck, this is new for me. She isn't a quick fuck-and-leave girl. I see that now. I like her. I mean really like her. Maybe I can just explore a little and come back and see her.

She's looking at me sheepishly. "I, I, I have never done that before. I'm not sure what to do."

"Shit, baby, you don't have to do anything you don't want to. I won't think any less of you. In fact, I admire you for not just diving on me like all other women do."

"I think, oh… I don't know John. I feel stupid. I don't know what to do. If you, if you guide me, then I would like to try with you." She's on her knees on the bed in front of me but sitting back on her feet, and she's looking at the bulge in my trousers. Fuck, yes, I do want her to do that, but first I think I need to make her feel good.

I smile at her, and I lean forward. "Come here, Red." I bring her closer to me, and I kiss her properly. She responds. I take the bottom of her t-shirt and start to lift the hem up

"Is this okay?" she nods yes. I lift it up, she puts her arms up, so I can take it off. She has perfect tits. I throw the t-shirt on the floor, and I cup her tits in my hands, squeezing. I play with her nipples between my thumbs and she gasps. I pull the cups down so her tits are hanging out, and I lean in and take one in my mouth while playing with the other one.

"Oh god, that feels amazing." She's panting while I play. My mouth alternates between them, giving both the same attention. My hand travels down her side to her waist and the button and zip that are on the side of her trousers. I undo the button and start to pull the zip down. Her hand suddenly clasps mine to stop me. I suck her tit and bite her nipple gently with a bit of pressure. She lets go of my hand, and I continue undoing her trousers.

Once they are slack, I move my hand to the front, and I cup her pussy through the material and start to stroke with my finger. She starts rubbing backwards and forwards, trying to get some friction. I keep sucking her tits, groping one, sucking the other, and then run my hand back to the waistband and make my way into her pants. She's soaking wet for me. I stroke her clit a few times then dip a finger inside her. She's gasping now, with her head thrown back.

"Oh shit, John, don't stop. Oh my god, that all feels amazing." She starts to move faster on my hand, trying to get me deeper. I put two fingers in her, then three, and stroke her clit with my thumb, and still suck her tits, biting her nipples harder each time. She explodes. I mean literally explodes. She screams so loudly, grabbing my hair and forcing her tit further into my mouth. She wants more, so I bite harder still. She's pulling my hair and almost jumping up and down on my hand, her juice just dripping from her pussy. She grabs my head and stills me. She's panting hard, trying to get her breath back, and I can feel her pulse racing against my head. When she releases my head, I look up at her. She has a sheen of sweat on her top lip and on her forehead. I lean forward and lick the sweat from her lip. I'm so fucking turned on by her right now. I have never in my life felt this way. I pull back and look at her. I mean really look at her. She's gorgeous, just glowing from her orgasm. She must have been shaking her head because her hair is a bit wild. She looks fucking beautiful. I have never thought that about any woman before. Fuck. I'm screwed. I'm going soft.

I slowly pull back and remove my soaked hand from her trousers. She's watching me closely, and I bring my fingers to my mouth and lick them like lollipops, sucking her juices from them. Her eyes widen at what I'm doing. She looks like she wants to devour me. I take a finger out of my mouth and put it in hers. She sucks it and moans. "That is what you need to do my cock. Just suck it like you are my finger. Just take as much as you can in your mouth, suck and lick." She's doing exactly that to my finger.

I start to pull her trousers and knickers down. She gets off the bed and shimmies out of them. She's standing naked in front of me apart from the bra still holding her tits high up. I get off the bed, and she reaches for my shirt and starts to unbutton it. I let her undress me. I'm enjoying myself for the first time ever during sex. It's always been such a dirty chore for me after my parents. But this is different somehow. I can't pinpoint why...

She slides my trousers down my legs, letting my cock spring free, and he doesn't disappoint me. She just sits and stares at him, licking her lips. She needs to put her lips around him before I burst.

"Wow, I don't think that will fit in my mouth—it's huge!"

I smile at her. "Oh, you will be surprised where he fits, baby." I pull her up to her feet. "I'm going to lay on the bed on my back. I want you to get on top of me, but I want you facing my feet so your arse is in my face. I'm going to lick out that pretty pussy of yours while you suck my cock." She's just staring at me like a deer caught in headlights.

"Can you do that, baby? Do you think you would like to try? I told you we don't do anything you don't want to do."

"Yes." She nods frantically. "Yes, I want to. Oh god, I want to so badly." I laugh at her enthusiasm, then get on the bed on my back and pull her onto me so she's straddling my body with her arse near my head. Shit, this is perfect. I don't think I will last that long. Suddenly, she tentatively licks my cock. I think I chose the wrong thing to do. I wanted to see her face, but I can't from down here.

"It's okay, baby, he won't bite. You can lick, suck, and you can stroke my balls at the same time if you like?" She giggles a bit. I love that sound. Did I just think that? Fuck. She licks him a few more times. He's wet from pre-cum, and she licks it all off.

"Mmmm, you taste quite nice, John," she whispers. She's driving me nuts. Then she does it. She has her hand firmly wrapped around my cock, and she puts it in her mouth. I can feel the back of her throat. Shit, I didn't think she would ever get that much in. She starts to bob her head up and down, sucking and licking and getting right into it. I start thrusting up, getting lost in it. Her hand is rolling my balls around, and she's not being gentle. I'm sure she's bullshitted me. She must have done this before. Is she another fucking whore? NO. Don't go there.

I manage to pull her back slightly so her pussy is right above my face. She's dripping wet. I can see the juice coming out of her pussy. I lick at it and circle her clit with my tongue. She bucks a bit, and I pop out of her mouth. "Fucking hell" she screams.

"Don't stop, baby." She puts me back in her mouth and carries on. I suck her clit a bit more, then I insert my tongue into her pussy and wiggle it around, all while sucking her juices. I start thrusting with my tongue, just like I am with my hips. I have my hands on her arse, and I'm spreading her arse cheeks. I start to circle her arsehole with a finger. She stills.

"It's okay, baby, just enjoy it all."

She carries on sucking. I play with her arsehole a little and move one hand near my mouth. I remove my tongue and replace it with two fingers, then I flick her clit with my tongue and suck. She's doing the same to me on my cock, sucking, and then scraping her teeth along it. God, I'm going to explode. Fuck.

"I'm going to cum, babe. You can either swallow or stop. Your choice, but it's going to happen nowwwww," I scream out with my release. She sucks and sucks, and she swallows it all. Well, fuck me! For someone who said she has never done this before, that was fantastic. I continue to suck her clit and pump my fingers in and out. She screams out her release louder than before. I lap up all her juices as they pour out of her. She stills and collapses on top of me. We both lay there for a while, trying to catch our breaths and come down from the high. Well fuck, that was the best thing I've ever done and enjoyed. I have never in my life enjoyed any part of sex before. It was just something I had to do to get a release. I even avoided going down on a slut, and usually, I never did. But with her, with Red, it was just different in every way, I can't explain. It was fucking fantastic.

I think she has fallen asleep on me, but she moves slowly and gets off me awkwardly. She can't look at me and tries to move past straight to the bathroom. I grab her hand and pull her back on top of me but facing me. "Hey, what's wrong?"

"Nothing."

"Yes, there is. Look at me." She slightly lifts her head and looks at me really shyly. I put a finger under her chin so she looks at me full on.

"Red, tell me what's wrong. Why can't you look at me?"

"I feel really dirty doing what we just did. I feel embarrassed. I feel shy. I don't know, John. I don't feel like we should have done that. I don't know you. I never swear, but you made me swear. I feel so ashamed of myself. I feel like a slut, John, and I'm the furthest thing from one of those." I pull her to me so her head is on my chest and I hug her.

"Baby, that was fucking amazing. You were fucking amazing. Please don't feel bad. Tell me. Did you enjoy any of what we just did?"

She lifts her head to look at me. "All of it was amazing, John. You made me feel fantastic. I've never done anything like that or ever felt anything like that."

"Then don't be embarrassed for enjoying it. Don't feel shy, especially after what we just did, and please do not say you feel dirty when what we both felt was out of this world amazing. I can honestly say, hand on heart, that was the best blow job I've ever had and enjoyed, and I don't want to blow my trumpet here, but I have had a lot, baby."

"Urghh, why did you have to say that? Am I just some sort of easy ride for you? Are you some kind of manwhore? Oh, shit what have I done?" She sits up covering her face with her hands and shaking her head. "I think you need to go, John. Sorry, but now I feel cheap and nasty as well."

"Baby, I didn't mean it like that, and no, I'm not a manwhore. Just that growing up, you know, girls would throw themselves at me, and come onto me, what male would refuse? I swear, you are the first girl I can honestly say I enjoyed every fucking minute doing what we did. Please don't feel cheap and nasty. It was beautiful, and you're beautiful. I don't want to ruin what we just did." She looks down and starts playing with her hands.

"I don't know, John. I think I feel cheap because I've never done that before, especially with someone I only just met. I have only ever had sex once before with a so-called boyfriend, but he finished with me saying I was a lousy lay. I suppose I just feel inferior because you're obviously experienced. I'm sorry, it's just my insecurities." She laughs nervously, which I find kind of cute, which is weird. I never find women cute. Who the fuck am I right now? Saying all this mushy shit and actually meaning it for once. God help me.

I pull her in close to me. "Let's just have a cuddle before I leave. I have work in the morning. I'm sure you do as well, keeping the hordes of businessmen caffeinated for the day. Can I ask how old you are, Red?"

"I'm twenty-four. How old are you? I blow out a breath and rub my hand over my face. Shit, she's young, but I suppose, not too young. I'm thirty-three now, I think. I don't know for sure as I never had birthdays as a kid, but I remember once my mother saying something about me being thirteen, and I kept count from there. I don't want to lie to her again, so I tell her.

"I'm thirty-three, Red. Is that too old for you?"

"No, not at all. Am I too young for you?"

"No, I don't think so. To be honest, I have never really bothered with age. I've never celebrated a birthday." She gasps at that. Shit, too much info, there will be questions now.

"You don't celebrate birthdays? Is that religion or something?"

"No, it's just we never had any money when I was growing up, so my parents never bothered with birthdays."

"I'm so sorry, John, that must have been hard. Are your parents okay now though?"

"They died when I was a teenager. They were in an accident."

"I'm sorry, John. Do you have any brothers or sisters?"

"No, I was the only one. We didn't get on, so I don't miss them. It is what it is." She goes quiet then, so I start to get up to use the bathroom. She gets off me and lets me go. I pick up my trousers and take them with me. I've turned into a right pussy tonight with Red, but I feel really comfortable with her. I've never felt comfortable in anyone's company before. I would even like to stay and I have never wanted to stay with anyone. I really enjoyed being with Red tonight. It's made me feel normal for the first time in my fucking life. I never thought I would have any felings like these until her. What has she done to me.

I think I need to leave now. I have plans to make. Being here tonight with Red has been so good that I haven't thought of the bitch once. Now, just like that, she's back in my fucking head. God, I need her gone for good. Then maybe, once my head has cleared, I can concentrate on spending some time with Red. I've never wanted to spend time with someone because I can—only because I needed to before.

"I think I better get going now, Red. Is that okay with you? I've had a great time with you tonight, baby."

"Oh, yeah, sure, John. I had a great time too."

"I will see you again soon, okay?" I put a piece of wild red hair behind her ear and stroke down the side of her cheek. I lean down to pick up my shirt. She comes towards me and starts doing the buttons up. I stroke her arms and kiss her forehead. She looks up at me, and I bend to kiss her lips. They're all swollen from earlier, and she looks sad.

"Is this it then, John, are you just saying you will see me again because you will come into the café or because you want to see ME again?"

"I want to see YOU again, Red, but I'm not making any promises. My life at the moment is a little complicated, and I wasn't looking for any kind of relationship. Can we see what happens and where this goes without making any promises?"

She hangs her head. I lift her chin up to look at me. "Red, please don't think I just used you. I just have shit in my life to sort out, and it would be unfair to make you any promises right now. I really hope we can see each other again. You have no idea how good you made me feel tonight, and for that, I thank you." I kiss her again. I grab my suit jacket, put my shoes on, and leave her standing there. I feel like a complete wanker.

The last few hours have been bliss because I just got lost in her and didn't have to think of anything else. Now I think I want to explore this thing with Red. Can I do that with someone? Have a life with them knowing what my past is like? I don't know, she's making me question everything I thought about women. Maybe there are some good ones out there, and I've just been in the wrong places to see it.

I head back to my place and the closer I get, the more despair I feel, and the bitch starts entering my head again.

Once I get back, I quickly change. I'm still on a high from Red so I do a workout. I haven't checked my computer for a day or two, and I don't even know if the bitch has sent me a message or not. I've been so consumed with following her and so angry at her for sleeping around when she was arranging a date with me. The fucking whore has to die. I need her out of my life. She's consuming me, making me remember everything my parents did to me. I'm living in a hell, which is why being with Red was so refreshing. She wasn't a whore.

I'm smiling as I fire up my computer, but my smile soon drops when I see I have a message from the bitch.

> Lewis,
> I'm sorry about this weekend, but I would love to still meet up with you. Is next Saturday okay for you? Shall we meet at The Dog and Partridge on Winster Lane? It's a lovely little country pub. Let's say at 7.30 p.m.
> Let me know if this is okay for you. I look forward to hearing from you.
> Katherine.

Fuck her! I reply.

Katherine,

Yes. This Saturday is fine for me and the time and place are not a problem. Look forward to finally meeting you.

I do hope your family are all well. I hope your niece is over her ordeal. What a shame, the poor little thing.

See you Saturday

Lewis

Why is she changing the place to meet? This strikes me as strange. Maybe she's trying to keep it casual because she is screwing someone else. I need to find out who it is she's screwing. I search her profile on Facebook, and on the dating site. The dating site shows me who is following her, but looking through them, I can't see anyone that resembles the tall guy she was with. There's nothing on Facebook either. She's not active there at all really. Shit, why the change? What does it matter? I'm not waiting till Saturday anyway. Tomorrow is the day for me.

Katherine

I WAKE UP IN THE MORNING, and the first thing I do is check my phone to see if there is anything from Lewis. My heart beats fast when I see I have a missed call from him. The call was at 10.45 p.m. last night, just after I fell asleep, typical. Strange he hasn't left me a message though. If I couldn't get hold of him, I would either leave a message or send a text, but there is no text either.

No message and no text tells me he has to speak to me in person, which can only mean one thing, he doesn't want to see me again. My heart sinks thinking about that and about how good we were the other night. Is he really just another typical arsehole stringing me along?

What am I going to do about FL now?

Has FL replied? If he hasn't, then I won't go on Saturday and that will be that.

It's not even 6.30 a.m. yet, and I need a coffee. My head is banging from all this already. It's Wednesday. I have a lot to do today. I can't be worrying about real Lewis or fake Lewis.

In the kitchen, I fire up my laptop while waiting for my toast and coffee, and my heart sinks as I see there's a message from FL. Please be cancelling. Please be cancelling.

Oh no! He can't wait to meet me on Saturday. I'll message him back later tonight when I'm home and tell him I've changed my mind and don't want to meet him. I can't go through with it, not now, not ever, not after the real Lewis was using his lovely tongue on me the other night.

There's a message from Alf, and he's scheduled to start the project when we are ready.

I fire back a message and tell him we need to set up a meeting for Friday this week if he's available at 4 p.m. I send Dave and Tom the same message. I need to get started on the warehouse project sooner rather than later as time is money in this game, and I need the distraction.

I head out to work. I know I have a meeting this morning with someone looking for an apartment, then I have a conference call with that odd couple again.

I'm missing Clive, and Chrissie is going to be off for a while. I'm glad Clive will be back on Friday. I could do with someone to talk to about Lewis. I can't stop thinking about him and how I fell for his bullshit. I really thought he meant what he said. He was so genuine. Why do I choose the pricks? I fucking fell in love with him in less than a week for crying out loud. I feel betrayed, heartbroken and angry all at the same time.

The morning flies by. I keep checking my phone just in case Lewis does call or message, but I don't know why I'm bothering, only to be told it was fun, but no thanks.

I get a call from a guy called Mr Flynn—a property owner. He's heard about me and has some buildings on the market he thinks I might be interested in. I haven't heard of him, but he says I was recommended to him by an estate agent that I had used before.

They sound perfect and right near my warehouse project. I jot down the details he gives me and arrange to meet him there at 3.30 p.m.

I put all the details in my planner on my computer and phone. Where's Clive when I need him? He would be so proud of me.

Still nothing from Lewis. I'm not going to look again. I'm not interested now. Okay, that's a lie, of course I am, and I keep looking. I'm terrified of what he's going to say.

I decide to leave the office at about 2.15 p.m. to give me chance to pick up a coffee on the way to the tube station. If I get there early, it also gives me a chance to take a quick look around. I decide to change into my flat boots and also have my thick long duffle coat—much better for visiting old buildings than heels. I grab my Luis Vuitton scarf, hat and gloves.

Once off the train, I head to the meeting—the farther I walk, the worse the buildings and the area get. I think these buildings are too far gone for me to be able to make them into anything. They are derelict and in my opinion, should be knocked down. I turn a corner and head for the building on 67 Horseferry Road, which is the farthest building from the road. I start to walk around the building and to be honest, I'm a bit scared. This is the type of place the homeless, druggies, or gangs would hang around. It's not near any sort of life, there are no street lights, and it's getting darker. In fact, I think I need to leave. I feel really uncomfortable here, and I have a bad feeling in my gut.

As I move away, I see a door open on the side of the building that's nearest the water's edge. I stop and listen to see if I can hear anything inside. It's deathly quiet. I peek in, very wary. The place is a mess. I slowly edge farther into the building. There is just dirt, broken glass, oil drums, rubbish and debris all over. There is graffiti on the walls, and the beams and floorboards are hanging down from the floors above, you can see the holes and right up to the upper floors.

Some pigeons scare the crap out of me as they take flight. "Fuck!" I shout out loud, then smack my hand over my mouth. I check the time. Its 3.25 p.m. I hope this Mr Flynn turns up soon, then I can get out of here. I don't like this place. I feel like I'm being watched. I turn around to leave, finally too creeped out to stay, and I startle as I see a figure standing at the end of the room I'm in, by the doorway. I didn't realise I had walked in so far. The way he is standing, watching me, with his hands in his pockets, sends shivers down my spine. He's very tall and well-built from what I can make out.

"Hello, there, are you Mr Flynn?" I shout across to him. I scan the room and realise he's standing in front of the only exit from the building. Shit, fuck, what if it's not him and it's some psycho? He doesn't move, except I see a slight nod of his head.

"You must be Miss Porter?"

Thank god for that. He is who I'm meeting. I start to walk in his direction to meet him properly and shake his hand. The hairs on the back of my neck are standing up, and I have a really uneasy feeling. The closer I get to him, though the more familiar he looks to me. It's very dark in here, the light outside is dimming, and it's turning to dusk. I should have arranged this meeting for the morning, knowing there wasn't much daylight left, but I wasn't thinking straight.

Damn, Lewis, he's got me all in a twist.

As I get nearer, I see he's in jeans. He has a dark bomber jacket on and a baseball cap that is pulled low over his face, and he still has his hands in his pockets. I'm shitting myself, and I'm still thinking about Lewis!

"Well, Mr Flynn, I have been looking around, and I have to say, this building is probably best just being pulled down, and you selling the land for development, which to be honest isn't really my thing. I like to renovate old buildings if I can, and not build new. I feel I may have wasted your time. I'm sorry about that, but thank you for thinking of me." He doesn't speak. He just stares at the ground as I get closer. He's a bit weird. He hasn't even looked at me. I can see the closer I get that he looks really tense. Just before I reach him, he says, "Stop where you are!" His tone terrifies me. His voice is so deep and very hostile.

"Excuse me?"

"What didn't you fucking understand about, Stop. Where. You. Are. Bitch?" I was flabbergasted. Shocked. Did I hear him right?

I stop, frozen. "I'm sorry, Mr Flynn, but I think I should leave."

"Oh no, Katherine, you little whore. You're not going anywhere." I stand rooted to the spot, shocked at what I'm hearing. Who is this guy? Why is he calling me a whore and how does he know my name. I start to take a couple of steps backwards.

"I said stop where you fucking are. Do you not understand what I'm saying to you? I thought you were a smart woman, but obviously, I was wrong. STOP. FUCKING. MOVING!" he shouts so loud at me that I do as he asks, but I jump when some pigeons take flight from his screaming. Fuck. I don't know what to do. He's blocking the only way out of this room. There are broken windows, but they are too high up.

He moves his hands from his pocket. I can make out he has gloves on, and he also has something gripped in one hand, but I can't see what it is. He slowly raises his head slightly to look at me, but I still can't make out his features properly in this light. From his stance and his stature, he really looks familiar, and I'm trying to wrack my brain as to where from.

"Cat got your tongue now, whore? Do you have any idea who I am?" I just stare at him, not speaking. I don't know what to say. I don't know who he is. Suddenly, he starts to move closer to me. I can see some more of his face. I must look startled, my eyes wide and my mouth open. Oh my god, it's Lewis, but it's not Lewis. I'm confused. Is it him? How and why is he here and being like this? No, it's not my Lewis, but it could be. It's his face, that's for sure. Is it him? Shit my mind's playing tricks on me. Could Lewis have a split personality? It is him. It's Lewis. Same features, build, everything. But it isn't, how can it be? Surely I would know. Would I? I mean I barely know him, but somehow i just know it's not my Lewis.

My Lewis—that's a joke.

"I've seen you before," I say trying to think where. I'm staring at him.

"Answer me, whore. Do. You. Know. Who. I. Am?" he says, emphasising each word.

"No, no I can't place you, but I have seen you before. I know I have. Why do you keep calling me a whore? What have I done to you?" He steps right up to me and grabs my cheeks with one hand, squeezing my face hard. He's hurting me. It feels like he's going to snap my jaw with the strength and the grip he has on me. I'm staring into cold dark eyes. His face is just like Lewis's, but the lines are much harder and his eyes darker. I can't make out the colour in this light. He's also broader in the shoulders than Lewis, but his height is the same. I'm so confused. He must see the quizzical look on my face.

"You've been talking to me for weeks, you whore. Stringing me along all this time while fucking other men. Why would you do that?

You're all the same—dirty fucking whores. Fucking anything that pays you attention. You're the fucking double of my filthy whore of a mother. That's why you need to disappear." He shoves me backwards by my face, but I'm just thankful his hands are off me.

He looks down for a bit before looking me straight in the eye, and it suddenly hits me.

"You were the guy in the deli last week, and the guy watching me yesterday. I've seen you around a few times the last couple of weeks. What do you mean I've been talking to you for weeks, stringing you along?"

"Yes, that was me. I've been following you and keeping my eye on you. I saw you with that other guy the other day. You're a filthy whore. Why would you do that when you were arranging to meet me? Why would you screw other men?"

"Wait, what do you mean arranging to meet you? I don't even know you." He hits out with his hand, backhanding my face hard. It stings badly, and my eyes start to stream.

"We were supposed to meet last Saturday, you stupid fucking bitch, but you cancelled on me with some stupid family excuse. Was that all bullshit so you could screw someone else?" I open my mouth in a gasp. This is fake Lewis. How can this be? I put my hand over my mouth in horror. "You're fake Lewis?"

"Who the fuck is fake Lewis?"

"You, you're from the dating site. You used Lewis Clancy's pictures as your own. I realised when I met him for real. But you could be his twin—the resemblance is unmistakable."

"You stupid bitch, I picked that picture because he looked like me, so I used him. How was I to know you knew the real guy? Was that him coming out of your place the other morning, you whore?" He gets right up in my face, spitting with anger like all this is my fault—whatever this is—I have no idea. My cheek is still stinging from the slap and the grip he had on me before that. I'm terrified. He looks demonic as he stares at me until something flashes fleetingly across his face—something like regret, but I'm not sure.

He turns away from me and takes his baseball cap off his head. I can see his hair is tied in a bun. Seeing him without the cap, I can tell it isn't Lewis, but my god, they are the spitting image of each other. How can that be? Lewis doesn't have any brothers that I know of? Maybe he has a cousin? Maybe he lied to me. Maybe this is him. Fuck, I'm so confused.

He has his back to me and is running his hand back and forth over his hair. He hangs his head, and it looks like he has it in both of his hands. He's shaking his head, then grabbing at his hair, muttering to himself, but I can't make out what he's saying. I need to find a way to get out of here, but if I try to get past him, he will just grab me. I look around, seeing if there is any way I can make a run for a window, but they are all too high. Shit, I'm screwed. I don't know what he is going to do to me. He's so angry. He's been stalking me for god knows how long, and he thinks I'm a whore and I remind him of his mother.

He suddenly turns around and stalks towards me. Oh, shit I don't like the look on his face. He tears my hat from my head taking some of my hair with it. I cry out in pain. "Don't make a fucking noise, whore." He snatches my hair and starts to pull me to the corner of the room. I grab his wrists, trying to get him off me, but he just drags me, nearly yanking my hair out. I can't grip him properly because I still have my gloves on, but I'm no match for his strength, even if I can get loose. When we get to the corner, there's a chair I hadn't noticed before and next to it is an oil drum. He pushes me down onto the chair, grabs my neck and starts squeezing tightly. I'm fighting for breath. This is it, he is going to kill me. I feel dizzy from the lack of oxygen, and think I'm going to pass out. He grabs some rope from the top of the oil drum and ties my hands together behind my back and then to the chair. Then he ropes my legs together and to the legs of the chair. I can't move. I need to pee, but I doubt he will let me use a bathroom, even if there was one in here. I try to squeeze my thighs together, but it's difficult.

"What you trying to do there, whore? Are you getting off on this? Is this turning you on? You like a bit of rough, do you? Is that why you're trying to press your thighs together? Fucking unreal, you dirty whore."

"NO, you stupid fuck. I need to pee."

Whack. He slaps me again.

"Don't you dare call me stupid, you fucking whore." My eyes are streaming again.

"Don't cry, bitch."

"What have I done to you? Why are you doing this to me? I don't even fucking know you. Let me go, you fucking arsehole."

Whack.

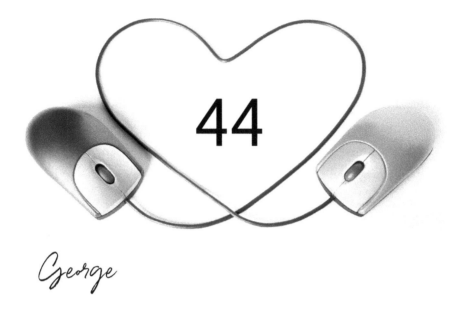

44

George

FUCK, FUCK, FUCK! WHAT have I done?

I fucking punched her in the face. She was questioning me. It was all too much, and I saw the red mist again, but it disappeared fast. Fuck, I may have snapped her neck the way her head went back. I bring her face forward and watch to make sure she's breathing. I want to make her suffer first, don't I? Why am I questioning myself now? What I felt with Red last night made me really happy. I want to feel that again. If I fuck up here and get caught, that will be the end of me. I will be put away, and never see Red again. I don't want that. Fuck, why did I go back to Red's last night? If I hadn't, I wouldn't be questioning what I'm doing. This is what I've wanted for so long. To get this bitch and get rid of her. But seeing this bitch close up like this, I realise she isn't my mother.

Why have I never seen it clearly like this with the others? When I killed them, it was during the red mist, but it never cleared until after

I'd done it. This one is the closest looking to my mother, which is why I started all this to get rid of her, but in herself, she is nothing like her. I've fucked up again like I always do. My fucking mother and father have ruined my life. It's one big fuck up.

Am I being a pussy? I do need to get rid of this bitch before she does what my mother did to me. I'm so confused. I don't know what I want any more. I have always wanted this. I have always been filled with so much repulsion and hatred. Now, after Red, I'm questioning everything. I never like any women but Red is different, and I want to get to know her. Maybe not all women are the same? Maybe my time with Red last night showed me they are not all the same. Red stirred up feelings in me I have never felt before. I think I need to let this bitch go or at least not kill her for now. I wanted her to pay. All this time I wanted her to pay. Now I have her, I feel regret. Regret for all the others I killed before—except my fucking parents. I will never regret them. I feel like I'm going out of my mind. So fucking confused right now.

She knows that guy—the one who's pictures and name I used because he looked like me.

She said that's who she was with the other night. He's the guy she's been seeing. Did she think he was me? It's all fucked up. It's making my head hurt. No, she said I was 'fake Lewis', so she knew I wasn't real. That's why she changed the meeting place on Saturday. Was she setting a trap?

I pace, holding my head, trying to talk this all through in my head, but it's so confusing. Do I want to kill her and get rid of her now that I KNOW she isn't my mother? There is no red mist now. When I think of red mist, I automatically think of Red, and how sweet she is. Fuck, I'm fucked. Does that mean there will be no red mist anymore as long as Red is in my life? I can't cope with this. I don't know what to do.

She starts to moan, which means she's coming around. Shit, what do I do? If I let her go, she will report me, and I'm sure the police will be able to trace the dating site back to me. It's too late. I will have to get rid of her. It's her or me. I want to see Red again. Fuck, I really do. I'm going to have to finish this whore like I've wanted to for weeks and take my chance. I have this oil drum to hide her body in. I can leave it here and hope no one finds the body for a long time, and I can move away somewhere safe and take Red with me.

"What happened. Where am I?"

Shit, she's coming to. I take her scarf from around her neck, and I put it over her eyes and tie it tight so she can't see me. Then I move quickly to the end of the room to watch her.

"Why is my head throbbing? I can't see what's going on? Ouch, my head. Please, is there anyone there. Please, why can't I see? Let me go!"

I start to pace back and forth at the end of the room frantically rubbing my face in my hands. She can hear me, but she doesn't seem to remember. Maybe that's a good thing. I need to think what to do. There's no choice is there really?

My only options: I can leave hoping she doesn't remember anything, or I finish her and take my chances.

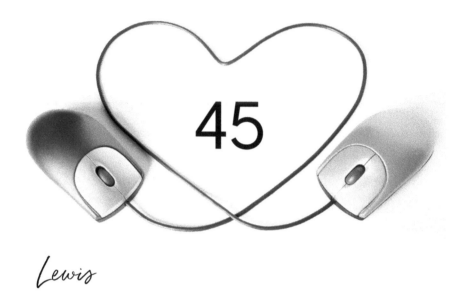

Lewis

I WISH THIS DAY WOULD END. IT'S BEEN a long ass day, and I can barely concentrate, which is making it even longer because we have to keep re-doing the takes. It's all on me. My head is elsewhere—thinking about Kate. Wondering what she must be thinking. I have been here since 6.30 a.m. on location at the Palazzo. I have barely had time to take a piss, and when I have, I didn't have my phone on me because Luce had it like she usually does on set. I really want to check to see if Kate has messaged me—she must have seen my missed call when she woke up. I hope she's messaged me back.

It's 10.30 p.m. by the time the director calls, "it's a wrap." I should be excited at that, but I'm not. I just need to speak to Kate. I rush to find Luce to get my phone from her, but the lady from wardrobe tells me Luce left at 9 p.m. and went back to the hotel. Shit, what did I do to deserve this? I get changed as fast as I can and head out to find the car to take me back to the hotel. When I get out front, I see the car along with three of the models that were on the shoot with me, and the paparazzi also there, waiting. Shit.

I run to the car, skidding round people to avoid bumping into them. I yank the door open and tell the driver to hurry back to the hotel. The door opens again, and the three models get inside with me. Shit, this is all I need. I try not to be rude when I ask what they are doing?

"Coming back to the hotel with you, Lewis. Wrap party with you, in your suite..." the first model says suggestively. She runs her nails along my thigh, getting higher. I slam my hand on top of hers to stop her going any further. I can't remember any of their names. I've stayed away from them all day. I didn't want to be snapped with them and for it to be all over the tabloids back home, but fat chance of that not happening now. Great, more explaining to do.

"I'm sorry, ladies, but I'm not having a party in my suite. In fact, I'm going to pack up my shit and get on the first flight I can, to get back to see my girl, who I've missed so much. So, if you don't mind, I will get out at my hotel, and the car can take you back to your hotel."

"But, Lewis, we heard you always like to party after your shoots. We were hoping you would like to party with all three of us. We've heard you can handle that." They all start to giggle, and she goes back to stroking my thigh.

"Look, ladies, I don't want to be rude, but I don't care what you heard, I'm not interested. I have a girlfriend, who I'm in fucking love with, and I will not do anything to jeopardise my relationship with her. So, please spread it around that Lewis Clancy is well and truly fucking spoken for." I glare at all three in turn. They are all beautiful and if I hadn't have met Kate, then no doubt I would party with them, but not now. No way. I love Kate and would never mess that up—unless I already have, of course.

My flight isn't until tomorrow, but I'll try and be on the first flight I can get out of here tonight, no matter how much it costs me. If I can't speak to her on the phone, then I will see her in person.

As soon as the car pulls into the hotel drop off area, I'm out of it fast and running to get to my suite. I can't wait for the lift, so I go for the stairs—all seventeen flights. I storm into my room, luckily the door is open, as Luce is there packing for me. My phone is on the table. I grab it to check it. NO Fucking messages. What the fuck. She really is pissed at me.

"I've nearly finished your packing. I figured you wanted to leave as soon as you could, so I re-arranged the flight, and you have a car coming for you in thirty minutes to get you to the airport."

"God, I could kiss you, woman. Thank you. You're forgiven for taking my phone and not leaving it for me." I smile at her as I rush into the bedroom to get changed. I phone Kate as I go. It rings out, no answer and goes to voicemail. I don't care if she's in bed, so I ring again and still no answer. Fuck. I will just have to go and see her.

We're in the car on the way to the airport. Luckily, as it's a private jet, we are straight onboard. I try her phone again but nothing. She must be able to see I'm phoning. The phone is not turned off because it rings for a bit. Shit, why won't she answer? I shoot a quick text.

Lewis – Hey, beautiful, will you please pick up your phone and speak to me? I really need to talk to you urgently. Xx

We are about to take off, so I try her again, and it rings—just as I'm about to give up thinking it's going to voicemail, she answers the phone.

"Kate, oh, thank fuck for that. You've had me so worried, sweetheart." No answer.

"Kate, beautiful, answer me, please. I'm so sorry." I'm straining to hear, but with the noise of the jet, it's difficult. I swear I hear whimpering and muffled sound, but can't make out if anything is being said. I look at the phone to make sure I'm still connected and can see we are.

"Kate, Kate are you there? Please answer me?" I can still only just make out faint noise. It sounds like moaning to me. I look at the phone again. Am I hearing what I think I'm hearing? Holy fuck, is she in bed with someone else and has knocked the phone on, on purpose, so I can hear her?

"Oh god, Oh god!"

Well shit. I definitely heard that all right. She's fucking someone.

Would she do that? No, Kate isn't that kind of person, is she?

"FUCK!" I hear her shout and there is no doubting that word. She obviously is that kind of person. I had her pegged all wrong.

How could I have got it so wrong?

I don't really know her though, do I?

No, she wouldn't. I think I know her well enough in the short time I have known her, but I'm questioning myself now. I'm so fucking confused, and my head is all over the place.

I think I want to throw up. I got it all wrong. She played me. She somehow bewitched me and made me feel sorry for her with the stories of her past boyfriends. It must have all been bullshit. Telling me she doesn't trust. Yet she trusted me, how convenient. I bet she does this to all the guys she meets on that dating site. Is that site even real? Did she make up all the catfish stuff? I mean what are the chances, right? Everything is so mixed up in my head, trying to make sense of it all. I can't listen to this muffled noise of her fucking someone else. I need to just tell her to go to hell and hang up and try and forget about her. Go back to screwing the VS models instead, but then I hear her voice very faintly, "Fake Lewis." And then the line goes dead.

What the hell?

46

Katherine

I'M IN SO MUCH PAIN.

My face and head are killing me.

Everything is fuzzy.

What happened. Where am I?

I can't see a thing.

I can feel my phone vibrating in my back pocket, but I can't move my hands. Fuck, I'm tied up.

Who has tied me up?

I wriggle in my seat, trying to pull on my hands to loosen the ties, but they are bound tight. I can't move, which means they are also tied to something. My phone stops vibrating. Whoever tried phoning must have hung up.

What was that?

I heard a noise?

Someone must be there.

It sounded far away though.

"Hello, who's there?"

No one speaks. I moan as I move my head. It hurts so badly. Oh god, I feel like it's going to explode. Shit, why can't I remember what happened?

"Owww, Oh god," I moan again. I try to move my legs, but they won't move either. They're tied up tight, and hurting.

"Oh god. Oh god," I cry out. Panic is setting in. I start to hyperventilate, breathing so hard that my chest hurts along with everything else. I'm trying to remember where I was and what I was doing.

"FUCK!" I shout. Why can't I remember? There is something about FL in the back of my mind, but I don't know what it is.

"Fake Lewis…" I mumble out loud to see if it rings any bells, but it doesn't. I start wriggling again, trying to loosen my hands and legs by moving my bum around on the chair I'm obviously sitting on. I scream out loud, and I hear a shuffling sound again.

"Hello, please help me. What happened, where am I? Owww, please. It hurts."

Still nothing and the movement I thought I heard has stopped.

I'm in so much pain. Moving my mouth to speak is making it worse. It feels like all one side of my face is swelling up and it's making it hard to move my mouth and jaw. I feel like someone has hit me in the side of the head and my cheek with a hammer. Oh god, what if they have? What have they done to me?

"Pwese 'elp me." I can't speak properly now. I start to shiver. I'm not sure if it's because it's freezing here or I'm in shock, probably a bit of both. I feel so tired. I just want to sleep. I must try to stay awake though. I'm straining to hear anything because I have a buzzing in my head and ear. My eyes are so heavy. I need to sleep. Maybe if I just close my eyes and sleep this will all be a nightmare, and I will wake up from it soon. So, so, tired.

47

George

She's passed out again. Thank fuck for that. It gives me a bit of breathing space.

She was disoriented and couldn't remember what had happened. If she wakes up again and still can't remember, I'll leave her here. She'd better pray someone finds her. If she does remember, then fuck it, I will just have to finish her as I intended.

I don't want to though. I want all that shit to stop now. I know I'm fucked up, and what I have done is fucked up, but Red has made me realise there is more out there. I don't have to do this anymore. If I can get out of this shit today without killing her, I know it's a sign—a sign that I need to stop and see where it goes with Red.

Will I tell Red about my past? I don't know. I have to learn to trust before any of that, maybe in time, I can tell her. Not about the killings, fuck no, never that, but about how I grew up?

I also need to do some research on Lewis because I've been told before that we could be brothers, this bitch even said his twin! It's why I used his name and pictures to draw in the whores?

Fuck, what does that mean?

Are we related in some way?

How will I find out?

I have no idea how to find out.

This is screwing with my head big time.

"Where am I? Pweas someone, I need help. Is anyone there? Pain, so much pain."

She's started mumbling and stirring awake again, but she can hardly speak. Her mouth looks so swollen. Fuck. I stay as still as I can and take shallow breaths to see if she actually wakes up. She doesn't stir again. She's passed out once more.

I THINK BACK TO my early years, but I don't seem to be able to remember anything from before my new life day. That seems to be the first memory I have. It's like it just happened and from then my life was hell. It was the only time I had a cake. My parents sang 'happy new life day' to me. It was the only time they ever sang to me. I sang that song to myself for years and years. I still sing it to myself now.

Happy New Life Day to you,

Happy New Life Day to you,

Happy New Life Day, dear Georgie Porgy

Happy New Life Day to you.

Happy New Life Day to us

Happy New Life Day to us

Happy times we will have

Happy New Life Day to us us us us.

Now I know why; they were going to have a lot of fun. I was only there for their enjoyment. Were they my real parents? I've thought about that a lot, but have no idea how to find out. That fucking song makes sense if I think about it. It's like they were celebrating, saying I had a new life, and so did they. Fucking hell, could they have stolen me from somewhere or bought me, or someone gave me to them? God, my head is a mess.

I need to get out of here.

I need to think.

I need to find out the truth.

I sit down on the floor with my back against the wall and think about what I need to do.

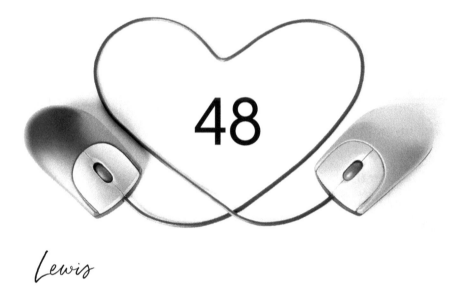

48

Lewis

Fuck! She mumbled 'fake Lewis' before the line went dead? What did that even mean?

Was she with fake Lewis, fucking him, was that it?

No! I don't believe that for one minute.

Then why the fuck am I thinking that? I'm tugging on my hair. Shit, this is so fucked up. What do I do?

Do I say screw it and screw her. Let her come to me? Or do I go to her place when I land? She's burrowed so deep into my heart in a week that I'm scared shitless of losing her already.

"Lewis, what's wrong love?" Luce asks, sitting down in the seat opposite me.

"Luce, I have no idea. I don't know what to do or even think."

"What do you mean? What's happened? Have you got hold of Kate?" I just look at her, vacant.

"Lewis you're scaring me, what's wrong?"

I explain to Luce all about the muffled noises on Kate's phone and tell her everything about Kate being catfished and fake Lewis. The more I talk it out, the more I get scared, and I can see the concern on Lucinda's face too.

Fuck what if something has happened?

What if he is there with her?

"Shit, we need this jet in the air now. I need to get back home now, Luce. I need to go to her place."

"Oh god, Lewis, should we call the police?"

"How can I call the police? What do I say to them, Luce? Can you go to my girlfriend's apartment and see if she's fucking someone? I don't know who else to call. Her PA, Clive is away until Friday, and she doesn't have anyone else except her brother, but he lives far away."

Just then the pilot comes on and tells us to buckle up as we are ready to take off.

I'm so frustrated not knowing what's going on and all my mixed up thoughts running through my head.

Luce leans forward and grabs my hand and squeezes it.

I put my head in my hands, and I actually cry. "As soon as we land, Luce, I'm going straight to Kate's place. Hopefully, Harry will be on the door tonight, and I'll make him go up to her apartment with me to see what's going on."

"That's a good idea, Lewis. The car will be waiting for us when we land. Don't worry about the luggage, I will get that all sent to your hotel, and I'll come with you to Kate's."

"Thank you. I don't know what I would do without you."

I can't relax all through the flight—it's the longest two hours of my life. Once we land and the stairs are lowered, I practically jump them, landing on the tarmac of the hangar, and running to the car. Luce isn't far behind, probably knowing how agitated I am with every minute that passes. I give the driver the address and ask him to get there as quickly as he can, but it's at least half an hour's drive.

I pull my phone out and dial Kate's number. I wait, not breathing, but she doesn't answer. It goes to voicemail.

"FUCK!" I shout and dial again. This time, when it goes to voicemail I leave a message, "Kate, baby, pick up the fucking phone now. Please? I'm going out of my mind with worry. Please ring me back. Just let me know you are at least safe. If I know that, then I will leave you alone if that's what you want." I hang up, and I wait with the phone in my hand and my legs jumping. Luce grabs my hand and holds it, giving it a squeeze every now and then. There isn't much either of us can say. I try Kate again—voicemail.

"Kate, for fuck's sake, please, please just let me know you're safe. Please, baby. I love you so fucking much. I'm going out of my mind with worry." Still nothing.

We finally approach Kate's apartment building, and I'm out of the car before it even stops. I hear Luce asking the driver to wait for us just as I'm entering the building.

"Harry, have you seen Kate at all tonight?" He jumps back at my voice and directness.

"No, son, come to think of it, I haven't seen her at all since last night, which is most unusual during the week. I haven't left the desk at all."

"Harry, look. I know it's not usual, but you need to get me into her apartment now. I think something's wrong. It's an emergency." He looks at me in surprise.

"I can't do that, son. I'm sorry. Let me try her apartment phone."

"Fuck!" I grab my hair and pace while he tries her phone. I call the elevator to save time. The phone is ringing and ringing, I can see by the look on his face. The elevator pings and I head for it as it opens.

"You can either come up with me now and open her door, or I'll go on my own and break the fucking door down," I tell him. He races around the counter and gets in the lift at the same time as Luce, eyeing me warily.

"Look, Harry. I know you don't know me well, but that's my girl. I love her, and if anything's happened to her, I will never forgive myself. I need to see if she is in her apartment and if she's okay. I've been trying to get hold of her all day. The phone connected earlier, but I was in Venice, and there were strange noises that I couldn't make out. I just pray she is safe." I hang my head down.

"Look, it's okay, son. I have the master key card here. I will open her door, and call to her before anyone goes in, do you understand?" I just nod because there is no way in hell I'm not going into that apartment as soon as he opens the door. Fuck, this lift is slow.

"Come on, come on, for fuck's sake."

Finally, it arrives on the top floor. I'm out of the doors before they are fully open, and banging hard on her door with my fist. I can't hear anything inside. Harry has the key out and opens the door

"Ms Porter. Hello, are you home? Kate, love, are you in?" Nothing.

I barge past him and run into the apartment. She isn't in the living area or the kitchen. I run to the bedroom, nothing, nor in her bathroom.

"Shit, she isn't here." I stand in the living area, gawping at the window, running my hand through my hair.

"Where is she?" I try her number again, but again it goes to voicemail.

"Baby, please text or phone and let me know where you are. I'm in your apartment with Harry. I need to know you're safe. Please, baby, I love you so fucking much. Please let me know you're safe." I hang up and drop to the floor where I stand. I sit there, on my knees, leaning back on my feet with my head hung and the phone in my hand.

"Come on, Lewis, get up, love. Sit on the couch, and let's think where she could be. Do you think she will be at her office?"

"Fuck, why didn't I think of that?" I pull up her office number and ring it. It keeps going to answer machine, so I keep trying, then leave a message to phone me urgently.

"Lewis do you know her PA's phone number? I know you said he was away but maybe he can shed some light on where she is."

"I don't have his number unless Kate has it in her home office."

I head to her office. I can't see her laptop so she must have that with her. I find an address book in her top drawer of the desk. I go to C because I don't know Clive's surname. Nothing there. I will have to search through it now to see if I can see a Clive, and there it is: Zane & Clive. I hope this is her Clive. I phone the mobile number, and it rings and rings. Fuck. He maybe won't pick up if he doesn't know the number. I hang up and try again. I know if I ignore a call and the phone keeps going, I answer. Finally, a voice, "Hello who is this?"

"Hi, is that Clive?"

"Who wants to know?"

"It's Lewis Clancy. Kate's boyfriend."

"Lewis! What's wrong?" He's panicky, so I know I have the right Clive.

"I don't know, Clive, which is why I'm trying to reach you. Have you heard from Kate at all tonight?"

"No, I haven't, what's going on, Lewis. Where is she?"

"I'm trying to find out. I can't reach her. I'm at her apartment and she's not here, or answering her office phone. I have left a lot of messages on her phone, so even if she was in Chelmsford she would know I have been calling her."

"Hang on. Let me check…" I can hear him booting up his laptop.

"Hold on, she actually used the fucking planner for once in her life. She had an appointment at 67 Horseferry Road at 3.30 p.m. this afternoon to meet a Mr Flynn about possible new buildings to renovate."

"Fuck, I hope nothing has happened, surely she can't still be there at this hour in the morning? Something's not right. I need to go, Clive. I have your number on my phone. If I find her, I will let you know." I hang up on him needing to check it out. I have a bad feeling in my gut.

I run out of the apartment shouting to Luce to call the police and have them go to 67 Horseferry Road to report a missing woman in danger. It's a long shot she's there, but I can't take any chances.

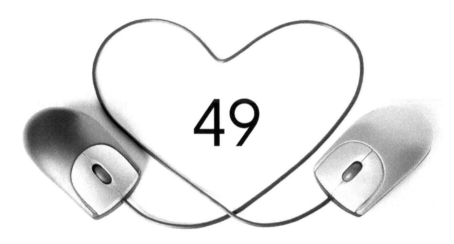

49

Kate

I FEEL SICK AND SO TIRED.
I feel like I've been hit with a truck.

Is that what's happened?

Am I in a hospital or something?

Am I even alive?

My head is throbbing, my face feels swollen. I can't see, and I can't move. It's freezing, so I can't be in a hospital. My lips are cracked and sting as I try to lick them, and my mouth is dry. I can't hear a sound.

How long have I been passed out? It feels like hours.

Was that a shuffle again?

"Hello, is someone there? Please say something, please help me." Nothing, no noise.

Where the fuck am I?

Who has done this to me? I don't remember anything. I'm crying, and it's hurting my head.

"I don't no what you want with me, whoever you are, please just let me go."

I'm sobbing now, but my throat and mouth are so dry that I want to stop crying, it's making my head worse. My arms and legs are numb.

I just want to sleep again.

I'm so tired and weary.

I just need to sleep.

50

George

SHE JUST WOKE AGAIN BRIEFLY AND still doesn't remember. Thank fuck for that. She heard me move and knew someone was here, but she didn't know who. The bitch was pleading to be let go. Now she's passed out again. Do I take my chance and leave her here and hope she doesn't ever remember? Even if she does, she doesn't know my name, and I can get rid of my computer. I'll just throw it in The Thames. No one will be able to trace me then.

I start pacing again, rubbing my head and face. Yes, I'll leave her here. If someone finds her, then she will be fine. If they don't, she may die anyway from hyperthermia, but that's not on me then. I won't have actually killed her myself. All I did was hit her and tie her up.

Yes, I can leave now, get rid of any evidence, then head to Red's. See if I can stay with her for a little while, persuade her to move away with me. Not abroad, I don't exist, so can't get a passport, but maybe we could move to Manchester? Somewhere away from here.

I head out of the room as quiet as I can. I don't want her to come around again. I move through the next room, heading for the exit door that is open when I see lights reflecting on the wall. They're moving, but the windows are high up, and I can't see outside. They are car headlights—I can hear the tyres on the gravel outside. The car seems to be moving very slowly. I run towards a window, dragging a box I can stand on. I can just about see out. Fuck, there is a car coming to a stop. I think it's near the door I need to go out of. Who the fuck is it at this time of night? I doubt they have security around these run-down buildings.

I jump down, breathing fast. If I hide, they might find her, and then start to search the place. I need to see who it is. Can I take them out? I'll see how many there are. I head quietly towards the exit, keeping close to the walls and scurrying along in the shadows. I hear a car door close, so I stop and listen. Just one door. Whoever it is, they are on their own. That goes in my favour. I hear footsteps— slow, cautious footsteps. I stay still. I'm not far from the exit. I can see the open doorway from here. If someone comes through that door, they won't be able to see me unless they shine a light straight on me. I crouch low to the ground in the dark shadows. I see a light getting brighter, coming towards the door. They have a torch with them, shit.

A tall figure comes into view, but I can't see who it is. They're holding the light up and shining it around, trying to make out what's inside. The figure steps into the building. If they bypass me and go through to one of the other rooms, I can maybe sneak out through the exit. My heart is pounding in my chest. Fuck, I don't want confrontation. I just want to get out of here.

The figure starts to move forward. I can tell it's a male as he walks past me. He isn't close to me, he's a good 15-feet away, and he hasn't shone the light my way. I don't move. I won't move until he leaves this room, then I will make for the door.

He stops. Shit, has he heard me?

Am I breathing too loud?

He shines the light around the room. I'm crouched so low to the ground that he still doesn't see me when he faces this way. I can't see his face because of the light, but I can make out his build, and he is as tall as me and quite well-built. He starts forward again in the direction of where the bitch is.

"Kate, Kate, are you here, baby? Kate, can you hear me?" Fuck, it's him. It's Lewis. How the fuck did he find her here? Did she tell him she was coming here? He sounds really distressed, panicked even.

He goes through the doorway at the other end. I can still see the light from his torch. I could make a dash for it now and get the fuck out of here, but I'm curious. I want to see him. I want to see if he does look like me. I listen, trying to control my breathing so I can hear. I'm straining. I need to move closer. I head towards the doorway he's gone through. Stupid fuck, why don't I just leave? They will never know then. But curiosity gets the better of me.

I'm at the doorway he went through. I know where she is, and he's gone into the wrong room. There are so many rooms in this building—it could take him a while to find her. I know exactly where he is because of the light. I stay low to the ground, and in the doorway, just peeping so I can see him. He's creeping in and out of the rooms. I decide to go through the doorway while he's in one of the rooms farthest away from me. I get closer to the room the bitch is in. I can't hear anything from that room. I think she must still be out cold.

"Kate, baby, please answer me. Are you in here, Kate? You're scaring me. Please, make a noise if you can hear me. Anything. KATE, KATE!" he shouts loudly, getting more frantic as he does. I hear her murmuring. He doesn't hear her he isn't as close as I am, but I know if he keeps shouting, she'll come around and make a noise.

I start to move towards the room where she is. I'm still hugging the wall, staying in the dark shadows. Just then, he steps out of a room. I freeze, not knowing if he's seen me or not. He isn't moving. I want to turn around and look, to see if he's noticed me. I turn my head very slowly as he points his torch in my direction. He's seen me. Fuck, he must have heard me breathing.

I stand upright slowly and turn my body around to face him. We stare at each other. The torch is low, near his tummy, and I can see his face a little clearer now. He is me. I can see the shape of his eyes, his mouth, his nose. It's like looking in a fucking mirror. He has long hair and has more stubble than I do. He's also wearing glasses. He must be thinking the same things as me, I see his brow crease and the puzzled look on his face. He hasn't said anything, he's just standing, staring at me. He lifts the torch higher, to look at me properly as he edges nearer to me. I can't see his face now because of the torch. He's getting closer though. Shit, what do I do or say?

"Who the fuck are you?" he says as he gets nearer. I don't speak. I need to get out of here.

"I said, who the fuck are you? Where's Kate? What have to you done to her? Why are you here?" He starts to walk a little closer to me. I step back. I don't want him to get a clear view of me. If he does, I will have to kill both of them.

"Who the fuck are you? It can't be a coincidence you being here. Answer me, goddamn it. Who the fuck are you?" He is still edging cautiously closer towards me, and I try to step back, but then I stop. I can see him clearer. Holy fucking shit. He does look just like me. I'm frozen to the spot. He's close to me, and I see the confusion on his face again as he looks at me and tries to register what he is actually seeing. He can see me now as clearly as I can see him.

"You, you look like me. How, how do you look like me? How can that be possible? Why are you here and why the fuck do you look like me? ANSWER ME!" he shouts loudly.

"Hello. Hello, who's there." The bitch speaks, we both hear her at the same time. He lowers the torch, and his head jerks to the room she's in. He looks anguished and confused, but he doesn't hesitate. He runs in the direction of her voice. He can't deal with me because he needs to get to her. I step to the doorway of the room she's in and watch.

"Kate, Kate, baby. Thank fuck. Kate, it's Lewis." He's running towards her.

"Lewish, Lewish help me Lewish." She's trying to shout back to him, but her voice is so croaky and it comes out as a whisper. I watch from the doorway. I watch him as he gets to her and kneels down in front of her.

"Oh thank you, thank you. Baby, you're okay. I've got you now." He is untying the scarf gently and removing it from her head slowly so as not to startle her. He's being so gentle with her, as though she may break. I'm watching this, and I feel a pang of jealousy. I want that. All I ever wanted was someone to love me like that. I hang my head.

Suddenly, I hear another noise, like car tyres again. I have one last look at them in the room then I scurry away again, along the walls of the building in the dark shadows. I can see the car lights moving, so whoever it is this time hasn't reached the building just yet. If I'm quick, I can maybe get out of the exit door before they pull up. I can cut across, but they have to go round.

I make it to the door and slip out, scurrying along the outer wall and keeping low to the ground, just as the car is rounding the corner. I manage to get to the end of the building before the car stops. They won't have seen me as Lewis's car is in the way. There are two cars now, and I can see they are the police, then an ambulance arrives. He must have called for the police on his way here. They all get out of the cars and run into the building. I can hear shouting. I need to leave before they start to search the area.

I slip away as fast and as quiet as I can.

51

Lewis

Who is this guy and why the fuck does he look like me? I'm stunned and rooted to the spot. I don't know if my mind is playing tricks on me because I'm so tired, and terrified, that I'm hallucinating. I just can't comprehend what I'm seeing. He is me. He has the same build, height, and features as me. I can't make out his hair, he has a baseball cap on, which is my usual attire outside, but there is no mistaking he is my double. How is that possible?

I hold the phone up and shine the torch on him to get a better look.

"Who the fuck are you?" He doesn't speak. He just stares my way, but he can't see my face with the torch light shining in his face. He's just staring, quizzically. He tilts his head slightly and squints a bit as if he's trying to put together the similarities between us.

We aren't just similar.

We are each other.

We are the same.

We are identical.

"I said, who the fuck are you? Where is Kate? What have to you done to her?" He doesn't speak.

"Hello. Hello, who's there?" Fuck, it's Kate. I turn and run to where the voice came from. Fuck this guy. I need to get to Kate. I run into the room, holding my torch up. I see her in the far corner on a chair. Fucking hell.

I reassure her that it's me as I untie the scarf from her head and remove it slowly, so she can allow her eyes to adjust. I see her face, and I wince and hold the torch up to her. Her cheek is so swollen that her eye is practically closed shut from the swelling, and her lips are bleeding. She looks a mess, but she still looks beautiful to me.

I see her hands and legs are tied to the chair, so I start to untie them slowly, trying not to cause her any more pain. She winces as I start to free her. I try to massage her shoulders as I bring her arms slowly around her front. She must be in so much pain. Fuck knows how long she's been tied up like this, but it has to have been fucking hours.

"Baby, I'm so sorry I didn't get to you sooner." I'm staring into her face. I think she can see me through one eye.

"Lewish"

"Shhhh, don't try to speak, baby. I need to get you out of here. Can you nod for me?" she nods slightly but winces.

"I'm going to lift you off the chair. Then I'm going to carry you out of here. If I give you my phone can you shine the torch for me so I can see where we are going? Just keep your arm on your body but hold the phone in your hand if you can. I know you're in pain, baby, but I'm here now. I've got you." She nods slightly again.

I put the phone in the hand that's resting on her knee. I get my arms under her legs, behind the knees, and I lift her into my arms. She winces slightly, and I see the tears streaming down her face. But, like the strong woman she is, she shines that torch for me so we can make our way out. I have no idea if the guy has gone or if he is still there. He might have a gun or a knife, but it's a chance I have to take. I just need to get her out.

I cautiously enter the doorway

"Shine the torch around for me if you can, baby. I need to make sure it's clear." What I mean is, I need to make sure he isn't lurking waiting for us, but I don't say that to her. Fuck, which way did I come in? I was so consumed with trying to find Kate, I didn't take note of the way I came in, and there are so many rooms leading off rooms. I stop to think. I turned right. I think it's this way. Please be this way. I need to get her out of here.

I hear noises and stop to listen. Voices. Shit, what if there were more than just him in this building. Did he do this to Kate, or is this where the homeless or addicts hang out, and he saved her from them? I have no idea, but I'll think about that once I have her out of here and safe. She is my priority right now. I've stopped, and she's looking up at me with shock on her face. I think she thinks we are in trouble.

"It's okay, baby. I've got you. I won't let anyone else hurt you, I swear, Kate." I step to the side, into the shadows, as I hear the voices getting nearer. I need to stay out of sight with her just in case.

"Baby, can you hide the light from the phone please, so they don't see us here?" She tucks the phone under her top so the light isn't visible. It's so dark that I can barely see her.

I see a light coming our way, and I hear someone shout, "I'm checking this side. Mr Clancy, Mr Clancy can you hear me?" Thank fuck for that, it must be the police.

I step out just as the voice comes through the doorway with his torch. "Over here," I say and Kate shines the light to show where we are.

"I've found him," he shouts out over his shoulder, and more come running our way. I see the paramedics come rushing in, they go straight to Kate to take her from my arms, and start assessing her.

I follow them to the ambulance, all the while I'm looking around to see if that guy is still anywhere. I don't mention him to the police. I need to find him and find out who he is first. I also want to wait for Kate and see what she remembers about it all. I ride with her in the ambulance to the hospital holding her hand all the way.

"Baby, stay awake, okay?" I tell her about Venice and apologise for not being in touch. I know she's not really taking it in. I'm just talking to keep her awake.

When we get to the hospital, they rush her into an examination room. I give them all the information I have, which isn't much. Luce arrives and puts her hand on my arm as I'm leaning my head in my hands.

"Lewis, is Kate aright?" she asks me. I turn to her, and she grabs me and hugs me. I cry again—the second time.

"Yes, Luce, I think she'll be all right. She's battered and bruised, and they think she has a concussion and hyperthermia, but she's alive, and she will mend. They've been asking me all kinds of info about her, Luce, but, I know nothing about her, yet. I love her so fucking much. I was terrified at what I would find in that building."

"Shhh, it's okay, Lewis, she's safe now. You saved her. As for not knowing anything about her, well you have all the time in the world to find out now, thanks to you." She always knows what to say to make me feel better.

We stay there for what seems like hours in the waiting room before a doctor comes in.

"Is Lewis Clancy here, please?"

"That's me," I say shooting out of my chair.

"Ms Porter is asking to see you. You can go in now. She's in room 105 just down the hallway."

"How is she Doctor?"

"She is in pain but she will be fine Mr Clancy."

"Thank you, Doctor." I turn to Luce who has stayed with me all this time. She nods at me and smiles. "Thank you, Luce. Can you do me a favour and let Harry and Clive know we found Kate, and she's safe. They will be worrying about her. You go home and get some rest. Love you, Luce, and thank you."

I head down the hall as quickly as I can without actually running. I slowly open the door to Kates's room and see her small battered body lying there.

"Oh, baby," I say approaching her bedside. She opens her good eye, and I see the hint of a smile on her face, but she winces in pain. I lean down and gently place my lips on her forehead, lingering there.

"Baby, I see you're in pain. Don't try to talk, okay? I've got you, Kate. I've got you, and I'm not leaving you," I say stroking her hair on the top of her head as I lean in close to her face. I see a tear rolling down her cheek on the good side. I wipe it away with my thumb and just hold her undamaged cheek, gently caressing it with my thumb.

"I was so scared, baby. I couldn't reach you. I've never been so terrified in my life, but I'm so glad you're okay. The doctor said you're going to be fine." I lean in and brush my lips gently over her swollen lips, no pressure, I don't want her to feel pain.

She has her arms resting on her tummy, and I can see the welts on her wrists from where she was tied up. I feel so helpless. I need to find out if she is hurt any worse than this.

I stay there with her, taking my shoes off and climbing on the bed next to her and just holding her while stroking her hair. She falls asleep after a while, which is good. It's what she needs. She must be exhausted.

The door opens, and a nurse comes in to take her observations. I don't want her to wake Kate up.

"I have to take her observations. I'm going to have to ask you to leave, sir."

"No," Kate says from beside me. I face her, and she's trying to shake her head.

"It's okay, baby, I'm not going anywhere. They will have to physically throw me out. I'll just get up so the nurse can take your observations." I see the panic in her eye as I start to move. The nurse looks at me as I get up, and I see the recognition on her face. She knows who I am. She doesn't say anything but sets about doing what she needs to on Kate.

"Can you tell us what Kate's injuries are?" I ask her while she's writing in Kate's file. She looks at Kate who nods slightly to give her permission.

"Kate has a concussion, which is why we need to keep her in hospital for the day. She has a fractured cheekbone and eye socket with swelling to her eye and her mouth. It looks like she has taken several blows to the face and head. Kate doesn't remember what happened, but memory loss is quite common with a concussion. She also has welts on her wrists and her legs from being tied up, but there are no other injuries." I let out a breath I didn't know I was holding. Hearing she has been hit several times to the head and face has me furious inside, but I don't want Kate to see I'm upset.

"Will Kate remember what happened?" I say looking straight at Kate.

"We don't know at this point. Her memory could return, but

sometimes people never remember. The brain has a funny way of blocking out trauma for some."

"Thank you, Nurse,"

"You're welcome. Her observations are good. Her temperature is back to normal. I will pretend I haven't seen you. Visiting hours are long gone, but I get the feeling you are not going to leave quietly, even if I ask you to." She's right. I'm not going anywhere.

I go back and lie on the bed at the side of her. I just hold her until we both fall asleep. It's been a hell of a twenty-four hours.

52

Kate

I START TO STIR.
My head is throbbing.

I can't move.

I feel restricted.

What's happening to me?

I start to panic.

I have a really uneasy feeling. Something is wrong. I try to open my eyes, but my vision is blurry, so I lie still. I can hear something, someone, breathing. Fuck, where am I? I try to move again, but something really heavy is holding me down. I start to wriggle. I try to speak, but nothing comes out.

"Baby, Baby, shhh it's okay, look at me, Kate. Look at me, beautiful, it's me, Lewis. You're safe. You're in the hospital. Do you remember why you are here?"

I try to focus on his face. I can see the outline of it through one eye, but the other won't open. I concentrate on his voice. It soothes me.

I remember him talking to me at some point. It was his voice. It was soothing and calming me.

"Baby, I've got you. You're safe." Why does he keep saying that?

Why can't I remember?

What is happening to me?

He tells me I'm in the hospital. I was attacked at an old warehouse that I'd gone to view, near the docks. I do remember a little about being brought into the hospital, but nothing about what happened. I only remember Lewis. I nod my head to him to let him know I'm okay. He gets up, wets a washcloth, and comes over and ever so gently cleans my face so as not to hurt me. He pours me some water and puts the straw in between my lips so I can suck.

"I remember you and here but that's all." I sound terrible, I cant say my words properly, I hope he understands me. I lean back and close my eyes. He's stroking my hair. Why can't I remember what happened? The only thing I do remember is Lewis, but why?

53

George

I GET BACK TO MY FLAT AND START pacing around the small room, tugging at my hair. I stayed just long enough, at a distance, hidden, to see her carried out to the waiting ambulance. I can't get over how much he looks like me. My head is so fucked with all this.

She is going to be all right though, no thanks to me. I see now that my obsession with her just because she looked like my mother was wrong. Just like what I had done to the others who looked like my mother was wrong. Even though they were all whores.

I feel like a caged animal, like the walls are closing in on me. I'm so confused, but it's not just her and Red that are confusing me, it's him I'm confused about too. I can't stop thinking about us being the same. Even down to the length of our hair.

I have to get my shit together. I have no idea if the bitch remembers me or not. She may get her memory back and tell the cops all about me. I need to clear out and toss my computer in the river. I switch it on and clear all the hard drive. I don't have much shit, so it all fits in a duffle bag and backpack.

It's still early in the morning, and there is hardly anyone around when I get to the river. I throw my laptop in as far as I can throw it. I grab my bags and head to Red's place. I'm not sure if she'll be home or if she's at the café this morning. Either way, I will find her, and try and persuade her to put me up.

I ring the bell and wait to see if she answers. I ring again, getting impatient. I hear the bolt move on the door.

"John, hey, what are you doing here so early?"

"Hey, Red. I couldn't stop thinking about you, and wanted to see you before I leave…"

"Leave, where are you going? she asks looking at my bag and backpack, confused.

"I had to be out of my apartment today and thought I would get an early start. I'm heading to Manchester. I haven't found anywhere to live around here yet, and I need somewhere if I'm going to stay working here. I've taken a couple of weeks off so I thought I would go to Manchester and see if I can find a new job there and a place to live. I just wanted to see you before I left. After the other night, you're all I can think about. I told you my life was a bit complicated at the moment. I need to straighten some things out, but I couldn't leave without seeing you first." I look at her with such longing. I want to be in her so fucking badly. She's standing, looking at me, her gorgeous red hair is all loose and wild, and her green eyes are piercing in the morning light. She looks a bit taken aback. All I need is for her to invite me in. I know if she does, then I can work it so she'll ask me to stay. I want to stay. Fuck, this isn't like me at all.

"Do you want to come in for a coffee? I don't have to be at the café until noon today."

"That would be great. Yes, please, Red." I wink at her, knowing that's her weakness. I pick up my stuff and follow her up the stairs to her room. She goes straight to put the kettle on. I drop my bags, and I walk up behind her. I put my hands around her waist and splay my hands on her tummy and pull her into me. She gasps at my touch, and she puts her hands on top of mine.

I nuzzle into her neck. "Mmm, you smell so good, Red." God, I want to fuck her. She feels so good in my arms and this just feels right.

"Is this okay, Red?"

"Yes, yes, John. I'm pleased you came to see me before you left." She turns in my arms so she's facing me. My hands rest on top of her arse now, and she has her hands on my chest. She looks up at me sheepishly and licks her lips, looking at my mouth.

She wants me to kiss her. I can tell, so I bend and gently place my lips on hers, trying to gauge her reaction. She slightly opens her mouth, and that's all I need. I put my tongue in and deepen the kiss, caressing her tongue with mine. She moans. Fuck me. Now, I'm rock hard. She must be able to feel how hard I am against her because she's pressed right into me. I need to take this slowly. I break away and smile down at her.

"God, I've wanted to do that since I last walked out of here," I say to her and watch her blush. She looks stunning when she pinks up like that, absolutely gorgeous. Now I'm back here, I just want this with her, and who knows, dare I say it, but maybe a normal life.

She turns to finish the coffee. I still have my arms wrapped around her, and she giggles. I love that sound.

"What you laughing at, Red?"

"Just you. You can let me go, you know, while I make the coffee. It's not like I'm going anywhere."

"But I don't want to let you go, that's the problem." She turns with the coffees and stares at me with a quizzical look on her face.

"Then why are you going to Manchester, John?"

"I thought I could find somewhere to live here, but from what I've seen so far, I can't afford anywhere. Manchester might be more affordable, and it's a fresh start for me. I'm sorry, but I don't have much choice at the moment. I don't have anywhere to stay around here now." Did I lay it on thick enough? I look at her with a sad face. She also looks sad, and thoughtful. She walks and puts the coffees down on the little table. I walk behind her, and as soon as she turns around, I take her face in my hands and lean in for another kiss. She grips my hips, pulling me to her, and I moan into her mouth. She moans right back. I break the kiss.

"What are you doing to me, Red?" I say leaning my forehead on hers, still holding her face in my hands.

"The same thing you're doing to me, John." She closes her eyes and sighs in my face.

"I don't want you to go. I'll miss you, and I don't even know you."

"Same here, Red. I've only just found you." I move in for another kiss. This time I take it deeper. Heavy breaths, tongues duelling, one of my hands back on her arse kneading and squeezing, the other running up her back. She has her arms around me, both hands now on me, pulling me as close as she can to her. I can feel her nails digging into my back. She can feel how hard I am, and her moans are coming out faster. I lift her up, and she wraps her legs around my waist. She starts rubbing herself on my rock-hard cock. I walk towards the bed, but as I reach it, she pushes back and looks at me with a serious face.

"Hey, sweetheart, what's wrong?"

"I don't do this, John. I don't want you thinking I do this all the time, and that I'm some sort of hussy. I don't know what happens when I'm with you. I just seem to lose control.

I'm sitting on Red's bed with her on my lap, legs wrapped around my waist and her pussy resting on my cock. We still have our clothes on. I need to see if she wants to stop now. As much as I want to be inside her. I need to think about her feelings. That's a new one for me, fucking hell, I have never thought about a womans feelings. I know she isn't a whore. She stopped it going any further the other night. She's looking down, embarrassed, and she's thinking about it. I don't want to stop. I grab her chin gently and tilt her head up to look me in the eyes.

"Hey, look at me. I don't think you're a hussy at all, Red. If you don't want to go any further, then that is fine by me, sweetheart. I won't think any less of you. I like you, and I want you, but you decide what you want. We don't have to do anything. Just holding you and being with you is enough for me."

She's looking straight at me. "Don't go. Stay here with me. Even just for a day or two to sort out what you want to do. Stay as long as you like." Bingo. Hook, line, and sinker.

"I'm sorry, John" she looks embarrassed, "I didn't mean to blurt that out and put you in an awkward position. We don't know each other at all and I ju…" I stop her rambling with my lips, letting her know it's okay. She breaks away after a few minutes but can barely look at me.

"Red, look at me. If you don't mind me staying a few days, then I would love to. I want to get to know you more. I can't do that in Manchester, can I? I don't want you thinking I only came here for that though. I really wanted to see you before I left. I didn't want you thinking I was a jerk that had fun the other night and then disappeared for you never to see me again. I'm not like that and would never want to hurt you. You've got into my head, Red. For reasons I can't yet understand, but you are in my head, and I want to see where this goes."

She has the biggest smile on her face. "Oh, John." She flings her arms around my neck and gives me the biggest hug. Fuck, that feels so good. It really warms my insides, and makes me feel wanted.

"Is that a yes? You want me to stay?" I ask her laughing as she's nearly strangling me.

"Yes, Yes. God yes, John. Thank you for not thinking bad of me."

"Never, sweetheart." With that, I kiss her hard. This time, I'm not going to stop unless she tells me too. The kiss turns a little frantic. She's kissing me back, moving her chest close to mine. I take this as a sign she wants to do more. I run my hands to the hem of her top. I start to lift it, and she breaks the kiss while I take it off over her head. She reaches for my t-shirt and does the same to me. I let her, watching her face as she does. I see the look on it—pure lust as she takes me in. Her hands start roaming all over my chest, gently caressing me. Very gently she traces over my tattoos.

"So beautiful, John. You're like a work of art. All these wonderful tattoos." Wow, she's saying I'm beautiful. I've never had anyone say I was beautiful before or look at me the way she is. She continues tracing over my tattoo's very gently in awe. Her fingers, gently tracing all over is making me feel all tingly again, and she is making me feel loved. I have never had feelings like these in my life. They are strange but nice.

"You're beautiful, Red." She lifts her head to look at me. She's blushing. I raise my hand to her lips and run my thumb over her bottom one. It's swollen from our kissing. I move my hand down her neck and to her breasts. I stroke her nipple through her bra, and her breath hitches and she shudders. She's still gently caressing my chest, and as she flicks over my nipples, I take in a breath, and she smiles. She leans forward and starts to lick my abs, then flicks my nipple with her tongue. Jesus, I think I'm going to cum like some fucking teenager. She sits back up and looks at me. My turn.

I lower the cups on her bra so her gorgeous tits hang out—so full and so real. I fondle both of them in my hands. She sits up, straightening her back and pushes them towards me more, then she leans back slightly, resting her hands on my knees, behind her. I lean down, taking a nipple into my mouth, and suck while playing with the other one, rolling it with my thumb and finger. I swap, taking each tit in my mouth in turn. She is breathing heavily now, almost panting. I watch her face as I suck, the ecstasy written all over it.

"Fuck, Red. You are gorgeous, and I fucking love your tits. So real and round and heavy. Perfection."

She has her head tilted back, and she starts rubbing herself on the seam of my jeans over my cock. I bite her nipple—not too hard but hard enough. Then, with my free hand, I start moving down to the waistband of her skirt. I need to get her out of it.

I let her tit fall from my mouth, and I gather her skirt and pull it upwards so I don't break the connection of her rubbing my cock. She sits up straighter and helps me lift it over, and I throw it on the floor. I stare at her. She is perfect, sitting on my lap, smiling at me just in her bra and panties with her knees either side of me, resting on the bed. Fuck.

I take a nipple back into my mouth, sucking and nipping. She starts panting and moving again, rubbing harder. I move my free hand down between us, and I stroke her pussy through her panties. Fuck me, she's soaking wet. I start to flick at her clit gently, then rub and then flick again. She leans back again, resting her hands on my knees, lifting slightly to give me full access. Her panties need to go. I grab the side and rip them off. I release her nipple and bring the ripped panties to my nose and sniff before I throw them. I then go back to her pussy and run my fingers into her folds.

"Oh, John. Oh, God." I put two fingers inside her, and she starts lifting herself up, and pushing down, faster and faster as I finger fuck her. I want that on my cock. I want her jumping up and down on my fucking cock.

"Shit, Red. I can't wait any longer. Red, look at me, are you ready for me to take you?"

"Yes, John, now. Yes, please."

She is sucking on my neck and moves down to my nipples again.

"Red, baby, if you carry on doing that I'm not going to last. Are you ready for me, Red? Say it to me, baby 'cause I can't wait another minute to be inside you."

"Yes, John, I want you inside me now."

I manage to stand up from the bed still holding Red by the arse. I turn and lay her down. I get a condom from my jeans pocket before I pull them down. I rip the packet open, as she watches my every move. I slowly roll the condom on my rock hard cock, watching her face all the time. She licks her lips. Her breathing is ragged, and her eyes are wide. I don't want to just fuck her, that's what I would normally do. I want to do this right.

"Red, I want to take this slow with you, sweetheart, I want to look into your eyes as I take you. I want you to watch me. I've never 'made love', but with you, I want to. I want to experience what it's like with you. You're in my head, sweetheart, but you're also in here," I say tapping over my heart as I climb on the bed above her. I raise up on my elbows so I don't crush her, and I suck on her bottom lip. I grab my cock and run him up and down her folds, over her clit, making him wet with her juices. I position him at her entrance, "You ready, sweetheart?" She nods yes and smiles at me. Her eyes are full of wonder. With that, I start to edge in gently. She said she wasn't very experienced, and I don't want to frighten her.

She grabs my biceps, takes in a breath and closes her eyes as I breach her entrance, I still. "Speak to me, sweetheart. Are you okay? Do you need me to stop?"

"God no, John, don't stop, please no, I want more of you." She lifts her hips up slightly, which edges me in more. Fuck she feels good. I go in deeper, then stop when I go in as far as I can. She opens her eyes and looks straight into mine.

"There she is, my girl. Keep your eyes open, Red. I want to see you, sweetheart. I want to see your face as you cum for me. I want to see the ecstasy in your eyes. Can you do that?" She nods yes, biting her bottom lip.

I start to swivel my hips gently, round and round, and she lifts her hips and juts her tits out. I take one of the perfect globes into my mouth, still watching her watching me. I let it pop out of my mouth as I start to push in and pull out, right to the tip, then back in again, slowly and gently. It's fucking torture. My instinct is to slam into her so fucking hard and just pump away, but I need this, it feels so different, I still have the control, even going slowly, I still have the fucking control.

It feels fucking amazing—watching her, watching me. I see the awe and the ecstasy. She starts to pant, and I feel her walls gripping my cock tighter. It feels amazing. I won't last much longer. This is pure bliss. I have never in my life felt anything like this. It's always been a chore to me, but for the first time I feel it, I feel all warm, I have feelings for her. She is close. I feel her. I feel my cock getting bigger as I get nearer my climax. "Sweetheart, I need you to cum for me. I'm so fucking close. Can you feel that? Can you feel him growing inside you?"

She arches her back and screams, "Oh fuck, John. You feel so good, I'm so close, fuck, fuck Johnnnnn" She explodes with her orgasm, screaming my name, and it's the best fucking sight I have ever seen. Her eyes are rolling back, she is shuddering underneath me, her legs tighten around my waist, and she is pulling me in as deep as she can by my arse. That's it, watching and feeling her gripping my cock tighter and pulling me in deeper has me exploding. I pump and pump, spilling my load, swivelling my hips, as her scream goes on, calling my name.

It takes us both forever to come down from the high of the orgasms we just had. That was something completely different for me. I have feelings of being wanted and feeling cherished and dare I say it loved. Is that what it feels like?

"Hey sweetheart, are you okay there?" I try to move off her so I don't crush her but she grips tighter. Her face is buried in my neck. I feel her shudder and sniff, then I feel wet on my shoulder. Fuck, she's crying. Did I hurt her? "Red, sweetheart, look at me. Why are you crying? Did I hurt you?"

"Fuck Red, you're scaring me here. Look at me. Did I hurt you?" She looks up at me, and she's smiling, but crying. "No, John, you didn't hurt me. These are happy tears. I have never felt anything like that before. I feel so overwhelmed by it all. I'm still trying to come down from the high my body is on. That was the best feeling in my life." She looks shy again. "What is it, baby?"

"You made me swear, again, I never swear, John. I feel embarrassed."

"Well, if it's any consolation, you swearing and calling out my name as you cum is the best fucking thing I have ever heard." I lean in and kiss her.

We stay on the bed just holding each other for some time and I love the feelings of being wanted. Fuck who am I? We then take a shower together and explore each others bodies as we wash. I want to take her again but she has to get to work, "Fuck Red, look how hard I am for you. I want to take you up agianst this wall now, hard and fast, but it will have to wait till you come home tonight. I promise you though it will be fast and it will be hard, but then I will make love to you all over again. Can you handle that Red?" She nods at me with the biggest grin, grabs my head in her hands to lower my face to her level and she kisses me so sweetly. "I can John, and I look forward to it."

We arrange to meet back here after her shift for dinner. She gives me a spare key and use of her things, including her laptop.

This woman is awakening new feelings inside me. I kind of like it. She's giving me a new perspective on life and women in general.

54

Lewis

I NEED TO MOVE, BUT I DON'T WANT to disturb Kate. We'd both fallen asleep as soon as I'd laid with her. I hear movement and a trolley being wheeled, that must be what woke me. I have my back to the door, so I don't know who has come in. I look at Kate, still sleeping. I get so angry when I see the swelling on her face and the bruises coming out more and more. I want to punch someone. She looks so peaceful right now but then she must hear the trolley, and she flinches. I can see the panic building like earlier. The panic until she remembers where she is. "Shhh, baby, I've got you. I'm still here. You're safe. You're in the hospital." Her breathing is ragged, but she's calming down, listening to my voice. Her good eye starts to open, and I watch with a small smile as she tries to get her focus.

"Hey, baby, how you feeling? Is your head still hurting?" She nods slightly.

"Hi, Katherine, I'm your nurse, Julie, and I need to take your observations if that's okay?" I slowly get up and move off the bed to let the nurse do what she needs to do.

"Baby, I'm just going to the bathroom while the nurse is here, okay? I won't be long. I promise I will be back soon." She nods her head slightly at me.

In the bathroom, I splash water on my face. I look at the time. It's 4 p.m. already. I need to see if they are going to release Kate or if they are keeping her in overnight. I don't want to be away from her for too long.

I head to the coffee machine, then head back to Kate's room. The dinner trolley has arrived, and they are just giving her some soup to suck through a straw. The nurse is just finishing up as I enter. "How's she doing, nurse? Do you know when she will be released?"

"She is doing great, actually. All her observations are good. The doctor will be in to see her soon, and he'll decide if she can be released."

"Great, thank you." I walk in and take over from the lady trying to give Kate her soup. "Here, let me do that," I say taking the cup and straw from her. Kate looks exhausted.

I smile at her and stroke her head before I lean down and kiss her gently on her forehead.

"You're going to be fine. I promise."

Kate falls back to sleep, and I sit in the chair next to her, I must have nodded off myself because I startle awake when the door opens. A doctor enters the room, I get up and stroke Kate's forehead lightly. "Hey, baby, the doctor's here to see you." She wakes up and gives me a smile as best she can, and I move away slightly to give them space.

The doctor takes her file. I stand back as he looks at me. "And you are?" he says.

"Lewis, Kate's boyfriend,'" I say a bit sternly because of his glare.

He tells Kate that all her observations are great and that there are no other concerns. Kate nods at his questions showing she understands what he is saying.

"Ok, Lewis. I am happy to discharge Ms Porter if she has someone to watch over her for the next seventy-two hours. She will need someone to keep an eye on her and wake her periodically. The swelling should start to subside in the next day or two. Ms Porter will need to come back next week and have an x-ray on her face to make sure there are no bone splinters in her cheek."

"Can you do the x-ray now?"

"No, we need to wait for the swelling to go down first."

"I see. Yes. I will be taking care of her," I say keeping my eyes on Kate the whole time I speak to the doctor. He turns to look at Kate, and she nods to let him know that what I have said is correct.

"I will get the discharge papers ready and make up a prescription for some strong painkillers and ask the nurse to make the appointment to come back to the fracture clinic next week. You take care, Ms Porter." She nods, and he turns and leaves.

I help Kate get up and out of bed, trying not to jolt her, knowing how much pain she's in. I get her dressed, and an hour and a half later, I'm pulling into the parking garage at Kate's apartment. We walk into the foyer, with me keeping my arms around her waist. She's doing great. Harry is at the front desk, and he looks up as we come through the garage door. He runs out from behind when he sees us. "Katherine! Oh my goodness. I'm so glad Lewis found you. We were so worried." Kate tries to smile at him and nods slightly. I kiss her temple gently, and she leans into me. Harry darts to call the lift for us.

"Thank you, Harry. I'll speak to you later when Kate's settled." He nods at me and holds the door open as we enter it.

We get into the apartment, and I steer Kate straight to her bedroom.

"Would you like me to run a bath for you, beautiful?"

"Please," she says nodding at me. I sit her on the bed and go into her en-suite and run the bath. I pour some lemon bubble bath in, and I make sure it's not too hot then head back into the bedroom. I kneel down in front of her.

"Come on, let's get you out of these clothes and into the bath." She looks at me with her good eye, and she looks devastated. I see the tear running down her cheek. I wipe it with my thumb.

"Sshh, baby, don't cry. I promise it will be all right. Once the swelling has gone down, you will be fine. Come on, let me help you." I stand up and gently pull her up. I unbutton the shirt she has on and slip it off her shoulders. I kiss each shoulder gently and then her wrist where the welts are from the restraints as she watches me. I kiss her cheek on the good side and breathe her in. I take her shoes off then undo the button and zip on her suit trousers and slowly ease them down her legs. I kiss her knees as I do and look up at her looking down at me.

"You are beautiful, Kate. I have never seen anyone more beautiful than you." I see the tear slide down her cheek again, so I kiss it away. I gently pull her to me, she rests her good cheek against my chest, and I cradle her head gently. I feel her sob and her breath hitch. I feel so fucking helpless.

I wonder if she is remembering something. I pull away and marvel at the beauty stood in front of me in just her underwear. I take her hand and lead her to the bathroom. Once at the bath I take my sweater of over my head and then undo my jeans and slide them and my boxers down, so I'm completely naked in front of her. I see the quizzical look on her face. I don't say anything, I just step behind her to unclasp her bra, and then I gently remove that and her knickers.

I scoop her up in my arms gently as I get up. "I'm not going to drop you. I'm going to step into the bath with you, is that okay?" She nods yes to me. I step into the bath and lower myself down, holding onto her. I sit with my back at the end of the bath and put Kate gently between my legs and lean her back into my chest. She sighs as the water and bubbles cover her. I grab the sponge from the side and dip it into the water and gently start to wash her shoulders and neck and down her front. She flinches slightly as I move over her breast. We haven't even made love yet, but this feels so right to me. I know she's insecure, but I hope she doesn't feel it now.

"Baby, just relax. I can feel how tense you are. I want to take care of you. That's all. Nothing else. Although, I'm not sure my cock has got that message because you're just so damn beautiful." I know she can feel my cock hard against her back, but there's nothing I can do about that. I would be lying if I said I didn't want her. I'm desperate for her, but I can wait, no matter how long. I continue to gently wash her all over.

"I'm just going to get out and grab you a towel, so I can get you dried and into bed. Have you remembered anything from last night? Do you know who did this to you?"

"No. I only remember you." She shrugs. I wonder if it's the other guy, who appears to be my identical twin, that she is remembering, but I don't say anything.

I stand up and lift her out of the bath, gently placing her on the floor. I take the towel and start to dry her softly until I get to her lower belly, then she leans down and takes the towel from me, looking embarrassed. I wish she trusted me. I know and respect that she's not ready to start anything sexual. I take her wrists in my hand and kiss them both where the welts are, then kiss her palms. She reaches out and strokes my cheeks, then looks me in the eyes. "Thank you, Lewis. Thank you for everything." She's finding it hard to speak, but I understand what she's saying.

"You never have to thank me, Kate. I just want to look after you and make you better." I smile at her trying to make light of the situation. She smiles as best she can at me.

"Come on. Bed! You need to rest. I'm going to see if you have any soup and if not, I will run to the deli you like and get some." She nods, and I scoop her up again and take her to the bed. She puts some pyjamas on and curls under the covers.

"You stay there, and I will go find soup. If I have to go out, I won't be long. Try to sleep a bit."

I head to the kitchen and find a tin of chicken soup. Great, now I don't have to leave her. I warm the soup, and I phone Luce. I update her and tell her I'm in Kate's apartment. She confirms that she's cancelled all my appointments for the next week to leave me free to concentrate on Kate. She's also going to come round with everything I need from the hotel. I don't know what I'd do without her.

I take the soup to Kate. She's flat out, but I need her to eat. I gently stroke her forehead

"Kate, baby, wake up. I need you to eat to help you recover." She starts to stir. I smile down at her. "I'm sorry, beautiful, but I have your soup. You need to eat it—you need to build up your strength to heal."

Kate has drifted back off to sleep when Harry rings to let me know that Luce has arrived.

I need to talk to her and tell her what happened. She's the only person I trust with my life, and she may be able to give me some ideas.

"Shh, Luce, Kate's sleeping. Thank you for bringing my things. Do you have time for a coffee? I need to talk something over with you."

"Yeah, sure. What's wrong? You look stressed out and worried."

"Fuck, Luce, I'm in a bit of a pickle and don't know what to do." I run my hands through my hair. I go and make the coffee for us, then we sit, and I tell her all about my twin.

"Wow, have your parents ever said you were adopted or that you had a brother?"

"They never said anything to me, Luce, that's what's confusing. It was like I was looking in a mirror."

"Oh, Lewis, I think you need to look into your past. You can go to the national archives and see what you can find out. Or, go and see your parents and ask them outright. That is going to be the easiest way. I know you're hurting right now, but you need to find out for your peace of mind."

"I was thinking of hiring a P.I. to look into it for me. What do you think?"

"You could if you don't want to ask your parents."

"I don't, yet. I think I need to find out for myself and then approach them, and find out why they have never told me. I kind of feel betrayed, as though my life has been a lie. God, how many emotions can one person go through in less than a week? It's exhausting?" I lean forward with my head in my hands. I feel so drained.

"Hey, why don't you try to get an early night and have a good sleep, then tomorrow think again about how you want to go about this. Just remember, Lewis. I'm here for you, always, and anything you need just let me know. I can even come and sit with Kate if you need to go out."

"I love you, Luce. You know that, right? I couldn't survive without you."

After I see her out, I head straight to the bedroom to make sure Kate's okay. She's still sleeping.

I lean against the doorframe of the bedroom, and I watch her sleeping. She flinches occasionally, but she doesn't wake up. I should stay in one of the spare rooms, but I don't want to leave her. I want to watch over her and make sure she's okay during the night. If we just get tonight over with then I'm sure she will be fine. The doctor said seventy-two hours.

I get into bed very slowly so I don't disturb her. She's lying on her back, and I lay, facing her, watching her until I drift off to sleep.

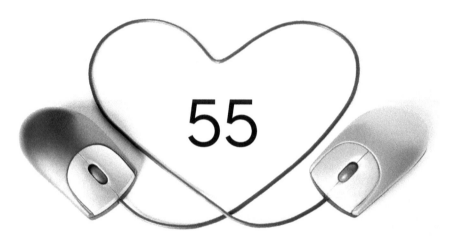

55

Kate

"KATE, BABY. SHHH. YOU'RE okay. You're safe. I've got you, beautiful. Calm down.

Lewis. It's Lewis. I open my eyes and try to focus. I blink a few times until I see his beautiful hazel eyes hovering above me in concern.

"Lewis." I free an arm from the quilt and stroke down his face. He looks pained, and he looks tired.

"I need a wee," I tell him my speech sounding a little better.

"Ok, what the lady needs, the lady gets," he says to me as he gets off the bed and comes around to my side to help me. I think I can walk, and now he's got up of the bed, I can move the quilt. I see the clock on the wall. 1.30 p.m.

Lewis sees me looking. "Wow, we have both slept for nearly eighteen hours."

I go to the bathroom and then stand at the sink to wash. I look in the mirror in shock. It's the first time I've seen my face, and I look hideous. The bruises have really come out and most of my face is black. One side of my face is all puffed out, and my lips are swollen. I can open my bad eye a bit more than I could yesterday but still not fully. My eye is black and very swollen.

I have tears rolling down my cheeks. Lewis comes in and gently gets a washcloth and wets it. Before he begins wiping my face for me, he leans in and kisses both my cheeks, taking my tears away.

"Baby, you are beautiful. I know you're hurting, but this will all be gone in a week or so. Kate, look at me. I don't care what you look like." He gently takes my face in his hands.

"Do you hear me, baby? You. Are. Beautiful. I know I have only known you a week, but..." he takes a deep breath, still looking at me.

"Ah, fuck it. Baby, I love you. I know it's too soon, but I knew it the moment I laid eyes on you." He looks startled at the look of pure shock on my face. The tears are coming thick and fast now. He brushes them away with his thumb.

"God, I'm an idiot. I suppose that wasn't the thing to tell you right now, hey? I'm sorry. I'm so sorry, but I do, with all my heart, and I want you to know I'm in love with you. I nearly went out of my mind when I couldn't reach you." He pulls back to look at me. I nod gently at him and reach up to stroke his cheek to let him know I understand. He leans into my hand and kisses it.

"Come on, let me wash you, then we can get you into some clothes to cover that gorgeous body up because my cock is screaming to be in you." We both look down where he is tenting in his grey sweats. He blows out a breath. "Yeah, I know, but what can I say? You're gorgeous. I know we have to wait but try telling him that." He laughs.

He is so sweet, and he looks embarrassed. "Thank you," I say to him softly. I don't want to tell him I love him until I can say it properly. I want him to hear it, not guess at what I'm saying. He grabs the washcloth and very, very gently washes my face. I try not to wince, but I can't help it. He washes and kisses, washes and kisses, trying to alleviate the pain. It works.

I get dressed, and we eat some porridge. I don't want to go to bed, so I sit on the couch, and he puts a blanket over me. I must have nodded off because the next thing I know, I'm being woken up by stroking my face. "Hey, wake up, sleepyhead." I open my eyes and see my gorgeous Lewis standing smiling at me. Just to the side of him is Clive.

"Oh, sweetie, how are you feeling? I got the next flight I could after Lewis phoned me." He looks heartbroken

"I'm okay. Thank you for coming."

"Baby, while Clive is here with you, I'm just going to nip out for a while. I want to get you some soups, and I have a couple of jobs to do. Is that all right with you, Clive?"

"Yeah, sure Lewis, I will stay for a bit and talk her socks off. She can't really interrupt me now, can she?" He winks at me.

Lewis leans in and kisses my good side on the temple. Clive has gone to put the kettle on.

"See you in a bit, beautiful. I love you," he leans in and whispers in my ear.

God, I am so in love with him.

I can't talk very well, so I sit listening to Clive talk about his holiday and about how he and Zane have decided to get married. I'm so pleased for them. He is my best friend, and I want him to be happy. I must nod off again while Clive is talking away because I wake to Lewis whispering in my ear.

"Hey. I have some more painkillers for you to take. I went to the deli and got some homemade leek and potato soup. Are you ready for something to eat?" I nod gently to him. We spend the evening watching the TV with Lewis sprawled out on the couch and me cuddling into his side. I keep falling asleep. I feel myself floating at one point then realise it's Lewis carrying me into the bedroom. I don't fully wake up, but I feel him put me under the covers. I do remember him waking me a couple of times though, throughout the night, to make sure I'm okay.

The next few days fly by. They mainly consist of Lewis looking after me, then me sleeping, eating, and having Clive and Luce come and visit. The times they are with me, Lewis does errands. The swelling is really going down now, and I'm able to talk a lot better and open my eye more.

I feel a lot better and can shower after protests from Lewis that he's not leaving me alone in the shower, which results in him coming in the shower with me and washing me.

To be honest, I can't wait to get down and dirty with him. You would think after the trauma I had been through, it would be the furthest from my mind, but when you have the most beautiful man in the world caring for you all the time, telling you he loves you every chance he gets and his cock obviously dying to get inside you, it's hard to deny the feelings.

56

George

L IVING WITH RED IS SO EASY. Better than I thought it would be. She's easy going, and she is always ready for me. I have never wanted anyone as much as I've wanted her these last few days. I can't wait for her to walk through the door every day. We've been out to the pub a few times for something to eat and go for walks in the park. For the first time in my life, I feel normal. She still calls me John, and I don't know how to tell her my real name, but I'll work round to it somehow. I've had to be cautious. I've expected the police to come knocking every day.

I tried to find out some background info on Lewis, but I can only find the PR stuff, and I'm at a loss as to where to go from here. I need to know if we are related somehow. We're identical—how could we not be?

While Red has been working, I've been stalking again, only this time stalking *him*. I thought he would be staying with *her* after the attack. I messed her up pretty badly, and I do really regret it. I'm just thankful Lewis came along and found her so I don't have another death to add to the list.

I followed him a few times, mainly to the deli, but a couple of times he went to another office building not far from the Olympia. He got the tube, so it was easy to follow him there. The office building was huge. I had no idea who he was seeing or what he was doing there, as I kept my distance.

I'm back there now, waiting to see if he leaves her apartment and where he goes this time. I've been here a while, and I'm freezing. It's been like this most days. I decide to head to the café to get a coffee and see Red's smile—it always lights up my heart. I smile back at her then take my seat near the window. She brings me a coffee and gives me a kiss. I try to take the kiss deeper, but she pulls away saying she's at work, but I love how she blushes so much. I love how I affect her. She has no idea how she is breaking down wall around my black heart. I never thought it possible.

"How has your day been, Red?"

"Much better now you're here. I miss the way you smile at me, John. You make me feel so special every time you look at me."

"You are special, Red and don't forget it." I tap her lightly on the backside and she giggles. I love that fucking sound. I hear the door go to say someone has just come in.

"Customer, Red." She sighs. I know she doesn't want to leave me. I'm looking out of the window, but I know she hasn't moved from my side. I look at her, wondering why, and the look on her face instantly worries me. She looks at me, then looks towards the door, then back at me again. Her mouth is hanging open. I turn to look at the door to see what she's looking at, and I freeze. Fucking hell, he's standing there, and he's looking straight at me. Fuck, what do I do now? I drop my head, hoping he doesn't come over, but I know damn well he will. Why else is he here? Another couple of customers come in, which is good. "Red, you have customers to serve, baby." That breaks her from the trance, and she moves towards the counter, looking at the both of us as she goes. I look back at him. He's as shocked as I am. He starts to move and heads towards me. FUCK.

He comes to the table and pulls out the chair to the right of me. I don't think either of us know what to say. He has a baseball cap on as if he's trying to disguise himself.

"So, where do we start with this?" he says to me. I look at him properly for the first time.

"Fuck, this is freaking me out." I don't have a cap on so run my hand through my hair.

"Yeah, I know what you mean. Why were you at the old building? Did you have anything to do with attacking Kate?"

"Fuck no. I never touched her. I was walking in the area and saw a car pulling out at breakneck speed, so I went in to see why. I knew it was a derelict building and thought it was really strange." I've prepared this answer if asked about the warehouse, providing she doesn't remember me, which I can assume she hasn't.

"You just happened to be in the area? There is nothing around there, so why would you, who just so happens to look like me, be just in the area?" I'd thought about this as well.

"I go around the docklands looking for scrap metal to sell to metal merchants. It helps me pay the rent. I went into the building to see why the car sped away so fast. I heard a moaning and saw a woman tied to a chair. She mumbled something but I couldn't make out what. I was about to go and help her when I heard a car arrive, and I panicked. That's when you arrived, and I hid. I didn't want to be accused of something, and I thought if you found the woman, then she would be safe."

"What kind of car was it that sped away?"

"Fucked if I know. I don't own a car and never have. I don't know anything about cars. All I can tell you is it looked black, but then it was dark." I should be proud of myself. I sound so fucking believable, even to me. He just sits there staring at me. It makes me really uncomfortable, and I fidget a bit in my seat. "Fuck, man, this is so unreal. Where the fuck did you come from? Why do we look the same? Are we related? Brothers, cousins. What? Did you know I would be here? It's a bit odd that we run into each other again, don't you think?"

He just stares at me. I look around and see Red watching us. There is no one near to hear us, which is a blessing. "Yes, I knew you were here. I hired a P.I., he followed you. He said you had been following me the last few days. Guess you're as curious as I am. He's looking into our identities but hasn't found anything yet. My parents have never mentioned I was adopted or that they had another child, and I don't have any cousins as far as I know. What about you. What do you know?"

"Fuck all. I don't remember anything from before around four-years-old. It was the first and only time I had a cake for my birthday. All I remember is my fucking whore of a mother singing Happy New Life day to me. I mean, what the fuck is that all about? I know now it should have been Happy Birthday, but I didn't know at the time." I decide to tell him what my life was like. I turn to see Red watching us. I ask her for two coffees. Turns out we both drink it the same way. She's standing, looking at the both of us. I know this must be confusing to her—I told her I had no family.

"Red, I will explain this to you when we're home, okay, baby?" I say patting her gently on the backside. I see Lewis raise an eyebrow.

"You two are together?" I nod. A couple of coffees later I've told him all about my life, only missing out the part where I killed my fucking parents. I told him they died in a car crash, which is why I don't like cars. He hasn't said much the entire time. I think he's shocked. I don't know why I feel the need to spill it all to him. I believe we are definitely twins. We both have black hair, which weirdly is practically the same length, we both have the same eyes, but he wears glasses. The only difference is my tattoos are visible.

He tells me about his life. That he was the only son, and he loves his parents, although he is angry at them for not telling him he had a twin. He doesn't know if he was adopted or if they gave one of us away. He's going to find out. He tells me how successful he is now and that he's in love with the woman I attacked and that she was badly beaten and left with a fractured cheekbone and eye socket, and lots of swelling and concussion, but that she is going to be okay. He says she can't remember anything at all about that night, apart from him, which they find odd. Obviously, she thinks I was him. I tell him my name is George or at least I think it is unless it was changed by my parents.

After three coffees and a heart-to-heart, it's time for him to go. He needs to get back to Kate. He asks for my number so that he can let me know what he finds out.

"John, are you okay?" Red asks rubbing my shoulders. I didn't hear her approach. I'm so wrapped up in my thoughts. She's now massaging my shoulders.

"No, Red, I don't think I am, baby." I let out a long sigh.

"He looked really familiar, John, and not just because he was your spitting image, which he was. I've seen him before. Is he your twin or something?"

"Let's talk about this at home, Red…" I need to work out what to tell her and how much to tell her. I get up, kiss Red, and leave. I need a bit of time to think.

57

Lewis

Ⓘ WALK BACK TO KATE'S, MY MIND RUNNING away with me. I can't
wrap my head around what George told me about his childhood.
I just can't comprehend someone living like that. I don't understand
it, and to be honest, my heart breaks for him. What a life, if you can
even call it that. He didn't give me specifics, but I knew from what he
was saying that both his parents sexually and mentally abused him.
I could see the hurt and anger in his face and the sorrow in his eyes.
He wasn't lying to me, that much I could tell, and why would he? We
seem to have a connection, which is weird, it's the first time we've
spoken to each other or seen each other properly.

I don't know what to make of his story about him being there
that night Kate was attacked. Is that even believable? I can believe he
was collecting metal to make extra cash, but that he just so happened
to be there at that exact time AND my twin, what are the odds? Was

he the one who attacked her? If it was, I'll kill him myself, but I don't know.

I'm walking slower now, trying to fathom all this out before I get back to Kate's. I need to tell her about George. I have to tell her that I think she remembers him from that night, not me. I also have to tell her it looks like we are twins, that I have no idea of the circumstances, and I have a meeting with my P.I. tomorrow because he has some new information for me.

I need to get back now, she has her team coming for a meeting soon about her warehouse project, and I want to be there with her so I can find out more. It really intrigues me, and I love how excited she is about it.

I'm so happy that she is getting better. I haven't tried anything with her, and I won't while she's in pain. She's getting a little frustrated, which I find really endearing. It makes me so fucking happy that she wants me nearly as much as I want her. In truth, I don't know how much longer I can hold out, knowing she's ready for me.

58

Kate

I START TO GET ANGSTY AFTER A WEEK at home. I want to get back to work. I start at home, working with my team to get the warehouse project up to date, ready for work to start.

Lewis is here during our meeting. He's taken a great interest in the project, listening to us and also contributing with ideas he has. I love that he is interested and wants to stay and participate. When the guys leave, he looks a bit worried.

"Hey, handsome, what's wrong?" I ask as I approach him and wrap my arms around him.

"Sorry, I know it's out of my league all this. I hope you didn't mind me staying for your meeting. I see how excited you are about the project, and I just wanted to experience some of that with you." He looks at me sheepishly

"Oh, God, Lewis, no. You don't know how happy I am that you took an interest. I felt so proud sitting there with the guys and you, wanting to participate. You have some amazing ideas, and at this stage, before the work starts, it's the best time to make any changes. Thank you for your input. I loved it. Just like I love you." I blush. I can feel the heat creep up my neck as I stare looking for his reaction to what I just said.

He's staring at me, confused, as though he's trying to register what I just said.

"Did you just say you love me?" he asks with the biggest smile on his face.

"Huh huh," I say, nodding with a big grin on my face matching his.

"I love you so much, Lewis…"

59

Lewis

Fucking hell. She just said she loves me! She said she loved my input like she loved me. I'm in awe, and I just stare at her before I attack her mouth. She tastes so good. I'm going to get addicted to her. She moans in my mouth, which makes me moan right back. Fuck, my cock is rock hard. I need to stop this. It can't go any further. I step back and immediately regret it when I see the hurt, anger, and pain flash across her face. I grab hold of her hand. "Baby, just sit down, there's something I need to tell you." The look of horror on her face tells me she thinks this isn't good.

"It's okay. I just have some info I need to share with you." She lets out a sigh of relief. I know exactly where her mind went—she thought I was going to end things, but she couldn't be further from the truth. I need to restore some faith into her. I'll make it my mission. I'm not letting her get away ever. That's one thing I know for sure.

I head to the couch, pulling her with me. I sit down and make sure she sits next to me. I lean in, and kiss her gently, then pull back so I don't take the kiss deeper. I let out a sigh—she's looking at me with so much worry on her face.

"Baby, I love you. I fall deeper and deeper in love with you each day that passes, and it's fucking killing me not to get inside you, but I will not inflict more pain on you—"

"You won't, Lewis," she interrupts me. I put a finger on her lips to keep her quiet.

"Listen. I've found some things out since your attack, and I want to tell you what I know. I will never keep any secrets from you, and I want you involved in my life, and I hope to God you want me involved in yours."

"Lewis, what is it? You're starting to scare me. Are you okay? You're not ill, or anything bad, are you?" She looks at me, shocked.

"I'm not ill," I shake my head, "the night you were attacked, I ran into a man in the derelict building." She pulls back from me again, looking horrified.

"Was it the man who attacked me? Oh God, Lewis, why are you just telling me this now? Have you told the police? Do we know who it is? Do I know who it is?" She gets up off the couch and starts pacing the room, with her hand running through her hair.

I get up to stop her. "Baby, come and sit, and I will explain." I pull her back to the couch and sit her down next to me again, keeping hold of her hands on her lap.

"I haven't been keeping it from you. I just didn't know who it was until today. I met him just now, I…"

"You know who attacked me?" She interrupts again, shouting, but immediately winces. I pull her to me and cradle her head gently to my chest.

"Shhh, don't shout. It hurts your head, and no, I don't know who attacked you." She looks up at me confused. "If you stop interrupting me and let me tell you." I smile at her kissing the tip of her nose

"Go on," she says.

"I saw this man in the building near the room you were tied up in. I thought he was your attacker, but you called out, and my first thought was to get to you, so I ran into the room where you were, and he ran away. The thing about him is… Fuck, it's hard to even say this out loud, it sounds so absurd, but he was my twin." She looks at me dumbfounded.

"What do you mean, he was your twin? I didn't know you had any siblings and why would your twin be in the same building I'm attacked in, on the same night, at the same time?"

"Well, that's what I have been trying to find out. I don't have any siblings that I know of, but Kate, he was my fucking double, it was like I was looking in the mirror. I asked who he was, but he didn't answer, as he was in as much shock as I was. That's when I heard you and ran to you." I take a deep breath and run a hand through my hair and over my face, taking my glasses off.

"I didn't have much time to think about him at the time. I was just relieved I'd found you. I didn't tell the police because what would I say? That I saw a man identical to me and he ran off? I hired a P.I. who has been following this guy, and it turns out this guy has been following me since your attack. My P.I. phoned me today to say this guy was in the café across from your office, so I went to confront him. He was as shocked to see me as I was to see him again, face to face. Neither of us know the circumstances, but there is no mistaking we are identical twins." I explain to Kate, George's explanation about being in the warehouse and why he left when he knew that I'd rescue Kate. I take another deep breath. Kate is just looking at me. I don't think she knows what to say.

"Do you think he's telling the truth about not attacking me?"

"Honestly, I don't know, baby. I suppose there could be a chance, you know, I believe in everything happens for a reason."

"Me too," she says softly.

I tell her all about the conversation I had with George and about his childhood and the strange connection we seemed to have. She's crying as I tell her. She puts her hand to her mouth to try to stop the sobs. I lean forward and kiss away the tears.

"It's so sad, Lewis. I cannot imagine any child having to live through that. Do you believe him?"

"Yes, I do. I can't explain why, but I knew he was telling me the truth. I felt his hurt, his anger, his anguish, and his sorrow. I felt it in here," I say putting my palm to my heart.

"I wanted to cry for him. It's so confusing. To find out I have a twin and to find out about the life he lived while I had amazing parents who loved me so much." She leans in and kisses my nose brushing the hair from my face.

"I'm so angry at my parents right now, Kate, for never telling me. I feel my life has been a lie."

"Can't you go and ask them, Lewis? They will most likely have all the answers you need?"

"I don't want to just yet. I'm too angry, even though I know it would help me, but I want to find out what my P.I. knows first. I have an appointment with him tomorrow. He has some new information for me. Do you think you would be up for coming with me, baby?"

"Of course I will, Lewis. God, sweetie, I don't want you going through this alone. Lewis, I. Love. You." She says emphasising each word. I fucking love this woman. I lean in and kiss her. I'm the vulnerable one now, and she takes control, I can't stop her. The kiss deepens quickly until we are both gasping for breath. We sit, forehead to forehead once we break apart, breathing deeply and smiling at each other.

"Baby, I think I'm addicted to you," I tell her.

"Too late for me, handsome. I'm already there." She leans in and kisses me again. This time Kate grabs my t-shirt and starts pulling it over my head.

"Baby, I don't think I can stop if we start this. Please, please tell me if your pain gets too much. I'm not comfortable with knowing you're in pain." She leans in again

"Make love to me, Lewis. I can't wait any longer."

Just like that, I'm done for. I get up off the couch and pull her up to standing, scooping her up into my arms. She squeals and laughs, putting her arms around my neck. I lean in and take her mouth again, walking us to the bedroom.

I sit her down on the end of the bed, leaning down to kiss her again and she immediately makes a play for the buttons on my jeans. I stand up and let her undo them. She then caresses my chest, circling my nipples, and pinching them, gently at first, then tracing my pecs. She leans forward and kisses my belly button and licks the V leading down to my cock. Fuck, that feels so good. She stops and looks up at me with awe all over her gorgeous face.

"God, Lewis, you are perfection. How have I got so lucky to have you? Tell me this is real. Tell me I'm not in some kind of coma imagining this. Tell me, Lewis, because you are like an angel stood looking down on me right now. Have you been sent to wake me up?"

I get her head in both my hands, and I lean down and kiss her eyes, her nose, and her mouth.

"Baby, you have got that so unbelievably wrong. You are the angel looking at me. You are the most beautiful thing I have ever laid eyes on. It's me that has got lucky, not you. This is real, my beautiful Kate.

This is us right now and hopefully for the rest of our lives. I've found my angel, and I'm not letting you go for anything. Do you hear me? I love you so fucking much, it hurts in here," I say tapping my chest where my heart is. "I have never felt like this about anyone in my life. You're it for me." I feel so emotional. I feel my eyes well up. I see a tear escape Kate's eye. I lean down and lick it from her cheek.

I need to worship her body and let her know how true my words are. I lean down and pull her t-shirt out of her jeans and slowly lift it over her head, making sure I don't jerk her while doing so. I'm worried I'm going to cause her pain, but we both want this so badly. She lifts her arms so I can take the top off.

"Beautiful," I say looking down at her. She blushes and tries to cover herself up. "Baby, I've dressed and undressed you. I've showered and bathed with you and washed every part of your perfect body clean. I've even licked and tasted you. Please do not be shy with me. Please do not try to cover yourself up in front of me. You are gorgeous."

She lowers her arms and dips her head. I lift her chin and lean down to kiss her lips, reaching around the back, unclasping her bra and gently pulling the straps down her arms, throwing it to the floor. I grab her hands to stand her up. I take her tits in my hands, and they fit perfectly.

I squeeze them and play with her nipples, still kissing her. She breaks and leans her forehead against mine. I smile at her because she looks so shy right now. I lean down, take a nipple into my mouth, and swirl my tongue around and around while still playing with the other one.

"Oh God, Lewis. I need you." With my free hand, I slowly move down to the waistband of her jeans, and undo the button and pull the zipper down. I edge my hand down the front, to her folds, and slip my finger through her—she is wet—it's so hot.

"So wet and ready for me," I say around her nipple. I find her clit and start playing with it. I then travel down and plunge my finger inside her. I move it in and out, then back to her clit, spreading her juices around, still swirling my tongue around her nipple. She's holding onto my shoulders tightly, her nails digging into me. She bucks forward and moans loudly. She's gasping hard, and I feel her breath on the top of my head. I let her nipple drop out of my mouth with a pop.

I look at her. "Baby, let me know you're all right." I panic, worrying about her being in pain.

"Yes, yes, perfect," she pants out with a smile on her face.

"Look at me, baby. I need to see your eyes." She opens them and stares straight into mine, and I can see ecstasy and love staring right back at me. I take her mouth again, plunging my tongue into it, duelling with hers. I thrust back inside her with two fingers, in and out—she's gyrating on my hand. I try to pull her jeans down with my free hand. I break the kiss. I want to watch her cum. I want to watch the pure ecstasy, but I also want to make sure she isn't in pain.

When I stand straight, she grabs onto my arms to keep herself upright, her nails digging in harder the nearer she's getting to her climax. She starts to shimmy, helping me take her jeans down. She's now able to spread her legs wider to give me more access. Fuck. I need to taste her. I lower her to sit back on the bed. She is so close now. I still have my fingers inside her, stroking her inner wall. She feels amazing, but I want my tongue in there, tasting and sucking her dry.

I kneel on the floor in front of her and lay her back gently. She's panting hard, and we haven't taken our eyes off each other.

"You still okay, baby?" She nods at me. I lower my head and watch my fingers moving in and out, in and out. She's soaking wet, and my hand is covered in her juices. I can see her swollen clit. I look at her and smile. "So fucking beautiful. I need you to cum on my tongue. I have to taste you again—my very own supply of Kate honey." With that, I take her clit in my mouth, and I suck. I lick, and I suck, and I pump in and out with my fingers. She is close, writhing on the bed and gasping for breath. I can hear her muttering over and over, "Oh my God. Oh my God." It spurs me on, knowing she's in ecstasy because of me. I remove my fingers, replacing them with my tongue. I want to taste her cum. I play with her clit with my wet fingers, and that's all it takes. She explodes on my tongue, crying out, her back arching off the bed, gripping the quilt in her hands, her head bent back. She tastes fucking spectacular. She's squirting in my mouth, and I can't lap it up quick enough. I hold her legs down wide open, and I keep sucking and lapping until it's all gone. She's settled back down on the bed with her arm thrown over her eyes. I crawl up over her. I need to make sure she's all right

"Are you okay, baby. Does your head hurt? Look at me. I need to see your face." She removes her arm. I'm above her, looking down onto her gorgeous flushed face. She's smiling, her eyes smiling right into mine. My cock is like granite, but I need to make sure she is okay to carry on. She looks the happiest I have seen her. "Baby talk to me." I start to worry about her head.

"Mmmmm, Lewis, I'm more than okay. I'm perfect. You just completely obliterated me. In fact, your magical tongue just cured my headache. I love your tongue almost as much as I love you." I'm so relieved.

She pulls me down to kiss her, and she sucks on my tongue as it enters her mouth. I can't help but moan, as I start rocking against her core.

"Baby, let me get my jeans and boxers off. They are a bit of a hindrance at the moment, in case you hadn't noticed." I grin at her. It's my turn to look like the Cheshire cat. She licks her lips as I get them down to my thighs, releasing my cock.

I start to move back onto the bed. My cock is like a divining rod, pointing straight at her pussy. I slowly kneel on the bed, and crawl up her body, licking and kissing my way up her legs. I kiss over the top of her pussy then up over her stomach. She jolts up and grabs my neck, pulling me in for a kiss and lowering us back to the bed with me on top of her. She moans as my cock rubs against her clit. Fuck, I don't think I'm going to last. He's expanding already, and he's not even inside her yet.

"Baby, do we need a condom? I'm clean. I got tested before I met you, and I haven't been with anyone since my results. I want to be inside you with no barrier so fucking badly, but it's your call, beautiful. Are you on the pill?"

"Yes, and I'm also clean. I haven't..." She breaks off looking to the side.

I bring her face back to me and kiss her gently. "It's okay baby. You don't need to tell me."

"It's just I haven't been with anyone for a long time. I'm on the pill to help regulate my periods." She's looking at me, blushing again. God, I love it when she blushes. It's so endearing.

"I would like to feel you, Lewis. I have never done that before. The few times I have had sex, I always insisted on a condom. I trust you, and I want to feel all of you." She looks so shy.

I retake her mouth and plunge my tongue inside. I'm lined up at her entrance, just a little push, and I'll be in. I have my hands wrapped under her arms, holding her shoulders. I break the kiss

"You sure about this, beautiful? I'm not sure I can hold out any more. I think I'm going to embarrass myself again. Something about you makes me act like a teenager." I smile down at her. She nods at me and smiles the biggest smile. I slowly edge in. She gasps, so I stop, but she's still smiling at me. She arches her back, lifting her hips, asking for more. I push in harder. She gasps again, looking me straight in the eyes. The love I see is euphoric, and I mirror it back to her. This, right here with her, is my heaven.

"Fuck, baby, you feel so good. You okay?" She nods again, and I push harder until I'm fully submerged into her tight, wet pussy. She's so wet for me again, and she feels so soft inside like silk on silk. I start to move, slowly at first. She's absorbing all of me, and it feels fantastic.

I start to rock in and out, picking up the pace. She's clinging onto my arms, digging her nails into me. I'm gripping her shoulders, giving me the leverage to push farther into her. I rotate my hips on the next push in, and she arches her back. She's panting hard, and she keeps eye contact with me all the time. Fuck, I think I'm going to cum.

"Baby, I'm not sure how much longer I can hold out. You are fucking perfection in every way. You feel so amazing. You need to cum for me." I rock and twist harder, two more pushes in, hard and deep, and she screams out my name over and over. She literally explodes on my cock. I can feel the tight walls of her pussy wrapping my cock like a fucking glove. She's gripping me, not wanting to let me go. My cock explodes like never before.

"Ahhhh, fuck, Kate, fuck, fuck, fuck..." I can't help the cursing. She's gripping me tightly with her arms and her pussy. I'm pushing and pushing hard, my cum squirting until I still above her. I bury my head in her neck, sweat pouring off me. My cock is still jerking inside her like she is draining every last drop from me. We stay like this, holding on to each other tightly. I'm kissing the sweat from her neck, and she's doing the same to my shoulder. I look up into her eyes. She looks fucking beautiful—glowing—but not just that. She looks content, happy, relaxed, and serene. But tears are streaming down her cheeks.

"Baby, are you okay? What have I done? Fuck, why are you crying? Did I hurt you? Please, tell me what's wrong. Do you need your painkillers?" Shit, what have I done to her? I knew I would cause her pain. Fuck. I start to get up, but she pulls me down to her mouth and kisses me deeply. She breaks the kiss, but she's still crying.

"No, Lewis, you didn't hurt me. I'm not in any pain." She reaches up with her hand and runs it over my forehead. "You look so worried, handsome. You did not hurt me, honestly. I'm sorry for crying. I'm just overwhelmed with love. These are happy tears. That was phenomenal. I have never felt anything like that. I can't put into words the way you make me feel. I love you, Lewis, so much.

It scares me that we hardly know each other.

It scares me that you will run a mile now you've had me, no matter how much I trust you. It scares me just thinking I may lose you. I'm so mixed up and confused by my feelings. That's what the tears are about. But make no mistake. I'm in pure bliss."

Wow, this woman has turned my world upside down. I kiss away her tears. I smile at her, then kiss her with as much passion as I can.

"Baby, that was phenomenal for me too. I have never, and I mean this from the bottom of my heart, I have never ever felt like that with anyone before. I love you, but in truth, I am also scared about how fast my feelings for you have hit me. I'm scared that I might lose you. But baby, the way your pussy milked my cock and gripped him, you have no chance of losing me ever."

I lean in and kiss her again. My cock is at full attention already, still buried deep inside her. I start rotating my hips. I'm ready to go again. I hope Kate can take another orgasm. She moans, grabs my hair, and lifts her hips to let me know she's on board. I break the kiss, lean back, grab behind one of her knees and lift her leg so it rests on my shoulder. I start frantically pushing and twisting. I can feel her start to grip my cock, so I know she's close. My cock is throbbing. I need to cum. I play her clit with my thumb, and that's all it takes, she detonates around me again, screaming my name over and over. I explode inside her, pumping and pumping as her pussy grips me. Fuck, she is gorgeous when she cums. Her face is pure ecstasy. I can't stop watching her. I release her leg, and I roll off her to my side. I'm exhausted but in the best way possible. She moves nearer, and I put my arm around her and pull her to my chest.

"I love you, beautiful."

"I love you too, handsome."

We are silent for a while, both catching our breaths. We drift off to sleep, both exhausted, clinging onto each other.

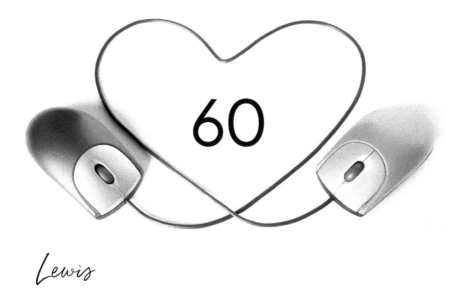

60

Lewis

WE SLEEP WRAPPED AROUND EACH other. I gently get up of the bed and use the bathroom. When I come back, I stop at the door and look at Kate who's awake, leaning on her side, propping her head up with her hand, and smiling at me—still very naked. I lean against the doorframe and cross my arms over my chest. I am still naked too. I don't care. My cock is standing to full attention at the sight of her. She takes all of me in and licks her lips, her eyes dragging up my body. I look over her shoulder to see what time it is and am shocked to see it's 9.30 a.m. I can't remember the last time I slept in until that time. I know from the look on her face that she wants me and that makes me feel all soft and gooey.

"See something you like, baby?" I grin at her and start to head for the bed. She laughs at me

"Yes, you."

"How are you feeling today? How is your head? Any pain?" I need to know before I take her again.

"Actually no, nothing. I said you had a magical tongue. I think you also have a magical cock."

"Well, beautiful, I have that appointment with my P.I. at eleven so how about you get your beautiful backside of the bed and take a shower with me?" I crawl onto the bed and lean in to kiss her. "That way, I get to have you again in the shower, and we get clean at the same time. It's a win, win. What do you say?" I land another peck to her mouth.

"Sounds good to me, handsome," She quickly gets up on her knees and leans down to kiss my cock. Fucking hell, this woman is going to kill me.

"Shower. Now," I order her and swat her backside as she moves past me off the bed. I get up to follow, and she swats my arse back.

"Right. it's like that is it?" I grab her by the waist and haul her over my shoulder. She's laughing hard, and she taps my arse a few more times as I walk us into the shower and turn on the water. She screams as the cold water hits us both.

I let her slide down my front very slowly and take her mouth as the water warms. It soon becomes heated, and I take her up against the shower wall. I can't get enough of this woman.

We finish washing and then dry each other. I love how her confidence has grown with me already. Kate heads to the kitchen to do some scrambled eggs on toast for us. I pour our coffee while she dishes out the food. We just flow and work well together.

"Lewis, why do you think no one has ever mentioned your twin? I mean, you're famous, so wouldn't you think people would recognise him, thinking that he's you? I think it's really strange that it's never been brought up."

"I thought the same thing, and George even said he was surprised about that, but I think with his visible tattoos all over his arms, and more growth on his face and I wear glasses a lot so people must have realised he wasn't me. Plus, he looks mean, moody and angry the times I've seen him. I think he is permanently angry with the world or that was the impression I got."

"Hmm. You ready to head out, or we will be late? You kept us too long in the shower." She winks at me.

"You complaining, baby?" I wink back at her, get up, grab my wallet and her hand, and we head out to my meeting.

We've just left the meeting with my P.I., and I'm heading to the café to meet George. I'm not sure it's a good idea to take Kate with me to meet him yet.

"Baby, would you be offended if I went to the café to meet George on my own? I think he is trying to come to terms with all this, as am I. I think if it's just me it would be better." I hope she understands. She looks at me and gives me a small smile.

"Of course, Lewis. I was going to suggest you go on your own. He won't want me there when you're telling him something like this. I'll head on home and meet you there later. I have work to do anyway."

"I love you, beautiful. You don't know what it meant for me to have you there while I got all that information." I give her a kiss, and we head to the tube station. When my PI told me that my parents are my real parents I was so relieved. I was gripping Kate's hand tight, but she didn't complain.

I get to the café, and he's sitting at the same table. I walk in, and the girl behind the counter nods at me. I nod back and head to George. He knows I have news, and he's looking apprehensive. I pat him on the shoulder lightly, and I notice he flinches.

"Hey, George, thanks for seeing me. I thought you would want to know as soon as I got some news."

"Yes, thanks, Lewis. I have to say I'm fucking shitting it about what you found out. Just tell me first. I need to know. The vile creatures who brought me up, were they really my parents?"

I shake my head. "No, George, they were not your parents." He looks at me startled. His mouth hanging open as if he is going to speak. He suddenly drops his head into his hands, and he cries. I can see his shoulders rising up and down. Fuck, he's broken. I pat him on the shoulder to show him my support, and he doesn't flinch this time.

He then grabs a napkin from the table and blows his nose. "Sorry about that. It's just you have no idea how I feel hearing that. I feel like the weight of the world has just lifted from my shoulders. What they did to me, the things they made me do to them… All this time, I have felt so filthy,vile and disgusting. I thought it was normal growing up. I thought all parents did that. I fucking hated it, but I had no idea. I never met another person until they died when I was sixteen. So I never knew what normal was." He looks down at his hands—they are shaking. He picks at the skin around his thumb and chews his lip.

I proceed to explain to George that he is my twin and that he was abducted from our pram when he was two. My mum had us in the double buggy and left us outside our local shop, which she often did because it was too hard to manoeuvre a double buggy around the small aisles. She always looked out of the window at us to make sure we were okay, and that particular day she saw a woman pulling George from the buggy.

There was a van parked by the side of the road, and the woman jumped in with George. My mum couldn't get to it in time.

There was a massive search for George, but there were no witnesses, and my mum didn't see the woman clearly. My mum fell into depression and ended up in hospital for a long time. It took her two years to come back to life and realise she had a son that needed her. They decided to move away to the other side of the country. I told him we were born in a small coastal town call Flimby not far from Carlisle, but my parents moved me to Kent in the aftermath of the abduction. I don't think they wanted me to find out, to protect me. George was never found.

He looks distraught. "What a fucking mess. Are your parents still around?"

"OUR parents. Yes, they are. They live in Penzance. I've been thinking about this. I don't want to tell them over the phone. I thought we could go and see them this weekend, and I can tell them face to face, and then you can meet them. If you want to think about it, I understand. It's a big thing. I have no idea how mum will react..."

He looks at me, confused "What do you mean? That she won't want to see me?"

"Fuck no. But it's going to be a massive shock. I don't want her descending into depression again." We stay and talk for a bit more, and it's kind of weird, but it's great knowing I have a brother. I tell George I'll be in touch. We shake hands and grip shoulders. I pull him in for a hug, patting his back.

"Great to meet you. George. Oh, one other thing. Your birth name is John."

He looks at me and bursts out laughing. "You're fucking shitting me. John? My name is John, so I'm John Clancy? Wow JC! Well, it's better than fucking George, that's for sure. I've always hated that name. Call me John from now on. George is dead."

I nod and slap his back. I head for the door then turn. "See you soon, John."

I head home to Kate with a bounce in my stride. That went better than I thought. I feel really good. I have an amazing woman who I adore and love so much, and I find I have a brother—not just a brother, a twin.

epilogue

Two Years later

Kate

I CAN'T BELIEVE THE DAY HAS ARRIVED for my warehouse conversion to be officially opened. The buildings are amazing. All the apartments are luxurious, but the penthouses are magnificent. My vision of them has exceeded all my expectations. I fell in love with them so much that Lewis and I are having the penthouse in building one. We move in this weekend, and I can't wait.

Lewis and I have been together for two years now. I love him and have done since the day I laid eyes on him in my office. Needless to say, I quit the dating sites after my attack, and I have never heard a peep from the fake Lewis Catfish guy since. He just disappeared from my life completely.

Lewis moved in with me after my attack and never went back to his hotel. We just got into a routine—we just fit. I had another offer on the apartment next door that I couldn't refuse. Telling Lewis was the best. "Lewis, I know you were still interested in the apartment next door, but I just accepted an offer on it that I couldn't refuse." I looked at him all businesslike as his face dropped and he looked really pained and hurt.

"Oh."

"Oh?" I said raising my eyebrows.

"But baby. I thought that would have been ideal for us. Was I wrong? Don't you want me near you?" He said the last bit so quietly, I only just heard him. I could see the sadness and hurt in his eyes.

"Well, handsome." I stepped right in front of him so he could see my face. I was trying so hard not to smile. "I just thought, what a waste of time, you buying next door—you've been living with me for eight weeks now. You'll probably just be here all the time anyway. I was wondering if you wanted to make it permanent? Living here with me?"

I was the one then looking at him sheepishly, trying to gauge what he was thinking. His eyes darted all over my face, and I wasn't sure what exactly he was looking for. He didn't speak. I started to panic thinking it was the wrong decision, doubting myself. He made me wait what felt like hours then broke out in the most amazing smile. He lifted me up, spinning me around. "Baby, thank fuck for that. I was wondering how I was ever going to leave here and leave you. Thinking about my own place now after living with you, well, it was killing me. Beautiful, there is no place I would rather live than with you—wherever that is. I love you with all my heart. Thank you for making me the happiest man alive right now." He had me raised above him so I was looking down into his face, resting my hands on his shoulders, then gradually lowering me to kiss me.

I have already sold twenty-seven of the forty apartments. They were bought off-plan. I could not be happier with the way it has all gone and the hype surrounding it. I suspect a lot of the interest has to do with my gorgeous famous boyfriend, who is also my partner in the project.

After I sold the apartment next door and Lewis officially moved in with me, he asked me if I would like an investor/partner on my project. He really enjoyed being involved and came up with great ideas, so thought the next progression was to come on board if I agreed.

I loved the idea of him being my business partner, so we got a contract drawn up by our lawyers. He has been hands on right the way through, giving lots of input and even getting his hands dirty when Alf would let him.

I grab my stuff, wondering where Lewis is. He should be here now, ready to leave with me to head to the opening of the buildings by the Mayor. I wanted to see him beforehand. I have something for him, a little surprise. It's going to have to wait until tonight now. I grab my phone from my bag to ring him to see where he is, but see I have a text message from him.

Lewis – Baby, sorry I'm running late. My agent had more to discuss than I realised. I'll head straight to the opening from here. It makes more sense. I will be there on time for the opening, I promise. Love you, baby, so much. Always yours. See you soon. Hope you're excited. X

I was only hanging back waiting for Lewis, so I shoot a quick text back on my way out of the door.

Kate – Okay, handsome. It makes more sense rather than trying to get back here for me. I'm so excited and so happy. I have the best partner in the world by my side. Please try to get there on time. Preferably earlier if you can. I have lots to do to make it perfect. Love you more than life, sweetie. You are my life. See you soon. Xx

Everything is spotless. The caterers have arrived and are all set up. Clive and I have got the ribbon ready to put across the opening at the gates, but I'm still waiting for Lewis. I text him again.

Kate – Hey, handsome, are you on your way? Just getting worried. The Mayor will be here soon. Love you. Xx

Lewis – Be there in about 10 minutes, baby, sorry. Love you. X

Great, he should be here before the mayor then. More guests are arriving. The press are here, milling around with Clive, taking pictures in the communal areas, the other penthouse, and a couple of the apartments.

Lewis – Hey, baby. Where are you? I have just arrived, and it's bedlam. I can't see you anywhere. Love you. X

Oh great, I can breathe now, I was getting worried.

Kate – Oh, great. On my way down now. Will meet you near the gates to put the ribbon on for the mayor to cut. Love you. Xx

I chuckle to myself looking at our texts. No matter what we text, we always say love you.

I head to the gate and see everyone is already there. I spot Lewis immediately, talking to the Mayor. He spots me as I approach. He looks worried and a bit pale. I hope he feels okay.

I lean in to give him a kiss. "Hey, handsome, are you okay? What's wrong? Has something happened?"

He gulps and smiles at me. Only it's not his usual smile and doesn't reach his eyes. It's a bit strained. "Hey, baby. I'm fine. I have the most beautiful woman in my arms, and we are just about to open our very first project as partners. I'm more than happy." He leans in to kiss me again. "Everyone seems to be here. The Mayor is ready. Shall we get this show on the road?" he says but still doesn't look right at me. I think he's nervous.

I greet the Mayor while Lewis ties the big red ribbon up. The opening begins. I'm so excited. Lewis is stood behind me with his arms wrapped around my waist and his chin on my shoulder. The mayor announces the opening of Unus and Duo and he cuts the ribbon. I squeal and jump up and down excitedly. I turn to kiss Lewis, but then freeze on the spot.

Lewis is on the floor.

Lewis

As KATE TURNS to me, the shock on her face is priceless. She looks up at first, then sees me down here, on one knee, holding a blue Tiffany box open with a brilliant white emerald-cut solitaire diamond on a platinum band. It's simple, but elegant, just like Kate. Her mouth is hanging open as she tries to register what she's seeing.

"Baby, I know I'm hijacking our opening here, but I couldn't wait any longer for this. Katherine, you are the most beautiful person I have ever met, inside and out. I love you more than life itself. I couldn't imagine a life without you by my side. From the moment I laid eyes on you, I knew you were the one. You've put up with all the attention I get from fans and you never complain when we are out and get stopped. In fact, you volunteer to take the pictures." I laugh at her, but I'm shitting myself. I can't gauge her reaction. She's still stunned, only now her hand has gone to her mouth, so I carry on. "You have the kindest heart I know, and have graciously given it to me. I promise to cherish it forever. You have made me a better person. You complete me, and I adore you. I want to not only have you as my best friend and my business partner but in my life forever. Katherine, will you please do me the greatest honour of becoming my wife?"

Her hand is still at her mouth, but she is now trying to hold in the sobs. She's crying hard with tears running down her cheeks. Oh no, have I done the wrong thing? Are they good tears or bad tears?

"Baby?" I say with a shaky breath. I'm sure I must look panicked,

"Oh, Lewis. Yes, a million times, yes. I love you so much." I take the ring from the box and put it on her finger. She throws herself at me, knocking me onto my backside as she climbs on my lap, kissing my face all over, then kissing me on the mouth. There are loud cheers and hollers and cat whistles. We are lost in the moment, forgetting everyone is standing around us. Kate buries her head in my shoulder, embarrassed.

"Baby, you have just made me the happiest man alive," I whisper in her ear.

"I can't wait to start the next chapter of our lives, in our new apartment, and I cannot wait for you to be my wife. You're so beautiful. I love you so fucking much." I'm sitting on the floor at the entrance to our new building conversions with the love of my life on my lap having just agreed to be my wife. The best day ever.

We get up and carry on with the opening. Kate has a few groups of potential investors to show around. I talk with the Mayor before he leaves and some of the other guests. Clive is busy making sure everyone is looked after while they wait for their turn for a showing with Kate.

She makes her way back after her second showing, and I manage to grab her for a quick kiss.

"How is it going, beautiful?"

"Couldn't be better, Lewis. I have sold seven more and have another nine interested, and I have two more groups to show. At this rate, we are going to sell them all. I'm so excited." She leans in and gives me a kiss before heading to the next group.

Our removal company arrives with all our stuff. I decide to make a start on unpacking while Kate is showing people around. I head up to our apartment and start moving the boxes into the rooms they belong. Needing a break, I go up to our rooftop garden. I just sit there for a bit, thinking about the different direction my life has taken and is taking. I need to tell Kate about my meeting this morning and the decision I've made to cut right back on the modelling. I get more enjoyment being Kate's business partner than I do modelling now. It's given me the best life, but now, I want more. I want Kate, and I want a family with her.

I think back to meeting John and the circumstances surrounding him that still haunt me—finding Kate after her attack. But I gained a brother from it. I get on great with John, and we keep in contact a lot, even though he and Red moved to Manchester. Once mum and dad got over the shock that John was alive, we managed to rebuild our relationships. All four of us. It was such an emotional time. John and I stayed with them a few days and they talked nonstop. John did tell them about his childhood, which devastated them both, especially mum.

I introduced John to Kate not long after, and it was awkward initially. He was so distant from her and wouldn't speak to her. It made Kate uncomfortable. She thought she had done something to upset him. Luckily Red was with him, and Kate spent most of the evening talking to her. I didn't know what was wrong with John, he was very distant, but denied it when I approached him. Thankfully, he started to relax around Kate, joining in with her conversations, and they actually got on quite well after that, which was a relief.

I'm still in the garden when I hear footsteps on the stairs. I know it's Kate straight away. I can always sense when she's near. I turn and am stunned as always by her pure beauty.

"Hey, my beautiful fiancée, come here," I say patting the seat next to me.

"How did the last showings go?" I ask pulling her into my side and kissing her head.

"Fantastic," she says beaming at me. I see she has brought up an ice bucket with a bottle of champagne, two glasses and some orange juice. I grab the champagne.

"With the last showings we've nearly sold them all, and get this, the penthouse has sold!" She has the biggest smile on her face.

"I'm so proud of you, baby. You are so damn talented, and you're all mine—my wife to be!" I say smiling from ear to ear as I lean in to take her mouth. It gets heated as always, and she pulls away before we get to the point of no return. I start to open the bottle of champagne, but Kate puts her hand over the other glass to stop me from pouring. "Orange juice for me, handsome." I look at her quizzically, and she laughs at me.

"I have something for you too, my husband to be. I was hoping to give it to you this morning before we got here but your meeting ran over. I'm glad it did now because this is the perfect time, here, on our rooftop garden, on our first night in our new home."

She reaches into her back pocket and pulls out a gift for me. I take it from her and unwrap it to reveal a long black velvet box. It looks like she's bought me some jewellery. I gently open the box, trying to work out what it is I'm actually looking at because it's no piece of jewellery. Kate is tense at the side of me. I look at her with a frown.

"Baby?"

"Oops," she says turning the white stick over so it's facing the right way up. I look down and see the word on the stick: Positive. Holy fuck, we're having a baby. My eyes automatically well up. Is this real? Can this be happening? I look up at her. She's crying, smiling, and nodding her head, yes, to let me know it's real.

WOW. My life is complete. What more could I want than this right here?

John

MY LIFE HAS turned around completely, and it all started with Red. Her coming into my life just at the right time. I fell in love with her gradually. Or maybe I did at the start but didn't recognise what love was. Fuck, my life was a mess. I know for a fact, if I had not gone back to Red's that first night, I would have killed Kate. Yes, it's Kate now, not bitch or whore. Getting to know Kate after attacking her was tough. I felt so much guilt for it. None of them can ever know what I did.

I was cold to her the first time we met. I couldn't bear to speak to her. It wasn't because I still thought she looked like the whore I thought was my mother, but because of what I did to her. I felt so much remorse. She still doesn't remember that night. I live with the fear that someday something will trigger her memory. It's a fear I will live with along with the remorse I feel for taking those other women's lives for looking like my fucked up abductor. The fear I have inside every minute of every day that the police will find me.

Lewis is a great bloke. I have come to really trust and like him, but it took me a bit to get to that point. I had to get past the resentment. Why wasn't he the one who was taken? Why was it me?

He took me to meet my real parents—he was my rock through

that time. It was hard walking into that room and seeing those two strangers fall apart when they saw me. It broke their hearts, hearing all about my childhood and what I went through. I told them everything, well apart from me killing the fucked-up bastards, of course. I think I wanted to hurt them for never finding me by telling them all about the sexual and mental abuse. I didn't know these strangers, and I wasn't ashamed to tell them everything the fuckers made me do. I know they felt terrible, in fact, Beryl, my mum, had to run out of the room to throw up. I know I wasn't being fair, but then it wasn't fair I was abducted, and I wanted them to feel some of what I felt. I wanted to make them feel guilty.

I soon realised they'd been through hell and have lived in hell all this time. They told me everything they did to try and find me, for months and years. They showed me a box full of everything that belonged to me and all the newspaper clippings and the documents from the police reports. It was so surreal knowing I had these parents that I never knew. Parents that loved me more than life but couldn't help me in any way.

After a few days with my parents and Lewis, I kind of let the anger simmer away. I realised they were not to blame for my abduction.

Red and I got serious. I did some work on Lewis and Kate's warehouse project to get me back on my feet. Lewis also got me some modelling jobs with him, which paid really fucking good. More money than I had ever seen. We didn't do many, but they enabled me to accumulate a small nest egg to move to Manchester and set up with Red in our own dream, a café to run together.

Both Lewis and my parents kept telling me to go to the police about my abductees. I told them it was pointless, the bastards were both dead, and I had never seen anyone else, so it died with them. They understood and agreed. The main reason though, was there was no way I going to be interrogated by the fucking police. If the police knew about me, and the bodies were ever found, there would be no question it was me.

I didn't want to hang around too much. I was still terrified of the bodies being discovered.

I'm the happiest I have ever been in my entire fucking life. I now have birthdays with birthday cake and everything. Red goes all out when it's my birthday. I fucking love her. I can never marry her, but I can make her mine by proposing, which brings me to right now.

It's the anniversary of our first ever night together, its been 2 years. I know this because Red has been subtly reminding me. I've arranged for Lewis, Kate, and my parents to come down for a little party. None of them know I'm going to propose, except Lewis. He phoned to tell me he'd just proposed to Kate and that she was pregnant, and that gave me the idea to ask Red.

I told Red the café was closing early because we had a small party to arrange for a customer who came in earlier today while she was out. I'm in the kitchen, starting to panic. Lewis just texted that they are two minutes away. I'm hiding in here, and Red is out front. I hear a knock on the door. This is it. I check my pocket to make sure I have the ring. I hear voices and Red squealing.

I walk out and see them all hugging and greeting each other. I get down on one knee next to the sideboard that houses all our teapots and crockery.

"Oh my gosh, I can't believe you're all here. Does John know you're all coming?" She turns around.

"John, John. Ohhh…" she drifts off when she sees me there on the floor. Her hand flies to her mouth.

"Yes, Red, I knew they were coming," I say smiling at her.

"John, what are you doing down there?"

"Well, Red," I say bringing my hand out from behind my back.

She gasps when she sees what's in my hand. "John, what is that?"

"I think you know what it is, Red. I love you, and you know we can't have a real wedding, but I still want to ask you to marry me. Red, will you be my fiancée? We could have a ceremony, and you could get your name changed because I love you, and I want you to know that I want to spend the rest of my life with you." The next thing I know, I'm on my back. She's thrown herself on me crying her fucking eyes out.

Yes, I will be your fiancée. I love you so much. I'm so happy. Yes, John. Yes. Yes. Yes!"

I smash my mouth to hers, forgetting the others standing there. I start rubbing her back and heading down to her arse.

"Erm, John, we have company," she says pulling back, we both start laughing.

"Here, Red, let me put the ring on you. Make it official." I grab her hand and put the ring on her finger.

"Erm, John. I wanted to talk to you about something, and well, I think this is the best time really…" She's blushing, really red like she does when I do bad fucking things to her.

"What's up, Red?" I say, lifting her chin with my finger. She can't look at me, and she glances back to the smiling faces of my family.

"John, we're going…" she stops, and now I'm worrying.

"Red, what is it? You're fucking making me panic here. Spit it out, Red, for fuck's sake."

She takes a deep breath. All of a sudden she shouts. "We're having a baby." She looks down, then looks up sheepishly. I'm stunned, shocked, and just sitting still on the floor frozen in place.

"John, say something to me. John, you look really pale, baby." She looks straight into my eyes. I suddenly grab her and squeeze her to me. I can hear my mum crying in the background.

"Shit, John, say something to your girl," Lewis says to me.

"I'm going to be a dad?" I whisper in her ear. Red nods her head at me biting her bottom lip

"Bloody hell, Red. Me? I'm going to be a dad? I love you so much." I grab her to me and kiss her hard.

"Are you happy, John?"

"Absa-bloody-lutley, Red"

My parents come over, and my mum crouches down and gives us both a big hug.

"Oh my word, I'm going to be a grandma to two babies. I can't believe this. You and Kate both pregnant."

"Erm, mum." Lewis tries to get her attention. She looks up to him. He has Kate tucked in his side, and they look at each other smiling.

He turns back to us all. "Make that three babies and who knows?" he says looking at me and Red. "It could end up being four," he says smiling with the biggest fucking smile on his face, looking at Red.

She looks shocked. "Oh God, it could be twins, couldn't it?" she cries. Holy Fuck. I have never in my life been this happy. Ever.

"Well, brother, you know they say us twins do everything the same. What are the chances both Red and Kate being pregnant at the same time? It seems to be our thing, these unusual occurrences. Like brother like brother, as they say." There he is again, grinning. I'm so thankful they all came into my life.

"Do they, Lewis? I have no idea, but I love the way my life is going. I love having you all in my life. A life I could never have ever imagined having. Thank you, all of you, you will never know what this means to me." I look at Lewis and smile. He pats my shoulder smiling back and nodding at me knowingly.

The big flat screen TV is on in the background just behind where

Lewis is standing in front of me, and as I'm looking at him talking, it catches my eye. The sound is muted, but the picture on the screen is an ariel view of some woodlands. There are lots of people in view, all in white coveralls. It's all lit up, and there are a couple of white and yellow tents erected. I must look like a deer in headlights, and I'm sure I must have paled. What catches my eye is the box at the bottom of the screen and the scrolling words that I keep reading as they move along.

BREAKING NEWS—CONFIRMED—SO FAR THIRTEEN BODIES HAVE BEEN FOUND IN WHAT LOOKS LIKE A MASS MURDER GRAVE IN TOTTENHAM MARSHES, NEAR LOCKWOOD RESERVOIR IN LONDON. POLICE THINK THERE ARE POSSIBLY MORE BODIES TO BE UNCOVERED.

OH FUCK.

The End

More about Lynda

Lynda lives in Cheshire in the UK with her husband Peter and cat Bailey also with two grown up daughters and an 11-year-old granddaughter. She runs a successful financial business with her husband.

As a young teenager Lynda used to read horror books with a love for everything Stephen King and James Herbert. She has always wanted to write and even wrote horror stories at age 13. A little later she started reading Jackie Collins and Jilly Cooper and has always had a love of books. This then exploded with Twilight and Fifty Shades as it did with most people, oh, and the introduction of E-Readers.

In her spare time, she has a season ticket for Manchester City Football Club and goes to all the home games. Loves going to concerts and the theatre. She goes to the cinema at least once a week. Then when the weather is nice you can see her gliding down the road on her Harley Davidson 1200T motorbike.

Travelling is also high on the agenda and her dream is to visit every state in the USA.

Acknowledgements

I wouldn't have done this without the help and support I got from a few people.

First my Husband who made time for me to write by running our business. Stuart Reardon, my second bestie who spurred me on telling me I could do this and not to be a chicken. Also, for the lovely images on the cover.

Jane Harvey-Berrick Author, for your help and support.

The friends who read the book and gave me feedback, Andrea S Roberts, Sheena Lumsden and my lovely sister Jackie for her ideas.

My Editor Claire Allmendinger for guiding me through and being patient with me.

Sybil Wilson from Pop Kitty for the amazing cover.

Emma Hayes & Stuart Reardon for the cover images.

Cassy Roop from Pink Ink Designs for the fantastic formatting and making my words look pretty.

Thank you.

Lightning Source UK Ltd.
Milton Keynes UK
UKHW021618260319
339930UK00002B/21/P